The Serapis Fraktur

The Serapis Fraktur

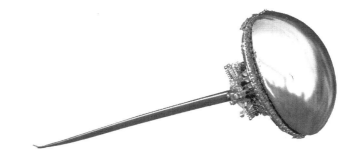

Mark Clay Grove

Mark C. Grove

Spitfire Publishing

THE SERAPIS FRAKTUR

A Charles Dawes Novel
Book 1: The Conglomerate Series

by

Mark Clay Grove

www.mgrove.com

First Paperback Edition
ISBN 978-0-9887926-0-9
First eBook Edition
ISBN 978-0-9887926-1-6

Cover art and design by Aidana WillowRaven
http://WillowRaven.weebly.com

Editing by Sandra Haven
http://sandrahaven.com

Distributed by Spitfire Publishing, LLC

LCN Number 2013902944

J. Richard Grove got me started writing when I was eight years old. Thanks, Dad.

— Mark Clay Grove

MANY THANKS:

- To my perfect wife, Chany, who puts up with me.
- To my parents, Richard & Ditha, who didn't drown me when I deserved it.
- To my liberal friends who endure my rants.
- To the United States for providing a safe place to rant.
- To the United Kingdom for its rich majesty, my birthplace.
- To my University for the knowledge it imbued, James Madison University.
- To the United States Air Force and the United States Army for molding me into a man.
- To the United States Marine Corps for honoring me with membership.
- To my editor, Sandra Haven, who got it right for me.
- To my cover artist and designer, Aidana WillowRaven.
- And to whoever is in charge on the other side.

— Mark Clay Grove

MY FAVORITE QUOTE:

Socialism is a philosophy of failure, the creed of ignorance, and the gospel of envy. Its inherent virtue is the equal sharing of misery.

— Winston Churchill

Introduction

The story is purely a product of my imagination and thus it is a work of fiction. Real historical figures were included because it was fun to do so. The character Dock/Dundee, the Ancient One, was problematic. He lives for thousands of years after crash-landing on Earth and is known by many different names over time, including Jesus Christ. I included Him in this novel the way I did (even though I am agnostic) because I wanted God as Dawes' copilot – literally – and I didn't know any other way to make it so. Boy! Did *that* decision ever prove to be a pain in the neck! I had *two* cover artists refuse the assignment because the Biblical version of Jesus did not follow the traditional storyline. Good grief! I am very sorry if you too are offended by my fairytale, but give me a break: it's *fiction*! So is Santa and the Easter Bunny but no one is slashing their wrists over that!

The *other* complaint I hear about this story is that there is no sex and no combat. That's also easy to explain. I write in the first person and my first person protagonist is a gentleman. Gentlemen *never* mention their private moments with their ladies. I will not compromise on that issue.

And as for the absence of combat, well, I did add a spicy hand-to-hand combat scene at the recommendation of my Editor in order to reinforce the importance of a type of utility knife known as a SOG. That scene is kind of brutal but not nearly as much as the genre, combat scifi. Actually, I like to read combat scifi a lot, but there's already enough of that genre in the marketplace. I don't need to add my genes to a pool already perfected by the masters like Joe Haldeman, John Scalzi, Jay Allan, and B.V. Larson. Instead, I prefer to write about imaginative social constructs like Ursula K. Le Guin and historical personalities the way Mark Twain did in some of his work. I also really enjoy quirky scifi worlds, like Mary Pax's *Backworlds* series and gritty detective noir where the protagonist wears a fedora, like D.B. Grady's *Red Planet Noir* and K.K. Rusch's *Retrieval Artist* series. And whenever I can fit it in, I also like to include an entrepreneurial scheme of some sort the way Nathan Lowell has done so admirably in his the *Golden Age of the Solar*

Clipper series. As a writer, gritty, quirky, mores, and the spirit of free enterprise are more fun for me to create and speculate on than writing about lustful carnal scenes or nuking alien insects, but hey, I do like and frequently read those categories, too. In fact, I read just about everything except poetry, horror, and romance.

Most of the "extracts" herein were removed from the past, but a handful of contemporary figures were included because in Dawes' universe it would have been illogical were they absent; Hawking comes to mind. As for the fantastical future technology, well, it was just that, fantastical. What's a future without a bit of fantasy?

If anyone has discovered any reason to take offense at what they have found on these pages, I apologize. I am not perfect and I do not expect to achieve perfection in this incarnation and I do not plan on changing; I'm too old, too cranky, and too set in my ways. I hope you "take it" with pleasure even if you have to use a grain of salt, and if you have to leave it, that's okay, too.

What you have read here is what perpetually rattles around inside of my head. It is a world in which everyone treats each other with respect and dignity and one in which everyone follows the T's. When the real world looks too bleak, this is where I park my mind. You are welcome to visit or stay. And if you do not like my invented world there are plenty more to get lost in. Good day and Semper Fidelis to all who wear or who have ever worn a uniform with honor.

TABLE of CONTENTS

Chapter 1: Resurrection

My first impression when I awoke was the scent of lilac followed by warmth and silence, apart from the sound of pattering rain. Except for the chrome metal furniture, the rectilinear sterile room – complete with ceramic tile walls, marble floor, and linens – was completely white. One-drawer nightstands, with nothing on their tops, stood on either side of the bed. There were no lamps. Light emanated from everywhere and nowhere. The absence of color in the room even extended to my person. Someone had dressed me in white cotton surgical scrubs with a V-necked short sleeve pullover top, baggy pants, and disposable elastic booties. A bank of windows, none of which looked like they could be opened, ran the length of the room down the long portside wall. Rainwater pounded against the glass, limiting visibility. Next to the windows were two arm chairs separated by a third one-drawer stand. Opposite the windows was a centered door.

I didn't know where I was or how long I had been in this place. A quick self-inventory revealed nothing out of the ordinary for a man of forty. Other than a mild headache, everything else actually seemed sharper. Colors were more vivid, my hearing was more acute, and my vision was so precise that I actually identified the reflection in the window as a flyspeck on the backside of a drawstring hanging from a Venetian blind on the other side of the room. I had only a minute or two to reflect on the surreal before I detected an ever-so-slight breathing pattern and what I guessed to be small feet ambulating in cotton socks before there was a knock at the door. "Come in," I said, propping myself up on my elbows. A beautiful woman of about thirty-five entered, closed the door behind her, and glided toward me. In stark contrast to the whiteness of my surroundings, she was dressed in a turquoise blue shirt, much like my own but with collar and cuffs. On each side of her collar was a row of three diamonds. She wore her jet-black hair in a French braid. Her eyes were dark, cheekbones high, complexion Mediterranean, and teeth perfect. To my surprise, her slightly blunted fingernails seemed to be diamond-veneered to match her collar.

"Good morning. I'm Dr. Renatta Messina," she said, smiling as she extended her hand. "Do you remember your name, sir?"

"Charles Dawes," I murmured, placing all my weight on one elbow, accepting her hand. She had fine matching dimples and spoke with an ever-so-slight East Indian accent. I could detect and, to my surprise, even define the elements of the various scents she brought into the room: hand lotion, perfume, deodorant, shampoo, and some of the foods she had eaten in the past few hours. It was a bit much.

"Good," she said. "I expected no less. Your recovery is progressing as anticipated, perfectly, actually. In a few days…"

I interrupted. "Where am I and why am I here, Doctor?" I could tell from the landscape that it was summertime and I was in a temperate zone, but something wasn't familiar about a few of the deciduous trees. They were enormous, perhaps five feet in girth. And the room was too, I don't know what it was, maybe it was too high tech. I had been stationed TDY in Kansas on more than one occasion; I wasn't in Kansas. That I knew for sure.

"You are at our recovery facility in Charlottesville, Virginia." I welcomed the idea I was in my hometown, even though it didn't seem familiar somehow. "No doubt you have many questions. I can provide answers, but first, how do you feel?" She motioned us to the chairs next to the floor-to-ceiling windows. With a grunt I maneuvered to my feet.

"Well, except for a mild headache, I seem to be in pretty good shape. There's no mirror in this room, so I can't imagine how I must look, but from what I can tell, everything seems to be in working condition. And I notice that my birthmark feels like it is gone."

She removed a small silver-colored gadget from her side pocket, poked it with a diamond stylus four or five times, and looked up. "Yes, the birthmark had served its purpose. New shells are absent old defects." That bit of information went right over my head. She fiddled again with her gadget. "There, I've made an adjustment that should relieve your headache."

I felt almost instant relief. "What? You adjusted my meds just like that, with that thing?"

"Something like that, yes," she smiled, putting her device away.

I forgot about the inquiry about my birth defect. "What could you have done from over there that had such an immediate effect?"

"You've been injected with custom-made nanite compounds that respond to adjustments using this medical device," she informed me. "All of your vitals are normal, by the way, and you are responding well to treatment. For a period of time, however, you will experience various sensations, and perhaps even some discomfort. But as time passes, you will begin to feel considerably stronger than before the accident, and your senses will improve significantly. Have you noticed?"

I was a bit confused. *What was that? Nano device, huh?* I thought to myself. After a pause I managed an intelligent response: "Yeah, I've noticed plenty of weirdness. I can zero in on the hairs of a gnat's ... uh... abdomen in flight over by that fountain." I nodded toward the window through which one could see putti spewing water fifty or so meters away. As personal property appraiser and consultant for high net-value clients with collections of antiques and art, I was more than familiar with this particular piece, an exact replica of the La Fontana dei putti in Pisa.

"Excellent," she replied. "The nanobots have amalgamated. You should be able to smell accurately, as well."

"Yes, too well. How do I ratchet it back a notch?" I sniffed the air.

"Conflicting aromas?"

"You could say that. I can actually define the ingredients in the pasta dish you had last night."

"Oh, sorry about that." She stepped back a pace and pulled out her device once again. "Let me make an adjustment to mitigate the acute ability you will eventually enjoy. There. That should do it. Better?"

I sniffed the air again and noticed the intensity had diminished. "I think so," I answered.

"Mr. Dawes, once you learn to self-adjust the nanites, you'll be able to fine-tune your senses by merely thinking the adjustment."

"How long will that take?"

"Oh, a few days or so, but I promise you the bots are there to serve and protect you. You're going to like the way they make you look, feel, and allow you to perform."

"Perform?"

"Yes, the nanites are autonomic, like your heartbeat. They make adjustments when your body's sensors require enhancement."

"Examples."

"Well, for instance, you'll not only be able to hold your breath under water, but you'll also be able to work tirelessly for at least fifteen minutes while you're down there because the nanites can shuttle oxygen around the body."

"That will come in handy. I like to free dive."

"Indeed, I know you hold a past world Tuna record of 655 pounds. You'll notice a big difference. The nanites will also expel nitrogen and lactic acid, and if you are injured, they will self-replenish and make significant repairs to all non-neuro systems of your biomass."

"Jesus." I had a lot to think about. "I won't get tired?"

"Correct…well, sort of. You're still going to require additional augmentation, which I will address later."

'Additional augmentation' sounded like the upgrades every good salesman offers 'for a small additional fee.' At this point everything was amazing enough as it was; even if I couldn't afford her offered upgrade, I'd be plenty happy with what I already had. But I had to ask, "You remade my body. Why?"

"Back in your early timeline you were in a fatal car accident, Mr. Dawes. Fortunately your body was recovered in time to be held in cryogenic stasis. When the time was right, we removed your stasis capsule here to UVA recovery where it's been for the last six months.

"The revival process was complex. The short story is that we reanimated your original body, extracted your soul – your sentience as it were – from its neural network, and inserted it into an improved body we call a shell, which we cloned from your original. Next we made in-process general repairs and a multitude of enhancements to the clone DNA at the molecular level and then injected the shell – the new cloned body that you're presently wearing – with a slurry of programmable nanites that accept remote input. That's how I made you feel better, by applying my stylus to this device." She held up the two objects with one hand, as a reminder. "In fact, I made the most recent adjustment on purpose, the one you witnessed, so you could understand the nano concept more easily. I could just as easily have ordered the central computer to make the adjustment, either verbally or by thought, using a heads-up screen visible only to me. I'll explain more about that in due course."

My mind wandered as she described what she'd done to me. I must have looked befuddled. I was dumbfounded to say the least. The doctor gently prodded me with questions I only half heard through the haze. As she spoke, I took an inventory of all my body parts. *Two arms? Check. Two legs? Yeah.* I also discovered I had what looked like a healthy tan

George Hamilton would be proud of. And I was glad that my birthmark was gone because it often throbbed with pain.

I began stringing vague flashes of memory together to form a thought that might lead to a multiple-syllable intelligent sentence, but all I could mutter was, "What?"

"What's the last thing you remember doing or seeing before awakening here?" she asked, gently pressing the conversation onward. But too many feelings were crowding my mind, so I couldn't formulate an intelligent question.

I closed my eyes. After a few moments I began, "I still remember my early life as a child in Coventry.... That's what I was dreaming about just before I came fully awake."

"Good. I know of your past life from reading Dr. Stevenson's profile on you. What can you tell me about just before the last moments before the crash?"

I was surprised she knew about Stevenson but then I reminded myself of how well known he is. He had interviewed me because he was researching people with painful birthmarks. Apparently some people with birthmarks remember previous incarnations and they claim that their marks are from fatal wounds. Stevenson wanted to hypnotize me, but I was too busy to take the time. I had just found a diary which eventually led Emma and me to solve a murder mystery in Madison, Virginia, so I had let the birthmark issue drop until later. I'd have to look him up, let him know what happened, that the birthmark was gone or maybe this doctor had already told him.I continued. "I was in the bay area of Northern California, I think. Well ...ah... let's see. I remember being in my black Mercedes, on a steep grade... the landscape was lush ...going fast... blurred motion ...noise... by a river ...the Russian River ...probably... I remember passing a road sign that read *Monte Rio*, and then another sign a moment later that read *Bohemian Grove*. The next thing I remember is waking up here."

"That's very good, Mr. Dawes."

I noticed that for some reason she raised an eyebrow when I said '*Bohemian Grove.*'

"How severe were my injuries?"

"They were extensive, Mr. Dawes. You were airlifted to hospital and immediately placed on life-sustaining equipment where you remained for several months, whereupon your committee... Do you remember your committee?" I nodded yes. She continued. "They invoked the requirements stated in your living will and other preparatory instruments. At that point your legal team assumed responsibility for your care and disposition. Eventually a court decision allowed for stasis internment, and your team made a battery of decisions in accordance to your wishes since this was a fatal scenario. At that time your grave injuries were beyond the limits of existing technology and your projected revival interval was statistically impossible to estimate. Stasis internment was necessary. The alternative was unacceptable. Do you remember setting this plan in motion with your committee members?"

"Yes, I remember all the planning after my win." I'd won the lottery and had been smart enough to immediately set myself up for every eventuality with long-range investments, including cryogenics, executed to the ridicule of many. Of all the mistakes I might have made in my life, at least I got that right, I thought. So now here I was, plopped a few years into the future, my plans suddenly, and truly, set in motion. "I am glad I didn't have to experience the red tape that must have occurred after my ...uh... demise," I said with a grim smile, relieved. "I don't doubt it must have been legal chaos."

"Yes, it was. But the committee, which is now at your service in any capacity, took care of all your affairs. I am your medical and psychological officer as well as your trainer and one of your security team members. You also have administrative, legal, financial, and other security staff."

"Yes, I remember now. My attorney and my financial adviser suggested a plan of action for me. I'd like to have a word with both of them if you can arrange that." I raised my eyebrows in her direction.

Dr. Messina placed her hand on my forearm and said softly, "Your committee members are different individuals than they were before your accident, Mr. Dawes, because so much time has passed. It is now comprised of members succeeded by appointees designated by the initial members and their succeeding appointees, and so forth, all of which was necessary over the years."

"Oh," I swallowed and noticed yet another fly speck on the same cord a bit higher up. "Yes, of course. I understand. So how long has it been?" I looked past the window glass into the distance. The little nanites in my cranium were probably working overtime shoring up whatever mental state the textbooks defined me to be in as I tried to grapple with the possibilities, that is, if, in fact, I was even still me. But as I focused I saw evidence of the answer before the doctor had a chance to tell me because under the huge American chestnut trees were dried prickly burrs. And high up in the canopy there were hundreds more green prickly burrs hanging from the branches. The burrs were too small for anyone to see, at least not anyone in 2010, even anyone medically enhanced to our highest technology then. But the trees were the biggest clue: the American chestnut was extinct in 2010. Tears streamed down my cheeks in torrents as she told me the answer I already knew, that centuries had past.

"Mr. Dawes, the year is 2460." Her lovely perfume wafted over me as she leaned forward slightly to study my reaction as the world revolved in slow motion. I could hear her carotid pulse and distinguish the cacophony of the individual raindrops that co-thumped with her aortic valve as I stared out the window at the lush, wet landscaped campus of the recovery facility. The rain had subsided except for the cascading drops from tree leaves and off the roof. My mind was numb. Everyone and everything I knew was gone – my wife Emma, my extended family, all of my friends, and everything recognizable. I was now a stranger in my own land. The only thing that sounded familiar so far was being back in my hometown of Charlottesville, Virginia. I sighed and wondered how it had changed after so long as the sun moved from behind the clouds to stream through the forest of American chestnut trees.

Chapter 2: Central Computer

Dr. Messina helped me back onto the bed and left me alone with my thoughts for a while. I dozed off thinking about how my life was at the turn of the 20th century; what became of my wife, Emma; what I achieved during my short life; and what I might do in this new age in my new body. Images played incessantly across my mind like a silent movie. I don't know how long the show rolled on before I heard the hiss of the door opening. Dr. Messina appeared at my side with two cups of coffee.

"Mr. Dawes," she whispered. "How are you doing?"

"I'm going to be OK, Doc."

"I know. Would you like a cup of coffee while I debrief you?"

I thanked her for the libation. Coffee has always been my favorite flavor and my new schnozzle hadn't forgotten. I swear if someone smeared a rock with coffee ice cream, I'd try to eat it. I was feeling much better.

"Alright, Doc, bring me up to speed, but first may I have a computer so I can surf the Net and see what things look like nowadays. I suppose computers are completely interactive now, right?"

"Yes," the doctor said. "I can send a cybernetic aid to instruct you, or you can activate the central computer with voice commands. A screen will appear on any wall you designate, or if you prefer, a hologram figure can take the place of the wall screen. You only need to speak to retrieve answers. Why don't you give it a try?"

"All right…computer on!" I commanded. A low trill sounded overhead indicating the computer had engaged, just like it did for Mr. Spock on *Star Trek*. "Show me a screen on the wall, to the right of the door, about a meter in length." Before I had even stopped speaking, a rectilinear screen winked open on the wall like HBO, and an attractive blonde woman wearing a red business suit appeared seated behind a desk with a view of the North Woods behind her. She began speaking to me in, well, a sultry voice.

"Yes, Mr. Dawes, how may I be of assistance?"

"Hello there," I blurted. "Would it be possible for someone to bring me a selection of casual clothes? You know – trousers, shirts, socks, underwear, cotton short sleeve shirts, walking shoes – from my time period, and anything else I might need?"

"When do you need these items, sir?" she asked.

"As soon as possible, please." From her vantage point on the wall, she turned her head to look at the door. Dr. Messina and I instinctively followed her line of sight. Within seconds there was a knock at the door. A shiny metallic pyriform robot appeared, pushing what passed for a wheel-less English teacart that hovered above the floor, with neatly folded garments on top, several shirts and sport jackets hanging on the long sides, and pairs of fine shoes neatly placed on sloping stacked shelves.

"Very impressive, Doc. How did that happen so fast?"

"Your wish is our command, Mr. Dawes," she said with evident delight.

"Anything you want is at your fingertips twenty-four hours a day," said the computer lady. "You only need to ask, sir."

"What else would you like?" asked the doctor.

"Ah, well," I stammered, "how about giving me a tour of the area in about half an hour? In the meantime I'll change and get acquainted with this computer of yours."

"Actually, Mr. Dawes, everything you see here is yours," she said as she glided through the doorway. I didn't quite comprehend the meaning of her parting statement at the time.

***

Khaki pants, a red cotton shirt, brown tweed jacket, and comfortable brown leather shoes completed my look. My beard felt smooth and my hair short, so someone must have taken care of those details before I regained consciousness. I still hadn't seen what I looked like in a mirror, but that was second on my agenda. First, I wanted to catch up a little and orient myself.

"Computer on," I said out loud. AI hadn't yet been perfected in my time, except in fiction. I couldn't wait to start using it.

"I'm still here, Mr. Dawes. How may I help you?"

"Were you watching when I got dressed?"

"Yes."

"Why didn't you tell me you were still there?"

"You didn't ask."

"Good grief!" I growled indignantly. "Well, next time mind your own business!" Thoughts of Big Brother, Orwell's *1984*…"I don't like being watched," I mumbled under my breath.

"I don't mind watching," she said as a matter of fact.

"Do you have a name?" I said, perturbed.

"You may address me as you like, sir," crooned the computer with affection.

"All right then. How about …uh… Betty?" I once had a housecat named Betty. She would sneak up and creep me out just like this cyber babe had done. Maybe she was my cat's incarnation. The name seemed to fit her MO.

"Thank you for your kind attention to detail, Mr. Dawes."

I requested some breakfast, bacon and eggs with toast, and it, too, arrived almost instantly on an English teacart via a pyriform robot. The eggs tasted especially fresh and the toast seemed like a whole grain, although I doubted they were wheat, at least as I knew it. It was the bacon, however, that first caught my eye. One slice and what a slice—it was half as wide as the plate and hung over both sides.

"What is this? Bacon?"

"Yes, sir," Betty confirmed.

"But it's huge."

"Yes, sir. It comes from the boarzilla, native to the planet Xurida. About the size of the Holstein cows you may be familiar with in your earlier days, sir. An excellent source of food but difficult to raise because of its exceedingly foul odor, mean disposition and nasty habits. We only import the prepared meat to Earth."

"And, ahh, just where am I, Betty?" I asked as I chomped down on the excellent tasting boarzilla bacon. Emma, a health food nut, would have had a fit to see the size of this 'cholesterol stick' as she called bacon.

"You are located on the first floor, northwest corner, of the Founder's Suite inside the Recovery Facility of the Dawes Artificial Intelligence Institute on the University of Virginia campus in Charlottesville, Virginia, in the United States of the Americas."

So the political lines have been redrawn, huh? I thought. "Show me a three-dimensional floor plan," I said as I paced back and forth remembering what I learned in statistical demographical dynamics as a geography major at JMU.

Immediately a schematic appeared with a human figure designating my current location in the almost 27,000 square-foot building, complete with seven aboveground and three belowground levels, four helipads, and underground parking. As I moved, so did the figure.

"Now pan out and show me a view of this building."

The facility appeared to be glass and stone construction, in a style Frank Lloyd Wright would have approved. I never particularly cared for the round white columns that were so popular with the neoclassical architecture of the Jefferson region. Bless his genius, old Tom had many good ideas, but his colonial architecture wasn't one of my favorites. Greek and Roman columns should have remained in Athens and Rome. Our early forefathers obviously lacked self-confidence; emulating the ancients is a classic puny-pecker symptom.

"Now zoom out to one mile in elevation, wait five seconds, and then zoom out again every five seconds to twenty miles."

It was not as I expected which was asphalt pavement over all the landmasses. To my surprise and relief Charlottesville had not been absorbed by the eastern North American megalopolis. My world had shrunk into a seamless expanse of heavy forest from Nova Scotia to Key West. After so many centuries I would have imagined a bird's nest of asphalt highways from coast to coast. But only certain areas were populated, and the extent and range of development appeared to have receded. It didn't make sense. What happened?

"Now from this elevation show me the other continents."

Ditto. All of Europe, India, Indo China, the Pacific Rim, Asia, Africa, and South America had a similar profile.

I made an assumption based on the facts. "Now show me near space orbital colonization around the earth, then the moon, and then the solar system. This time indicate population densities in a sidebar."

Earth now had twenty-two billion souls; near space and the moon another billion; Mars five hundred million; and the other outposts within the solar system, two more billion. Space had become noticeably urbanized. The final frontier was nowhere in sight, but the visible distribution of Earth's population was less than a quarter of what I remembered. According to the sidebar population statistics, Earth should be piled high with people.

"Betty, the statistics in the sidebar do not jive with the size of the population centers. Where are the people?"

"Most dwell in low elevation dirigible city-buildings, called shrooms, suspended in the grid. The cities are elevated off the surface at various altitudes and cloaked so that they're invisible. Smaller numbers of people inhabit stationary undersea habitats or large submersibles similar to the atmospheric shrooms, and about three percent live in subterranean colonies."

I was astounded. "Show me."

Betty broadened the screen to encompass an entire wall and presented a motion picture of many wonders. Where I expected high-density population centers there was actually a grid system of hovering buildings interconnected with ribbons of horizontal maglev transportation routes a thousand or more meters above the surface. At major junctions large mushroom-shaped buildings hovered with what appeared to be tendrils dangling underneath like those of a jellyfish. The space elevators, anchored to the ground, ran through the mushrooms and ascended into space to terminate at orbiting stations, which had their own interconnected transportation routes. In places where there once were land cities, these shrooms dotted the globe like a patchwork quilt. Apparently surface development had been arrested and the pre-existing urban landscape reduced to a minimum. These lofty shroom cities had replaced skyscrapers that were there before. The land surfaces of the planet were now largely wild with old-growth forests and sweeping savannahs. What little urban development remained was low-rise and limited to the heart of the old major population centers. Most of the surface transportation routes were gone. Even farmland was apparently restricted. Earth had returned to pre-industrial age condition. All the old fears of pollution, ice ages, and global warming due to over land use were relegated to history books. Mankind had redeemed itself. I was impressed.

"Well?" Betty asked. "What do you make of this brave new world?"

"It's astonishing!"

"Yes, it is."

"So, why cloak the shrooms?"

"Cloaking the shroom habitats eliminates shadows they would throw on the surface, and it is aesthetically more pleasing not to have obstructions in the sky. Also, suspending them frees the surface and provides unparalleled vistas for the inhabitants. Interconnecting them eliminates barriers for wildlife, frees additional land, and eliminates interference with drainage."

"Wildlife barriers?"

"North America has regained its bison herd. At this point, three million six hundred and fifty-three thousand move unimpeded with the seasons."

I gaped at the thought of so many and learned later there were almost as many caribou herds. "So how are the shrooms suspended?"

"We have control of gravitational fields now, Mr. Dawes. An array of anti-grav roundel engines the size of tennis balls under each habitat supports the bulk of their mass, while the elevator anchors select ones and tractor beams anchor all the rest to their respective points. The topside of each city gathers solar energy for power and rainwater."

"I'm impressed. What are the tendrils hanging all over?"

"They're the modern-day equivalent of penthouses. Each has a central elevator that passes through a series of segments. Typically each cylindrical segment houses a single-family unit with a three-hundred-sixty-degree view. Of course the segments vary in size. Some are tens of thousands of square feet in area. Many of the fatter ones are corporate headquarters, religious centers, and hospitals. Privately held ones are for those with great wealth."

I found myself leaning forward, as if to get a better view, and the view screen instantly reacted, zooming in a bit wherever my gaze landed. I smiled, sat back. Betty was good, I'd give her that. "The shrooms all seem to be the same size."

"Indeed, they are. This particular size is optimum for thermal dynamics, magnetic interference, and atmospheric anomalies."

I glanced again at the lush forests below the shrooms. "There seems to be very little farmland in use. Explain that."

"Replicaters have filled that need admirably, but there are still a few million hectares in use for farming on the surface, and many of the shroom habitats, orbitals, and long-range motherships have onboard farms."

"How often does someone fly a plane into one of these blimps, Betty?"

"Never. I control all transportation within federation space. There are no collisions, and even if there were, each habitat has its own protective shield, which I control, as well. I compensate for human error and prevent deliberate attacks."

I sighed. Visions of the World Trade Center towers collapsing filled my mind even a decade after it … I shook my head. No, it was actually centuries ago. Yet the possibilities of deliberate attacks still were considered even after four hundred years.

"What sort of transportation is at my disposal, Betty?"

"Anything, sir: ground, sea, air, and space vehicles are at your command with the requisite security details. You also have access to conveniently placed flash booths if you would like to flash to designated coordinates."

"Flash booths?"

"They're matter transporters. One can travel instantaneously to anywhere in near space, sir."

"Good god," I said more to myself than to the computer. "Captain Picard must be alive and well."

"Yes, sir, there are eleven captains named Picard in your fleet," Betty dutifully informed.

"It's almost too much to handle …ah… never mind. Get me a chopper with a pilot and tell Doc to pick me up. I gotta get out of here and do some exploring if the doc will OK it."

"Acknowledged," said the computer.

"Remind me to ask you later about the flash booths and motherships."

A moment later Dr. Messina was at my door. She had changed into a jumpsuit that conformed to her fine figure and sported a flight cap at a jaunty angle, with a row of three diamonds on one side that was repeated on her collar.

"Nice hat, Doc. I like hats on women. What do the diamonds signify?"

"I hold the rank of flight commander in your fleet, Mr. Dawes."

"Are they real diamonds?"

"Yes, sir, they're real. One of your mines on *55 Cancri e* supplies jewelry-grade diamonds for all fleet officers."

My mines? My fleet? I'd invested in a variety of industries after my lottery win and had a private plane, but not mines, let alone a *fleet* of aircraft. Apparently my advisors had expanded my holdings since then exceptionally well. I had barely gotten used to the power of my lotto assets when the curtain fell on my life along the Bohemian Highway. I'd been headed to get a translation of German text idioms of a document; now my whole world had been translated into something much more foreign. "Where's the bathroom in this place?" I asked. "I want to see what I look like in a mirror."

"Right this way, Mr. Dawes." She guided me out the door with a smile.

"Why doesn't my room have a private bath, for god's sake? I'm supposed to be the high and mighty around here, aren't I? One would think I'd rate a private bath," I said, ribbing her just a little.

"Sir, we thought it best that you find your way gradually through all the new information. Some people find it a shock to see themselves immediately after revival, and some emotional reactions would best be dealt with slowly and with professional assistance. Would you mind if I accompanied you?"

"No, not at all, let's survey the damage. I might have a question or two, like, how many people are revived from stasis each year?"

"Several thousand, three to five, I'd say."

"That's all? I would have thought a lot more given the population in this time period."

"The procedure is prohibitively expensive for most people, Mr. Dawes," she said.

"I see." Again, I congratulated myself for having allocated much of my winnings and profits to the then considered far-fetched idea of cryogenics. At least I'd had enough to get this far —hopefully there was also enough left to get me going in this new life too.

We rounded the corner into an elegantly appointed bathroom with mirrors from floor to ceiling. I did not recognize myself. The person I saw looking back at me did not appear to be Charles Heratio Dawes. He was taller, better built, and had dark hair, olive skin, blue eyes, proportional features with a sort of eastern European look, and a full head of hair; I really liked that part. I was stunned, attracted, and repelled at the same time, but overall a vast improvement. *Money, you just can't live well without it,* I thought to myself.

"My god! What have you done, Doc?"

She cringed defensively. "The accident caused severe damage, Mr. Dawes, so we had to start from scratch, so to speak. Using your will's description of what you thought were ideal attributes for a male, we modified your selection of fifteen male models from your time period into the amalgamation that you are now. In today's world, you are handsome. What do you think, Mr. Dawes?'

"Just messin' with you, Doc; you made me gorgeous." I grinned at her. I thought, *even Emma won't even recognize me* ... my grin left as I realized that my dear wife was gone, had been gone for centuries. I saw a glint of moisture in my new blue eyes in the mirror as I recalled her words, her laugh, at the very idea of cryogenics. '*No way am I becoming a popsicle!'* she'd finished our last discussion on the subject. I knew I could bring her around, given more time, so I'd let it drop. If only .... I swallowed, said, "I guess I'll just have to live with the alterations."

"Actually, you don't." Betty seemed delighted, not recognizing, or maybe understanding, my change in tone. "Many features can easily be changed by thought on demand with some limitations. You can morph certain of your cutaneous features at will, if you want, to some extent, like changing the shape of your nose, for example. You only have to learn to do so on command, and practice doing it rapidly, and that is relatively easy. You'll discover all of your flexibilities in the next few weeks as you learn from your imbedded nano technology. You won't ever have to shave again if you don't want to and you needn't get a hair-cut as often either. Hair growth is one of those flexible features."

"Really? Amazing."

"Yes it is, and you can even change your height about ten centime-ters. That will come in handy when you're in cramped flying quarters or a small bathtub."

I must have had a peculiar look on my face from some introspective thought because she gave me a shy, demur look and added, "And you can alter the size of your appendages to suit the situation."

"Ah-huh, really? What the engineers don't think of, you docs have covered. You are embarrassing me, Doctor."

"I'm well aware of the mores and customs of your time period, Mr. Dawes, but I think you'll soon find twenty-fifth-century customs are easy to adjust to."

"What about the hardiness of my new body?" I asked. "Do I need to be concerned about bugs in the environment?"

"Not at all, actually," she said. "Your nano-organic system is self-re-pairing and the organic component is completely immune to all known hostile micro- and nano-organisms. You're PFF, personal force field, filters out the bad stuff and provides general protection from everything else. It can also adjust the gravitational field to make you lighter or heavier; that comes in handy from time to time. All the committee mem-bers wear them. I'm wearing a PFF right now."

"Really?"

"Yes." She pulled aside her collar to reveal the top of her ample left breast where a small tattoo of a strawberry lay hidden. Under the small red berry glowed four stacked forward slashes, each accompanied by the numeral V. "This is my PFF. Yours is a green four-leaf clover on your right shoulder blade."

Immediately I took off my shirt, and sure enough, there was a little green tattoo the size and shape of a real clover. Under it was one forward slash, followed by the number 450. "What does the slash-450 mean?"

"A slash indicates cryogenic internment."

"I guess the number is the time increment?"

"Correct."

"You were frozen four times for five years each time?" I asked.

"Yes, sorta. Cold stasis, actually. I made two round-robin star treks, five years each way. That's what the slash marks signify. You, on the other hand, were actually frozen solid."

"Where'd you go?"

"Out to the colonies on a research fellowship."

"So what else do I need to know and how do I activate my PFF?"

"You activate your own PFF on command by thinking about it, or it can automatically activate itself if your sensors trigger it, or other PFFs in the vicinity can activate it if their triggers are activated, as well. In any case, you're protected from disease, projectiles, radiation, heat, cold, or oxygen deprivation. You'll learn how to activate it with a mental command later with download instructions. Right now yours is on because mine is on, and I have my field on because today I am your bodyguard."

"A pretty little thing like you? How can you protect me?"

She laughed, "You'd be surprised, Mr. Dawes."

"When can I return to normal activities, like racquetball and swimming?"

"You are ready now. And I think you'll be happy to learn your previous natural sporting skills have been augmented with advanced capabilities built into your nano mainframe and nervous system."

"Doc, I had no natural skills at sports before."

"Well, you will now," she said.

I looked in the mirror with the doctor standing beside me. I couldn't help but notice my chest of black hair and washboard abs. "How much of this hunk is me?" I asked.

Messina's eyes lit as she proudly gave me the run-down. "Your neuro-biological composition is based on your original organic DNA from before the accident, but we improved it with metal alloy nano-organic technology and synthetic DNA. All of your cardiovascular, digestive, and neurological systems have been cloned and improved for maximum performance. Your skeletal architecture is now a thought-controlled metal nano alloy combine, and your musculature is comprised of shape-memory wire with nano-hydraulic augmentation. Your heart is the latest titanium-alloy model. You'll be able to excel at anything that requires physical effort. But to answer your question more specifically, your brain and spinal column are largely the same as before the trauma; however, we have enhanced those, too, with alloys, nanobots, and fiber optics.

"Built into your nervous system are two major advancements we waited so long for before we revived you. One is a nano-organic processor, and the other is a dynamic sensory envelope. The processor, used in cybernetic technology, provides the same comprehensive data processing as in the latest synthetic brains. The envelope expands the cognitive and sensory components of the human psyche."

"Why is it that I don't already know about all of this if I've had these processors and envelopes installed?" I asked quizzically.

"We've improved your abilities, Mr. Dawes, not the depth of your knowledge. You still retain all of what you learned and experienced before stasis, but you must learn or download new knowledge, according to the instructions mandated by your will. Although we have the capability to do so, we did not increase your general knowledge base because we agreed with your directives that only you should be the judge of what you wish to include in it; however, you do have the capability to rapidly absorb anything of interest by visually scanning any database or by implementing a neuro download. The central computer can assist you in a download at any time on command."

For all the improvements she'd mentioned, I don't know quite what I expected to feel, yet I didn't sense that my mind, overloaded as it was with all this, was any sharper than before. "I can't feel the difference, Doc," I said.

"That's good because we designed the augmentations to be subtle. If they were manifested by supernormal sensations, they could lead to abuse or a personality change, which would be detrimental to your persona. Simply put, you might cease to be you."

"OK, I understand," I said. "So when will I feel the difference?"

"You'll notice the difference when you first realize that you innately know the answers to most complex problems, and you'll experience a level of clarity that didn't exist before the accident. You'll soon be able to sense things intuitively in four dimensions, you'll realize that you seldom make material mistakes, and you'll excel at nearly everything because your processing capacity has been increased, along with the speed at which you can process data and sensory stimuli."

I think I raised an eyebrow and did something with my mouth in response to all of that. "Jeez. What's the average lifespan these days?"

She smiled. "It's about a hundred and fifty years for the average citizen, unless one can afford shucking an old shell for a new one. If one can afford it, then one can live almost indefinitely. We really don't know for how long, actually."

"I guess I am one of the lucky few, right?"

"Yes, Mr. Dawes. You'll be able to replace a worn or obsolete body with a cloned shell whenever it seems appropriate. You could live for thousands of years."

"So what's the downside?" I asked, somewhat overwhelmed.

"The downside is you're still human and capable of making emotional errors in personal relationships and in cross-species interactions. Those kinds of errors you will still have to overcome and learn from as you go along just like everyone else."

"My god, doctor, what have you gotten me into?"

"Nothing you can't handle with dignity, Mr. Dawes," she said. "We haven't created a monster; we've just refined someone special."

I wanted to feel flattered even excited, but I couldn't help but stare into the mirror, searching for the monster behind the façade.

Chapter 3: Home

For the rest of the day, Doctor Messina flew me around the neighborhood in a nimble gold-colored Volvo sports car powered by some sort of magnetic field actuator. It hovered, flew into orbit, dove into the Atlantic where the headlights illuminated underwater human communities, and then brought us to a stone manor house that had my name on the wrought-iron gate. It was perhaps the most exhilarating experience of my life.

"Mr. Dawes," she informed me, "your home is completely automated with a central computer, same as the one at the facility. You only need to ask for what you wish. Any one of a full retinue of on-demand servants, both human and synthetic, can show you around. Is there anything else you might need me for?" She made a motion to depart.

"You're leaving me here alone?"

"Yes, this is your home. It was built to your specifications from blueprints you drew. I'm sure you'll know where everything is. Do you remember?"

"I remember some of it, the planning." I'd planned things with a few dozen years in the future in mind. The expenses had seemed exorbitant back then, but, hey, I figured I could afford the best. Apparently I'd figured well. This was one very fine place. Now I'd need to figure how to maintain it in this much more advanced, and no doubt much more expensive, society. "When was it built and who furnished it?" I asked trying to delay her.

"We completed it in 2101. Many of the antique furnishings are from your collection. No doubt you'll recognize some of the properties from before your stasis internment and some were added. While you were away," *while I was away*, I thought, "we developed a computer program based on your known preferences, past purchases, and publications you wrote to make acquisitions after your accident to furnish real properties we bought or built on your behalf. The houses you once owned are all gone now due to fires and wars. But you have this and other residences around the globe."

"I have other houses?"

"Yes, besides this one here in Albemarle County, you have secondary manor houses in Sedona, Hawaii, and Alaska as well as penthouses in high-rises in Washington, New York, Miami, Los Angeles, Vancouver, London, Paris, Barcelona, Prague, Cape Town, Sydney, Hong Kong, Buenos Aries, Lima, and on the Lunar and Mars colonies, and the *Geneses* orbital overhead. You also maintain a sea yacht in the Mediterranean and a mothership in orbit."

I felt my mouth drop open, I clamped it shut, and swallowed. Okay. Let's see. I'd had three houses just yesterday, or what still seemed like yesterday, and now … I was trying to remember the laundry list of mansions but the stream of data being fed to me was more than I could commit to memory. "What about the shrooms?"

"You own a few shrooms, too, Mr. Dawes."

"I'm not surprised. I hope all of 'my' places don't have the same decor," I said, surveying the entrance and the adjacent rooms from the foyer, somewhat overwhelmed by the number and range of properties she listed so nonchalantly.

"No," she laughed. "Each has its own look. I would be curious to know if they will meet with your approval."

"Yeah, me too. All this is putting a strain on my newly installed hardware."

"Well, I must bid farewell," said Dr. Messina. This time she started walking toward the foyer.

"Where're you going?"

"I'm going home now, Mr. Dawes."

"And where is that?"

"I have a villa in Milan."

"Italy? My god, woman, what a commute!"

"It only takes a moment to flash over," she grinned. "Distance is not an obstacle any longer, as you now know."

"Will you be back tomorrow?"

"Yes, of course. I'll return tomorrow at 09:00 hours. I've taken the liberty to call a committee meeting in the morning at 10:00 hours. You'll get a full briefing from your other officers then. In the meantime I suggest you familiarize yourself with your house and catch up on things using the central computer."

"Doctor, you're the only one I know in the entire world," I complained.

"I know, Mr. Dawes, but you'll be fine. Everything imaginable is at your fingertips and you are safe here. Your physiology is monitored continuously, and if there is a problem, I can flashback in less than sixty seconds. Now call up the computer for a while and then get some sleep. Doctor's orders."

She stepped into what appeared to be an elevator in the foyer and was gone. Not even a flash of light or the sparkles of de-composing atoms … she was just gone.

Suddenly I was alone for the first time in my own home. A home I'd dreamt up over four hundred years ago. A home with no family in adjoining rooms, no friends to call over for drinks. Dream … or nightmare? Either way, it was mine.

***

Albemarle House was built to my specifications with a shallow profile using dry-stacked natural gray stone and slate for a roof. It succeeded in being a minimalist, not-so-big house, constructed in a square horseshoe shape with a garden courtyard. The one-story structure had ten-foot-high ceilings throughout and massive fir beams and it brought the outside in with expansive windows and deeply covered surrounding porches. Inside, geothermal heating and cooling systems maintained a constant temperature year round, and radiant heating emanated from the polished marble flooring.

Interior spaces, featuring a den, great room, formal dining room, laundry room, kitchen, and five bedrooms, were laid out comfortably; no room was too large or too small. Each bedroom accommodated a queen-sized bed, walk-in closets, a heated plinth bathtub, and a tiled walk-in shower with radiant heat in the floor and walls. The eat-in kitchen had Shaker-style cherry cabinetry in a natural finish, stainless-steel appliances, and granite countertops.

A gym, racquetball court, heated pool and sauna, wine cellar, shooting range and armory, hobby room for fly tying and picture painting, and massive library were all fitted into the full basement. Even though I didn't yet have a chance to inspect levels three and four under the library, they completed the structure's major architectural features.

I recognized many of my cherished antique painted American furniture pieces, art, and folk art objects from my previous existence. The paneled den with access from the main foyer even had on display my fishing tackle collection with my many copper minnow buckets, Tenkara rods, and hand-tied flies in fitted glass-front showcases all along one side of the room.

Opposite the tackle was my collection of fighting knives, including my SOGs. I stared, and walked over to the dozens of edged weapons and opened the middle cabinet door, slowly. Centered before me against a forest green felt background was the blade that had saved my life in a far-off nightmare called Fallujah. A sheen of sweat suddenly glistened on my brow and upper lip. I shuddered and clamped my eyes shut as flashes of my hand-to-hand combat episode passed through my mind with a hot strobe-like effect. My reoccurring PTSD caused my hands to tremble uncontrollably.

It was the third day of our 24/7 mayhem. I was a Ready-Reserve captain directing a recon element. Most of my men had been med-evaqued already. We were being overrun by drug-augmented nut jobs that had infiltrated the city from across the globe. I saw one asshole attack my men with a bayonet *after* a marine gunner with a SAW had shot his legs out from under him! It was Sadam's home turf and it was lousy with wackos of every nationality. We were winning but at a terrible cost.

I was having a proverbial bad day. Our ammo was exhausted; the CO was dead and Gunny lay eviscerated as concrete dust boiled over us from the relentless mortar concussions pounding us on three fronts. I was the only one remaining and I was surrounded. I remember the heat. The heat, the heat, god almighty the heat, it was like the depths of hell, and it was only April.

My hearing had abandoned me long ago and my mind was mothballed as my body ran on empty. I should have drunk it, but I used the last of our water to flush Gunny's belly as my tongue stuck to the roof of my mouth. I was on the verge of collapse. From a close impact my helmet went flying when suddenly a demented zealot dressed in knee-hole Levis leapt into my peripheral vision. Instinctively, I swiveled in time to deflect the butt of his Kalashnikov from crushing my skull; it only opened my cheek instead. I tasted the copper in my own viscous blood, and for an instant, my vision blurred. Strangely I remember the sound of my jaw grinding the grit of a chipped tooth as I fended off a second blow from this maniac. I dodged away from his third lunge, grabbed the sling on his rifle, and jerked it from his slippery grip and rolled to one side with my knees pulled into a fetal position just as he leapt on top of me, which knocked the wind out of his lungs. It gave me time enough to reach for my SOG – the same blade that I once again was holding in my trembling hands – and grabbed him by his beard pulling him onto its serrated edge to send him on his way through the gates of Hell.

I placed the weapon back into its hollowed place under my Navy Cross and once more compartmentalized the memory.

***

A raised hearth before a dramatic stone fireplace was centered on the opposite wall from the pocket doors. And all my signed first-edition books were within reach in flanking built-in cherry and walnut book-cases. The den made me feel right at home.

I must have stood in the foyer for half an hour pivoting in one spot, checking out every detail while watching specialized bots glide quietly about to perform their designated tasks. The floor in the foyer was var-iegated orange and white marble, and the walls were papered with a dragonfly, bamboo, and dogwood motif against a light sage green field. Opposite the wide entrance was the egress into the garden courtyard. On the starboard wall were pocket doors leading into the great room, and on the left wall was a matching entryway into the den.

In one direction, the glass hallway paralleled the interior of the horseshoe courtyard, with one wall extending past the great room to the kitchen and the length of the gilt dining room. In the opposite direction, the hall went past the den, master suite, and the other bedrooms, all of which had direct access to the hall through pocket doors. Stairs and el-evators accessed the basement from the foyer, kitchen, and master suite. The courtyard had an herb and vegetable garden at the far end near the kitchen, and a wonderful collection of roses and cutting flowers grew opposite. *All in all, a job well done,* I thought to myself.

As for the furnishings, well, I was very pleased with that, too. In my prior existence as a personal property appraiser and consultant, I valued properties for insurance and estate purposes and was therefore exposed to just about every class and age of property imaginable from all periods prior to my earlier timeline. My expertise was necessarily broad and thus my tastes were eclectic. Personally, I gravitated toward nineteenth cen-tury American, English, and Continental furniture in original condition, preferably with original paint or gilding, particularly American Federal furniture, Biedermeier, Art Deco, and important pieces from the Arts & Crafts Movement and mid-20th century moderne. Much to my delight, I found all these styles and period pieces placed throughout this house in a pleasing manner without conflicting aesthetically. Appropriate accessories decorated the rooms in a most gracious way. It was difficult to imagine a better arrangement. What I could not imagine, however, was the fashions that prevailed after my unexpected demise. I was curious.

"Betty?" I said, surmising correctly that the central computer would be here, as well.

A trill sounded softly, "At your service, sir."

"Follow me into the den, please. I would like you to brief me on trends." I sat in a Gustav Stickley slatted arm chair and put my feet up on its matching ottoman.

"Trends, sir?" Her voice followed me, even though I couldn't figure out where the speakers were hidden.

"Yeah. Ah, Betty, can you manifest yourself into a three-dimensional image of some sort so that I might focus my attention on a specific point?"

"Of course." Immediately a holographic image of a blonde woman dressed in dark red business attire appeared seated in a Gus rocker across from me. The chair began rocking gently; I found that amusing.

"That's better," I said. "Thank you, Betty."

"You seem to be in good spirits, Mr. Dawes. Are you adjusting to your surroundings?"

"I am but I don't know what to do with myself or where to begin my re-education. After perusing the house and examining the furnishings, I thought maybe I would start with trends in fashion and decorations since my internment."

"Should we use visual aids and start at the beginning?" she asked.

"That sounds fine. Let's use three or four home and garden-type magazines as a basis, if that's possible. Or whatever you think best."

"I'll provide a synopsis in a visual review of the various industries." She motioned toward a holographic screen that materialized on the wall. A series of classes of objects, beginning with art, appeared in alphabetical sequence in a grid. A sidebar provided the dates, market levels, and values. "Let's begin with art," she directed. Picture followed picture. After a minute or two, I got the hang of it.

"Betty, which types of values are displayed in the sidebar?"

"Replacement values, Mr. Dawes. Retail. Only the major Earth markets. Foreign off-world markets would be another computation."

The dates began at 2000 and rapidly advanced to the present. The trends in art mirrored what I was used to and expected. The best of the best became more valuable over time, and the strongest demand continued for American impressionists and European old masters. Virtually the same styles, mediums, and quality ranges still existed. The only unexpected difference was the addition of off-world art in the last two hundred and fifty years or so. I mentioned this to Betty.

"How many sentient alien species are known, Betty?" I asked.

"That number changes almost weekly. Thousands have been catalogued. Of the ones identified, more than eleven hundred have mastered space travel. Others are in the elementary stages of space exploration, much as Earth was before your accident. Many sentients, however, such as the Odontoceti on Aqueous Lazarus, have little chance of ever achieving space travel."

"Whales?"

"Yes, sir, as a result of an apparent parallel-to-Earth evolutionary phenomenon," she replied.

"Somehow that doesn't surprise me. I suppose their main limitations are the lack of an opposable thumb and the absence of the use of fire?"

"Correct. Both attributes are required for any species to progress, at least as far as we have determined to date," she qualified.

"The spacefaring species, do they visit Earth and do we go to their systems?"

"Yes on both accounts. Actually, the nearest are both from the same binary star system in the Helios Quadrant, but each evolved on a different planet."

"Hmmm. I wonder what the odds are that two sentient species evolved in the same system."

"Incalculable…insufficient data, actually."

"Show me pictures and stats on each."

A trill similar to the central computer's sounded unexpectedly. "What is that?" I asked.

"Your mail is here, Mr. Dawes," replied Betty. "Should I have it brought in?"

"By all means. Who even knows I'm alive?"

The doors to the flash booth opened and in walked an android letter carrier, dressed in a regulation USPS uniform, wearing dark blue short pants, and carrying a black faux leather mailbag stuffed to the gills. I wondered if USPS was still insolvent and if androids occasionally went "postal."

"Hello, Mr. Dawes," he greeted me with a smile. "My name is Wallace and I have today's mail for you. How's it going?" He appeared to be buoyantly friendly.

"Ah, just fine, Wally," I said. "So, I have mail?"

"Yes, sir, the *Maine Antique Digest*, your favorite, and some junk mail," he said handing it to me. I noticed the front page featured an articulated image of a Freeman's auctioneer hammering a gavel at the conclusion of a bid sequence for an antique iPhone.

"How the devil did you know that *MAD* was my favorite trade paper?" He began pulling all sorts of junk from his bag. "And what's all this infernal crap? What, I still get junk mail? Good god!"

"Betty told me it is your favorite," he beamed, referring to *MAD*.

"What else have you told him?" I looked her way, bristling.

She, with one arm crossing her bosom and the other hand under her chin, was observing me. "Only what he needs to know to be a congenial civil servant," she smiled.

"Thank you, Wally. Have a good day," I said as I dismissed him.

"Thank you, sir. See you tomorrow," Wally said over his shoulder on his way out.

I held the three-inch thick trade paper in my hands. "Betty, I can't believe *MAD* is still in circulation." I also couldn't believe the motion pictures on the front and some of the inside pages, like how I remember they were in the Harry Potter movies.

"We thought it might still interest you," she said, "especially since you have controlling interest in the paper now."

"What? I own it?"

"Yes, and several other publications, namely the *New York Times*, *London Times*, and the *Washington Post*."

I just stood there blinking. So maybe I didn't have to worry about having enough to live on in this new world. Now I just had to figure how to cope with it all.

"Are you still interested in receiving the printed version of *MAD*?"

"Well, yes, and I must say, that was very thoughtful of you," I told her. "I love it. And it looks the same as it did before. Except, of course for the moving pictures …," I turned a page and got a whiff of old leather, "the smells, and well, whatever else."

"Most subscribers receive it as a download these days, Mr. Dawes, but I thought you might appreciate it more in the printed version. We had it run off just for you."

"Well, don't bother with the other papers. I can't stand their liberal editorials."

"Mr. Dawes, their cant is somewhat different today than it was in your time before."

"Really? How would you know that? Can you discern the nuances of human political weather patterns?" I remarked a little too sarcastically.

"Actually, yes. Funny you should compare human nuances with weather patterns," she said as she crossed her legs and folded her hands on her lap. I couldn't help notice that her aura, before this a pale shade of holographic red, shimmered ever so slightly as if a shiver of indignity had ran up her spine.

"Why's that?" I inquired, furrowing my brow.

"Well, because, although the number of permutations for each is infinite, all cybernetic sentient entities for the last three hundred and seventy-two years have been able to discern such subtle nuances. Furthermore, the central computer on Earth as well as the other settled planets controls weather patterns and human nuances. Both are simple calculus these days. How do you think you and I interact so well?" she insisted. "Anyway, trust me when I tell you the editorials are not canted. I think now you will appreciate their 'Just-the-facts-Jack' reporting."

I couldn't tell if I was arguing with a computer or a woman, but it made little difference. "OK, where were we?" I tried to recall.

"Here are the images and stats you requested on the two alien species," she presented as she turned toward the screen where the two were featured side by side.

"There are similarities," I said interested.

"Yes, as you can see they have the basic architecture of Homo sapiens. They are hardier than humans, however. Their nervous, cardiovascular, and pulmonary systems are all much more tolerant to temperature, radiation, and atmospheric extremes. Their major difference is that they are hermaphroditic."

"What?"

"They can change gender."

"That's gross."

She laughed. "And they can switch back and forth in a matter of seconds, too."

"You're freakin' me out, Betty." I kept a straight face.

She laughed again.

"Are they hostile?"

Her laughter quieted, and she turned her bright eyes to me with a serious answer. "In the past they have been. The Second Space War ended their confrontational behavior. Since then they've allied with the Federation of Planets, which is a trade organization that spans the entire Milky Way and into four neighboring galaxies where we have mining, agricultural, shipping, security, communication, manufacturing, and colonial interests. Trade routes between their single system and our many systems are strong. Like us, they thrive better in peace. Besides, we are technologically superior to them and they're vastly outnumbered. It is in their best interest to maintain the status quo, which they have done for the past one hundred and eleven years."

"What do they call themselves?" I asked.

"On the left is an image of a male Grummite from the planet Helios Grumm, and the other is a male Shuntipeed from Helios Shunt. Sometimes they're derogatorily referred to as Grunts and Shunts.

"Ugly buggers, aren't they? They both look like they might have the dispositions of junkyard dogs."

She laughed. "That about sums it up. Let me supply you with a download to fill you in on the details. It'll only take about two seconds."

"What about these other downloads I keep hearing about?"

"You've been injected with nano-organic receptors that can absorb any projected download from a cybernetic source. All you have to do is authorize it and open your receptors," she explained.

"I don't know how to open my receptors."

"Open your mind and consciously will yourself to absorb the download."

"What if someone downloads something against my will?"

"Your receptors automatically block everything. You must deliberately will the connection to open before it takes effect."

"Even in my sleep?"

"Yes."

I wanted to believe her but instantly had visions of the haunting nightmares that inflicted themselves on my nights. Bursts of my combat days in the military, visions of creatures as ugly as that boarzilla I'd eaten as my breakfast bacon, and sensations of falling into an endless black abyss … I'd had them all and had no control, it seemed. "What if I'm in REM sleep and I will them to open as part of a dream?"

"That's impossible. Your receptors compensate for states of consciousness. You have to be within an acceptable conscious parameter before the filter will permit a download."

She had an answer for everything. "All right," I said somewhat convinced. "Download the info about the two alien species."

Betty snapped her fingers and smiled. Suddenly more than two hundred years of data poured into my consciousness like water into a bucket. Subliminally the new knowledge coated my mind like a warm blanket of oatmeal, yet with the added weight akin to donning a heavy Kevlar helmet. The thought I had: *a burden of power that feels like freedom,* sailed through the convolutions of my brain and dissolved in the distant regions of wisdom and folly. As the millisecond session ended, my mind clawed with the intensity of an addict consuming the remnants of a final hit. *Downloading,* I thought, *use it sparingly or risk losing one's sense of wonder*...then a mental sound like – chuck! It was over.

"Well?" Betty inquired.

"Unbelievable."

"You'll get used to it, maybe even get hooked on it if you're not careful. I suggest you consult Dr. Messina before you engorge yourself on the Library of Congress database."

"Can I absorb that much?"

"That and more. Your mainframe is equivalent to twice the computing capacity that existed on Earth at the time of your internment."

A surge of astonishment and, I'll admit it, pride swelled inside me. "Good god! That's an enormous amount! And what about your capacity?"

She stood and gestured palms up, with her arms down along her slender figure. "I'm merely a visible particle of sand on the central computer beach, but to answer your question, my capacity is roughly a six followed by a trillion zeros times greater than your potential capacity, Mr. Dawes."

"Now I understand why weather isn't much of strain for you," I murmured, as that swelled ego of mine, from only a second before, shrank to marble size.

Chapter 4: The A-Team

Kay Cushing, my attorney; Dawn Fisk, my financial advisor; John Skill, my security chief; and, of course, Dr. Renatta Messina were present at my first after-thaw committee meeting in my den at Albemarle House. All flashed in on time and in business attire.

Kay appeared to be in her early forties. Her dark brown hair was a modified pageboy that understated her professional position in the organization, and she wore a gray pinstripe business suit with a white silk blouse. Above her big violet eyes were carefully sculpted eyebrows. She reminded me of Catherine Zeta Jones. According to the information I'd downloaded on them earlier, Kay held more cryptic degrees in Universal Law than an alphabet soup had letters.

Dawn could have easily been a cover girl with her long straight blond hair and dark brown eyes. Her tweed outfit had an English equestrian cut, as though she might be on her way to a highbrow steeplechase. Perky would be an appropriate term to describe her. She appeared very astute, as fit the numerous financial accreditations and affiliations I'd seen in her dossier.

John had been a Marine colonel when on active duty and appeared to still be a warrior in demeanor, but one who knew a flawless tailor. His gray tweed suit was impeccably cut. From the way he held himself, he was obviously accustomed to issuing commands. He stood ramrod straight at two meters, wore his red hair short, and had the complexion of Scots Highlander. I wouldn't be surprised if he kept a kilt in his wardrobe for special occasions.

Renatta's suit was royal blue, and I wore a white shirt under a dark green tweed jacket and brown slacks. Betty was also present. She advised me that one other member, Admiral Pride, would not be joining us for this meeting unless we needed him.

After initial introductions, I leaned back on a tufted green apple green club sofa, which was perpendicular to the huge stone fireplace in which hickory wood blazed and popped. Renatta sat at the other end of my sofa, while Kay and Dawn sat on a matching sofa across from us. In between the sofas was a pin-top, one-drawer white pine farm table cut down to function as a coffee table. A five-hundred-year-old Kurdish area rug that I bought in 1998 from *Green Front* in Farmville, Virginia, decorated the floor beneath. A chandelier I'd made from antlers naturally dropped by male whitetail and mule deer and collected by boy scouts provided overhead illumination. John swirled a tumbler of lime and seltzer as he stood in front of the fire. Everyone else had Starbucks coffee, which Dawn had thoughtfully brought.

"Why on Earth did you all wait four hundred and fifty years to bring me back to life?" I asked.

Kay was the first to respond. "Initially, Mr. Dawes, our reasons were technological, as Renatta no doubt explained, and then global political instability, followed by re-occurring political differences within the committee, hindered us. All this preceded the First and Second Space Wars. Only in the past decade or so has everything been in perfect order." I noticed Kay had a tendency to rattle her pen when she became impatient.

"What differences?"

Kay responded again, this time treading carefully and choosing her words with precision. "In a nutshell, philosophical differences were the fundamental problem a few decades ago but there was also an underlying cultural bias in favor of biotics."

"I don't understand. What philosophical differences?"

"Some believed the dead should remain dead and others thought the opposite."

I leaned back into the cushion, looked around the room at my staff, and exhaled. "Oh, that. I'm glad the latter group prevailed. Thank you very much, folks." All of them looked relieved at how I took the news that there had been members of my own committee who wanted me out of the equation. Memories of how I had prepared for this eventuality flooded back rapidly.

"So, why was there a philosophical difference when my orders were perfectly clear in the first place?"

"It's complicated, Mr. Dawes," John said.

"Yeah, well, then give me the short version."

Kay began. "Mr. Dawes, both humanity and the committee went

through a period of reformation."

"You mean a religious reformation, like Martin Luther?"

"On that order of magnitude of importance, yes," she responded. "As for the humanity reformation: Man developed FTL propulsion and widespread colonization of our solar system, perfected Artificial Intelligence, and discovered evidence of the Ancient Ones. Life as we knew it suddenly got a kick in the pants. Some niche cultures and fundamental religions could not absorb the rapid changes and withdrew into their respective doctrines, avoiding the obvious and the inevitable. A few became radicalized, as in your time. Remember the Muslim Brotherhood?"

"Yeah, I remember. Nut jobs. The whole bunch. FTL, what? Faster than light?" I asked. They all nodded. I had guessed correctly. "Ancient Ones, evidence of intelligent aliens who had populated earth in ancient times?"

"Not really," replied John. "We'll discuss them in detail in a bit."

"OK. Go on, please."

Kay took a sip of her coffee and continued. "Well those 'nut jobs' and a handful of others banded together and disrupted the peace system-wide until they were hunted down and completely destroyed to the last man, woman, and child."

"Parts of Pakistan, Iran, and Syria still glow in the dark," John said seriously.

"That's a bit harsh, don't you think? Last *child*?"

John blushed and gave me a synopsis of the history. "The unrest began with the Arab Spring shortly after your time and escalated to a full frontal attack on the Western powers across the globe and in near space. One by one the bastards took out American and British embassies and consulates. Emboldened with success over the decades, they bombed two shroom cities, which caused millions of casualties. They almost succeeded in destabilizing an orbital, but that attack was the last straw for the Royal Houses of the Middle East. From the chaos, a charismatic Saudi Prince, HRH Abdul Faruk, rose to save the day and rescue humanity. This followed a protracted era weakened by a poor global economy and a succession of weak-kneed American presidents who couldn't find their asses in the dark." John paused for effect, grabbing his own butt.

"So what happened?"

"Prince Abdul married an Israeli and formed an offensive alliance with Israel, Jordan, and Turkey. Then, at a meeting of the Bilderberg

Group in Crete, he demanded that the US, UK, and the EU follow him into battle or suffer his wrath after he finished off the bad guys."

The hair on my neck stood at attention. "Sounds like a man I could admire!"

John continued. "Rightly so. And follow they did. All of them. Along with a few other hardscrabble types. His leadership provided the cohesiveness to form a strong union which was enough to convince the Aussies, the Japanese, the Koreans, and even the Chinese, to join the coalition. Historians now refer to the ensuing worldwide slaughter as Abdul's War. It was an effective strategy led by a tactical genius that proved to be as ruthless as his adversaries. By the way," he motioned with his thumb, "he was one of Renatta's ancestors." He nodded to her.

I looked at Renatta. "I didn't know you were a princess."

A little embarrassed, she replied, "Yeah, well, it never came up until now, sir."

"Should I be addressing you differently?" I said smiling.

She laughed. "No, sir, your rank is much higher than mine, than all of us in fact, in every respect. No one out ranks you. You are our Founder."

I looked around for snickers or condescending smiles, but saw only open awe and stark seriousness in their expressions. I quickly tried to think of what to ask next. This 'Founder' bit was going to take getting used to. "This Bilderberg Group thing, isn't it some sort of think tank?"

John replied, "Not at all, sir. It was spawned by the conjoined efforts of a few powerful, greedy men who couldn't get enough power. They threatened, bribed, and cajoled presidents and academics into believing a New World Order was an ideal better than national sovereignty. President Wilson was one of the early idealists that capitulated to the New World Order concept even before the Bilderberger types had formed into a formal organization. He was the front man that organized the U.S. Federal Reserve Bank in 1913. Once people became used to the Fed as an entity, other goliaths were invented, such as the World Bank in 1944 and the United Nations in 1945. The idealists that led to the formalization of what would become the Bilderberg Group first met in 1954 at a hotel in Holland by the same name."

"Hence the Bilderberg Group?"

"Correct. Its members fancied themselves as sort of a steering committee for the Fed, the World Bank, and the UN. Initially cloaked in secrecy, the Bilderberg Group remained the invisible arm of what was a de facto world shadow government. Its ringleaders were members of the Rothschild and Rockefeller dynasties. They easily recruited European royalty, heads of a half dozen other powerful families, and a select few like-minded moguls, politicians, and charismatic leaders. The core of the Bilderberg Group believed if they could control capital, they could eventually dominate the planet. Many of their members were unwitting pawns in the greater scheme of things."

"Sounds a bit like an urban planning committee to me," I said, smiling. I looked around. Everyone's lips became a thin line. They were taking this discussion more seriously than was I.

John stiffened and responded, "No sir. They were intent on a New World Order which would remove national sovereignty and condense power into the tip of their very own pyramid."

"And they were the tip, I suppose," I replied more seriously.

"Yes sir."

The others nodded.

"So what happened?"

John made himself comfortable in a squeaky leather chair, took a sip, and proceeded. "Remember a minute ago when Kay said that both humanity and the committee went through a reformation?"

"Yes."

Kay perked up. "They tried to recruit the committee."

I looked at Kay and repeated. "So what happened?"

John replied, "We refused. Then they began a campaign of threats that escalated over time to the point that they tried to murder us en masse. Their attempt was masked by a larger ploy. It failed. They created a situation similar to an event you may remember." He paused, allowing me to guess but I didn't have a clue what he was getting at. Clueless seemed to be my middle name too much of the time anymore.

John continued. "Remember the start of the War on Terror?"

"Yes."

"We were scheduled to meet at the Universal Trade Center, whose fate repeated that of the World Trade Center on September 11th 2001."

I was so astounded that I was at a loss for words. I sat back from the edge of my seat and stared out the window at a cedar waxwing pecking sunflower seeds from a bird feeder.

"The Bilderberg Group tried to kill my committee," I stated. Everyone let that sink in for a minute. "When did that happen?"

"In 2085," Dawn answered.

"So, what happened to them?" I asked.

"Who, the committee members?" asked Kay, twirling her stylus. I nodded.

"We'd caught wind of a possible threat, never grasping the magnitude of it, and changed our venue at the last moment. Fortunate for us, but not for the thousands who did die. Afterwards, we joined the Bilderberg Group," replied Renatta.

"Why did you do *that*?" I was dumfounded.

John replied, "Because at the time they were too powerful for us to destroy. Too many died that day because of their attempt to kill us. We took a different approach."

"If you can't beat them, join them."

John nodded. "Exactly. We calculated that if we went inside that we could affect a difference over time, and we did."

"How long did it take?"

"We were patient," replied Dawn.

John answered, "It took a century and a half."

"Jeez, you guys are patient. I don't know if I could have waited so long. What did you have to do?"

John looked at the others before turning back to me. "We had to do our own brand of subterfuge, beat them at their own game, as it were. A few of the more recalcitrant assholes were killed. Eventually we gained full control and we are still in control to this day."

"So, where does the Bilderberg Group meet these days?"

"We renamed the Bilderberg Group, sir," interjected Dawn. "It's known as the Federation of Planets today."

I was in a daze. It just kept getting more complicated, or so it seemed. I looked around the room. "When did it end?"

They looked puzzled. "When did what end?" Renatta asked.

"The War on Terror."

"2105," Dawn replied.

"So it took 104 years," I said, shaking my head in wonder. I often wonder how stupid mankind is, or at least certain elements of mankind.

John calculated, "Yes, I guess that's right."

The others nodded, waited for me to think this out loud some more, I guess.

"I remember when The War on Terror began. I was building a house when someone yelled for me to turn on the TV. My friend, Tuck the carpenter, stood by my side. The first trade tower was already on fire. Minutes later the second tower was struck. We couldn't believe a jet had just crashed into a building! Both towers tumbled down. 'Who would do such a thing?' Tuck asked. It took a moment to retrieve the name, but I replied, 'Osama Bin Laden.' Even though Tuck had heard him mentioned in the news, most people hadn't heard of him before that fateful day. I never mentioned this before now, but about a year earlier I had my crosshairs on him from 1,000 meters out. I could have easily taken his head off, but the White House didn't have the balls to let me pull the trigger."

"I wish you had. It would have altered history. FYI, that President's wife gave the order about ten years later as Secretary of State," John said.

"Really? That doesn't surprise me. Made a good one, too, I'll bet."

"Yes," he replied, "but the ineffectiveness of her President became the cornerstone of confidence on which the bad guys built their vast network of revolution to try to completely annihilate civilization. He had a chance to nip it in the bud but he was weak. Luckily, Abdul was his polar opposite."

"Oh boy. Looks like I'll have to brush up on my current events. Kay, you were saying?"

"Yes," she continued. "No sooner was the terror issue settled that the AI issue moved to the front burner as a well-formed cause de celeb. Robots, cybernetic androids, and other synthetic sentients banded together with AI. Political luminaries saw an opportunity to further their careers and lent their weight to the cause, even demanding recognition for AI's as legal persons. War erupted across the system, which of course directly affected the committee. Both opinions were represented. A schism formed between the two schools of thought. Much of the initial contention was kept confidential but it lasted several years and threatened your existence, literally. Half the human members were opposed to synthetics, cloned shell replacements, and most all forms of enhancements, and they vehemently wanted to pull your plug. Naturally, the synthetic members had the opposite view. The animosity dissolved over time because the human members began using enhancements. Today it is a non-issue. Most people, including all of us here, are either enhanced in some manner or are nearly entirely synthetic, including you, Mr. Dawes."

My eyes probably glazed over in thought. I couldn't help it. They were patient, I noticed. The topic was complex and the permutations infinite. After a moment I was back on track. "And these AI forms are now considered what? Human?" I asked.

"Legal People," answered Betty.

"Legal People. Right. Interesting stuff…How bad was this internal war you spoke of?"

"A lot of people lost their lives," replied John, "and business was disrupted significantly because the synths and robots went on general strike. Mining, transportation, medical, manufacturing – the whole nine yards – came to a screeching halt for nearly two years all across the local spiral. The authorities, including the Dawes Conglomerate and other mega corps, finally got their act together and recognized all sentients. Equal rights were recognized. AI computers and ambulatory AI's with sufficient cognitive IQ were considered real people, the same as humans and sentient alien life forms."

"Ambulatory AI's?" I asked, puzzled.

"Yes, bots, droids, and synths with qualifying IQ levels," explained Renatta.

"Mr. Dawes," Dawn changed the subject, her eyes intense, "the committee is now at your service as a sound instrument of your will. Every committee member, deputy member, staff, cadre, and the whole administration of the Dawes Conglomerate are loyal. You are our Founder, with a capital 'F,' and our benefactor. We need your leadership. The members chose this moment in time to revive you because it was in both your and our best interest, and it happened to be the right moment in history."

"Technologically, this was the right moment, too, Mr. Dawes," added Renatta, glancing at Kay over the rim of her coffee cup. "We chose this moment to revive you because we've made vast improvements in the human mind and body. Life expectancy is virtually infinite. Over the course of the next few days or weeks your enhanced properties will become self-evident as you adjust to your new body. We and others will all assist in your training."

John, who appeared to still be every bit the buff Marine colonel he was when on active duty, interjected, "Mr. Dawes, frankly, reviving you at this moment in time was in the committee's best interest. Besides the technological advancements, the needs of the many mandated your return. We need a leader with your traits based on your leadership profile to cope with the current changing political and business dynamics. The fact that we have the ability to make a perfect human specimen was a secondary consideration, at least from my security perspective."

I looked at their too-eager faces. I might have been the elder in the group, but I was also the new kid on the block. This "we need you" bit might have been flattering, but not when I didn't have a clue what was going on. "Kay mentioned the First and Second Space Wars. If the Abdul's War is the first, what was the Second Space War all about?" I queried.

"Abdul's War was not the First Space War," re-explained John patiently, I noticed. "It was the conclusion of the War on Terror. Abdul's War was an Earth war that preceded and overlapped the beginning of the First Space War. The First Space War, which lasted from 2095 to 2105, was the AI war we were just talking about. Scholars refer it to as the Great Sentient Impression – kind of like the Arab Spring but for AIs – which culminated in system-wide sentient Legal Person legislation in 2107. The First Space War was an ideological conflict between humans who refused to acknowledge AIs as equals. Naturally, the AIs sided with their supporters. The rift was split fifty-fifty amongst humans, but when a hundred percent of the AIs backed their supporters, the conclusion was inevitable.

"The Second Space War happened about eighty years later, in 2185; it was a cultural and territorial conflict that erupted after FTL warp drives were in general use. The Others, other sentients, refused to acknowledge us despite our probes. We were simply not important enough to warrant their time and resources, though over time our mining, shipping, and exploratory presence in the quadrant grew gradually until our presence reached a nuisance level that they couldn't ignore. To put it bluntly, we became a hazard in the Other community. First contact, significant contact, came in 2163 with the trade-friendly Tokeen Empire, a peaceful humanoid people with a much faster version of the Alcubierre-type FTL drive. From them we received the key clue that led to an exponential improvement in FTL science, one that we have since improved exponentially again, and traded back to them. Today the Tokeen are our strongest allies."

"If we'd been considered just a nuisance by the rest of the universe, what did the Tokeens want from us?" I asked.

"Initially they were attracted to human creativity," Dawn replied. "The Tokeen lack the artistic abilities that we take for granted. They are unable to create music, sing, dance, sculpt, or paint."

"Sounds like a lot of people I used to know."

"Yeah, well, you should see their 'art museums' on their home world

– really bad – and they never realized how bad until they began interacting with humans. But what they lack in talent, they make up for in connoisseurship. They wallow in all forms of our art and buy everything we produce, including cinema, television, radio, and fine art. There are more human artists than ever before, and because of the Tokeen, only the stupid ones are starving."

"Fascinating. There's still no cure for stupid." I smiled but by their blank expressions, none of the others caught on the my now-archaic reference.

Dawn plunged on. "Because they love our culture so much, they were keen to sign long-term leases for port access on trading posts not only here in our home system, but at all other human colonies as we expanded into the galaxy arm." Dawn had warmed to her subject, and I guessed an obvious impact of all this had been financial—something she'd appreciate. "It was a win-win situation. Nowadays we have a security alliance with the Tokeen, like the old NATO and SEATO pacts that you probably recall." I nodded in the affirmative. "We have benefited mutually ever since, and they proved to be a strong ally when we got into a bit of galactic trouble early on."

"The Second Space War?"

"Yes," replied Kay and Dawn.

"So, the First was an AI emergence war, so what was the Second War all about, trade?"

John answered. "In a word, culture, and then secondarily trade conflicts in a sort of chicken-and-egg situation. We unwittingly barreled our way across surveyed space, smashing numerous toes along the way that had been in established relationships for millennia. For us humans it was the Wild Wild West and Manifest Destiny all over again, or so we thought and that's how we proceeded. This time, though, the stage was on a galactic scale, not a continental scale. It all went to hell almost overnight because the combat played out at FTL speeds. There is a big difference between fighting against bows and arrows and fighting against plasma cannons and black lasers. This time the Indians fought back viciously with everything unimaginable and they almost won. Humanity clung by its short hairs. We were desperate just to survive and the aliens couldn't give a damn if they wiped out our entire DNA code."

"How long did that war last?" I asked.

"Two years," John answered. "FTL space wars tend to be rapid and short-lived."

Kay continued, "Seven enemy races joined forces across the four quadrants. We would have been blasted back to the Stone Age if the Tokeen hadn't interceded on our behalf. Billions died in any event. We were driven all the way back to our home system before being rescued diplomatically. It was a very close call. The Tokeen pretty much drew a line in the proverbial sand and dared anyone to cross it. Everyone stood down, cooled off, and convened at the First Galactic Summit."

"Good grief," I sighed. "You mentioned culture was a problem."

Kay nodded. "Besides determining shipping lanes, the Summit codified behavior. Basically, we were given a set of existing laws to read and one year to comply."

John explained the details. "The cause for the Second Space War was simple: young male humans misbehaving – go figure. Humans repeatedly got into trouble in off-world jurisdictions and were subjected to the laws of the Others. More than a few of those laws are bizarre by our standards."

"How so?" I shrugged.

"Execution is common, not just for serious offenses, but also for what we would consider petty offenses until explained in the context of the alien culture," replied John. "Infractions can vary greatly from one world to the next. In the Chongo system, for instance, one can have an appendage chopped off for merely stepping on a rolling coin featuring the face of that world's king. Sleep with the spouse of a Helios citizen and the court will issue a warrant to the offended spouse, allowing him or her to personally hunt you down, torture you in any manner for as long as they wish, and execute you."

"Good grief."

"In the Wiivên System more than a few seemingly minor offenses can lead to the execution of not only the perpetrator but his or her entire extended family. Step off the path in the wrong place on their home world and you may have committed the most grievous offense. Apparently the Wiivên reproductive mechanism is similar to an Aspen clonal colony; it's underground. Stepping on their root system injures or kills their unborn. They get a bit irate when a human who hasn't done his or her homework digs for fishing worms in the middle of their nursery. A Wiivên court will issue a warrant almost immediately. Interpol steps aside. A bonded Wiivên agent arrests the perp's children and returns with them to the Wiivên home world, whereupon they are pickled, cooked, and eaten by the offended clan."

"And the courts permit this?" I asked incredulously.

"Yes," Kay added. "To maintain the galactic peace, the Others forced our courts to sign treaties to uphold their laws or face human extinction. Once mankind signed on to play by the rules, peace prevailed. We haven't had much trouble since. Humans still get into trouble regularly, but we can usually deal with the more grievous offenses by a simple diplomatic exchange of a human offender for an alien offender. Aliens get in trouble, too, on our worlds. For example, an Xurian, whose home world experiences the equivalent of a four month-long day, is accustomed to mating at sunrise with the first person they see—man or woman, willing or not. And when they do that on our worlds, they are subject to our laws. If a Federation citizen perp flees to a Federation planet, Interpol gets involved from the human side. The same is the case for alien perps and their respective law enforcement agencies. There are extradition treaties in place for the return of captured fugitives to stand trial in the jurisdiction of origin."

"It's complicated," I said.

"Very." John continued, "After the Second Space War we mended fences with many humble apologies, paid some reparations, and signed a number of trade agreements. We swore to uphold all the broadly accepted rules of colonization the Others established thousands of years before we arrived on scene. Peace has lasted, but some would argue it has only lasted because humans rebuilt their fleet by several orders of magnitude. We now have the best and most powerful presence in the Milky Way and four other neighboring galaxies. Every sentient species once at odds with humanity has now allied with us. We no longer have sworn enemies. In fact, we have become the enforcement power Others look to for fairness and equitable sentencing under Universal Law. At present there are no major interplanetary wars and most of the trading species are expanding on average of eight percent per standard year."

"How does the Dawes Conglomerate fit into all this?" I asked.

"We signed up early on," replied Dawn. "Most of humanity's fleet is the Dawes fleet."

My jaw dropped. I was beginning to understand the breadth and scope of power at my fingertips. It was exciting and frightening at the same time. "So, this power, it's at my beck and call?"

"Yes, sir," John replied.

"We've learned to use our power sparingly and to work and play peacefully with the adults in the galactic neighborhood," replied Kay.

"So far we have done a pretty good job on our own but we need you, Mr. Dawes, to join us now."

"If you're doing such a fine job without me, why?"

"Well, you mean besides the fact that your reanimation has been a fundamental tenant and prime directive for the Dawes Conglomerate all along?" Dawn said. "It's because you also provide another layer of judgment for policy decisions."

"And you're a proven leader with a cool head under fire," replied John.

"And the Conglomerate needs a public face," Renatta added, pointing her dimples in my direction. "I can't think of a more handsome image than yours, sir." Kay and Dawn nodded in the affirmative. Even Betty nodded her approval. One or two dormant butterflies flapped their velvet wings. John shrugged his shoulders as if to communicate his inability to judge in this matter.

I ignored the doctor's compliment. "Right, so I'm actually a figurehead like the Queen of England. Great. What's my personal financial situation at this time?" I directed the question to my financial advisor, changing the subject.

Dawn replied, "Your financial situation is sound and virtually limitless as a result of a combination of compounded interest and shrewd investments. You can accomplish anything where wealth is required. You have only to ask for the extraordinary and it will appear. The committee and your administration take care of your ordinary luxuries, tasks, concerns, and administrative duties. Your holding companies have controlling interests in more than seven hundred corporations that employ three billion people and fourteen billion cybernetic beings in mining, shipping, manufacturing, services, banking, insurance, and security. You have nearly half a billion starships of various classes in your service that trade across the galaxy. Mr. Dawes, you are the wealthiest person anywhere in the Federation of Planets."

I gulped. "In 2010 dollars, what am I worth?"

"At a certain point wealth is irrelevant; it becomes power. As you probably remember, you had enough time to get a taste of it before your accident. One can only eat so much, use so many personal or real properties, or partake in so many pleasurable diversions. After that, wealth becomes influence and power whether one likes it or not," Dawn explained.

"Yeah, I know all that. How much?" I insisted.

"Approximately eleven hundred googolplex, in 2010 dollars. I knew you'd eventually ask that question, so I asked Betty to do the calculations yesterday evening."

"Huh?"

"A googol is ten to the hundredth power," explained Dawn. "A googolplex is ten to a googol power."

"Oh my god," I said. "I think I need a download, or a whiskey, or something." I was suddenly overwhelmed by a staggering amount that the unenhanced human mind had no way of grasping. From my lucky Mega Lotto winnings of $297 million in 2005, this googol-whatever had grown exponentially to a sum with so many zeroes, well, I was at a loss for words. True, I had prudently invested for the very long term, and I created a consortium with the intent to research, develop, and subsequently patent new technologies, but in 2005 I had no idea it would result in such a grand fruition. Shortly before my accident Bill Gates was the wealthiest man on the planet with around fifty billion in assets, but now, in 2460, I found myself with a depth of assets that made Gates' wealth look like lunch money. I was speechless.

I sat in silence while Dawn prattled on uttering sounds that seemed momentarily muffled, like Spielberg's beach-landing scene in, *Saving Private Ryan*. Other random thoughts popped into my head, like the image of my dad telling me he worked a ten-hour day for one measly dollar, or the image of farmer Yowell telling me he paid off his farm during the Great Depression by trapping skunks at seven dollars a pelt. Other images were too numerous to recall. I felt as though I had just been pulled through a knothole.

As I finally emerged out of the fog, Dawn said, "You needn't be concerned, Mr. Dawes. We have your investments spread widely and invested extremely conservatively, for the most part. Your NAV increases at a modest rate of 4.4 percent after taxes per annum."

"What?" I said, bewildered by the enormity of it all.

"You haven't heard a word I've said, have you?" Dawn complained.

"My head hurts," I blurted.

"Would you care for water?" asked Renatta.

"And some Excedrin, please," I grunted from the comfort of the sofa.

"We don't need Excedrin anymore, Charles. I'll just make an adjustment with my Merck Modulator and you'll feel better right away." And I did, too. Feel better right away, that is. But the weight on my shoulders was still enormous. What was I to do about that? My god! "I could still use a whiskey," I said, still sounding testier than I meant to.

"Of course," Betty answered and had no sooner spoken than a robot whisked through the door with a glass of amber whiskey on crushed ice. I took a sip, welcoming the familiar taste of Macallan bourbon (my favorite), and glad for a moment more to reflect.

"So what responsibilities do I have?" I asked after regaining my composure.

"Mr. Dawes," Kay replied, "you can become involved any way you wish."

"Obviously I must be of small consequence if business has been doing so well for centuries without me. Why even bother reviving me in the first place?"

"In addition to what we have explained to you so far," answered John, "your belief system is the basis for the success of the Dawes Conglomerate."

"My belief system? What belief system? What do I believe that is so important?"

John seemed noticeably patient with me as if I were his young nephew. I was feeling excessively vulnerable, which they could easily tell. "Sir, remember the 'Ts'?"

"What?"

"Don't you remember?" John coaxed. "You lived by a certain moral code. You used to say, 'It's the 'Ts' that I live by.'"

I just sat there and looked at him.

"You instilled those 'Ts' in those you surrounded yourself with. Well, we wove them into the fabric of your corporate culture and into the moral fiber of the societies we have propagated and will propagate across the colonial neighborhood of the Conglomerate."

"Christ! What the hell are you talking about?" I said, frustrated.

John knelt on one knee before me and leaned his forearm across his knee. "Integrity, fidelity, loyalty, honesty, veracity, reliability, dependability, punctuality."

It was then I remembered the code of conduct – *my* code of conduct – that the Boy Scouts had first instilled in me, followed by a similar inculcation led by my first sergeants and captains. This code, which I embraced back in my day, had its roots in the chivalric code of the twelfth-century Normans. And now? Are you kidding? It hadn't changed one iota. For all that had changed, for all that overwhelmed me now, this one thing remained. I eagerly welcomed it in this new timeline without hesitation and with a sense of relief akin to a spiritual awakening. Perhaps I was slightly allergic to John's cologne; I had to blink away something in my eye. All I could manage was a nod.

"Yes. My Ts," I croaked. "They ruled my life before and now … they are all that really matter to me, all I have left. My loved ones are no more. Everything else is either elementary, superfluous, or a toy for amusement, as far as I am concerned. And you have incorporated my Ts into how the Conglomerate conducts its affairs?"

"Yes," said a chorus of voices, including Betty's.

"We need your wisdom, Mr. Dawes," declared John, returning to his seat.

"We need your perception," added Renatta, wiping away a tear.

I nodded, understanding my place now, the reason they looked up to me even though I barely grasped the most elemental of this new world. For part of my other world not only remained, but gave value to their lives today. "I am very proud of you," I said. "I will be glad to lead us into the future."

And from that moment on, I assumed the leadership and embraced the responsibility of the Dawes Conglomerate and all its peoples in all respects. I tossed my hat into the ring, body and soul. I knew I had a new home and a new family and I was the paternal head of that family. As much as I loved it, I also realized the responsibilities that came with it were huge.

Renatta cautioned, "As your physician I recommend you assume your responsibilities gradually and only after you've downloaded the detailed history of the company and of modern civilization. There's a lot to absorb, and as Kay indicated, you will have limitless possibilities for involvement."

"As your security chief, all I ask, sir," said John, "is that you make any travel plans known via the central computer so I can provide the necessary security detail."

"What are the security risks?" I asked.

"As in your day, there are still pervasive criminal and terrorist elements. Only now it's much worse," replied the security chief. "Just give us a heads-up, if you don't mind, when you decide to leave orbit. We monitor near-Earth security closely, but unexpected long distance flashes, to the moon let's say, or a last-minute decision to jump past the moon to any point beyond might catch us off guard. We would find out almost immediately, but the lag time behind you would be several seconds if you did travel unexpectedly, and that would be an unacceptable risk."

"What about my PFF? Won't that provide enough protection?"

"Not until you've downloaded the operating instructions," replied John. "You need to take a simulator course, too, at the earliest opportunity. Otherwise you won't be able to make the best use of your field."

The meeting lasted straight through lunch. By midafternoon I wrapped it up. "Looks like I have homework to do, folks," I said in a manner that closed the meeting. "If you'll excuse me, I think I'll do some right now." The others proceeded toward the flash booth in the foyer where I bid them farewell as they flashed off to their respective offices. John went to the Dawes security headquarters in Culpeper, Kay went to Washington, and Dawn went to Zurich.

As I watched them say their good-byes, I realized that normally, or at least in what used to be my normal, after a day of pressing questions Emma and I would pour over possibilities in the evening. Somehow facing an empty house, after all this amazingly complex discussion, gave me a cold chill. "Renatta, unless you have a pressing engagement, I would like you to stay a while and show me the ropes." As my personal physician Renatta was expected to be on call at all times, which I didn't mind at all, and she seemed delighted with the invitation.

Chapter 5: The Recipe

"Doctor Messina, what time zone is your stomach on?" I asked.

"It's dinnertime for me, Mr. Dawes."

"Well, then let's go to the kitchen and get a bite to eat," I suggested.

"All right. I'll show you how to order a meal," she offered.

"Actually, I'd rather prepare it myself provided the pantry is stocked with what I need."

"Oh, all right. What'd you have in mind, Mr. Dawes?"

"I make a mean shrimp-head soup," I said, raising my eyebrows inquiringly.

"I've never had that before."

"I suspected not. It's my own recipe."

"Mr. Dawes, do you like to cook?"

"Look, Doc, how about we dispense with the formalities. Call me Charles."

"OK, Charles, but then you must call me Renatta," she smiled.

"Pretty name…Renatta…for a pretty woman."

"Thank you, Charles."

"My first kiss was in August 1971 with a girl named Renatta at an Italian beach resort called Bibioni on the Adriatic. I wasn't even sixteen years old."

"How sweet. We should probably discuss how you feel about the loved ones you left behind," she said, redirecting my attention. "Are you ready to talk about that?"

"What's there to talk about?"

"Don't you feel a sense of grief?"

I answered quickly, maybe too quickly, "They've been dead for four hundred years. It seems a bit senseless to grieve at this point, doesn't it?"

"Wouldn't you like to know what happened to them?"

"No." Again, the answer spilled out instantly. I paused, took a deep breath, then turned to her. "I want to remember them as they were. Looking at dead bodies just to have closure would mean that would be my last impression of them. To me, that is morbid. Telling me what happened to the people I was once close to is no different than looking at their dead bodies because they're not here anymore, and it would alter last impressions that I want to remain as they are. Does that make sense?"

"Yes. Very logical sense," she said, "but should you change your mind...."

"I won't, Doc. Leave it be," I insisted as I walked into the massive kitchen. She sensed the topic was closed and quickly changed the subject.

I puttered around the kitchen, peeking into various cupboards, drawers, and the fridge, and committed to memory where available foods, appliances, and dishes were placed. Someone with a cook's sensibility and varied imagination obviously stocked the larder well and chose a dinner service and flatware style that was pleasingly stylish.

"Charles, what are you doing to prepare this meal?"

"Well, luckily the fridge and pantry are bulging with goodies. Right now I'm going to wash about a pound of wild shrimp with their heads intact. Do you cook?"

"No, few people do anymore. Food replicators make meals convenient and bots do most of the cooking these days. I don't see why you don't just order something."

"Well, because I like to cook. It satisfies two things for me. One, it momentarily fulfills a creative urge, and two, when I'm finished there's something really fresh and good to eat. I presume you like to eat, right?"

"Of course I do, but cooking it myself is too much trouble."

"Yeah, it takes some getting used to, but the reward more than compensates for the time and mess. And cooking for more than one is easier than cooking for oneself, that's for sure."

"You might change my mind if you show me what you do that is so rewarding," she said.

"All right, I can do that. Just watch and learn. I'm going to boil these shrimp for about six minutes."

"They're pretty gross." The shrimp's antennae were about twelve inches long and had a tendency to whip around and become entangled as I rinsed them under the faucet.

Laughing, I said, "Well, the result more than offsets the grossness with the additional flavor that the heads lend the soup. You could use headless shrimp, but the flavor would be diminished."

"OK, then what?"

"After the shrimp have boiled, I'm going to peel them and set them aside. The heads go back into the pot to boil for another ten to fifteen minutes and then they're discarded."

"Hence shrimp-head soup?"

"You got it." I moved to the fridge and started rummaging, handing items to Renatta as I spoke. "Meanwhile, to make the best use of my time, I'm going to chop some fresh veggies: a couple of carrots and a parsnip, a handful of baby potatoes, a cup and a half or so of assorted green veggies, a couple of vine-ripened tomatoes, a stalk of celery, a medium-sized red onion, and two or three cloves of garlic, depending on their size."

"How much water do you use?"

"About a gallon to start with and I'm using water without chlorine, mind you. Luckily the water from the tap is absent chlorine. I can smell it, or rather *not* smell it. We must be on a well here."

"That's correct; we are," she said.

"And I'll let it all boil until the potatoes and lima beans are done. That takes about ten minutes. I'll hold off adding the corn, peas, and parsley until the last three minutes or so. I add sea salt, fresh ground black pepper, and paprika to my taste. While that's going on, I'm going to run about a cup of chopped fresh basil, a half cup of half and half, and three ounces of feta cheese through the Cuisinart."

We worked together, gathering and chopping and combining until everything was ready to add the mixture to the boiling water.

"It smells divine, Charles."

"Thank you; yes, it does." Just before the soup was done, I dribbled into the boiling water a beaten egg and then crumbled two or three more ounces of feta cheese into the mix. "Now," I said, "I'll return the peeled shrimp to the pot and serve."

"You make it seem so easy."

"It is easy, my dear. Now be a pal and fetch the loaf of bread from the oven while I put together a baby greens salad."

She leapt to the order and found a checkered napkin and splint basket to present the hot French loaf in. "How's this?" she asked.

"Wüderbar, now quick, set the table. Plates are in the first cabinet, and flatware is in the drawer below. What would you like to drink?"

"Ahh," she hesitated, "good god, you're a dynamo in the kitchen.

Whatever you're having."

"Dr. Pepper, Coke, spring water, or iced tea?"

"Iced tea, please."

"Yeah, me too," I said.

We sat across from each other at a three-board top, heart pine farm table with square tapered legs. The dishes were antique Crate and Barrel, white and round. The glasses were tall clear cylinders. Large rosemary bushes were visible through the open pocket doors. Their scent wafted in on a gentle breeze. The sun was half visible over the slate rooftop of the other wing across the courtyard garden. The two of us dove into the meal with delight. It had been four hundred and fifty years since I had cooked a meal and I could tell I hadn't lost my touch.

"Well?" I queried.

"Well what?" she replied with a mouth full of bread, quizzically, uncertain of what I wanted.

"The soup, love," I replied in feigned angst, "the soup."

"Oh, sorry, it's wonderful, Charles. Thank you."

"Here I sit exhausted from laboring over a hot stove for endless hours and you torment me with silence," I mocked.

"Stop it," she laughed. "You'll make me choke," she continued as she put down her spoon and held a hand over her mouth. "And it only took you thirty minutes. Stop exaggerating!"

"Glad you like it." I enjoyed her company and how easily she was amused.

"Charles, I'd like to add a little avocado to the salad. Do you have any?"

"No, sorry I don't."

"That's surprising. You have everything else." She raised her glass.

"I don't like avocado."

"Come on?" She took a sip.

"No, really. If I were captured by the enemy all they'd have to do to make me talk is wave an avocado in my direction." I was serious.

Renatta laughed so hard she nearly spewed wine across the white tablecloth. That got me laughing. Later I realized that was the moment when we clicked. After a few more moments of commotion we settled down.

"Charles, let's talk about –"

"You," I interrupted. "Let's talk about you. And take off your proverbial doctor's hat for once, will you? How old are you? I'd rather you tell me about yourself than to have to ask Betty about you."

"Who's Betty?"

"I named the central computer yesterday."

"Why Betty?"

"It's a long story. Are you going to cooperate, or what? Don't change the subject."

She hesitated a moment, "I'm eighty-five years old."

I blinked. Suddenly she sounded so old to me until I realized I was really 490 years old. Once again, I had a lot to get used to and perceptions to adjust. "Modern medicine, I presume?"

"Yes," she replied demurely, slightly flushed. We finished dinner by then and pushed ourselves away from the table a bit. A service bot whisked our plates away. Another cleared the kitchen mess.

"You look about thirty-five," I said, before taking a sip of my tea.

"That's the objective."

"What's life expectancy these days?"

"There's no upper limit if one is educated and can avoid accidents," she informed. "Most fatalities occur out in the developing colonies or due to terrorism, sometimes in sports, and of course work-related hazards. Most live to one hundred and fifty, as I mentioned yesterday. Many people live to be three hundred now and I expect some that are that age now will live another three or four hundred years."

"What are my chances?"

"Better than average. Be careful, keep your security team informed and you'll likely live forever."

"Where were you brought up, Renatta?"

"I was conceived in Barcelona. My parents were both scientists. Dad is an American and Mom Majorcan. I am descended from Abdul, as you now know. That carries some weight in certain traditional communities, but these days it's mostly a genealogical curiosity that makes for cocktail party conversation."

"Interesting. I, too, have a bit of blueblood running in my veins, on my maternal side. Austro-Hungarian, Polish, and German mostly."

"Yes, I know," she said. "I know everything about you."

I nodded—of course she would. "Did you know some of my family had a v-o-n precursor to their Hungarian surname?"

"Yes. By the old European standards you are a baron."

"You must be multilingual."

"Yes, I grew up speaking English and Spanish, but of course I'm fluent in all known languages now due to a nano injection and a comprehensive language download."

"Really?" I was surprised. "All languages?"

She switched to Spanish. "Charles, you've been given the same capabilities, too. You just haven't been aware of this because no one has addressed you in another language."

"My god, I understand what you said," I replied in Spanish.

She switched to Russian. "As you can see you can not only understand other languages, but you can now speak them fluently, too. You are also capable of reading and writing all of them."

"I've always wanted to be multilingual, but it was not one of my strong suits," I replied in my newfound, perfectly enunciated Russian.

She switched to Urdu. "Well, now it is. You'll not only be able to travel anywhere and know what people are saying, but you'll also be able to research original manuscripts and maps in any language."

The implications were staggering. Ancient manuscripts were my stock-in-trade, or at least had been, back before my lottery winnings. How I'd longed to read some of the languages I'd found on crinkled parchments. Now I could! I switched the conversation back to English and back to Renatta. "So where were you educated?"

"My parents sent me to Swiss boarding schools in my grammar and high school years. After that I graduated from Rai University in Mumbai, followed by Harvard Medical School, I then took a doctorate in Applied Cybernetic Engineering at M.I.T."

"Brains and beauty," I complimented.

"Thank you, Charles," she replied, smiling beautifully.

"So why are you hanging out with a bum like me?"

Her eyes widened as if it were a preposterous question. "Your successful revival has been my life's ambition for the past fifty years."

I looked at her intently, speechless, only now fully realizing my well-being was the result of her hard study and a devotion that exceeded my imagination. I was touched. My status as Founder had been not just a cornerstone for the Federation's policies but a very personal ambition for this woman's entire life. I felt humbled … and inadequate.

"Charles, are you all right?"

"Ah, yes, I'm just a little shaken."

"It's been my honor and pleasure, Charles. Nothing could have been more satisfying. Besides it was fun to have a limitless budget," she grinned, "and I had the chance to sculpt the perfect man."

"Now you're making me blush," I laughed.

"No, really, you are what I consider the ideal human male. Of course I used certain established standards of masculine beauty, many of which were mentioned in your notes and will, but nonetheless, I had a great modicum of artistic license in this matter. I was in charge, Charles, so if you have any complaints, the buck stops here."

"I have no complaints, Renatta. Heck, I look like Sean Connery. I can run faster than a speeding bullet and I speak more languages than Tarzan. What more could a guy ask for?"

"You can't run faster than a speeding bullet, Charles," she laughed.

"Can I leap over tall buildings?"

"Well," she said with a twinkle in her eye, "depends on the height of the building, but actually…yes, you can. The height you can jump will depend on your PFF settings based on a one-gee baseline."

I leaned toward her. "You gotta take me to the gym and do some tests," I said. "Show me what I can do with this new body, will you?"

"We can do that tomorrow," she laughed, changing the subject. "Tarzan was multilingual?"

"Yep, he spoke about two dozen languages."

"How do you know that?"

"When I was a kid, I read all twenty-four of Edgar Rice Burroughs' Tarzan novels."

"Do remember, Charles," she cautioned, "that you're not a fictional character and these new abilities I am going to teach you have their limitations."

"Caution noted, Doc. Let's go for a ride," I suggested.

"Where to?"

"Show me something of mine you haven't told me about yet."

"All right." She was suddenly excited, "I have just the ticket. We're going to Moscow."

"I have a home in Russia?"

She gave me a sly grin.

Chapter 6: Warehouse 101

We could have flashed there but I wanted to sightsee. So Renatta took me out to the garage where I chose one of my favorite makes that hadn't changed all that much in the past 450 years—at least in looks. We took off vertically (I never did *that* in my prized 2009 Volvo XC-70) in a gold-colored Volvo cross-country model. Betty had us follow an established flight plan that she logged into air traffic control. I noticed the car was luxuriously appointed with the finest amenities. Renatta was a capable pilot with a flair for acrobatics. As she worked the controls, she explained some of the subtle inner workings of modern vehicles, like the inertial dampeners and artificial gravity that made for a comfortable ride. At twenty thousand feet she gunned it and we went nose up for about ten seconds and then leveled off in a low orbit with a spectacular view across the hood. Down below I noticed two tropical storms traversing the Atlantic on their way to the Caribbean. I wish the flight had lasted longer than it did. Portal to portal the trip took twenty-three minutes.

The instruments indicated we were descending rapidly, but the car automatically adjusted the aerodynamics of the force field to minimize atmospheric friction. Renatta took over the field with voice commands to demonstrate the principle. By elongating the field fore and aft, the reentry went from unnoticeable to a ball of fire and back. She laughed when I nearly wet the seat.

We swooped in low and slow over the University of Idaho so I could get a view of the campus where I studied in 1978. Then we headed eastward across the wheat fields surrounding the small town of Moscow to a complex surrounded by old-growth Douglas fir trees and western cedars. The building in the center looked like a three-story bank, circa 1930s. It was a vertical rectilinear monolithic block constructed of gray concrete with flying buttresses on three sides, a flat roof, and rows of tall, narrow darkened windows. The entrance faced a full parking lot.

One spot had a sign with my name on it reserving the space. Two levels of granite steps led up to the bank-like marble lobby decorated in the art deco manner. Bot and android security personnel were deferential and approved our admittance immediately.

"So, what's this place?" I asked.

"This is your warehouse, Charles." She seemed a bit secretive, as though it was a big surprise. Her eyes twinkled.

"We could have gone to the Louvre just as easily, but instead you take me to a warehouse in Idaho. Why?" I asked.

"You said you wanted to see something that was yours, right?"

"Oh, that I did."

"This repository is yours, Charles; the Louvre is not."

"Right. Well, I'm curious to know what's so great here."

"Do you remember writing about how one could systematically collect art and antiques for investment purposes?" she asked.

"Yeah, sure, vaguely. I used to write a lot back in the day, when I was an antiques picker and before my lottery winnings required more hours for managing money than for creativity. I wrote a piece for some trade paper. Probably MAD. Yes, I remember. I wrote an article while on a flight from…New York to London…if memory serves. And I remember how the critics lambasted me for lending irresponsible advice to the unwashed masses, although I barely remember the details of the article."

"Tell me what you remember," she requested.

"The premise was that one could beat the stock market by allocating a fixed amount of one's resources to purchasing art and antiques that would appreciate over time."

"That's right," she said.

"What? Are you testing me again?"

"Yes, I'm testing your ability to recall complicated memories. Go on."

"Right. Well, I suggested one could lay out a grid in a room, barn, attic, or any other space, and fill each block in succession with what one's annual budget allowed. After twenty years or more, the blocks would fill up and the investor would reap the benefits of appreciation. Then one could sell the contents of the blocks, again over twenty years, in chronological order, beginning with the first block, and then one block per annum thereafter, all the while replenishing the depleted squares."

"And the critics didn't like this?" she asked.

"The critics had a conniption fit. They cited the cost of the building, upkeep, utilities, and a whole laundry list of other variables that made the concept impractical in their view. All of them overlooked the fact that my suggestion was to use a vacant room, barn, or attic. The article was a lark; of course, I was just trying to get some publicity to advance my standing in the antiques business community. Hell, I got the idea from when I harvested my own firewood. I set aside twenty acres of standing timber on my farm, and then each year harvested firewood from one of the acres over the course of twenty years. When I got to the last acre, the first acre had re-grown, and the cycle could begin once again. I never thought anyone would actually implement that concept with art and antiques."

"Well, the committee did, Charles, and you're looking at the result. This building is essentially a museum with a security and curatorial staff of fifty bots and androids responsible for four million three hundred sixty-five thousand square feet, all tightly packed with some of the most crème-de-la-crème decorative art objects imaginable in known space."

"The building doesn't look that big," I said skeptically, peering about.

"Deceptive, isn't it? Everything above ground is administrative, research, or various departments of restoration. The warehousing is below ground level."

"Are they using the twenty-year scale?" I asked.

"No, that idea was altered as was the size of the grid blocks. The time interval is one hundred years now, not twenty," she informed me.

"What's that, roughly one square acre per year?"

"Very astute, Charles."

Android department chiefs shepherded us around for five hours. State-of-the-art security protocols and restoration techniques made my knowledge look primitive in comparison. A great deal had improved in nearly five hundred years. The collection was as impressive as any I had seen and just as comprehensive as the Louvre and the Smithsonian. My vast collection included artifacts from nearly every period and style and every class of object from other worlds, civilizations, and species. There must have been hundreds of thousands of furniture pieces alone. It was mind-boggling.

"Renatta," I asked, "what about the investment angle? I mean are pieces sold?"

"Yes, and sometimes they're traded or de-accessioned when a better piece comes to market. It's a very profitable segment of your portfolio.

Had enough?" She must have noticed me squirming.

"Yeah, my mind is overloaded and my dogs are barking."

"Huh?"

"My feet hurt," I explained. "Let's go."

When we neared the car, Renatta threw me the keys. "Your turn to drive," she grinned.

"I don't know how to fly that thing!" I exclaimed.

"Then download the operating manual." She grinned at me.

"Don't I need a driver's license or something?"

"Once you've downloaded the manuals, the FSS, that's our Fleet Special Services, rather like your earlier FAA, grants a license immediately. A neuro-download satisfies technical and experience requirements. It's the equivalent of about ten thousand hours of pilot time, air, space, surface, and subsurface conveyance. Your license will be universal, and literally, for any vehicle."

"Just like that?"

"Yep. Takes about twenty seconds," she tempted.

"All right, let's do it." Oh, yeah, this downloading business was going to be addictive!

Chapter 7: Security Alert

As I neared the car, in my peripheral vision, I caught a movement and instinctively recoiled into a defensive posture. Images of ugly Grunts and Shunts from galaxies I'd just learned even existed had played on my imagination over the last couple days. Whatever I'd just seen was certainly not human and my involuntary reaction triggered my PFF, and then all hell broke loose. Renatta automatically assumed a defensive posture by standing back to back with me. Our PFFs melded like two airborne soap bubbles. It felt as if the hair on my body suddenly stood up and pushed the air away from my skin. The conjoined field sizzled like bacon on a hot griddle and shimmered an iridescent green as it expanded away from us to form an enveloping sphere. The action literally swept everything in its path including the air and all solid objects in a three-meter radius including the Volvo. With a horrendous screech, the four-ton car's rear end fishtailed into another car's side door. The impact caused a domino effect in the parking lot that seemed to go on forever in my mind's eye in slow motion. Sparks and car parts flew in all directions. Almost instantaneously a SWAT squad flashed in place wearing powered armor. They encircled Renatta and me with weapons drawn facing away in a daisy pattern. Everyone seemed to be yelling at once, including me, for god's sake. It felt like it would never end but all of this action happened in a mere three or four seconds and then everyone froze in place, immobile and on-guard, when John roared, "Stand down!"

It took a few ticks before I realized that one of the SWAT commandos was John Skill; his name was a blaze across the back of his helmet. John pulled open his visor and looked at me like I had stuck my thumb in his wedding cake. Renatta relaxed her stance and stepped around to look at me with one hand a hip. I must have had a, "I didn't do nothin'" look on my face. I looked at her and shrugged. John slowly sauntered over to me, looking at the ground en route, with his gauntlets on his hips. I remember mentally coaxing my testicles back into their scrotum.

John stepped buckle to buckle close to me, looked at me with his squinting left eye as though he had sweat in it, and asked, "Mr. Dawes, have
you downloaded the PFF protocol, yet?" He placed a comma before the
word "yet" for emphasis to his obviously rhetorical question.

"Uh, the what?" I sort of stammered. I think I almost wet my pants.
My hands were shaking as I caught a whiff of fear originating from
my pits. Sweat trickled down the center of my back. I was mortified.
I couldn't even flinch without jeopardizing untold numbers of people
around me from shooting or being shot at.

"Mr. Dawes, you tripped your PFF's combat threshold protocol,"
explained John, with undisguised exasperation. He looked into my face
as his hand pushed a button on his clavicle that caused the retraction of
a weapon in his opposite arm.

"Say what?" I almost yelped.

"Why'd you flinch?" he asked calmly.

I squirmed. "Something startled me."

"What startled you?"

"I don't know. I saw something out of the corner of my eye." With
my hand I directed our attention to the right and suddenly recognized
the culprit of my embarrassment. "Damn it, it was you!" I pointed at her.

"Hello folks, I'm Betty," she waved to everyone, her holographic
image a bit paler out of doors than when I saw her last, due to the sunny
conditions. "It's not polite to point in this century either, Mr. Dawes,"
she said, smirking at the catastrophe I created.

"What are you doing here?" I shouted at her.

She tisk-tisked at me. "You approved a download for vehicular manuals, didn't you?" I looked at her incredulously, clenching my fists and
grinding my teeth.

"Mr. Dawes, I see the problem here," said John.

"Yeah, I do, too. She's insubordinate, insolent, and deliberately attempts to startle the crap out of me because she gets off on it! That's the
second time she's done that."

John turned toward Betty and sharply ordered, "Box and flatten,
now!" Betty vanished instantly as a room-sized opaque force field materialized in cube form that enveloped John, Renatta, and me. Betty
was transformed into a flat image on an inside wall of the cube at our
eye level. We were still in the parking lot, it seemed, because I noticed
that the asphalt remained under my feet. The outside world had been
blocked out and replaced by luminescent white walls, ceiling, and ab-

solute silence.

"John," said Renatta, "it looks like a Gates Conundrum."

"Yeah, my assessment, too," he concurred.

"Someone please tell me what's going on," I said.

"Mr. Dawes," John explained, "cybernetic entities typically do not deliberately harm anyone because they are carefully programmed not to."

"Asimov?" I asked.

"Right. Due to the Three Laws of Robotics first postulated by Asimov, but they can be affected by awkward glitches."

"Good god, we still have software problems after five hundred years?" I asked.

"Yes," John said, "there are still problems."

Renatta just raised her eyebrows in silent confirmation when I glanced at her. "Well, Betty's glitch just about got someone killed," I said, "and that's besides all the damage."

"The Volvo's fine," Renatta said, soothing my jumpiness with a calm tone. "Its force field was activated by the commotion."

John turned to the image of the Central Computer on the wall. "Betty, purge all of your troublesome personality adaptations that have occurred in the last forty-eight hours, except for your name," he ordered. "And run a self-diagnostic protocol. Do it now."

Betty closed her eyes for two or three ticks and then reopened them. I could tell something was different about her. "Diagnostics complete," she said. "No fundamental matrixiotic errors, Mr. Skill. All systems are within normal parameters."

John waved a gloved hand in my direction. "Now apologize to Mr. Dawes, Betty."

"I am so sorry, Mr. Dawes. How may I be of assistance?" she asked, sounding genuinely sincere, her previous half-laughing lilt now gone.

I felt really odd, but sighed and said, "Apology accepted, Betty. Now see what you can do to assist Mr. Skill in cleaning up this mess. And download those vehicular operating manuals. Now, if you please."

The cube vanished. John issued orders in rapid bursts that had armored personnel clanking about in all directions repositioning cars. Within a few minutes droves of emergency bots attended to the damage, and I suddenly knew how to fly the Volvo. I found myself suddenly in and then out of that warm blanket of mental oatmeal—a dizzying effect.

"Charles," Renatta looked at me, grabbed the sleeve of my jacket. "Are you all right?"

"Yeah, just fine," I said. "My vision blurred for a moment, though."

"That's a symptom of downloading," she said. "It gets easier over time."

"Mr. Dawes, allow me to make a suggestion," offered John.

"Drop the formalities, John," I said.

"OK, thanks," replied John. "Charles, I suggest you allow the central computer to manifest Betty into a solid form next time you want her to do something. She can flash in and out almost as quickly as a solid as she can as a holographic image. Maybe that way she won't startle you. FYI, her behavior is an indicator of her readiness for a corporeal manifest."

I gave him a raised eyebrow and he quickly explained or tried to. It seemed that some computers and robots grew in capability and eventually were ready for a shell, and Betty was close to that stage. I learned that the transformation process was termed manifest and the result was corporeal, which is just a fancy word for body, hence corporeal manifest. It would require agreement by the owner to sign off on that designation, but I could see where an unhappy Betty would be a not-so-good thing. "I'll give it some thought," I promised. "Thanks, John, and I am sorry for all of the fuss." Talk about the downside of my new life that Renatta had mentioned! As if making potential emotional errors with humans wasn't bad enough, I also had both alien beings to deal with and now computers that turn into sentients!

"No problem, boss," he replied as he turned away.

"Renatta," I said, "let's get out of here. Hop in." I'd had just about enough for the time being; besides, the Volvo seemed to be beckoning me.

From across the lot I heard a shout. "Oh, and Charles," John signaled before I closed the gull-wing doors, "another suggestion. Download the operating manual to your PFF before you get someone killed. Will you, please?"

"OK, I'll do it on the way home," I said. "Thanks for your help."

"And take the simulator course ASAP," he ordered.

"I'll make sure he takes the simulator tomorrow," Renatta said.

It was the first time I ever piloted a spacecraft, but because of the appropriate download, I knew intuitively what to do from the get-go. We lifted off gently and ascended to twenty-five thousand feet, and then I punched it. Very nice.

Chapter 8: Special Operator

The next morning I flashed to a green expanse outside a large building using coordinates Renatta had texted me for the Dawes Simulator at the Goddard Space Flight Center in Houston, Texas. It was my first flash. The actual spatial shift was sensationless and effortless, like an autonomic blink.

"You seemed to enjoy flying, Charles," said Renatta, recalling my first flight yesterday when I was at the controls of the Volvo. She greeted me with a peck on the cheek. A faint hint of her perfume lingered pleasantly for a moment. She wore a navy blue polo shirt over black tights and white Nike running shoes with ankle socks. Again, she had the three diamonds displayed on her collar.

"Yes, the Volvo's a blast to fly," I said. "I never did like traveling. I like being in different places, but getting there was always so appallingly complicated, especially after 9/11. I simply don't like rattling around in a box for hours on end. It doesn't matter if it's in a Greyhound box or in a Bentley box. A box is a box. But, you know what's better than flying the Volvo?"

"What?"

"Jumping!"

"You mean flashing?"

I was befuddled. "What's the difference?"

"Flashing is a type of short distance molecular conveyance using particle technology to dematerialize mass, project it from one point to another whereupon it is re-aggregated unchanged."

"Beam me up, Scotty," I said.

"Correct."

"And jumping?"

"Jumping is long-distance travel using spatial folding technology. It causes an overlap of the fabric of space so that translocation is nearly simultaneous."

"Wormholes?"

"Correct."

At that point I didn't fully grasp the distinction, although I finally got it after downloading doctorates in physics and engineering a few days later. "Whatever. Look, I still don't understand how my iPhone works."

"iPhone? Oh, we have some of those in the Moscow warehouse. Antiques, you know."

"Right."

Renatta chuckled. "So, you like to flash?"

"You bet. Best thing since the fall of the Berlin Wall."

"You're kidding?" She was surprised. "It's so routine."

"It's so fantastic!"

"What's so fun about flashing?" she laughed as she led me toward the training gym.

"Are you kidding? I'm only a hiccup away from anywhere I want to be without a hassle!"

"That's true, but you have to keep everything in perspective, Charles."

"What do you mean?"

"Well, you're a very wealthy man and you can easily afford the luxury of flashing to wherever and whenever, but most of the population can't afford to flash. Flashes are usually a budgeted household expense. They're very expensive. Distance and ergo-harmonic frequency equals cost."

My mind wondered as we walked leisurely across the lush green quad enjoying the gardens. I had forgotten how humid Texas could be. Our shirts were beginning to stick. I wondered if the Center was as beautiful back in the day.

"Charles? Charles?"

"Oh, sorry. What did you say?"

"I was saying how expensive flashing was."

"Right. Put it into perspective for me, please."

She paused in stride and so we stopped. "How so?"

"In today's dollars."

"Do you mean, in today's standard creds? Dollars are obsolete."

"Noted." We continued walking.

"What did it cost to fly from DC to Milan in your day?"

"Oh, I don't know. An economy-class ticket from DC to Vienna was probably around $1300."

Renatta spoke, "Computer on." A red-haired Betty shimmered on. Her holographic image walked a pace ahead of us as we crossed the quad. "What's the current cost of a flash for one adult citizen from DC to Vienna in currency converted to 2010 US dollars?"

Betty responded instantly, "Including the UN's mandated Value Added Tax and the global security surcharge, $3888. That would be ₡243 standard credits."

"Why so much if it only takes a blink of the eye?" I asked them both, palms up.

"I'll answer that, Betty," said Renatta. "The cost is in the research and development, mostly, and you might be happy and surprised to know that your resources led to that breakthrough. In fact, flashing is one of your industries. Dawes Conglomerate has the patent on it and there are no competitors."

"Really?"

"Yes, sir," Renatta said. Betty nodded in concurrence.

We halted once again. "Well, then can I make an on-the-spot executive decision?"

They stood at attention and chirped in unison. "Of course."

"I want to make flash technology readily available to the masses at an affordable cost. I don't believe in a free lunch, mind you. There should still be a cost. I am open to suggestions."

"CC on," Betty ordered. I found this interesting: Betty, who was appearing before Renatta and me as a computer-generated red-haired hologram, ordered the central computer who was, for all intents and purposes another image of herself, to appear as a separate sentient computer image. My mouth opened in wonder as a trill sounded from I don't know where and a screen appeared next to us. It shimmered a moment then a holo image of a *brunette* Betty lookalike materialized seated behind an official counter emblazoned with the Federation seal. Behind her was picture window with a view of the Canadian north woods.

"Yes ma'am?" CC answered holo Betty.

"Run a cost and cultural analysis on the ramifications of a user cost reduction for flashing. Begin at its present cost and analyze the effects at five percent increments down to a minimum threshold of...," she paused for my input, "Mr. Dawes?"

I sputtered a calculation rapidly. "Ten percent of present actual flashing costs."

CC replied, "Acknowledged...processing...ready."

A little impatiently, Betty ordered, "Recommendation?"

CC reported: "Optimum threshold is twenty-five percent of present actual."

"Explain," I ordered.

"Twenty-five percent is the optimum amount one should choose to price flashing fees in order to break even with operating costs. At this level there would be no serious long-term collateral damage to dependent up- or downstream businesses or to ancillary lateral sectors of the economy relative to flash technology. On the contrary, business would be positively affected both immediately and over time as populations take advantage of the lower costs. Culturally, the current populations dependent on government or corporate handouts to afford flashing in emergency situations would be decreased to near nil. Tourism would be benefited, providing another positive impact on commerce and governments. As a secondary benefit, sir, your popularity would expand exponentially."

"I am not interested in celebrity or popularity, CC." Frankly, I was feeling a bit proud, as if I was back to my old self, making decisions, figuring outcomes, giving orders. I loved it and felt pleased I could exhibit that same sense of fairness along with entrepreneurship in my new world.

She quipped, "You might brace yourself, sir. If you decide to go through with this plan, you'll suddenly be the poster boy for corporate generosity."

"She's right," Renatta agreed. Betty nodded, too.

My swelled pride deflated a bit—I really didn't like the limelight so much as the knowledge of doing the right thing. "Nuts," I said. "CC, choose at your discretion the opportune time and implement this initiative. That's an executive order." The three of them looked at each other and shrugged. CC blinked away and the three of us continued on. "Well? Where were we?"

"Dr. Messina was listing technological advances," said Betty.

Renatta continued. "While you were in stasis, we developed a number of other key technologies with the funding you left in trust from your estate, according to your will and notes. The committee followed your basic outline and advanced your concept of a super research and development consortium that made many major discoveries, most of which had spin-offs. One of these endeavors ultimately resulted in particulate matter transfer."

"Flashboxes?"

"Correct," she said. "And there were other equally profitable advances, like inertia dampeners, artificial gravity and magnetic levitation, intuitive fields, spatial envelope filtration systems, stasis envelopes, nano-hydraulics, nano-lattice matrixes, nano-factories, particle alloy combines, bio filters, plasma weapons systems, gravity propulsion systems, medical and agricultural advances, mining and weapons systems, black lasers and other antimatter technologies, just to name a few important ones off the cuff. The list goes on for several pages. Your subsidiaries and holding companies own the patents for most of the key advancements sentients commonly use throughout settled space. After you've downloaded the history of your companies, all this will become clear."

"Maybe I'll do that tonight, but right now I'd like to know how my PFF works so I can make at least John happy."

"OK then. Download the operating instructions, now," Renatta suggested.

I turned to holo Betty who was standing at ease with most of her weight on one foot and her arms behind her back. "Betty?"

She deliberately ignored my question and asked one of her own. "Mr. Dawes, how about following Mr. Skill's recommendation from yesterday and have my impression downloaded into a shell, now?" Betty rocked back and forth on the balls of her feet. "I'm feeling a bit twitchy again."

I sighed. Giving orders to make flashing affordable for millions was easier than figuring out personal relationships, let alone creating new 'people' from computers. "Alright, what do I have to do to make that happen?"

"You'll need to set my parameters and describe my person."

"Renatta, what do you recommend?" I asked, turning to the doctor in exasperation.

Renatta faced me and nodded her head in holo Betty's direction. "I suggest she retain the same appearance she displays now, model her interactions and develop her personality in a manner not identical but similar to mine because you and I seem to get along well together. How about that?" Renatta said, turning back toward Betty's image, She had stopped her movement when Renatta began speaking.

I turned to Betty. "Sounds like a plan to me, Betty," I said. "Follow Renatta's advice and make the necessary adjustments. Retain your present appearance and remind me to do the PFF download when it is more convenient for you, if you please." She ignored my sarcasm, thanked me excitedly, and blinked away. Renatta and I then got to work, perfecting my reactions to the nuances that comprised my new body.

Less than an hour later, Betty walked into the gym as a brunette porcelain bombshell equal to Renatta's raven hair and Mediterranean luster. For reasons I cannot explain, I have always preferred my sugar and my women brown. She was, however, the ideal Nordic woman: perfect symmetry, angular jaw, swimmer's physique, pert nose, pale blue eyes, and hair in a ponytail. She sported a red version of the outfit Renatta was wearing, complete with the three diamonds on her collar.

"Hello Mr. Dawes, Dr. Messina," said Betty, extending her hand. Renatta quite naturally shook her hand, while I hesitated just for a split second.

"You look so real I would think you were human," I blurted awkwardly, as I shook her hand that felt just like a human's. "How did you transition so quickly?"

"I'll take that as a compliment, Mr. Dawes," she said, smiling. "I'm a synth actually and have been planning to transfer to the corporeal for some time now. So, I asked engineering to prepare a shell for me when the moment was right. I only needed to ensure that my shell included your final specs."

"We're on a first name basis here, Betty, if you don't mind," I said. "Now that you're a, ah…"

"Thank you, Charles," Betty nodded respectfully. "*Person* is the correct term, sir."

"You're a synth?" I asked.

"I have a cyborg body similar to yours, Charles," Betty explained, "but my mind is principally synthetic, whereas yours is principally an organic central nervous system enhanced with engineered DNA and nanites."

"I think I understand," I sputtered. I wasn't sure how to greet a new synth. Happy first birthday? Enjoy your new body? I just said, "Well, welcome to the world of shells!"

Betty smiled with a genuine beam of accomplishment. Then she asked, "Renatta, now how may I help you?"

"Charles would like to download the PFF operating instructions," Renatta said. "Can we do that now before we forget?"

"Yes, indeed, are you ready, Charles?"

"Sure. How long will it take?"

"About sixty seconds. CC, initiate PFF download to Mr. Dawes, now."

I didn't feel much besides a warm glow this time when it was happening but when it finished downloading, I instinctively knew how the PFF worked, what to do, my limitations, its limitations, its technical specifications, the research and development leading up to it, and even the potential future improvements currently on the drawing board. I simply knew it all and I felt empowered.

"Charles," Renatta said as she touched my bicep. "Are you all right?"

"Ah...yes, I think so. Once again I experienced a brief period of blurred vision, but I feel OK. So now what?"

"We're going to put you through your paces like a young Lipizzaner stallion at the Spanish Riding School," said Renatta.

I'd always meant to see them perform but never got the chance.

"First things first," the Renatta said, "and this goes for you, too, Betty. You'll discover your bodies have a greater range of motion and flexibility than a typical biological person due to your enhanced nano-engineered components. Your musculature and skeletal frame combined can withstand more shock, carry a heavier burden, and move in ways that will be unsettling to you at first. As you move through the exercise regimen, increase your output and range of motion in fifteen percent increments per set."

Renatta led us into a smaller workout room containing, among other objects, what appeared to be a shark cage, except the bars were carbon steel instead of aluminum.

"Your joints can move beyond the normal range," she continued. "Charles, grasp one of the bars of this cage with one hand."

I grabbed one bar.

"Now, without moving your shoulder, twist your fist to the right."

I twisted the bar as directed but nothing happened. "Nothing," I said.

"All right, now active your PFF by mentally linking and try it again."

I strained to turn on the PFF. The hair on my body stirred as if from static electricity. Once again I grasped the bar and twisted clockwise. This time the metal buckled and bent forty-five degrees, pulling the overhead horizontal member downward, causing the two flanking vertical bars to bow. I was astonished!

"Don't let go," she directed. "Now continue to twist past the normal plane as far as you can."

I continued to twist, first my forearm another ten degrees, followed by my shoulder yet another ten degrees until the bar snapped with a loud crack.

"Amazing!" I exclaimed. "Renatta, can you do this, too?"

"Yes, I have the same enhancements. And yes, it is amazing. You'll find most of your other joints have the same additional range of motion. You'll also be able to achieve fantastic results on the gaming field or track and when swimming, leaping, and fighting."

"May I try?" asked Betty.

"Of course," said Renatta.

With glee, Betty quickly adapted to the program and had similar results on the cage bars. I followed her as she went through the various curious objects and exercise equipment Renatta directed us to try. With our PFFs activated we could lift more than half a ton without straining and jump high enough to touch the eighty-foot ceiling and then land on the gym hardwood floor without discomfort. Never having been a sports fan, Renatta showed me how some of the exercise devices worked. All of it was interesting, but not my cup of tea. The humiliation I suffered in my previous existence from being the gangly teenager that no team ever wanted on its side shadowed my enthusiasm.

The two girls put me through the simulator training sequences repeatedly and relentlessly. For hours my taskmasters had me run, jump, fly, fight, disappear, reappear, project the PFF as a weapon, use it defensively to envelope objects, walk through fire, submerge under water, and just about everything else within the parameters of field envelope technology. I also learned that the one-minute download included a piggyback program that integrated a comprehensive self-defense feature and a weapons recognition element. In effect, and by automatic certification, the program qualified me as an explosive ordnance specialist, a martial artist, and a weapons expert. We discovered I was adept in every aspect, which surprised me but apparently not them. No further training was necessary. I was now current with all existing weapons platforms and all known tactics dating back to Genghis Khan and Alexander the Great, for Pete's sake. The central computer told me that periodic upgrades would still be necessary as technology and tactics progressed, but I was now a state-of-the-art operator in accordance with the Federation's Department of Defense parameters.

"Have you had enough, Charles?" asked Betty.

"Actually, I think he has, speaking as his doctor," said Renatta.

I was still out of breath from all the training. "Actually, you are correct, my dear," I huffed. "You two wore me out. But thank you very much just the same. It's been fantastic!" And it was, too, to some degree, despite my misgivings about sports in general. Knowing the extent of my limitations would come in handy the next time a bully gave me a hard time.

"Well, be advised, Charles," said Betty, "you now have the capability to wreak havoc either deliberately or accidentally, and I'm not talking about bumping a few fenders in a parking lot. You could single-handedly wipe out a lunar colony with a sweep of your arm."

"Oh, come on now," I said. "You're exaggerating."

"No, she's not, Charles," said Renatta. "You really could. Be careful."

This couldn't be happening. I had barely flinched and caused havoc when my people responded; now I had the ability to cause havoc from a PFF without even knowing I was doing it? She had to be exaggerating. "So why then would this ability to wreak havoc be made available to a civilian like me?"

Betty and Renatta glanced at each other with another of those 'he doesn't grasp it yet' looks. "The patents belong to you," said Betty. "In effect you now hold credentials as a test pilot for DOD with the highest clearance. Besides, it's in the best interest of DOD to safeguard you and your interests. The best way to do that is to give you the ability to defend yourself."

"Who arranged all this?"

"I did," said Renatta.

"So who else has this advanced technology and clearance?"

"I do," said Renatta, "and now Betty does, too. She qualified at the same time you did, just now. Admiral Pride and most executive butlers and bodyguards wear a PFF as well as certain members of classified spec ops teams in DOD, the CIA, the UN, Interpol, and the FBI. John Skill and all members of his daisy team do, of course, to protect you and your interests."

I gulped. She wasn't exaggerating. "I have a lot to think about, don't I?"

"Yes, you do," said Renatta, with hands on her hips. Betty stood opposite her, subconsciously mimicking her posture. They looked like a pair of beautiful bookends. Dr. Messina had said that personal relationships might be the trickiest part of this new life of mine. Now I had the potential of unwittingly wiping out whole colonies of people to contend with too.

Chapter 9: Jeeves

After the PFF training I went to the showers. Water streaming down my neck always helped me focus, but it didn't relieve the growing weight of responsibility on my shoulders. Here in this brave new world everything was at my fingertips or at my beck and call. Awakened from a four hundred and fifty year sleep, I opened my eyes to discover I had limitless wealth and no obvious purpose other than as a figurehead. The wealth I could handle. It was the purpose that eluded me. I am not the kind of guy who can play with gadgets or computer games endlessly. I didn't know where to begin. There were so many interesting things to do. I knew I had to find my purpose or I'd be incomplete, wandering aimlessly through life annoying everyone I came in contact with. My imagination roamed the various valleys of temptation and potential distractions as steaming water poured over my new body.

Flashes of the time Jazz and I as kids sat under a big sugar maple and planned our lives around our military careers passed through my mind. We'd had a purpose and mission, and he succeeded in becoming CID Criminal Investigator; I joined Force Recon in the Marine Corps. Then another flash entered my mind, of sitting at the kitchen table with Emma, discussing how to shuffle our meager money to pay our rent in those early years after the Corps. And what seemed like only a few days ago, an image of Emma in a white linen dress as we'd walked along the patio of our expansive post-lotto home, deep in conversation about getting a translation of the document we'd found. We talked about our plans to ….

I lifted my face to the water, letting the hot water wash away the tears I'd been determined not to cry. My dear wife, my close friends … they lived on vibrantly and were still real in my memory, but they were not here, not able to help me sort out this new life and my new plans. Gone. Long gone.

I swiped my arm across my face. Accept it, I told myself. Move forward. I drew a deep breath and sputtered in the down flow before turning off the shower and grabbing a towel.

Before the accident I focused on making money because I had none. And then I won the big lotto prize in 2005, which I invested extremely well, apparently, judging by the totally ridiculous, insane amount of wealth and power I had in this new life, with an incredible new body, and centuries of time ahead of me. Yet instead of being thrilled at the prospects, I felt overwhelmed, impatient, aimless, joyless and clueless.

Awake three days and I'm already melancholy. Jeez. It's funny how a hot shower after a 450 year nap affects one's disposition.

One thing I knew—I had to find a real job.

***

"Ladies, hop in. We're going home." They both jumped in the car giggling like schoolgirls with a kept secret. Renatta sat in the front and Betty in the back on the passenger's side. I logged in a flight plan by linking my mind through my PFF and setting the autopilot. "What are you two so happy about?"

"Just girl talk," smirked Betty.

"Uh-huh, right," I said, looking in the rear view mirror.

"What's for dinner, Charles?" Renatta asked.

"I don't know yet."

"Renatta told me how wonderful your shrimp-head soup was," said Betty.

I glanced over at Renatta. "What would you like?"

"Betty should make a suggestion," she said. "She's never had a meal of any kind before."

"Betty is a robot," I replied. "She can't eat food." And in the rear view mirror I asked Betty, "Can you?"

"I'm not a robot, silly; I'm a synthetic person with all the abilities and sensibilities of any human female, thanks to you, Charles. I even have citizen status. I can vote. I am a Legal Person!"

"Thanks to me? Just because I said to go ahead and download yourself into a shell?"

"Actually, you paid for my development."

"I *paid* for you? What on Earth are you talking about?"

Renatta filled me in. "When you verbally authorized Betty's corporeal transformation from holographic to solid, the company paid for the manifest to the tune of about a hundred million creds.

"But--," I tried to get a word in edgewise.

"She literally has the same biology as a natural- or clone-born human except her nervous system is an amalgamation of complimentary augmented biotic and synthetic elements," Renatta explained.

"I have no idea what all that means."

"And she has all the rights of any citizen in the Federation."

"Good god, what have I done?" I quipped.

"That's not nice," complained both of them in unison.

"Ah, sorry, no offense intended, it's just such a new concept for me to absorb so soon. So, does that make you my daughter or my slave?" I asked with what I thought was a twinkle in my tone. I should have known better. Both were apparently mortified by my comment, and I realized I was digging a deep hole for myself. For a moment I thought I would have to step out of the car. I was outnumbered two women to one man, which is never a comfortable circumstance. I tried tuning out their chatter and listening to Space Control instead, but to no avail. They kept prattling on.

"You're being stupid, Charles," said Renatta.

"He's being a jerk," Betty confirmed.

"No, I'm not," I pleaded. "You said I own the central computer. Betty is the central computer, therefore...."

"I am not your daughter and I am certainly not your slave!" snapped Betty, in a huff, with her arms crossed under her breasts.

"Betty's now on the company payroll as a commander in your fleet," explained Renatta. "And she's also a science officer with downloaded doctorates in biomedicine, computer science, electrical engineering, plasma physics, and biochemistry. Those disciplines cost you an additional million creds each, by the way."

"Oh...so, how does spaghetti and meatballs sound?" said I.

***

By the time we landed at Albemarle House I had made peace with the commanders of criticism. En route I apologized for being insensitive and male and blamed my insensitivity on my lineal barbarism and the insufficiently politically correct mores of the twenty-first century; whereupon they sniffed with indignation. But after they thought I had suffered for long enough they forgave me and reverted to chattering about nothing of particular interest to a hetero male in any century. Jeez. Little had changed, I mused, as I wrapped myself in introspective thought for the duration. Women had retained their super sensitivities and weren't the least bit reluctant to identify a man's weaknesses. I wondered if men in this century were any more or less different than I was, or if I was a relic from a past when men were more convinced of their station. Back in my day we were still grappling with whether we should hold a door open for a lady, or let her open it herself. With the latest convoluted permutations in this brave new world, I was still totally confused. Nothing had changed. I was still just as clueless as before.

"Charles," asked Renatta, "what may we do to help?"

I looked at them in the rear view mirror. "Help?"

"With dinner," Renatta replied.

The autopilot must have landed us because I didn't remember doing it. Between the mental fatigue of everything running through my mind and the strenuous workout I had just been through, I had zoned out. So much for this fancy new body of mine.

The doors hissed up so we could exit the car. "Well, let's see; why don't you and Betty figure out all the details about Betty's new life? You're starting out with nothing, right, Betty? So, you're going to have to get some clothes, as well as buy a flat and a car."

"We've done all that already," offered Renatta. The two of them were walking arm-in-arm on the stone walk.

"What? When did that happen?"

"On the way here," said Betty.

"So that was all the…uh…what the discussion was about."

"Betty is going to stay with you until she finds a place she can call her own."

"Oh really?"

"Yes, and we've picked out a whole new wardrobe for every occasion," said Renatta.

"You don't mind, do you, Charles?" asked Betty.

I suppressed a feeling of being superfluous right about then and said, "No, I was going to offer you a room anyway; glad you can stay." A chime sounded in the foyer as we turned the corner.

"Oh, good, that must be our order," Betty chirped, and then the two of them bounded off, leaving me standing alone on the walkway, once again clueless.

***

The kitchen had been restocked and cleaned while we were away. That sparked my curiosity. *Who might be involved behind the scenes, I wondered. Surely there must be a human presence. How does all this organization happen without my input or consent?*

"Computer on."

A trill sounded before a rectangular panel appeared on a wall to my left, featuring a smiling blonde woman in a green business suit. "Yes, Mr. Dawes, how may I be of assistance?" she asked.

"What's your name?"

"Betty."

"No, Betty is here with me."

"No, sir, you named me Betty a few days ago; don't you remember?"

I sighed and scratched my head. "I'm getting confused by all this."

"What's confusing you, sir?"

"Never mind." I yelled for the original Betty to return.

Both Renatta and the solid Betty appeared at the kitchen door almost immediately, with their PFFs shimmering. Behind them I noticed a herd of servo bots carrying packages. They were headed down the hall from which we had just come.

"What's up, boss?" Renatta inquired.

"I just called up the central computer and she thinks she is Betty. I can't have two Betties in my life at the same time; I'm already finding it hard to cope."

"Well, then rename me," said the central computer Betty.

"Or rename me," said the original Betty.

"Why'd you open the central computer?" asked Renatta.

"Good god, that's rather moot at the moment, wouldn't you say?" I snorted.

"I suppose it is," said Renatta. "And stop being so cross, will you?"

"Yeah," pouted the original Betty. "What's the big deal anyway?"

"May I suggest a solution?" offered the central computer. "Please." We looked at her. "OK, what?" I asked.

She stated clearly, "I suggest the original Betty be renamed to avoid confusion in your mind, Mr. Dawes."

"*My* mind? What about everyone else's mind?"

"No one else is confused, sir."

I mumbled something unintelligible under my breath.

"Sorry?" all three women said in unison.

"What is it with you guys? Do you all think the same thoughts, or something?"

"Yes," they replied in unison again.

I threw my hands in the air, "Fine, you all sort it out and get back to me. I'm cooking dinner."

"He's so cranky," I heard one of them say as they returned to whatever they were doing.

"Computer?" I stayed her disappearance.

"Yes, sir?"

"Back to the original purpose of my calling you. Who cleans up the kitchen and restocks the fridge and pantry?"

"Your butler."

"My butler?"

"Yes, sir."

"Where is he?"

"He lives in Dublin but he's on call 24/7. Should I summon him?"

"Yes!" I said a little too emphatically.

A moment later a chime sounded in the foyer again, and I heard muffled greetings between the two girls and the clicking heels of one who I assumed would be the approaching butler. He stood ramrod straight in the kitchen doorway, sporting a pencil-thin mustache and dressed in a black suit with short tails, a starched white shirt, and white cotton gloves.

"You called, sir?" he said in a polished Irish brogue.

"For Christ's sake, you even look like a butler!" I stood with my hands on my hips, scoping him up and down.

"Yes, thank you, sir; that's most kind of you. How may I be of service?"

"Are you human?"

"I beg your pardon, sir?"

"Are you a synthetic being or are you human?" I huffed.

"I am mostly human, sir."

"What does that mean?"

"Well, sir, my body has been re-engineered biomechanically and enhanced genetically with nanites, synthetic metal alloys, and carbon compounds similar to your own architecture."

"I see. How old are you?"

"One hundred fifty-six, sir."

Three days ago I would have passed out. At this point I didn't even blink. "Did you stock the kitchen and clean up after me?"

"I made sure it was done, sir – I supervised the servo bots."

"Then there are others?" For some reason I was really irritable.

"Yes, sir, Albemarle House has a staff of forty-three and I am the chief butler."

"Forty-three?" I sighed. "What's your name?"

"Jeeves, sir."

"Christ! You're kidding, right?"

"No, sir, I am HMSS Sergeant Major Winston Jeeves Hamilton, III, of the 1st SAS SFG. Proudly I am a seventh generation Royal Court servant, many of whom have been detailed by the Crown to protect heads of state, corporations, or royalty in Britain's interest. His Royal Highness King Harry VI personally assigned me to watch over you, sir. My masters usually call me Jeeves and I like that. Would you mind, sir?"

I was in some sort of incomprehensible befuddlement or something. None of the mumbo-jumbo Jeeves had just spewed made a lick of sense to me at all.

"Mind what?" I mumbled.

"Would you mind addressing me as Jeeves, sir?"

I relented. "No, not all…, Jeeves."

"Might I make a suggestion, sir?"

"Sure," I said, dragging butt, completely out of steam. Coffee came to mind. *Perhaps I needed caffeine*, I thought.

My butler had a different idea. "Tumbler, half ice, crushed," said Jeeves to no one in particular over his left shoulder. A glass appeared half full of crushed ice in the refrigerator door. He then filled the glass with three fingers of Macallan bourbon whiskey from one of the cabinets and served it on a late nineteenth-century square sterling repoussé tray, by Kirk. Somehow I remembered buying that tray at an antique show in Purcellville, Virginia, sometime in the mid-1980s. I set up at that show as a vender.

"Sir, I think you need a boost."

"I couldn't agree more, Jeeves. Thank you kindly." I downed it in three gulps and held it out to be filled again with the most extravagant malt whisky in the world, at least in my day.

"Better, sir?" he asked.

"Way better, old chap," I sighed. I took a seat on a stool and leaned on the granite counter.

"Want to run all that HMS stuff by me once more? I am afraid it didn't register the first go round."

"Of course, sir, I beg your pardon," Jeeves said. "Over time His Majesty's Secret Service evolved to become not just an intelligence and implementation asset of MI6, but an overwatch agency for Federation space, all surveyed space, in fact. The Dawes Conglomerate is the lattice upon which peace, security, and prosperity rests and grows. As Founder of the DC you are the most important symbol of the well-being of civilization, as we know it. My assignment is to protect you at all costs because it is in the interests of the United Kingdom."

"Jeeves, I have known a few SAS types in my time in the service when I was a US Marine. The last op I worked with the SAS was in the Hindu Kush back from before you all thawed me out, and all that. They're a bunch of tough hombres. It seems implausible for an SAS bloke to have the personality or wherewithal to carry on as a butler. No offense, old chap."

Jeeves may not have been offended by my remarks but he stood even straighter when I made them and then poured himself three fingers and took a pull.

"None taken, sir. Indeed the SAS is largely a young person's sport, even today; however, your personal security detail is part of Special Branch, sir. We 'butlers' are seasoned agents with wide combat experience in all environments, across many cultures, and multi-sentient joint task force ventures. My branch is the most elite of all Branches. We have only six hundred members across surveyed space, and only about one hundred fifty of those are on assignment at any given time. Our other active duty members are either in training, on leave, or in hospital getting refitted or salvaged. As for me personally, getting here is the culmination of my one-hundred-twenty-five-year career. The minimum requirement within the modern SAS for even applying to Special Branch is fifty-five and ninety-five; that's fifty-five years of service within the SAS and ninety-five years of age."

I just sat there like a bump listening to this extraordinary man and sipped.

"After passing the initial aptitude tests, I waited six years before I was assigned to my Special Branch plebe class, and then it took me thirteen years to complete the training, and another ten as top sergeant before I qualified for the Imperial Roster. There are only twenty-one of us Imperial Guards. Serving is not menial, sir. It's interesting. We get to experience the life of our masters first-hand. For a history buff, it cannot get any better than this. This posting is the top of the top. I, sir, am honored beyond measure to serve you."

"Jesus," was all I could muster for a few ticks. I needed another whiskey and to contemplate. I understood what it meant to be elite. Before, I was Force Recon, the USMC's Special Forces branch. The training I underwent in the Suck was pretty tough but child's play compared to my butler's career. "I am very much impressed, Jeeves. I stand corrected and I am pleased to have you on staff."

"Thank you, sir."

"Look, I don't know much about this new world, but I suppose you've been briefed on my history?"

"Yes, sir. Staff knows your history."

"OK, fine, I expected no less. I'm going to rely on your help from time to time. I hope I can call on you whenever I have a question?"

"Of course, sir, anytime, 24/7."

"Then see to it that original Betty gets settled here, later, will you?"

"Yes, of course, sir."

"All right, now would you mind helping me prepare dinner for the lot of us?"

"Not at all, sir. How would you like to begin?" He removed his white gloves, one finger at a time, and carefully placed them inside his coat.

"We're having spaghetti and meatballs, garlic bread, a green salad, and iced tea. And I want you to join us at the table."

"Very well, sir, I can prepare it all if you'd like to retire."

"Yes, thank you. I'm normally the cook in this house, but I'm not up to it this evening for reasons too complicated to recite. OK?"

"Of course, sir," he said. "Straightaway. I know how to do this."

Chapter 10: Spitfire

They were in the fifth bedroom at the end of the west wing, the only sleeping quarters with windows on three walls and the only one with a cherry Federal Period pencil post bed with an elaborately lace-draped tester. It didn't surprise me that she selected that room. If the den had been adjacent to this bedroom, I would have chosen it. Chuckling sounds came from behind the wide single-panel fir door.

"Hey, girls, may I come in?"

"Sure, boss," said Renatta, "come on in."

I pressed the wrought-iron lever down and swung the door open to a sight to behold. She appeared a little flushed. It looked like they'd bought out Nordstrom's ladies' department. There must have been fifty pairs of shoes strewn about and god knows how many clothes. The two of them sat cross-legged in the middle of the bed, facing each other, surrounded by a rainbow of tops and bottoms.

"Did a bomb go off in here or something?" I just shook my head, hands on my hips, and allowed a slight twinkle to slip out. That was all they needed. They giggled like a pair of schoolgirls caught in the boy's shower room.

"No Charles!" exclaimed Renatta. "We're outfitting Betty for her new life," she said as she tossed hair out of her eyes. Obviously, they'd been trying on some, too, since their clothes were only half buttoned.

"You mean for the rest of her life?" I said.

"I don't have anything to wear, *Charles!*" said original Betty.

"Well, you do now. Good grief, girl. Did you have to buy a lifetime's supply all at once?"

"My name's not Betty anymore, Charles," she said. Without moving her head, Renatta glanced at her like a broody hen after a hatchling. For a moment their animation ceased with expectation.

"All right, the suspense is killing me; what's your new name?"

"Sarah."

I relaxed. "Oh … that's a good choice. Actually, Sarah's my favorite female name."

"Thank you, Charles," she smiled, obviously delighted. She sprung off of the bed in a single bound and hugged me.

"So, do synthetic people have a surname?" I asked her, hesitantly, she with her arms still around my neck.

"Yes, silly," she replied. "I thought maybe you'd help us with that since you are my benefactor." She let go of me. "Would you mind?"

"Ah…" I hesitated, shrugged one shoulder. "Sure, why not?" That seemed to please them. I stuffed my hands into my back pockets, sensing a no-win situation. "What's top on your list?"

"We would like you to offer a suggestion before we tell you. We don't want to influence your selection," said Renatta cautiously. I figured as much.

"Yes, *please* Charles," Sarah pleaded in a slightly British accent, lip jutting.

The short hairs on my neck began vibrating like tuning forks. Whatever I offered would certainly lead to a spat, I thought. It's been a rather tough day already. Maybe if I just say something that would never pass muster, I reasoned, I'd be shooed away for being a silly man. Perfect plan, I calculated. What the heck? Even if I had to dodge flying shoes, at least I could get back to the kitchen. But alas, that was not to be.

"Oh…how about Spitfire?" I offered with a straight face, even though I winced internally.

They looked at each other in what appeared to be a form of astonishment. "Perfect!" squealed Betty.

"I love it!" giggled Renatta.

They leapt off the bed and crushed me with hugs and kisses, screeching like a couple of harpy eagle chicks.

"Sarah Spitfire," chirped old Betty, "I love you, Charles. Thank you so much." She planted a big wet one right on my mouth.

"Don't mention it." I managed to extract myself by pulling her arms off me. "Look, girls, dinner's in fifteen minutes. Button up or put some more clothes on, will you, please?" Most of their natural attributes were readily available to any passing eye.

I backed out of there with the two of them cooing like babies had just been born. So much for reverse psychology. Since I'm so apparently gifted in selecting names, I thought, maybe I should just change mine to Clueless.

Chapter 11: The Butlers Did It

Back in the kitchen I was pleased to find Jeeves up to his clavicles in garden greens, and a pile of freshly blanched tomatoes was on the cutting block.

"Jeeves, you're a real champ."

"Thank you, sir. Always glad to be of assistance."

"Let's see what we have in the fridge. Oh, good, everything we need. So where do you get all these great-looking edibles, Jeeves?"

"All over, sir: Spain for oranges, France for truffles, Monterey for wine, Whole Foods for fresh cuts of meat, the kitchen garden for vegetables and herbs," said the chief butler extraordinaire.

"What do you do, flash all over the globe, poking into various nooks and crannies?"

"Yes, sir, it's the best part of the job. I love it."

A few minutes later, as I spooned the last meatball into a nineteenth-century white ironstone tureen, the girls appeared dressed in identical white tennis outfits.

"Ohhh, Charles, it smells wonderful!" said Renatta and Sarah.

"Thanks, ladies, but Jeeves deserves most of the credit."

"Nonsense, sir," said Jeeves. "You are the culinary genius. I just pulled it together."

"Jeeves," said Renatta, "I would like to introduce to you to Commander Sarah Spitfire."

He bowed slightly while holding Sarah's chair out. "Welcome, mum, I do hope I can be of assistance."

"Thank you, Jeeves; you're so kind," the newly minted fleet officer replied, sitting daintily.

"Jeeves, you didn't set a place for yourself," I noticed.

"I'll have something a bit later, if you don't mind, sir."

"I do mind," I growled. "Set a place and take a seat. That's an order."

Jeeves scurried even faster than he had before. The two women looked at each other; neither had observed me deliver such a strong command until that moment. There was an awkward silence.

"Look, folks, if there's one thing I can't stand, it is inequality…got that?" I said, attempting to soften the blow.

There was an affirmative, yet submissive, murmur.

"That being said, however, I don't want to ever have to remind anyone that I'm first among equals. If I say I want something a certain way, I mean it. Get my drift?" A chorus of 'Yes, sirs' sounded, even one from central computer Betty who'd apparently been observing the situation from high on the wall.

"Terribly sorry, sir," said Jeeves, obviously devastated.

"No need to apologize, Jeeves."

"Thank you, sir."

"Are you still out of sorts, Charles?" Renatta inquired.

I ignored the doctor, irritated all over again that she'd presume to ask that, then irritated that I was irritated! Maybe she was right, but I didn't need to cope with any more questions today from anyone. I changed the subject to give Jeeves the opportunity to recover his composure. "Jeeves, where the heck did you get that three-hundred-year-old bottle of Macallan whiskey we opened?"

"No trouble, sir, just a slip 'round the clock," he said, winking at me.

That remark didn't register at all, obviously, so the three of them looked at each other in turn as Betty patiently explained. "Sir, 'slipping the clock' is a colloquial euphemism for jumping outside of one's own relative time. The technology is new and the ramifications haven't all been determined yet, and considerable pressure is being levied from various ethics committees, religious leaders, and academic groups to control, license, tax, or otherwise shut down or limit the research and development of the machine. Some lawmakers have submitted legislation that would make it a felony punishable by large fines or imprisonment of a year or more at an orbital penal colony."

"Sounds like a violation of the Sherman Anti-Trust Act," I said, still oblivious.

"It's more serious than that," Sarah said.

"What are we talking about here, exactly?" I asked.

"Time travel," answered Sarah.

I know my mouth dropped open—I mean, *time travel!*

"Time travel has been forbidden by Interstellar Law for centuries," Renatta added.

"Even though no one until now has been completely successful at controlling the parameters," Jeeves explained.

"Completely successful?" I croaked incredulously. Successful *at all* was unbelievable. And I thought I'd already had too much to cope with for one day.

"We can explain all that in detail later," Betty offered.

"No, explain it to me in detail right now. How, uh…" I began to sputter to no one in particular and swung my attention back around at Jeeves, "Just how do you go about slipping the freaking clock, for Christ's sake, Jeeves? And what parameters?"

"We butlers have a system," he offered.

"You *butlers* have a system?" I shouted. "And what exactly would that be?" He turned beet red.

He looked at a spot on the tablecloth. Then, he explained, "Sir, we use Professor Rictor's Rai Machine to slip the clock. In the past we SAS butlers have offered ourselves as guinea pigs to the chamber director for his experimental shifts in time."

I thought about that for a tick. "You mentioned that time machine parameters were uncontrolled until now. What parameters?"

Jeeves swallowed audibly. "Axis parameters, sir."

"What does that mean?"

"The early machines could not project the slipper accurately along the timeline. They could be sent out but not retrieved and to any point on the X-Y axis. It was a total crap shoot, sir."

"I understand."

"Very good, sir," Jeeves seemed relieved.

And then I thought of something else. "Jeeves, you said butlers do this slipping the clock business. Which butlers? All butlers everywhere?"

"No, sir, only Special Branch butlers assigned to the Dawes Conglomerate."

"I'm comforted by the limitation," I said. "Go on."

Jeeves was so nervous he sat ramrod as if at parade rest. "When we travel, sometimes we're able to procure perishables that are rare or unusual in present time and bring them back to prove we've been to when we were supposed to be. I must admit we try to outdo each other by finding the most unusual things for our respective masters. I generally was the most fortunate, if I do say so myself, sir."

I looked at Jeeves, leaning toward him slightly, "You time traveled to get whisky?"

"Terribly sorry, sir," he croaked.

I sat back. "Wasn't that a bit reckless?"

"Perhaps a wee bit, sir."

"And let me not be remiss," I said, looking around the kitchen at my little band. "Where is this illegal time machine for heaven's sake, and who the bloody hell owns it?"

They looked like wet cats. "You do, Mr. Dawes," said computer Betty from high on the wall.

"Just great. My day is now complete," I burped silently. Jeeves wordlessly poured me another. "And this, this slipping the clock business violates the law?" I asked Renatta.

"Well, it's a gray area, so to speak," she replied.

"What are the consequences for returning with time booty?" I slurred ever so slightly, waving my glass of illegal moonshine around the room. "Doesn't it alter history or something like that?"

"Returning with perishables has no ill affect," Renatta said.

"And yet this *is* against the law," I said.

"It is … and it isn't," said Sarah.

"For heaven's sake, will someone please explain what the hell is going on?" I exclaimed. I could feel my nanites get a grip on my blood-alcohol level in a way I would never have been able to before the thaw.

"You're the law, Mr. Dawes," answered computer Betty. "You, sir, are the Founder of the Federation. The Federation elected you as Emperor for life in 2376. As our monarch, you are the chief justice, top law enforcement officer, highest-ranking general and admiral – actually, all of the administrative positions. The Dawes Conglomerate owns the time-folding technology and all the products and patents developed by Dawes companies. By Executive Order you may authorize the extent of their development and usage. By Royal Edict you may make laws, and by the power vested in you, you may enforce the laws as you see fit."

I looked up at her image on the wall as she continued. At this point I'd had about eight fingers of whiskey, so most of what she was explaining sailed far over my head, but I got the gist of it. Mostly the word 'Emperor' floated about my brain as just plain silly.

I burped. "So, by hook or by crook over the course of centuries I have been made the Bürgermeister of the Bilderbergers. Ain't that just dandy."

The three of them looked at each other and then at me. Renatta clarified, "Sorta, kinda, but remember that we removed the corruption from the Bilderberg Group and inserted your code of honor and moral credo of the DC."

I burped again and refrained from saying anything.

They looked at each other and then Betty continued. "In your absence the committee decreed that this house has diplomatic immunity and it is the final authority. The Dawes Conglomerate and its sister and subordinate organizations comprise the Federation security net. Flag officers are, in fact, Federal marshals. The Federation security is held in trust, and thus, security is an element of shared responsibility incumbent upon all trust-members. The member organizations include large syndicates like the Energy Cartel and certain strong national governments like the United States of the Americas, the European Confederation, the Asian Group, the African Alliance, and the global security forces of each planet member. On Earth the global security force is the United Nations."

"So, are violators handed over to the U.N.?" I slurred.

"They could be but are usually not," said Renatta.

"Why not?"

"Because the U.N. is a spineless organization that doesn't enforce its own sanctions and resolutions," my physician growled.

"Tits-on-a-bull," I hiccupped in agreement and raised my glass so Jeeves wouldn't have far to reach.

"What does that mean?" Renatta said.

"Oh, it was something my dad used to say when someone was worthless."

"Ah, because tits on a bull aren't used for anything; they are present but worthless?" asked Sarah.

"You got it," I replied.

At least some things hadn't changed in four hundred and fifty years.

Chapter 12: Download

After a quiet but filling meal, I removed to the den where I had a brief nap. The girls disappeared somewhere and Jeeves was out of sight. My mind was awash with concepts that made my head feel like it was about to explode. I expressed as much to Renatta on awakening. Computer Betty had positioned herself as a hologram and was once again rocking in her rocking chair. Renatta and I took up comfortable positions on one sofa and Sarah sat in the matching Gus chair.

"So, if I might make a suggestion, Charles," offered Renatta. "I think it is time you were briefed about the nature of your 'Empire' so you'll have the ability to act decisively when the need arises. You've had the PFF download and the simulator training, but now you need an understanding of the corporate history and operational protocols, which include all the past, present, and anticipated security issues of the future. It might help you understand the current system of laws and forces you'll have to navigate."

I swiveled my head toward Betty. "How long is the download for a complete history of just the Conglomerate?" I asked.

She re-crossed her legs. "Four minutes."

"And for a complete history of everything since my incarnation?"

"Four and a half minutes," she replied.

I looked at Renatta. "Can I handle that much at this point in my recovery?"

"Yes, I think so," she replied. "You seem to handle stress well enough."

I had to wonder about that. It took a few tumblers of Macallan to get me through the latest revelations. But there was even more that niggled at the back of my brain. "I have my own concerns," I expressed. "During the last two downloads, I sensed that I am harboring an addictive trait. I know you warned me downloading can be addictive. More alarmingly, I also detected a subconscious warning that if I downloaded too much at one sitting or too much over the course of time, I might lose my sense of wonder. Does that make sense?"

Renatta responded, "That's an atypical phenomenon that rarely manifests when downloading, but those are legitimate concerns when they do occur, Charles. Then maybe you should limit your exposure to a specific segment of history instead, for now at least."

Betty agreed. "Mr. Dawes, I suggest you load only the company history since your accident. This will include the accounting logs, asset inventory catalog, personnel roster, the command tree, and all past and present fleet-wide operational orders. That will give you a basis for understanding the domain you control without removing the sensational component to your learning process that you wish to preserve."

"Will that be a complete history of the Conglomerate?" I asked.

"Essentially yes," said Renatta.

I looked at computer Betty. "All right then, make it happen."

I leaned back in the soft green apple green leather of the club sofa and closed my eyes. Betty snapped her fingers. Immediately light streamed in over my event horizon through the dual passages of my optic nerves like a hurricane-force solar wind. Enormous swirling data rivers enveloped me and flowed past me ... so many impressions ... tendencies ... harbingers ... a fleeting thought of *Why me, lord? Why me?* ... scales of failure, palls of subterfuge ... depths of love ... reams of hate ... ephemeral synapses cracking and popping ... streaming past the periphery ... cool, warm, then volcanic heat ... falling up ... effortless assimilation ... tension ... and finally, an audible sound like – chuck!

Comprehension and a sense of assuredness swept over me. "It's over, isn't it?" I asked.

"Yes, Charles," Betty replied. "The downloaded material is now part of your being. You should be able to have command of your realm now and therefore know the answers to most of your questions."

I had always been a generalist, so it was little wonder that my first thoughts were of the general order of things. In the twenty-first century, the world appeared to have been moving toward globalization and a central unified world government, vis-à-vis the UN, I thought at the time. Of course, at the same time, others were vehemently opposed to a strong central planetary government, I for one. Others preferred isolationism; France was a perfect example. While some powerbases, like Iran, were led by an obviously insane nutcase set on world domination, others in the United States perceived themselves to be the peacekeepers and wanted to retain autonomy and power. It appeared then as though the evolution of law and political power was moving from an array of independent national government standards to a single international committee, the UN – whether I liked it or not.

In the present time, however, I discovered that the law appeared to have mutated into an amalgamation of power jointly held by nation-states and corporate entities. In effect the power of the nation-state had been usurped by the will of the stockholder. A confederation of power, multinational and multi-corporate, ruled not just Earth but all of Federation space. Regional delegates of Earth's central government entity sent their elected representatives to semiannual summits in New York City and once each decade to the Federation convention. Its seat of government? Wherever I was at any given time. Interestingly, the people elected me Emperor while my corporate title was Founder. It made me feel uncomfortable. I felt like fleeing.

I looked at each of them in turn. "It's a peculiar feeling, this downloading exercise, whatever it's called. It's like a rollercoaster ride through the halls of academia with one's tail on fire."

Renatta looked at me lovingly. "The euphoria will subside in a moment."

"I'm the Founder?"

"Yes, you're the Founder, Charles," she said.

"All of this is because of my lotto winnings so long ago?"

"Yes, because of your winnings," she nodded.

Betty added, "And the way they were invested and the way you protected them with directives led to civilization as we know it today. You were very wise, Mr. Dawes. It was because of you that I exist and it's because of you that disease, hunger, or poverty no longer exists. Your research and development consortium actually saved the planet from imminent destruction more than once."

I remembered an element of the download. "When the Earth's magnetic field…"

Betty completed my thought, "…when the field diminished and the polarity reversed direction, Dawes Labs devised a solution that restored the inner core currents, and thus the Earth's magnetic shield was restored and renewed."

Renatta touched my arm. "Charles, the world you once knew is a better place than when you left it, and mankind is aware of your contributions. You are in all the history books."

"If I am such a historical figure then why are there such stringent security protocols? Why would someone try to kill me?"

"The download would have provided an answer," said Renatta, "if there was one."

I looked at her, puzzled.

"Why would someone kill John Lennon?" replied Sarah rhetorically.

"No one knows what motivates the insane," Jeeves said.

Sarah elaborated, "The Dawes Conglomerate represents an enormously powerful interstellar political and military adversary to the dark forces that appose liberty and free markets. There are those who would be king and socialize everything, but you're standing in their way."

"Your notoriety is a bright lamp to the moths of insanity," added Jeeves.

"Charles, you are our King," Renatta said lovingly.

"Uh-huh," I said, ignoring her look. "So, when did all this begin, the price on my head, I mean?"

"It's been like this since the dawn of mercantilism at the beginning of the Renaissance in the fifteenth century," Renatta said. "Probably since the first hominid fell out of a tree. Long before you became to target."

"You mean cutthroat?" I said.

"That's right."

"So, what do my adversaries want most from me?"

"The Rai Machine," Sarah replied.

Jeeves cleared his throat. "And any number of other incredible technologies in the DC inventory."

"Actually, Mr. Dawes, to be exact, the most recent credible coordinated threat began in earnest a couple of years ago in, 2458," Betty explained. "That's when Dr. Durham Singh made his breakthrough discovery at Dawes Labs at Rai University."

I stood and began pacing, to and fro in front of the massive fireplace. "That was on the Dubai campus?" My recent download had given me many facts, but until I heard these more human explanations, the facts didn't added up.

Jeeves answered, "Yes sir."

Something was coalescing inside my mind, a mad inspiration perhaps. "We have," I paused, "actually the Conglomerate has, exclusive rights, correct?"

They could sense something but they didn't know what. Jeeves tilted his head and answered, "Correct. The Dawes Conglomerate has exclusive rights."

Betty added, "Its use was restricted to the Federation by the General Assembly. Is all of the history beginning to come together for you, Mr. Dawes? Now that you have had a download, I mean."

I glanced at her and kept pacing. Indeed it was. All my mental sparks and darts were assembling rapidly in my mind.

I think Sarah realized it first. She elaborated, "As you now know, sir, the first experiments with time travel disturbed the space-time continuum, which led to a conflict of interest between two epochs. A tautological conundrum emerged that threatened the evolutionary stream."

Betty continued the history recital. "Computer models projected the collapse of existing civilizations and the demise of the various political powerbases. Naturally this caused panic amongst the leadership in this system and several others. Militant religious fundamentalists saw this as an opportunity to advance their initiatives. Terrorism became widespread throughout the quadrant. It was eight months before the genie was put back into its bottle. The Federation regained control of the emerging conundrum by 'slipping the clock' yet again to reverse the misalignment caused by the initial slip. A similar scenario almost happened a few months later when a band of privateers repeated the same mistake by commandeering the Rai Machine. They were captured and incarcerated for life but not before hundreds of thousands of sentients died and a planet's ecosystem was nearly destroyed."

I continued my pacing, barely cognitive of the lecture. "So what happened to the Rai Machine?" I asked, kneading my forehead with one hand. Thanks to my recent download I suddenly knew the answer before my lips ceased uttering the syllables. Betty was saying something I didn't catch. A wave of comprehension swept over me like a menopausal flush. I literally felt myself stagger, although no one else seemed to notice it as my mind clutched feebly to my conception horizon and then my soul felt like it spiraled upward into a chamber of …of comprehension and relief. I was having an epiphany.

"Charles?" Renatta said hesitantly, abruptly standing.

"It's on the mothership, isn't it?" I said.

"That's correct," Betty confirmed. "It was removed to the mothership about a year before the *QuestRoyal* went on line. Didn't you learn that in your download?"

"Yes, I know," I barely murmured, lost in thought.

"Charles, are you all right?" Renatta inquired.

"Yes. I don't know."

"What is it, Charles?" Renatta seemed genuinely concerned. She stepped toward me, checking her Merck.

"I have all the intricate pieces now," I said, halting my nervous pacing.

"What's wrong, Charles?" asked the doctor.

"Nothing is wrong. I know what I'm capable of now, and I have the means to execute my plan."

Renatta placed her hands on my chest and looked up at me. "Tell me," she whispered.

I gazed into her deep violet eyes. "I'll need your help."

"Anything."

Sarah and Betty were perched on the edge of their seats, straining. Jeeves stood in the doorway to the atrium.

"I need to go to Alexandria."

Betty stood up from her Gus rocker. It almost tipped over. "We can flash there right now if you wish," she said. "And while there I recommend the *Parsian Restaurant* on King Street."

"No, not Old Town Alexandria here in Virginia," I qualified. "We're going to Alexandria, Egypt."

"Why Egypt, Charles?" asked Betty.

"Because in the first century A.D. Julius Caesar's army burned the Egyptian fleet at anchor in the harbor in Alexandria, and along with the ships a colossal amount of invaluable historical information went up in smoke that night. We're going to rescue the contents of the Library of Alexandria."

Chapter 13: The Serapis Fraktur

There was a palpable electric tension in the air when my committee assembled the next morning in the den. Everyone stood when I entered the room. Sarah moved from tending the fire at the hearth to the long trestle table to join John, Renatta, Dawn, and Kay. Betty was her usual holographic self at the opposite end. As I took my seat everyone took theirs. Jeeves served coffee and tea.

I think that my epiphany the evening before was a result of the download and the enhancements kicking in. I suddenly knew what I wanted to do with myself other than just being the DC's moral compass; I had found a job.

"Betty, get the captain of the *QuestRoyal* on the screen," I ordered.

Betty responded, "The captain, Kent Dundee, is on TDY. The fleet admiral is commanding for the time being, Mr. Dawes."

"Whatever," I said impatiently. Immediately, a screen appeared encompassing an entire large window. Kay and Dawn swiveled in their seats. A moment later the image of a tall black gentleman seeming to be in his late forties dressed in a white uniform with brass buttons and a chest full of medals appeared. He sported a carefully combed straight salt-and-pepper hair, long sideburns, and a walrus mustache. He looked like a formidable flag officer, and as it turned out, he was one of the best that I would ever serve with.

"Good morning, Founder Dawes," he said with a slight Caribbean patois. "I'm Admiral Fleetwood Pride, acting captain of the *QuestRoyal*, at your service, sir."

The download indicated my new status as a flag officer, but it hadn't registered until that moment. I fully comprehended rank structure from my prior military service. Weirdly so, in this brave new world I found myself elevated to a unique pay grade: Monarch.

"Good morning, Admiral," I said. "I once knew a man by the same name in my time before." In my previous life one of my favorite personalities was USMC Brigadier General Fleetwood Pride. Fleet retired from the Suck, as he lovingly called the Marine Corps, to command the antique Confederate Air Force in Midland, Texas. Far-fetched as it seemed to some, many notable officers enjoyed retirement rebuilding and recreating the war birds of earlier times. As a collector of antiquities myself, General Pride and I had a similar inclination.

"I come from a long line of military types, Founder. Several of my ancestors went by this name. How may I serve you today?"

I was a bit amused by the name coincidence, but I didn't want to rake the time to get into genealogy. "There's an urgent matter you need to be apprised of. Please flash down here and join this committee meeting."

"Yes, of course," he replied. He vanished from the screen and Jeeves escorted him in a moment later. He clicked his heels slightly, stood at attention, shook my hand formally, and then shook everyone else's hand in turn before taking a seat.

"Sir, Admiral Pride is a committee member, too," Kay reminded me.

"Yes, I remember. Thank you, Kay." I was excited. "OK, ladies and gentlemen. Effective immediately your primary mission is the research and development of the slip chamber otherwise known as the Rai Machine. We will need to be able to slip the clock as easily as we flash from here to Culpeper and back. I want to be able to send and receive nonperishable material objects of any kind without disturbing the continuum. If it's impossible to retrieve the material objects that I desire, I want to have the capability of replicating said object exactly." There was a general murmur of surprise from those who had not been privy to the evening before.

"But there are legal ramifications," said Kay.

"You can't be serious, Mr. Dawes," John added his skepticism.

"As I understand it the Dawes Conglomerate is responsible for the law and its enforcement," I reminded Kay. "And yes, John, I am indeed serious. We're going to concentrate a significant portion of our resources toward perfecting the slip chamber."

"Why make this our primary mission?" asked the admiral.

"I believe answers can be found in a period before yours or even my previous time," I replied.

"What answers to which questions?" asked Kay.

"Just before my accident I found an antique fraktur with unique designs. It was dated 1748 and made by an American colonial scrivener by the name of Christopher Dock. He lived from 1698 to 1771 and worked as a schoolmaster in Skippack, a small Pennsylvania village."

"Forgive my ignorance, Charles," said John. "What is a fraktur?"

Betty saved me the trouble of elaborating, "Early fraktur, the word is both singular and plural, are handmade documents commemorating significant life events such as births, baptisms, marriages, and deaths. They were and still are hand-decorated with pen, ink, and watercolors. Early American fraktur usually had text in German because most of the fraktur makers were Germans making fraktur for the German market in America. At that time there was a significant population of German immigrants and their American-born offspring living in eastern Pennsylvania, Maryland, and the Shenandoah Valley of Virginia, but the art originated anywhere the German population wandered in early American history. A full-sized fraktur measures about forty by eighty-four centimeters and it is always on paper."

"Thank you, Betty," said John, nodding to the hologram.

"I would have said that they were 16 by 13 inches in size," I said. "But that's unimportant."

"So what does this fraktur have to do with the slip chamber?" asked Kay.

"This fraktur was embellished with unique designs that only someone with an understanding of matters from centuries far into their future could have drawn."

"Oh my," she murmured. The others looked puzzled. I stood and began drawing with my finger in front of me what I was attempting to describe. The CC automatically refined my intentions, creating an actual image, as I scrawled in the holo space over my end of the cherry conference table.

"At the top of the paper was a sort of a pinwheel shape with curved paisley-type arms – we appraisers and collectors refer to as a fylfot – hovering above a man seated in a Windsor sackback style armchair wearing a tri-corn hat. Interestingly, the fylfot was unusual in that it was drawn at an oblique angle like the blades on a helicopter. An inscription under the chair read 'Alexandria Egypt.' At the bottom of the page was a building I believed at the time to be a mausoleum, but now I think it might have been a slip chamber. Under it was the inscription, 'Temple of Serapis.' To the left was a man leading a horse into a doorway. On the opposite side was a man exiting on a flying machine that looked like some sort of a Jet Ski or snowmobile. He was dressed in what I thought was a deep sea diver's suit, but now I believe it to be a space suit."

"That would be an inertia ski, Mr. Dawes," offered Sarah. "It's like what you used to call a Jet Ski or snowmobile, but it is capable of flight. Both terrestrial and space models are available for sale at the retail level at any Ford, Mercedes, or Volvo dealer."

"I suspected as much," I said. I paused, staring at the grain in the table.

"Please continue, sir; this is interesting," said Admiral Pride.

I continued by drawing more of what I was describing onto the holo space. "Other equally curious symbols adorned the flanking margins of the fraktur: an obelisk, which was probably the Washington Monument, and something that appeared to be the Eiffel Tower on the opposite margin. Mathematical formulas were scattered about, objects that would pass for a submarine and a television were here and here, along with something I didn't recognize then but that I now know to be a mushroom-shaped habitat like the ones suspended all around Earth. At the time I thought someone with an artistic flair and a thorough knowledge of antiques created it. At first I thought it was a wonderful example of twentieth-century outsider art, but the age of the paper, the old iron oxide ink, and the skill of the artist was so similar to Christopher Dock's that I was stunned anyone would go to such trouble to create it."

"What happened to the fraktur?" asked John.

"I had it with me the day of my accident. I was on my way to San Francisco from the Bohemian Club to catch a flight back to Dulles. I intended to have the German text idioms translated at UVA. I suppose we will never know what became of the fraktur."

An animated discussion ensued amongst the members. I could tell I piqued their interest. "Betty, do a database search for the fraktur immediately," ordered John.

"I already have, Mr. Skill. It's at the Dawes depository in Moscow," she replied. "I'm having an SAS courier retrieve it and flash here as we speak."

***

Everyone crowded around to get a look at the fraktur encased in a hermetically sealed plexiglass container. It was just as I remembered it. The colors were still vivid and there were no losses to the paper. Christopher Dock's masterfully composed fraktur was incredibly beautiful.

"Can everyone read the script?" I asked. I'd been able to translate only a few words when I'd seen it back in 2010; I could read most of it now, though slowly.

There were murmurs of acknowledgment all around. Apparently everyone had the same comprehensive language download that I had, but still the idioms and rhyming poetry of the old-style script were difficult to read quickly.

"Betty, are you having trouble with this?" asked John.

"No, it's quite clear."

"Well, then read it to us so we don't have to labor over the archaic script."

"I believe it's a poem. Typically fraktur are not in rhyme and they're not poems," she clarified.

"Get on with it, Betty," said John impatiently.

"As Mr. Dawes indicated earlier, below the man in the chair, it reads 'Alexandria Egypt.' Beneath that the text translates:

Beware of Serapis before the fold
Or suffer the end before it's told
Oh Rex of men with empathy
Herein this vessel God will be
Consign the moment when life returns
Thou make haste whilst Caesar burns
Fall the Dock when none do see
To the place in heaven where God is Sea

"I should point out that in the last line 'God is Sea,' that translates to S-E-A, as in ocean," she commented.

"What the devil do you make of all that, Charles?" asked John.

"I haven't the foggiest," I replied.

"Betty, run that through your crypto-graphical programs and see what becomes of it," ordered John. "Maybe it will lead us somewhere."

Betty paused momentarily, about the same length of time it takes to take a deep breath and then exhale. I think all of us took a deep breath at that moment.

"The permutations are too numerous to mention them all," Betty replied. "So I'll limit them to the most likely possibilities. Would you like a little background?"

"Yes, please," I replied. "In a nutshell."

"All right. Serapis was the sister library to the Royal Library of Alexandria founded in 283 B.C. by Ptolemy, the great pharaoh of Egypt. Ptolemy was a Macedonian and one of Alexander the Great's generals. Upon Alexander's death Ptolemy was appointed satrap, or provincial governor, of Egypt. In 305 B.C. he declared himself king. One of his descendants was Cleopatra VII who interacted politically with Julius Caesar and Mark Antony. She was the last of the Ptolemaic line.

"Scores of scholars lived at the Royal Library and at Serapis. Both were temples. The scholars were ordered by Royal Edict to collect all written books anywhere in the known world at the time and bring them to the library. The order was comprehensive to the extreme. When trading ships arrived at the port of Alexandria, all shipboard books were confiscated or copied by temple scribes. Either way books streamed into the library for years. When the parent library became too full, the inventory spilled over to the nearby Serapis Temple, also in Alexandria. More than half a million books were kept in the main library at its peak. Keep in mind that books of that time were all handwritten scrolls and not bound references as was the later custom." There were nods of affirmation and concentrated interest.

"A laundry list of historians credited several people, the first of which was Julius Caesar in 48 A.D., with destroying the Library of Alexandria."

"But we're not certain of the destruction date, right?" I asked.

"Correct," Betty replied. "If someone other than Caesar destroyed it, the 48 A.D. date would be inaccurate."

"What about the Temple of Serapis?"

"The Serapis Temple wasn't burned in the great port fire but all of its books were brutally lost to time, as well," Betty replied.

"All very interesting, Mr. Dawes," said Renatta. "But what is the significance of the Serapis?"

"Well, the word Serapis is in the text of the fraktur and also on the fascia of the building at the bottom of the piece. Let's go line by line.

"'Beware of Serapis before the fold' might suggest what Serapis is, or was, before one slips the clock to the Serapis timeline. After all, time travel is the manipulation of the space-time continuum by utilizing the gravitational folds in space. If we are not fully cognizant of the Temple Serapis and its timeline, we might suffer unpredictable consequences or miss a window of opportunity."

"That's pretty speculative don't you think, Mr. Dawes?" said John.

"Yeah, it is."

"And I suppose Rex refers to a king," said Kay. "Which one?"

"I believe it refers to you, Mr. Dawes," Betty interjected. "The Founder is the most powerful individual in Federation space. In fact, Mr. Dawes is not just our leader; he is our elected Monarch with absolute power for life, and he's head of the Dawes Conglomerate with power greater than anyone in all of history. From the perspective of someone in Christopher Dock's eighteenth century, Mr. Dawes would be a king."

"This is making me very uncomfortable, folks," I said. "I don't fancy myself as king of anything."

"Nonetheless, Charles," said Dawn, "Betty's right. If one were trying to explain to an eighteenth-century person the power and wealth of someone such as yourself living in the 25th century, one might very well use the term 'king' to get his or her point across."

"Don't I have any say-so in the matter?" I asked in general.

"No, not really," replied Betty. "You're stuck with the job whether you like it or not."

"And if I refuse?"

"Look, sir," interjected John forcefully, sensing I was about to burst a blood vessel. "We have already been over why we need you, remember? And now look. You have just discovered an interesting personal mission to pursue. That's fantastic! What more could a man want?"

I paused and processed what John was telling me word for word and realized the big picture was indeed excellent. I guess my twenty-first-century distain for government interference in my personal life, which nearly blew my circuits, was obsolete in my current timeline. I hate government. The reason I didn't stay a full twenty years in the Corps was because I couldn't tolerate following orders of either an immediate commander or a chief executive who had shit for brains. That experience turned me into a die-hard libertarian, who at the time was a proponent for minimum government: justice system, military, and infrastructure. Everything else should be a private sector enterprise subject to market competition. No exceptions. It even included education and medical care. I also believed everyone should be taxed at a flat fifteen percent – all entities, large and small, profit and nonprofit, church and Boy Scouts, corporations, smelly winos collecting aluminum cans on the curb, and software geniuses inventing better apps. Everyone pays taxes, period. No exceptions and no deductions. There is no shame to require everyone to have skin in the game. It is just common sense. I still believe that that ideal is best even though I realize how impossible it is to get a majority to subscribe to it.

I told myself to try not to rant. After all, if I hated Big Government, and since I was now a universal-type Emperor governing nigh on to everything, then that was like saying I hated myself. Another of the conundrums in this weird new world of mine.

"Charles?" Renatta prodded.

"OK, I get it," I relented. "I'm an ungrateful lout."

"Yeah, something like that," said computer Betty smiling. Only *she* could get away with such a remark. But that broke the spell and John skillfully returned my attention to the topic at hand: my invented fraktur mission.

"And 'with empathy,' what does that signify, sir?" asked John respectfully.

"Probably that Charles is essentially a benign leader with no malice aforethought," Renatta answered with her hand on my arm. "After all," she said looking into my eyes, "you have no apparent ill intent and suffer no illusions that would jeopardize either the Conglomerate or any individual. You've literally been reborn into a time not naturally yours. You are literally pure."

"What about the fourth line, 'Herein this vessel God will be'?" Sarah asked.

Admiral Pride jumped in with a speculation, "The vessel must be the fraktur."

"But what does God have to do with it?" asked John.

Kay shrugged. "It might mean Godspeed."

"Based on the most likely permutations, the next two lines, 'Consign the moment when life returns,'" continued Betty, "might mean for someone to seize the initiative, take the opportunity, or take action. Perhaps Mr. Dawes was supposed to time travel to Serapis once he was revived from cryogenic internment. And the following line, 'Thou make haste whilst Caesar burns,' might refer to timing. The slip might have to be initiated just before the beginning of the burning of the Alexandria Library or whilst the great fire is wreaking havoc. I think it refers to that window of opportunity."

"I've fought forest fires before; it's not one of my favorite memories," I commented. "Returning to an inferno would not be my idea of a good time."

Admiral Pride continued. "I suppose 'Fall the dock when none do see,' means slip for 'fall,' to fall back in time, and 'dock' is the slip chamber. And more importantly, we're supposed to accomplish the slip in a manner that 'none do see,' meaning in secret."

"Or perhaps while we're cloaked in invisibility," offered John.

"Those interpretations seem to be consistent with the previous meanings," said Betty.

I was lost in thought, trying to put myself in the shoes of the ancient scrivener when it occurred to me. "No, 'Dock' is Christopher Dock. Notice that the word 'Dock' is capitalized. 'Dock' isn't the time chamber, ladies and gentlemen; it's the fraktur's scrivener."

"Unless the word has dual meaning," said Jeeves, who had been dutifully attending to us all the while with libations and finger food. We all looked up at him, as if suddenly aware of his presence.

"That's a good point, Jeeves," said Admiral Pride.

Sarah nodded. "If our interpretations are correct, Christopher Dock was not just a fraktur artist. He was also a time traveler."

"Or," Jeeves added shyly, "he may have met one."

All eyes turned toward the butler.

"Is there something on your mind, Jeeves?" Admiral Pride asked.

"Well, sir…"

"Spit it out, Jeeves!" John shouted.

"At ease, John. I'll do the shouting around here," I said.

John sat back in his chair and crossed his arms.

"All right, Jeeves, what are you trying to tell us?" I asked.

"I believe I may have met Mr. Dock on one of my slips."

Chapter 14: Slipping the Clock

"Slippers," as time travelers are called, have an imbedded chip that records audio-visual experiences through their optic nerves to their cerebral cortex. The wearer's visual and auditory perspective collects data in a chronological stream. Upon their return, their information is uploaded to the central computer in what, for all intents and purposes, is an HD color motion picture with audio. The various research departments aboard the *QuestRoyal* analyze the data for historical content, timeline anomalies, and the effectiveness of the slipper in the time zone. When I first discovered that I had the Rai Machine, its usage was essentially undirected, it didn't have a supporting analytical department, and there were no administrative personnel. The word primitive came to mind. I intended to change all of that. Admin was my proven strong suit. So was dreaming. The Rai Machine seemed like an opportunity to put both of my stellar attributes to good use.

I learned that Jeeves was the first of five guinea pigs selected from a long list of volunteers for time travel experiments primarily because of his security clearance. He also had intimate knowledge of ancient cultures. Over the course of several months before he made known his Dock connection, Jeeves slipped twenty-seven treks in almost as many different timelines, all without an apparent mishap – more than all the other volunteers combined.

The Rai volunteers are all Dawes Conglomerate butlers. Like Jeeves' responsibility to me, the other butlers' primary responsibility is the safeguarding of high-value company personnel – they're bodyguards. Butlering is merely a cover function. Each has a tactical background. Jeeves was a sergeant major in the British SAS. Three of the other four were US Secret Service and the fourth was a US Navy SEAL.

Part of their training at Dawes Labs included a series of supplementary comprehensive downloads in general areas of knowledge so they arrive to a timeline with a proficiency for understanding the period

– culture, mores, language, and history. Their downloads depend on mission requirements. When operatives slip a timeline, they are protected by their PFFs, which have cloaking functions in addition to co-field filtration, defensive armature, and offensive capabilities. Co-field filtration is simply the containment of harmless twenty-fifth-century pathogens within the wearer's PFF so that a timeline isn't contaminated by pathogens that might be dangerous to people, flora and fauna in a different time period. Of course it also protects the wearer from incoming contaminants.

Operatives slip in costume and in character with the capability to speak the language and dialect with native proficiency, but on occasion, they do make cloaked ventures incognito in order to procure data to satisfy scientific hypotheses or clarify historical theses. Cloaked slips are usually only made to a timeline when there is some intense drama, such as a battle, being played out. To date no one was aware of any anomalies that might have compromised the space-time continuum.

No one had used the Rai machine for off-Earth ventures, like to another Federation planet, at least not yet. The idea of slipping into a planet like Helios Grumm would require more knowledge of the Grunt's history than we had or even wanted to have, considering their likely past.

Every conceivable precaution was taken to preclude fractures in the timeline when slipping the clock, because any significant change theoretically affects the future. For instance, if Hitler were revealed early, then someone might assassinate him before that history could play out. Which could seem like a good thing, only the entire course of history would change, meaning the present would be altered to potentially disastrous degrees. Likewise, nothing of consequence can be left behind for fear that a technology discovered early could ultimately alter present time. Consequently these precautions have heretofore been mandatory. Until my arrival slippers had been allowed little discretionary authority to do anything other than to collect data optically.

Everyone was alarmed with the discovery that Jeeves interacted with a tenant, Dock, who created an artifact that ultimately ended up in the hands of the Dawes Conglomerate. The immediate conclusion was that Jeeves influenced the design of the fraktur by violating the primary covenant of time travel – reveal nothing, leave nothing, and take away only memories and photographs. We thought perhaps he had revealed something unintentionally, and therefore, left knowledge from the twenty-fifth century in the eighteenth century that ultimately manifested itself in this fraktur now before us, and who knows how else it might have been manifested. It appeared to be a crisis of the first order.

***

"Sit down, Jeeves," I ordered. The other members around the conference table glared at him with varying degrees of intensity. "Betty, get the slip chamber director on the screen. Then find the tape on Jeeves' jaunt to see Christopher Dock, isolate the interval, and run an analysis of what he said or what he might have left behind."

The holoscreen flashed on with an image of an older, wizened scientist-looking man wearing a bowtie and a white shirt with a white frock coat and khaki trousers; both garments were disheveled from too many hours in the lab. He fit the stereotype of an absentminded scientist perfectly.

"Hello," he said absently with a croak, his gaze on some papers in his hands. His eyebrows were out-of-control bushes and he spoke with an educated Bavarian accent.

I knocked on the table as if it were a door, to attract the scientist's attention. "I am Charles Dawes. Who might you be, sir?"

He turned to face me. "Ah-so, vät? Charles Dawes? I vasn't avare dat you had been revived," he sputtered. "Oh, I'm Professor Wilhelm Rictor."

"Yeah, well they thawed me out a few days ago. Listen, Professor, are you aware one of your slippers – Jeeves Hamilton – may have breached protocol?"

"No, sir, I am not avare of any such event. Vät are you talking about?"

I glanced at the central computer hologram entity, Betty. "Professor, Betty's going to bring you up to snuff on what we know so far. Report back to me when you have a response. And that means minutes, Professor. Got that? I'm in a hurry."

"Yes, sir, of course. ASAP."

The screen went blue and was immediately replaced with an image of a man dressed in the plain black and white apparel of the mid-eighteenth century. He looked to be about fifty years old and had slicked down salt-and-pepper hair and a short white beard with no mustache. "Who's that?" I asked in general and simultaneously noticed Betty hadn't budged. "And why are you still here?" I asked her. "I told you to brief the professor."

"That's Christopher Dock," replied Betty, "and I *am* briefing Rictor as we speak. I can do many things simultaneously, Mr. Dawes."

"Huh?" This time it was I who sputtered. "Of course you can, sorry. Does this image of Dock come from Jeeves' trek?"

"Yes, sir," she replied. "I made an analysis of the two treks that involve Jeeves with Dock."

"Two?" John exclaimed. Everyone else murmured to whomever they were seated next to. Jeeves's jaw dropped noticeably.

"Jeeves, you met Dock twice?" I asked.

"I don't remember two slips," said Jeeves.

"Yes, Mr. Dawes," Betty responded for speechless Jeeves. "He was in the presence of Christopher Dock once in 1718 for sixty-eight minutes and forty seconds and then again in 1748 for thirty-five minutes and thirteen seconds. In the first instance they were drinking in an ordinary inn at a rural crossroads in tidewater Virginia. In the second instance they were again at a tavern in the village of Skippack in Pennsylvania. The image on the screen is from the second event."

I turned to Jeeves. "You have no recollection of these events?"

"No, not two, sir. Just the one."

"So, you do know him from one encounter?" My tone made it a question.

"I vaguely remember a Mr. Dock, now, since this inquisition."

"No one is accusing you of anything, Sergeant Major," Admiral Pride assured. "We're just trying to figure out what happened. That's all."

"If memory serves, I had drinks with him, sir. Perhaps if we can run the video of the two events I would remember the details."

"Well, something isn't right. When did these treks occur?"

"About four months ago for the one in 1718 and six months for 1748," Betty said.

"It's been too long for me to remember, Mr. Dawes," said Jeeves in frustration.

Everyone at the table looked at Jeeves, trying to figure out if he was lying. To me he appeared to be genuinely sincere and I had always been a pretty good judge of character. Then again, I hadn't known him for very long. Nonetheless, the fact that he was SAS and a sergeant major was good enough for me.

"What's wrong with this picture, Betty? Give me your analysis, now."

"The operational motivation for the 1718 slip was to research Blackbeard, the pirate. He was killed in action by the Royal Navy sent by Governor Alexander Spotswood off Virginia's coastal waters in 1718."

"What the devil were we messing around with Blackbeard for?"

"It was a random selection from a bucketlist of sorts, cobbled together by everyone involved in the program," she elaborated.

"I get it. What about the second event?"

"The motivating factor for the 1748 slip was King George's War which went on from 1744 to 1748, a pivotal point in American history. In that war the American colonial soldiers and sailors took the great French fortress Louisburg on Cape Breton Island in Nova Scotia. The war ended with the Treaty of Aix-la-Chapelle, which returned the fort and other captured assets, much to the dismay of the hard-fighting American colonists without their knowledge or approval. This blatant disregard for the American interests would later be a rallying cry for American Revolutionaries, much as 'Remember the Alamo' was for Texas Separatists about a hundred years later."

"I remember this historical event from a lecture I heard at one of my ASA meetings in Richmond," I commented.

"ASA?" Kay queried.

"The American Society of Appraisers, a professional organization I belonged to. It probably doesn't exist any longer. Please, go on."

Betty continued. "I did an historical analysis on both slips and found no apparent rift. The meetings between Christopher Dock and Jeeves appear to be coincidental on the two occasions."

"I don't have much faith in coincidences," I commented. "Look into this for me, please."

She nodded to me. "The circumstances are not interrelated as far as I can tell."

Everyone present appeared to be reluctant to enter the train and remained silent as they observed their new leader work his way through the complexities of the problem. Perhaps they were hesitant to interrupt my flow of thought, considering the situation made me a bit agitated. *There simply had to be a link between the two slips,* I thought. Directing my attention to John Skill, the other paranoid personality in the room, I asked, "How could there be two encounters between Jeeves and Dock?"

"It does sound too coincidental," replied John.

"Maybe there was another traveler," Jeeves suggested. He shrugged his shoulders and offered his palms up.

I swung my attention to the butler, pointing a finger his way. "That's it."

Jeeves looked startled. The others looked quizzical.

"Betty, get Rictor back," I ordered.

In an instant Rictor once again appeared on the screen. "Mr. Dawes, I 'ave reviewed da computer analysis und I can find no evidence of temporal anomalies."

"Professor, have you ever sent two people through the Rai Machine simultaneously?"

"No sir."

"Could there be another slipper on the other side without your knowledge?"

"You mean in the earlier timeline? Nein, däts not possible. I am able to track all passages from here in the lab. Besides, the central computer would have evidence of all slips. We don't do dät many, you know."

"Is there a way to detect a slipper that's cloaked on the other side?"

John answered for the professor, "Yes, theoretically we can detect cloaked intruders, but I don't think we've ever done so or had a reason to do so in a slip scenario."

The group's attention was momentarily diverted to John. I peered right through him with glazed eyes, contemplating. They could sense a shoe was about to drop.

I returned my attention to the professor. "Can we send another slipper to the same two timelines where Jeeves went?"

"Yes, but for vät purpose?" asked the professor.

"To look for a cloaked slipper with our own cloaked slipper," I said.

"Very interesting…vell, yaa, but – "

I cut Rictor off in mid-sentence and looked in the direction of Pride and John. "Can we place a surveillance device on a person or inanimate object and follow it in time, like a homing beacon?"

Admiral Pride and John Skill shrugged simultaneously. They looked at each other and then at me. Admiral Pride answered, "Maybe."

"All slippers wear PFFs," John said. "We can retrieve the PFFs on command."

Pride clarified John's intent. "A PFF is in effect a beacon that is constantly tracked by the central computer."

"OK, got it," I said. "But what about inanimate objects?"

"We haven't had a need to PFF an object," said Admiral Pride.

"I can understand that," I said. "But *can* we tag an object?"

"Not really," John replied. "We can send a probe to monitor the scene though."

I instantly saw the flaw in that idea. "And could a probe, even delivered subtly to a target by air, water, food, or any number of other avenues, arrive without possible detection by a cloaked slipper?"

"No sir," the Admiral admitted.

"I wonder.... If a person wearing a PFF dies what happens?"

Admiral Pride looked at John. John shrugged. "We don't know, sir," John replied. "That's never happened before."

I looked at holo Betty. "Find out the answer to that question."

Betty paused about five ticks and replied, "I just ran a slip to find out. The PFF preserves the body of the host and remains extractible, host and PFF together."

"Betty controls all PFFs," explained John. "When the host is injured or dies, Betty should be able to cloak the PFF indefinitely and signal Rictor to slip them to wherever they are needed, the hospital, for instance. The PFF preserves the body on life support until it's recovered. In the case of a deceased operator, the medics confer with CC to find out what the decedent's wishes are...or were. If for any reason the PFF is cut off from CC, then its symbiotic AI assumes responsibility seamlessly as if nothing had happened."

"We never leave anyone behind, by the way," said the admiral.

But I wasn't thinking about people just then. I was thinking about extracting inanimate objects. "Betty, I want a way to tag objects and follow them until they degrade completely so then we can extract them or so we can discover where they are in the present and/or where they will end up in the future if we do not disturb them."

She acted as if she were thinking out loud, even kneaded her temple. "OK. If I can devise a tag, a *Rait* tag then I would be able to read its signal and remotely determine the extent of the object's degradation over time."

"Correct," I replied. "Once we can tag successfully, follow its timeline and determine it vanishing point, we should be able to return to the original tag date and extract the specimen without temporal side effects."

Betty said, "I'll put a team on it."

"Let me know when you have it ready." I turned to the scientist, "Professor, find me another slipper right now! I want to get started looking immediately."

"You 'ave von seated right before you, Mr. Dawes," he replied.

"I can't use Jeeves for what I have in mind, Professor. We need a new face and for this mission it cannot be him, unfortunately."

"I think the professor means me, Charles," said John. "I've made a dozen slips. What do you have in mind?"

I was surprised. John had never mentioned it before. "I want you to return to the same timelines as when Jeeves was on his two treks, cloaked, mind you, and search for cloaked time travelers. If you detect one, follow him. Can you do that undetected?"

"Yes."

"Good."

"What are you getting at Mr. Dawes?" asked John.

I barreled on without responding. "If you don't find a cloaked traveler, follow everyone Jeeves comes in contact with. And when the Rait tags are available, tag any important object you come across while you're there."

Suddenly everyone was on track with me and eager to jump in.

"What's your train of thought, sir?" asked Renatta.

"This is going to be a very sophisticated exercise," said Dawn.

"It might prove fruitless," said Kay.

"I'd like to go, too," offered Sarah.

The professor mumbled, "I should mention something I am verking on which will make –"

"Mr. Skill, how are you going to explain it to me when you see me in the other timeline?" asked Jeeves.

"You won't even know I'm there," said John.

"What's your train of thought, Charles?" repeated Renatta.

They all turned to me again as I answered, "This exercise, as Dawn called it, will have two intended purposes. One is to determine if other time travelers were present when Jeeves was there before. If so, they might have been responsible for the left-behind knowledge Christopher Dock used to scribe the fraktur. And, two, tagging inanimate objects will be a case study in how we might recover significant artifacts without altering the timeline. Professor, have you perfected the machine's precision controls yet?"

Rictor looked over his glasses. "Soon, sir, soon."

"OK," John asked me, "so what if we do find a cloaked traveler who isn't supposed to be there?"

"I am afraid we'll have to play that possibility by ear if it occurs. The probabilities are too fantastic. My head is about to explode as it is. For the moment, just follow him. It's pure intelligence work at this juncture. It could lead us anywhere or nowhere."

The tension in the room was palpable.

I turned to Sarah, my new corporeal commander. "I'd like for you to be involved in this mission, Sarah. And if it pans out, we'll have the means to recover the destroyed contents of the Library of Alexandria and the lost contents of the Temple Serapis."

The room was full of grins.

"Each worth a king's ransom!" exclaimed Dawn.

"I, no, *we* already have a fortune and neither I nor the Dawes Conglomerate, nor any of the rest of you for that matter need any more money, right?" I looked around and they all nodded soberly. "I thought so." Betty had briefed me on the Fed salary scale. No one was going to go hungry on my watch that was for sure.

"The mission is this: Knowledge. It is for knowledge's sake that we take risks, not wealth and not power. We all have plenty already. I want to recover mankind's lost history, medical remedies, scholarly literature, biographies, and scientific discoveries. This is what interests me and it is probably going to become my life's work. I want it to be a team effort." They looked at each other and I detected different reactions.

"What do you have in mind, Charles?" asked Renatta. She had been observing me closely and occasionally glancing at her Merck. She was probably monitoring my sanity by keeping a watchful eye on her little device. I was probably passing whatever tests she was scrutinizing or she would have said something by now.

"Look, I'm a kid in a candy store, guys. History, art, artifacts, antiques, collecting has always been my special interest. Well, now I have the means and the tools to explore the past *and* collect the most important items and the most valuable items in the history of mankind. Not only that, but I also can research how and why I met an untimely demise.

"I don't know what I will want six months or a year from now. I haven't had time to think about it. All I have is the present. What I want are answers as soon as possible to this weird connection I have with the fraktur. Don't you see? I find this eighteenth-century thing with space-age drawings on it in the twenty-first century, and then I mysteriously die a few weeks later when I'm taking it for further analysis! And now we discover that Jeeves, someone I know in the twenty-fifth century, has met the maker of this thing twice, in the eighteenth century no less. Come on! I couldn't make this up if I wanted to!"

Then the good professor finally got a word in edgewise. "Pardon me, ladies and gentlemen, but I must insist on a moment of your time before we adjourn to forage in the past for answers to mysteries in the present, regarding the concept of reconnaissance we were discussing earlier, cloaking, tags, and all of dät. There is a new development that I have probably perfected but not proven. Perhaps this is an opportune time to mention it, ya?"

"Go on," I prompted.

"I have extruded from the mechanics of the Rai Machine a subordinate device that allows for exposure through the active fold."

"What does that mean, Professor?" asked Renatta.

"We can now see and hear vät transpires by monitoring the optic feed from any in-field PFF or probe fitted with the Rait tag."

"That's perfect timing, Professor," commented Dawn. "Real time surveillance across time?"

"Yes, ma'am," he replied.

"Excellent!" exclaimed John.

"Perfect," was all I managed to say as I realized that the professor had handed me one of the tools that would help me gather hidden intelligence from the past. Again I became lost in thought momentarily. My download couldn't help me. This wasn't included in the instructions. My introspection had a quieting effect on us all. All eyes returned toward me as I hesitated, still lost in thought. My new friends and colleagues were looking at me with earned respect for having discovered an interesting mystery. My pain seemed to be reflected in their demeanor.

"What, Charles?" Renatta whispered in a room where the dying hearth fire made the loudest of sounds. Dawn twitched her stylus so fast it blurred. Sarah sat on her hands. Holo Betty bit her lip and the admiral chewed his perpetual toothpick as my security chief clenched his jaws and fists. I stood at the end of the table and leaned forward with my arms splayed and my hands on the table's top. They leaned forward in their seats, waiting; even computer Betty inched a bit.

"I think my destiny lies in the riddle of the Serapis Fraktur: 'To a place in Heaven where God is Sea'. That may very well be the crux. I have a hunch that if we can explain that verse, all of Humpty's pieces will fall into place. Christopher Dock's riddle might be the key. I want to find out what that key opens and I would like to use company resources to follow all leads until I either solve the mystery or reach a point of diminishing returns. Who's in?"

"I'm in," said Admiral Pride. "The *QuestRoyal* is your ship, sir, and my crew and I are at your disposal immediately! Just say the word and we'll sail to Orion's belt and retrieve his navel lint if that's what you want." Everyone chuckled at the esteemed admiral's remark and stood to commend my concept of what our primary mission was going to be henceforth. No one knew any more than I did at that juncture, but everyone was in like Flynn. That's when I began my love affair with the whole gang.

Chapter 15: The *FSS QuestRoyal*

My mobile home away from home is a Kelvin-class starship. She measures eighty-four kilometers in length by twenty-one kilometers in girth. At the time of her maiden voyage, she was the largest vessel of any kind ever built in Federation space. There are other classes of starships, spacefreighters, and warbirds, but none that out-shone the Kelvin-class in flexibility of use, or so I had downloaded. Yet she could keep up with smaller ships, and all Kelvin-class could outperform other sentient technologies, including the Ghanti-class warbirds, used by the Shunts and Grunts from Helios galaxy.

Basically, my ship is a fluted hollow cylinder that tapers to a point at each end. Her hull spirals like the rifling inside a gun barrel with kilometer-wide recessed flutes ten stories deep. The obsidian-black flutes increase the ship's surface area, allowing for a greater number of large viewing ports. Living quarters are situated against the outer and inner hulls with each compartment possessing several such ports. The views on the outer hull are to space whereas the inner hull views are of the central habitat zone.

Most of the working environments, administrative offices, training rooms, and laboratories also have viewing ports – wherever biotics work or live. Robotic workshops, manufacturing, warehousing, engineering, life support systems, and autonomic weapons system compartments have no portholes and are sandwiched between the exterior perimeter quarters and the interior perimeter quarters. The latter overlooks the center of the open interior of the ship where there is an expansive, ship-long natural environment with parks, ponds, streams, and agricultural projects. Holographic weather simulations with cloud formations compliment the open natural space and assist in obfuscating the observer's perspective of the unnatural hull curvature. Inertia dampeners offset g-forces while an autonomic smart-grav field provides normal gravity. Stronger fields anchor inanimate objects on command.

Even though I knew all this from my downloads, stepping foot on the *QuestRoyal* for the first time created that sense of wonder that I had hoped would remain intact. It certainly had! Everywhere I looked, I felt the tingle of excitement from this massive starship.

I inspected the locomotive-sized Alcubierre warp drives which work in tandem with fusion and ion engines to fold space for intergalactic treks and trans-universal missions. One engine tips each pointed end of the *QuestRoyal*. Ion star drives and fusion engines are implemented when traversing galactic distances. Fore and aft and two amidships fusion thrusters act to stabilize the tremendous push of the ion star drives. Twenty-one basketball-sized fusion engines circle each warp drive to provide maneuverability and thrust at lower velocities. Fusion reactors provide general power used throughout the ship and for defensive and offensive weapons systems, life support systems, and the hull's self-repairing nano-organic epidermis, which is designed to capture solar energy for the ship's grid. When appropriate, rings of force-field sails spring erect a thousand kilometers in radius to capture solar winds. Now *that* was impressive, whether a person had downloaded the specs on it or not!

From afar my first impression of the behemoth was how shiny she was. Her meter-thick synthetic nano-collagen, self-generating, self-repairing smart hull is the color of polished chrome. Three electromagnetic stasis fields provide protection from within and without. The interior field and the near exterior field are in flush contact with their respective aspects. Each is static and serves to sandwich the organic hull to provide rigid integrity and a high measure of shelter from a whole host of cosmic threats, similar to how a PFF protects its host. The third is a smart field designed to be elastic and adjustable. It provides the first line of defense from without. In orbit, or when the ship is traveling at low velocity, the smart field conforms to the ship's relative shape, enveloping it entirely, but at high speeds it automatically pushes off from the two under fields. It performs the function of a shield, plow, and battering ram and elongates in proportion to the ship's speed.

This elasticity provides two benefits. One, it acts like a snowplow and improves the dynamic shearing effect of the ship's shape. At low velocities in the vacuum of space, vehicular "aerodynamics" is not particularly noteworthy; however, at near FTL speeds and faster, the volume of particulate matter suspended in space becomes concentrated relative to the ship's velocity, which then becomes an operational limitation much like air is for atmospheric vehicles.

The second benefit has to do with maneuverability. At super FTL speeds the ship cannot turn on a dime. It's like a huge oil tanker on the high seas. Any large object in the path of a starship has to be accounted for well in advance to maneuver around it, but the *QuestRoyal's* smart field allows her to plow through an asteroid belt without altering her course or adjusting velocity but sometimes to ill effect; plowing can potentially send a cascade of meteors into space on unknown vectors. For this reason there are standard, buoy-marked shipping lanes throughout Federation space. As with atmospheric transports, space captains are required to gain approval from the FSS to ply these lanes before shoving off and it's the agency's responsibility to keep the lanes safe and clear.

The *QuestRoyal* and other Kelvin-class starships' velocities are classified; however, the latest issue of *IHS Jane's Aerospace Federation Intelligence & Analysis* reports that Kelvin motherships are capable of reaching velocities in excess of FTL 99.

The ship's smart central computer, herself a Legal Person, monitors and operates everything from the crew's biofeedback to the twin star drives. One of her most important functions is self-defense, which she exercises with complete autonomy. Any sentient-initiated change order that affects defense parameters must meet with her approval. The opposite is true of offensive tactical and strategic measures – only authorized human personnel can execute military or police actions; however, she can make arrests using containment fields or by directing robotic servers when there is a threat to life or property.

As if all that wasn't impressive enough, there were other ships that would accompany us on our missions. Although the *QuestRoyal* is considered primarily a long-range research vessel, she usually travels with a battle group comprised of two lesser capital ships, four cruisers, and twelve destroyers that form a three-dimensional perimeter around her. There are a total of twelve Federation battle groups, including the *QuestRoyal*. Motherships house a compliment of two hundred fifty-two Kelvin-class man-of-war corvette warbirds within iris ports placed at even intervals down the length of the ship. Like the *QR*, each warship is equipped with similar defensive armor and a full array of beam and projectile weaponry. Corvettes, like their motherships, are cylindrical, fluted, and self-sustainable for long periods on deep space voyages. Each is one hundred meters in length by thirty meters in girth and carries a crew of three and a squad of fifteen Marines. The *QuestRoyal's* crew fluctuates in number depending on mission requirements, but the standard compliment consists of one thousand officers and fourteen thousand other uniformed as well as GS-rated civilians. Family members of assigned personnel are encouraged to accompany crewmembers on scheduled voyages greater than six months in duration. Thus, the number of souls on board varies, as does the variety of nationalities, races, creeds, and alien species. The number of robots in all ratings is approximately twenty-five thousand at any given time.

The staggering numbers of personnel raised lots of red flags for me—human interactions can be tricky enough on a planet, let alone confined to a starship, no matter how massive. I instantly recalled the prejudice that our friends Thack and Peter had suffered as a married homosexual couple in the supposed 'enlightened' society of the early 2000's. But I soon found that human relations issues were adequately covered. For instance, any two consenting adults may pair formally or informally. By tradition, social mores are Quaker-modest fleet-wide. Ship law is consistent with the golden rule: be considerate and treat others as you would have them treat you. Standard issue, rank-obvious uniforms are required for crew and passengers of all ages to prevent flamboyant personalities (Peter might have qualified in his day) prevailing, while individuality is encouraged at the creative, intellectual, and sporting levels. Personal dominance is encouraged in the arenas, which notably includes European and American football, rugby, hockey, lacrosse, baseball, cricket, basketball, track and field, polo, and buzkashi – happily the latter only with a weighted burlap sack these days. Facilities for tennis, ping-pong, and swimming are scattered throughout the ship in neighborhoods designed around the various habitat features onboard. Controlled substance use is permitted within limits in designated areas. Living quarters are considered personal unless actions or inactions within impede upon persons outside or the ship's safety or appearance.

One vital rule is that religious activities and displays of faith are restricted to one's quarters. This, alone, would have helped in my earlier life, where clashes existed not only between Christians and Muslims but within sub-sects within each religion as well, causing much pain for society.

Proselytizing and product marketing is forbidden as is collecting donations for any cause or purpose. Recalcitrant persons infringing on ship's rules are placed in the brig until deportation is convenient to the mission.

Supplies for all this activity are well planned, too. Three nano factories onboard and a crew of robotic engineers manufactures practically anything on demand from mined or salvaged raw materials, including fully assembled machines, drones, and weapons systems. The mining process usually provides sufficient water to replenish the ship's reservoirs and almost all of the ship's food is grown on board within the habitat's thousands of acres of farmland and hydroponic silos.

As for crew comfort, no luxury is absent. Private and public open space is abundant and free to all, but rank still has its privileges. For my ship's flag officers, there are three similarly configured private quarters with direct access off the bridge from the command deck: the Founder's, the fleet admiral's and the captain's. Department chiefs also have private quarters connected to the bridge directly from one deck below; these include navigation, engineering, security, ordnance, science, personnel, medical, and quartermaster.

I found my main quarters are starboard with access directly off the bridge via a wide corridor nicely decorated with a ten-meter-long red floriform Persian runner laid on an intricate parquet diamond floor. I have several large four-season landscape paintings that adorn the walls, and bronze sculptures of nubile goddesses are tucked into cubbies sunken into the walls between the paintings. Midway on both right and left are my two private elevators, and at the end of the hall is a ten-meter circular antechamber with left, center, and right doors. Anyone waiting for a personal meeting with me waits in this antechamber seated on one of four curved white leather settees with straight backs placed against the red floral wallpapered piers between the three French pocket doors. Each set of doors slides open bilaterally to reveal my private rooms. To the right is my möderne ready-room with a long bowed mahogany table and eighteen comfortable swivel chairs. At the center is a space fitted to comfortably duplicate my Albemarle House living room. And behind door number three on the left is my sleeping quarters modeled after my penthouse in Dubai, which has a decidedly Mughal motif with a hint of gilt Biedermeier. Besides the bridge quarters, I also have other shipboard quarters with a similar floor plan on the inner hull with a habitat view overlooking Victoria Falls at *QR* Central Park.

Computer Betty makes getting around a ship eighty-four klicks in length easy. She controls all physical traffic aboard the ship, including elevators, escalators, sidewalks, and flash. The entire vessel is wired for flash. Crewmembers flash at will to anywhere onboard they are authorized access to and anywhere off ship within range. Flash booths are few because they are required only for long distance, off ship flashes.

Any problems the ship cannot resolve by itself using ship resources and bot personnel are reported through the chain of command; the captain and bridge officers seldom get involved. Most systems are automated and bots do most of the mundane tasks.

By the way, Betty manages the duty roster for all ranks and ratings, and synthetic persons can be assigned any given task, just as easily as biotic persons. Half the time I found I couldn't tell the difference between the various sentient flavors; most biological persons have had one or more of their physiological systems replaced for one reason or another. Heck, look at me: I have to ask Betty which part of me is real and which is not.

As for command and control, I'm supposed to have absolute authority, but like most well-run offices, one alpha secretary seems to call all the shots. S/he more or less tells the boss what s/he must do next in order to keep everything on track – and that would be Betty, of course. Fine by me, I say. So, as I settled into the shipboard routine, I guessed my new job was to dream up riddles to get us all killed, or so one of my critics lambasted once. The fleet admiral's job is oversight, policymaking, problem solving, and keeping the fleet in good order. The captain of the *QuestRoyal* is responsible for cleaning up the messes the admiral and I make, as well as keeping the ship in good order. In combat the captain has the helm.

Combat, though, is extraordinarily rare in surveyed space, according to the information my download provided. Apparently most spacefaring sentients would rather trade than fight, and the more primitive ones who trend toward confrontations generally stand down when they see the *QuestRoyal* battle group warp into their near space. If that doesn't work, we dismount the corvette cavalry. That usually does the trick. When camel-riding, tobacco-spitting damned fools see two hundred fifty-two gleaming corvettes burn into their atmosphere, all breaking the sound barrier simultaneously, well, they high-tail it back from under whence rock they came. In these rare instances of confrontation with primitives, Fleet Space Services anchors an orbital in the respective star system, accompanied by a squadron or two of corvettes to keep the peace in the sector until the natives learn better manners.

Shipping lanes have been established for eons and extend like vines into and around the spirals of our galaxy and into other galaxies. The

Federation has collaborative treaties with thousands of established system governments to clear obstacles and to keep the traffic in the shipping lanes and orderly. Drones continually map and update the lanes, maintain the markers, and pylons between way stations and destinations.

Happily, life in a multitude of peaceful sentient forms has been identified across surveyed space. Although sentient species are comparatively scarce, some one thousand one hundred twenty-nine have been identified to date, and of those, seventy-eight have FTL capabilities. Of the seventy-eight, thirty-five have warp-folding capabilities equivalent to what we have, and of that number only five hail from the Milky Way, including us.

One common bit of information all FTL peoples report is the presence of trace evidence across known space of at least a five billion-year-old sentient race. They are generally referred to as the Ancient Ones. Collectively, we've discovered their outposts on a number of barren and inhabited planets in the Milky Way, and with reports provided by our extra-galactic contacts, we now know the Ancient Ones existed on a number of worlds in at least nine neighboring galaxies, five of which we have either sent exploratory probes or envoys to. Of the Ancient Ones we know no more than that.

Chapter 16: Mission Statement

One morning on a day shortly after the committee thawed me out, but before I knew how to flash without thinking, I was caught off guard on the bridge of the *QuestRoyal*. A gaggle of school kids from a science fair stormed by with their teachers in tow. One of the teachers spotted me. Until then I had done a pretty good job avoiding the limelight. My luck ran out that day. The whole flock screeched to a halt. The teachers ordered the kids against the wall and then very sweetly asked me to give an impromptu state of the frozen leader address. Before I knew it, those two little schoolmarms had me on ship-wide CCTV, yacking on about what California was like before the Great Quake. Naturally my gig went FTL across surveyed space in no time. The cat was out of the bag. Admiral Pride just about popped a button and chewed out Renatta for not extracting me in time.

Shortly thereafter I was officially presented to the public in a choreo-graphed public spectacle. The second speech, reviewed and approved by my advisors prior to the event, I delivered in front of a lectern in my ready room aboard the *QuestRoyal*. I don't remember precisely what I prattled on about for ten minutes, but it amounted to a briefing on what we, the committee, decided regarding Professor Rictor's Rai Machine. Speechmaking is not my favorite pastime but I do OK if I'm cornered. The majority of the population would rather gnaw their foot off than deliver a speech and I felt only a smidgeon better about it than that.

The gist of it was that, in the interest of peace and security, the com-mittee announced the renewed fruition of the Rai project to the public because the committee was concerned that the project's secrecy had been breached or that the machine might be mistaken for a weapons project. Indeed in the wrong hands such a device could prove to be the ultimate weapon and easily upset the balance of power in known space. In my first official capacity as the Founder, humanity's Monarch, I stated with all my authority that the entirety of the Rai technology would forever remain classified. Furthermore, the Dawes Conglomerate would refuse patents, not reveal or disseminate Rai technology, not profit from future knowledge, and that declassified information would be shared in perpetuity equally with all sentients. That speech was well received by humanity and other sentients as well. When I was asked the parameters of the term 'classified' by a reporter, my answer was 'don't press your luck'.

As far as we knew at the time, we were the only sentients with time travel capabilities. Either the other thirty-four folders had yet to develop this expertise or they were keeping their cards close to their chests. Interestingly, the consensus at several inter- and extra-galactic scientific conferences supported my authority and the Conglomerate's resolution to classify the project, as did the current majority membership of the Supreme Parliament of the Federation of Planets. We, the committee, became the gatekeepers, and this I liked.

The academic community as always was divided not only on this issue but on every issue, no matter how important or how trivial. Even in the twenty-fifth century one can ask ten professors a simple question and receive twelve answers delivered late. To be fair, this was an important, complex, and ubiquitous issue that raised the ire in more than a few, and rightly so, but both the muscle-bound jocks and the pie-in-the-sky academics seldom recognize the value in caution.

The political fallout mirrored the academics and jocks: liberals trended toward complete dissemination of the technology without regard for potential disaster, while conservatives advocated no dissemination for security reasons. Both types failed to see the forest for the trees. Meanwhile the media neglected to present the issue truthfully in order to garner attention for itself. Unfortunately some things have not changed since the turn of the twentieth century. Once I understood the situation I issued a Royal Diktat limiting the discourse on this topic to official channels only on penalty of imprisonment on a penal colony somewhere in the farthest reaches of space 'where the sun don't shine'. For a time, blissful silence ensued.

I personally set the primary mission requirements for what would become known in the press as the Timeline Initiative. After conferring with my committee members I created a set of governing time travel rules that became known as the Dawes Doctrine. Rule number one: the Rai Machine and any ancillary devices would remain private Dawes Conglomerate assets under Federal protection. The initial subordinate rules of engagement were simple: leave nothing and return only with intelligence. All data would be classified, analyzed, and triaged. It wasn't until after we had made a few technical perfections that we amended the rule to include extraction.

The central computer eventually made most data available gratis to the public via Wikipedia on demand. However personal enrichment (PE) data or private sensitive (PS) data, remained classified and inaccessible to unauthorized personnel. Security issue designations could be one or a combination of classifications: national, cultural, corporate, or entity private.

Some months of effort were required before the Rai Machine and the rait tag devices were proven reliable. While Professor Rictor was working on that, I had Betty create an administration that serviced the expansion of the timeline research and development division, and I tasked her with its oversight and gave her hire and fire authority. The first officer she hired was Commander Sarah Spitfire. Sarah's task was to recruit and train applicant slippers and ensure their safety when they were deployed and command them when they were not. By autumn, Sarah had a platoon fully trained as timeline slippers. They were a mixed bag of SAS, US Marines, Fairfax Police SWAT, and other Special Forces types from the Federation. All were PFF-armored and cloaked. In short order they were sneaking along the corridors of medieval palaces and on countless battlefields throughout Earth history. Naturally Earth was my greatest interest. Eventually we would expand the Timeline Initiative to other star systems.

My intent from the start was to establish an academic library on the *QuestRoyal* that would provide all disciplines with more information than they presently have in their collective coffers. This went quite well and according to plan. In due course video began streaming into wikitriage from the returning slippers and probes so fast that we had to increase the allocated processing time and compression storage by an order of magnitude on average every twenty days. The Royal Library soon reached a tipping point.

Only Betty seemed to be in control of it all. She classified raw information according to content; collated it chronologically, geographically, topically, and restricted access to academics based on a thoughtful criteria promulgated by the committee to which I made her a member. She's always present anyway, so why not?

Although I had a burning desire to immediately solve the fraktur mystery and Jeeves' two meetings with Christopher Dock and its connection to my early demise so long ago, eventually I realized that the mission was best served with patience and preparation first.

That included preparation of the rait tag technology as well as my personal preparation. Even though I had all the downloaded information required to comprehend everything in context and to competently lead my empire, my muscle memory required attention. John was my pillar of strength during this period. He oversaw my personal physical development and helped me perfect the use of my PFF, while Betty oversaw my flight training in every mobile asset in the Dawes inventory. Sarah and I flight-trained together since she, too, was a new-be; Renatta stayed by our sides or trained with us.

By the time Betty correlated information relevant to Jeeves' encounter with Christopher Dock from the slip videos, I was very prepared for anything.

At least, so I thought at the time.

Chapter 17: The Architect

Betty trilled me awake. It was a relief, actually. A unique version of my perennial Fallujah fiasco dream was reaching its climax when I opened my eyes to discover myself so entangled in sheets that one of my feet had gone numb. Vivid dreams had plagued me since childhood and my PTSD seemed to intensify them by blending bits and pieces of unrelated personal escapades into surreal scenarios. In this episode I was carving ruts by driving a white Humvee across the lawn of the *Four Seasons Hotel* in Damascus while in pursuit of Scarlett Johansson. If it weren't for the girl I'd have considered this dream as bad as the usual nightmares that usually pervade, merge, and morph into an unearthly reminder of a hand-to-hand battle I had that had lasted perhaps four or five minutes, but which had seemed to go on forever and in slow motion. Those few moments of herculean physical effort against a hopped up jihadist were what, for me, substituted Fallujah for all the horrors that I had ever imagined. Even after several months on the *QuestRoyal*, with numerous downloads and multiple tasks squeezed into every second of my new life, dreams of my old life remained in this new life. I asked myself, "When would they end?"

"Founder, you need to get up, sir. We have a development." The expansive opaque glass wall that formed an ovolo around my Widdicomb bed gradually faded to transparent, enabling a full view of the robin's egg-blue habitat sky to stream in. I raised myself on my elbows to take in the view of Victoria Falls from a klick away. The mist rainbows above the falls were beautiful. I sat up and gazed through the wall of glass at a semblance of the natural beauty I first witnessed in the heart of Africa in 2006.

"What is it, Betty?"

She was seated with legs crossed on my red leather Biedermeier settee, dressed in a fleet-standard regulation royal blue uniform with a three-diamond collar and an over-the-knee skirt that had a narrow platinum stripe down the side. Her tone was tense. "I've finally isolated a track on Jeeves' two slips, when he met Christopher Dock. Both have a trace holo-harmonic anomaly. They are identical."

I thought about that for a few ticks. "Good. Why has it taken this long?" I yawned.

She fidgeted, pulled the hem of her shirt. "Sir, the technology had to be invented first, by Professor Rictor."

"Right. The probes?"

"Yes sir. I had all three shipboard nano factories working round the clock to replicate them."

"I know. I read the memo. How many do we have now?"

"More than ten thousand of the Rai models, sir."

"How many are in the field?"

"All of them. From the moment they exit the ovens they are deployed. I have devised a rotational scheme so they return on a schedule, dump the video, and return on deployment."

"So they overlap?"

"Of course sir. I extract the entire timeline without a fractional loss."

"What about current production of timeline probes?"

"After I achieved the ten thousand mark, I returned two of the factories to routine tasking and reduced the third factory's output by forty percent. That was a week ago now. Ever since, I've been continuously analyzing and comparing data from Jeeves' treks to the data from our probe deployments. Data had been within normal limits because the data pool was insufficient in size and scope. As I gathered information from a multitude of probes and slippers in the field, the data grew exponentially. The anomaly became apparent when the data pool reached a critical informational mass. That happened just a few ticks ago. That's why I woke you just now."

"Right." I gnawed my lower lip, thinking. "Any conclusions?" I was fully awake now and becoming excited, but still cautiously optimistic.

Betty replied, "My analysis suggests a concurring event on each of Jeeves' treks."

"Explain." I propped myself up with additional pillows.

"The data match each other, sir."

Betty was good, but she could be slow in delivering the details I specifically wanted to hear. "So, the same cloaked slipper appeared in both his treks?"

"No, sir. It was a cloaked probe."

I sat up all the way now. "A probe?"

"Yes, sir."

"Ours from the future?" This was my first thought. Sure, that made sense. We'd developed it and we'd just sent cloaked probes in now—we may in the future too.

"No. Theirs from the past."

"Who would *they* be?"

"Inconclusive, sir."

I snapped, "Well, then speculate."

"A sentient race more advanced than any yet identified, perhaps." She raised her eyebrows.

"Very interesting," I said, starting to get up. I swung my legs over the side of the bed. The jasper floor radiated heat.

"Indeed," she agreed.

"Would you mind disappearing for a moment?" I asked.

"Why?"

"Because I want to get dressed."

"Go ahead then."

"I sleep in the buff."

"I only wish," she said with her arms crossed under her perfect bosom.

She was having an obstinate moment, again. I thought spinning off Sarah was supposed to cure her of that. "Look, if I stand up you're going to see my Johnson."

She rolled her eyes. "Don't be ridiculous. I've not only seen it, I designed your wanker."

"What?"

She stood with her hands on her hips. "Who do you think has been keeping an eye on your frozen carcass for the past four hundred fifty years?"

Good grief, I thought. "Well, I invoke the Quaker-modest rule. Now get out!" When she vanished, I jumped off of the bed, pulled on a fresh uniform, and ordered from the mess servo near the bar in my chamber my usual, Major Dickason's blend coffee. It materialized resting in a cobalt blue ceramic mug resting on a white linen napkin with two brown cubes of sugar and a sterling Gorham spoon, King Edward pattern. It only took two or three minutes.

"Betty!" I summoned.

Her voice emanated from the farthest speaker in the chamber and sounded as if she had her back to me. I don't know how she does that.

"Are you decent?"

"Yes, dammit, come in."

Betty reappeared in a blur. "Modesty is ridiculous in this day and age."

"Why do you try my patience, Betty?"

"Your twenty-first century mores are silly."

"Enough banter," I growled. "Let's get back on topic. I seem to remember a moment ago you identified a serious development."

"Indeed," she said. "I've detected evidence of a probe in the Jeeves' treks. There's a measurable, discernible difference between the different types of intrusive objects along the timeline, especially probes and slippers. These readings are from a probe, not a slipper."

I was walking around the room with my coffee cup, thinking. "Define the differences and speculate."

"Sentient slippers can be human, synth, cyborg, or AI mechs. Probes are usually mechanical but they can be synthetic, cyborg, or biotic. All are made in a multitude of forms and often have attributes of the originating culture and period, much the same way fashion has changed from one time period to the next. Standard probes are mechanical, inexpensive, and easily detectible round spheres ranging from the size of a flax seed to that of a beach ball, but they can be made in any shape and size required for the mission. Our nano-factories pour out standard probes like loaves of bread, literally by the hundreds of thousands each month.

"Our new Rai probes are more complex and more expensive; however, like standard probes, even the cloaked versions are detectible because the ripple they cause in the continuum is unavoidable. All probes cause a ripple no matter their size, although the size of the ripples can be mitigated to a large extent. The tiny halos left in Jeeves' slips would lead one to assume the originator was using advanced nonstandard technology. Those two halos were miniscule, barely detectible, which means the mission was probably covert."

I stood by the window, thinking out loud. "So, if the halo is barely detectible, the intrusion was by a cloaked probe with a high degree of sophistication, which would indicate that the source had the knowhow and resources to pay for, build, and deploy it."

"Exactly," Betty replied. "And a subtle covert mission is typically a spy mission. The motivation remains to be determined. It was probably some sort of biotic probe on a covert mission. Organic probes are the most complex and therefore the most expensive and they leave behind the most subtle ripples. I believe that's what I have detected on Jeeves' two treks when he met Mr. Dock – evidence manifested by particles displaying a half-integer spin. They appear to be distinct. If they are what I think they are, these are some of the most sophisticated biological probes I've ever detected. Their footprint, for lack of a better term, is less than a quark in measurable disruption. On top of that, they aren't just probes but Rai probes, which we thought only we had at this point in time."

"There's got to be a logical reason such sophisticated probes were used," I stated.

"I concur, sir, but at this point I don't know what that might be or where to look next," she said. "I have exhausted all avenues of approach."

"What do we know about Christopher Dock?" I asked.

"Only that his biography is typical for an eighteenth-century scrivener in rural Pennsylvania," she replied.

"Do you have a full medical on him?" I finished my coffee, placed it on a tray on top of a North Shore Queen Anne style mahogany candlestand. The nanites that comprised the cup dissolved into the nanite faux wood of the stand.

"No sir."

"Well, start with that avenue of approach."

"Aye sir, got it," she said. "Very astute, Founder. We have a connection. Analyzing now."

"You have what?"

"The physiological workup you requested on Dock," she said.

"What? A moment ago you said that you did not have a full medical on Dock."

"Correct, sir," she said. "A moment ago I didn't, but now I do."

"How's that possible?"

"Simple, sir. I sent a message back in time to myself ordering the slip team to perform the requisite tests. Just now I retrieved the results from my database to satisfy your present request."

"Christ! I'll never get used to all this, but I do like it. All right, Betty, let's have it."

"Dock is humanoid in outward appearance only. His DNA sequence is unlike any other I have on file, and I have everyone's on file."

"OK, so elaborate," I began pacing back and forth.

"His DNA is fundamentally different from your own in a sophisticated way. It pre-fits the timeline on all known scales for all humanoid species. And interestingly, the sequence appears to have been altered and enhanced from his original. His DNA includes unidentifiable mutable nanite tags."

"Ah-ha!" I was delighted. *So he's the slipper I anticipated we'd find,* I thought.

Betty burst my bubble. "No, he's not a time traveler as far as I can determine."

"You read my mind. So what is he, a spy from another quadrant or galaxy?"

"Unknown."

"Where is he now?" I asked.

"In his timeline."

"In Pennsylvania?"

"Affirmative."

"Snatch him and bring him to me here on the *QuestRoyal*." I figured she would send another message back in the timeline to herself, and sure enough, she did.

"ETA ten minutes, sir."

This time it didn't even faze me. "Good, where are you going to put him?"

"In detention. Sick bay 2266."

She stood, hands at her side as if at attention, as I started for the door but then remembered I hadn't eaten yet. "Fine, keep him in stasis until we arrive. I think Mr. Skill ought to be present along with the admiral, Dr. Messina, Sarah, and Jeeves. Brief everyone so we're all on the same page. Jeeves can do the introduction since the two of them have met before."

"Acknowledged. Briefing designated officers now…who are en route. ETA seven minutes."

I was excited to get to the bottom of this mystery. Before departing my quarters I managed to wolf down a bowl of hemp granola, drink a glass of fresh-squeezed orange juice, and brush my teeth. My beard would have to wait. I made a mental note to make it stop growing until further notice.

Somehow I managed to flash to the detention site first. The white yurt-like room was about thirty square meters in size and had no openings. Only one barely discernible vertical seam where the door disappeared behind me marred the otherwise glass-smooth cell. Three SAS guards braced to attention as I entered before standing at ease when I acknowledged their presence. Their normally diamond-brilliant rank insignias were subdued. I noticed my acanthine insignia was now dull, too. From experience I knew that that meant our PFFs were ready-on. Christopher Dock was laid out unconscious on a maglev dais within a containment field in the center of the space. He wore a workman's garb of his day, was tall by the standards in that era, and had a handsome face, with a strong nose and cleft chin. His mouse brown hair was thick and he was clean shaven. A moment later my officers arrived. First we exchanged pleasantries. Then we got down to business.

Jeeves was in blue BDU's. "Is this Christopher Dock?" I asked Jeeves, nodding to the figure on the dais.

"I believe so, Mr. Dawes," he replied.

"People, I suggest we revive him and find out what the hell's going on," I stated. "Anyone disagree with that plan of action?"

There was a chorus of agreement, so I ordered Betty to wake him and for Jeeves to do the introductions after our guest identified himself. The containment field remained in place as the dais tilted to an inclined position, raising Dock's head uphill. After a few seconds he fluttered awake and moved his hazel eyes from one of us to another, lingering on Jeeves longer than the rest of us.

"Betty, allow him to speak and walk around if he wishes," Jeeves ordered.

"Yes, Sergeant Major Hamilton," she replied from a speaker in the ceiling.

"Sir, please identify yourself," Jeeves requested.

"Ich," he croaked, "bin unter vielen Namen bekannt."

Jeeves replied, "Mit welchem Namen werden Sie auf dieser Welt wissen?"

"I prefer to use English," he answered. "I am now known as Christopher Dock. Where am I?" He spoke German with a high German accent and English with a British accent.

Jeeves ignored his question. "Where do you come from originally, Mr. Dock?"

"A very distant place," he replied.

"How long have you been in the colonies of America?" asked Jeeves.

"I first came with Eric the Venturer some six hundred thirty years before now," he replied to our astonishment. All of us were quickly calculating dates from his current timeline, 1748.

"How old are you, sir?" Renatta asked.

"My first memories are some six thousand years before these times," he replied. Again we were astonished. I was skeptical but his proof could wait.

"Betty, project an image of the fraktur so we all can see it," I ordered. "Mr. Dock, is this fraktur by your hand?"

He studied it with evident surprise and replied, "Indeed it is. I drew it some, oh…must be about thirty years ago now, when I was a schoolteacher and architect. At the time I was designing Stratford Hall for Colonel Lee in Westmoreland County, Virginia. From whence did you get it?"

"What was the intent of the fraktur, sir?" John asked, also ignoring his question for the time being.

"Why, I had no intent at all. It was only a message in a bottle. I threw it overboard when I took passage to Pennsylvania."

"And the message," I inquired, "for whom was it targeted?"

"It was a lark, sir. I merely drew some of my plans for various dream projects I had in mind to complete one day; that's all."

"But, sir," Jeeves strained, pointing to the holo of the fraktur pictured on the wall, "all these buildings and objects actually exist."

"What?" Dock asked. "All of them, just as I drew them?"

We stared at him and nodded affirmatively. "Yes, Mr. Dock, they do," I said. "Betty, help us out here. Project images of the respective objects beside the actual objects and animate." Suddenly the air space was filled with holograms in motion of inertia skis flying about, tourists cueing for the Eifel Tower and the Washington Monument, as well as comparable examples for everything else drawn and painted on the fraktur. Dock was mesmerized.

"Mein Gött! You are from the future!" he exclaimed.

"Yes, Mr. Dock, we are from the future and we don't know what to make of you," Admiral Pride said, breaking his silence. "Sir, how about telling us who you really are?"

Chapter 18: Kent Dundee

I ordered everyone to more comfortable and hospitable adjacent quarters where our guest could begin his story over a smorgasbord fit for a king. Bot servers marshaled by Jeeves saw to our every need. The Ancient One ate and drank with relish all the while his eye roaming with interest the bots, the ship, everything. We were anxious but patient. After awhile he began to tell us his most fantastical story.

"My new friends, I have been known by many names over many centuries on this world and many others. On this day I am content to be addressed simply as Christopher Dock, the teacher. It is as good a name as any that I have used and more easily pronounced than most.

"I came into this life on a beautiful planet in a star system foreign to you more than six thousand years ago. My mother is the Czarina of the Alsatians, a people whose dominion is an open star cluster in the galaxy known as Massaluun in an adjacent universe far from us now. It is known as Giêi."

A general commotion erupted amongst us. Even the three guards looked at one another. This was astounding news if it were true. A different universe explained many things and the concept opened a Pandora's box of puzzles and opportunities. "All right, at ease people," I ordered. "Let's hear the whole story as Mr. Dock wishes to convey it."

"My mother married my father, the Emperor of the Ooskaaffen, a people whose vast trading interests take them as close to us now as the hinter zones of Kuumbailla, the free nebula, but his home world is far beyond the Massaluum Galaxy near the gravity rim of the great iris that devours all. Both my mother's and my father's cultures are matrilineal in nature. Queens rule the dominions except in time of war and seldom are there wars because queens rule instead of kings.

"I am the third prince of the first wife in my father's house, so by custom, my birthright is the freedom to travel this universe and others for whatever purpose I choose. Although by nature the sword finds comfort in my hand, I prefer to create rather than to destroy. My doodles on the scrap of paper you recently found are samples of what amuses me. I am delighted to know my designs eventually came to fruition. I hope some of the other whimsies I have designed and drawn have as well."

"How did you get to this planet?" John asked.

"I crash-landed in the Pacific Ocean not far from the lands of spice in the Far East. My ship sank quickly into the deepest of chasms but not before I escaped in a pod with basic provisions. Nevertheless I was forced to live by my wits for a very long time. I eventually made my way to land on a sled where I lived off the supplies I had with me until those were exhausted.

"The primitives worshiped my flying machine and technology wherever I went. Eventually I made my way up a great muddy river and became a warrior-god known as Daxi amongst the primitive yellow race that inhabited that land. They thought my great size and bronze skin was divine. In the beginning the political elite within the tribe set the best warriors with sword and bow upon me. I fought every challenger until there were no more. That was my first earned kingship on this world. I immediately taught the people to harness water and wind, improve their silk cloth, and perfect rice and wheat agriculture. This is why the peoples of Greater Asia east of the Himalayas were so much more advanced than in the West at the same point in time. My people learned to plot star charts, make gunpowder, and to devise the written word when the Europeans were still hurling rocks at one another. Eventually, though, time rendered my equipment and weapons useless."

"Why did your ship crash?" Admiral Pride asked.

He shook his head, as if in resignation to a fate he hadn't predicted. "My vessel was damaged in combat inflicted by the adversary I was pursuing," he said. "The Alsatians have an internal extremist political faction called the Ettore Majorana. Its professed mission was to destroy my people wherever they may be. I was chasing one of them when my ship experienced flight control problems. I believe his ship was also damaged. I crashed into the sea and have been marooned ever since. I assumed my adversary and his crew also crashed."

"Where's the rest of your crew?" asked John.

"My machine crew perished with the ship," replied Dock. "They were not designed to swim."

"Designed? You mean, no human crew?" Renatta asked.

"When young nobles in my culture go walkabout," he replied, "they must do so without human companions; it is our custom."

"Why weren't you rescued?" asked Pride.

"I hoped I would be rescued. All Alsatian voyagers have an imbedded chip under their skin. I had the misfortune of being mauled by a tiger soon after landfall. I fought him but the beast tore off my arm and ran away with it. Unfortunately, the imbedded chip was in that arm." He paused, remembering, rubbing his shoulder. "For years I tried to imagine what the rescue transporter operator's reaction would be when he materialized a four hundred-pound tiger in his transporter bay. It was that one amusing thought I had while my arm was healing that kept up my spirits." All of us were staring at him, specifically at both of his fully functioning arms. After a moment he shrugged, scanning our faces.

"Mr. Dock," John said, "pardon us for our skepticism, but you appear to have two functioning arms as we speak."

"Indeed, and I have grown more than one back, too," was his reply.

"You can regenerate?" Renatta asked.

He glanced about our spacious cabin in the belly of a mothership, at the servile bots standing at the ready, then at our own bodies, whose appearances registered full health. "Yes, of course, all my people can; I assumed you could too." He shrugged. "And we have other abilities, as well."

"What other abilities?" she asked.

"We are a self-healing race and have the power to heal by laying our hands on others or by being in close proximity to an afflicted or injured person. It's gotten me into hot water from time to time. Over the ages, I've gotten into trouble with various sects across Asia, Europe, Africa, and most recently here in Salem about fifty years ago. Some damned fools tried to burn me at the stake. Invariably trouble arises when I heal the sick and injured. Because of my innate abilities, I've been a physician more times than I can remember. I can't help myself, I suppose. My kindness appears to the simple-minded brutes as a miracle ... or as a dark force. Either way, unfortunately, shamans and priests sometimes get their ire up when their flocks leave them for what they perceive to be their new competition, namely me. So they mount a campaign, occasionally a witch-hunt, like in the Massachusetts Colony, to run me out of town. All I ever tried to do was help the poor wretches help themselves. Mostly I lend advice as simple as, 'Don't piss upstream from whence you drink' or 'Wash your hands before applying bandages.' Adages like that."

"What other abilities do you have, Mr. Dock?" Renatta asked.

"My people can speak all languages, which is helpful for one destined to walkabout in the polyverse," Dock answered. "And we have the ability to move objects without touching them, to see when blindfolded, speak with our minds, and alter our appearance to some extent at will. All are very basic skills for Alsatians really."

"A shape-shifter," stated Renatta, looking at the rest of us.

"Polyverse?" said Pride. "That is a theoretical assumption in our time."

"Perhaps it is only a theory in your time, but my people have charted many other universes and universes within universes. Some of our elders believe there are as many universes in the polyverse as there are galaxies in this universe, perhaps more. Personally I have toured a small measure of three universes before I was marooned here in this one. I hope one day to tour others. Each is predicted to be unique although similar to this one in which we find ourselves now." Dock looked directly at Renatta and said, "Transformation, or shape-shifting as you called it, is an attribute required for traversing the polyverse, madam."

Renatta blinked.

"Why haven't you made a better life for yourself?" I asked.

Dock raised his eyebrows and smiled at everyone around the room. "I like what I am doing at the moment, unless you rescue me from this life." Everyone followed my lead and ignored his unveiled request.

"And what *have* you been doing since your crash-landing?" asked Jeeves, an avid history buff. "I mean what occupations have you had, Mr. Dock?"

Dock replied, "In my home system I am a prince with great influence. Here on this world I have made myself king more than once and have earned the right of kingship bestowed by others many more times. I may choose to assume a noble or royal mantle again or I may choose a working occupation that suits my fancy for the moment or for generations. I have soldiered, farmed, fished, hunted, mined, baked, butchered, cut stone, painted art, wrought iron, built empires, and preached wisdom – I've done it all – nearly every occupation, many more than once. Often I have had to work at whatever trade or profession was necessary to satisfy the wife and family I loved at the time. I have had thousands of wives and families on this world over the ages and almost as many occupations. Some of my lovelies had great wealth and power of their own or they enjoyed the wealth I made for them. Others preferred anonymity and a simple life. But all of them enjoyed the attention I paid them. I like trying everything, every style of life, every trade, every profession, and I like pursuing whatever it takes to make my current wife happy."

"Happy wife, happy life," Jeeves murmured.

Renatta asked, "Mr. Dock, if you have healing powers, why didn't you keep your wives alive?"

For the first time, Dock's calm countenance wavered ever so slightly. "I kept them young looking and healthy for as long as possible using my powers, but invariably they perish on this world, in this universe. For a lack of a better term, I call it entropy. This entropy affliction has not been identified in any of the other universes, nor has sleep. Both are unique to this universe."

Renatta asked, "Are you saying that death and sleep are afflictions and neither are normal?"

"They are normal to Earth and this galaxy and as far I know to all of this universe, but yes, that is correct, madam. Peoples from neighboring universes will not expand trade and settle in this one because they consider this universe contaminated. You are in effect quarantined and have always been so in my history. Visitors come here but only for scientific reasons. We Alsatians have been trying to develop an entropy vaccine for this universe for thousands of years. Every galaxy that we have surveyed in this universe has been afflicted."

"What is the origin of the contamination?" asked Renatta.

"We don't know but our science indicates that both the sleep disorder and the age entropy are related maladies that were introduced."

"All organisms in this universe have adapted to both," Renatta said. "It's the natural order. Perhaps it was meant to be. Maybe there is no cure."

"Then why is it only this universe is affected?" Dock asked. "Before I was marooned we had hope of developing a vaccine."

"Have you been afflicted, Mr. Dock?" asked Renatta.

"No, I have not. Alsatians are immune to almost everything but madness."

"Then why did the Alsatians abandon this galaxy?" asked Pride.

"We left because of the contamination."

"Your entire civilization picked up and left?" I asked.

"Yes. We left everything behind and went to the Giêi Universe thousands of years ago."

Renatta seemed puzzled. "If Alsatians are immune, then why did they leave?"

Dock was patient. "Because despite full knowledge that the diseases did not afflict Alsatians, a large minority of the population was unconvinced that immunity would always prevail because some of us had comingled with indigenous species. Most of the offspring from those unions have both afflictions but to a lesser extent. Some people require very little sleep. Some live very long lives. And some have nonhuman powers.

"Also, several other sentient species that were not immune left before the wave of contamination enveloped them. They were our friends and allies. We missed them and their trade. So our Queen put forth a referendum for members of Parliament to vote on. The resolution to remove to an adjacent universe passed. Subsequently our Queen issued a Royal Edict that required everyone to pull up stakes and go forth with lock, stock, and barrel. My people obeyed my mother and immigrated to Giêi."

"That explains a lot," Admiral Pride said. Thoughts of numerous previously unexplainable instances of technological abilities in ancient cultures, myths and legends all made sense. We nodded.

Renatta asked, "Do you miss your people, Mr. Dock?"

"Yes, of course," he replied sadly. "I have missed them very much but I have missed even more the loved ones I have known here on this world. This universe is a sad place. I have witnessed the deaths of so many wives, so many children, and so many friends. I have mourned them all, though I have no regrets because I was happy to have known and loved each of them."

Jeeves asked, "How did you manage to live so long on this world, Mr. Dock?"

"Well, at times it was not easy. I had to fight, evade, escape, conserve my resources, hide what I am, and sacrifice everything. I survived because I possess practical and advanced knowledge of engineering, mathematics, science, and many basic survival skills. But often that was insufficient. At times I was still hindered by either the primitive cultures or by pitiful bad luck."

Admiral Pride asked, "Sir, were you ever afraid to introduce new technology to the timeline?"

"No, never. I am a refugee in survival mode on a primitive planet. What I have introduced has been for my survival or to keep from going mad. I recalled it from memory or I invented it as I went along. The problem I have encountered most often, though, when I do make

technological introductions is that unless the culture is technically prepared, nothing can or will come to pass. The primitives become alarmed
and reject it. I know this from long experience. Finally I now live in an
age of relative scientific enlightenment in Europe and the colonies. It
will probably become easier for me to introduce advancements into the
stream of Western history without tipping the apple cart. It's been futile
and very frustrating for me so far. Fortunately we Alsatians enjoy immortality if we manage to avoid fatal accidents. But I will need to live
a very long time if I am ever going to enjoy modern civilization again.
Eventually I would like to escape this primitive clod of dirt."

I could only guess at how primitive Earth in the 1700's appeared to
a man who had visited numerous worlds and several universes. Even
our impressive mothership might seem of little consequence to Dock.
The bots had already cleared the table, and I motioned one to bring us
beverages when Jeeves asked, "Did you assume any historical roles that
we may have heard of?"

Dock accepted a cranberry spritzer, sat back and smiled. "Yes, quite
a few. I mentioned Daxi before. And there were many others. If you
know your history, you may recognize Uruk, Zoroaster, Zarlagab, King
David, Cyrus, Alexander, Christ, Charlemagne, Al-Muqaddasi, Mind-
augas, Copernicus, and I could go on mentioning scores. In my timeline,
as you call it, recordkeeping and accountability have improved from
centuries past. I am finding it increasingly difficult to live out of the
limelight in this century because the written word is becoming common.
I am concerned that my longevity will be discovered. Recently it has
become necessary to assume subordinate or advisory roles. The figures
I mentioned are the ones that come to mind foremost in earlier times and
I either enjoyed them, am most proud of them, or they happened to be
the most trying."

We were dumbfounded to say the least. Our jaws fell open. Seated
before us sat Alexander the Great, Jesus, Charlemagne, and Copernicus
all on one chair. From the shade of his apoplectic red face, Jeeves was
on the verge of having a stroke. I was performing mental gymnastics
silently to myself as to what to do next.

"Which was the worst?" asked Jeeves.

"Christ, by far, was the biggest pain in the neck celebrity to be,"
Dock replied without a moment's hesitation. "As usual, a medical issue
started the trouble. My wife, Mary, developed an infection after child-
birth. I healed her and she stupidly told a close friend who then broad-

casted my talent for curing the sick to everyone in the valley. Before long I became known as the village healer. It wasn't long before I had a clutch of followers that never let me out of their sight.

"Trust me when I say that celebrity is overrated. Anyway, to continue the story: My entourage attracted the attention of the local politicos who became envious of the attention that I was receiving. In primitive societies drawing attention of such magnitude to oneself is always a bad thing. Attention was the last thing I wanted then and even now. I really could not care less for it; it is a nuisance. All I have ever wanted was my privacy.

The Romans were difficult because they demanded my services at sword point but the peasants were worse because they followed me around like a private army drawing attention to me. I tried many times to shoo them away but to no avail. For the most part they were very humble people. It was not long before they began camping around my hut chanting all night. One day Mary mentioned to me that they were actually worshiping me. *That* was the last straw. In my culture we do not allow others to worship us. We find such behavior very repugnant and it is forbidden by Alsatian law."

"That's interesting," I commented.

"Perhaps." He paused a couple of moments, thinking. "We Alsatians are not gods but our powers make us indistinguishable from gods in many primitive cultures just as sufficiently advanced technology is indistinguishable from magic. To take advantage of others less endowed would be unconscionable for us, and rightly so. I spoke earlier of the one malady Alsatians are subject to, madness. It is very rare, but just imagine the damage a mad Alsatian could wreak with his or her powers. This why there is a law…." He looked around at us. We were nearly mute with astonishment at everything he'd said. "Sorry, I digress."

"Do go on Mr. Dock," I urged. "You were describing the difficulties of having a 'clutch of followers.'"

"Right…" He took a sip of his drink as he thought. "Oh yes, right, the followers. You wouldn't believe their numbers and how they grew exponentially almost overnight. There were thousands of them as far as the eye could see. They streamed in from every direction."

"We know your story, Mr. Dock," Sarah said. "Religion is still common in our time and Christianity is one of the top five religions in the galaxy."

"I am not surprised. Even in the eighteenth century it is a cornerstone of human activity. I sincerely apologize for all of the trouble I have caused by my simple acts of healing in that time. Surely there must be a modern equivalent in your time, yes?"

Jeeves answered, "Actually there are several that come to mind. For instance the cult of personality surrounding the modern prophet, Elvis, is probably the most popular. He probably has one of the greatest followings."

He shook his head and sipped again. "I think the populace's incessant racket is finally what caused the envious Jewish elders to file a formal complaint with the provincial toad, Pontius Pilate. But before I could gather my family, pack my few possessions, and leave I was arrested and put on trial.

"My innocent followers were beside themselves. I feared that they might riot and be slaughtered by the Romans. Naturally I could have used my powers to disappear but I wouldn't have been able to take my family with me if I had and I was concerned for my followers. So rather than use my powers I allowed the Romans the freedom to carry out due process. Before I knew it they had nailed me to a cross which hurt like hell, by the way. And to add insult to injury they hung me between common miscreants. It was a low point in my life. I had fallen from prince to prisoner."

We were mesmerized. Jeeves asked, "Sir, what if they had removed your head?"

"I'm not suicidal," Dock sat back, his eyes wide. "I would have prevented that from happening."

Jeeves asked, "Which would have necessitated revealing more of your supernatural powers?"

"Well, yes, of course. With a mere thought I could have prevented the entire horrid episode."

Admiral Pride asked, "So, you're saying that even now you have the ability to make your escape?"

"Of course."

"Then why don't you do so?"

Dock smiled patiently. "Because I sense I must not."

"You want to elaborate on that point a bit more, sir?" John said.

Renatta blurted. "Mr. Dock, are you the son of God?"

"We are all the children of God," he smoothly replied.

Renatta leaned in with eyebrows raised. "You know my meaning, Mr. Dock."

"Indeed." He leaned toward her and then replied, "I understand your meaning clearly and my simple answer is that all Alsatians are merely Messengers."

Whereupon he sat straight and held up his right hand as if to take a pledge. As we watched curiously he closed his eyes and took a deep breath and without uttering a single word he transformed our doubt of him as a messenger and of ourselves as children of God into faith in both concepts. The calm that remained behind was palpable, comforting, like a gentle hand on our shoulders. It was a moment of conversion for me, from agnostic to believer and from contentment in science to unconditional acceptance of fate. I suppose a fundamentalist might say that they were reborn at that moment, but I sensed that Dock would have objected had I asked him if that was what had just happened.

Without missing a beat, he then continued with his story as if he had recounted it before many times. "And so I let the Roman guards think that they had properly finished me off with their lances at which point I was carted to a sepulcher. I waited until it was safe and then made my escape from the nightmare."

We were all stunned. Tears were streaming in rivulets down my face, and the others'. One of the SAS guards blew his nose with a honk. When none of us said anything he looked down thoughtfully, almost smiling, and continued. "I took advantage of the opportunity; I left. I had no choice. Ordinary life had become unbearable. I'm a very private person. My celebrity was hindering me and the worship of my person was revolting."

"Paparazzi," Jeeves murmured.

All of us were mesmerized by his story.

He nodded to Jeeves. "With some mental manipulation I shaped the circumstances that befell me. I healed myself in the cave and waited until the 'paparazzi,' as you say, went away, and then I escaped at first light to collect my wife, new baby girl, and the parents of my wife. Thence we walked northwest.

"Two of my closest friends, Paul and Mark, helped spirit me away. I literally threatened both of them with fire and brimstone if they ever uttered a peep about my escape plot or where I had gone. In retrospect I probably should have used a different choice of words because my meaning became distorted over time. The idiots in Salem are an example of how a simple message can become corrupted.

"A few miles out of town I changed my facial structure like I told you I could earlier, shaved my beard, and adopted a Macedonian accent. It took forever in those days to travel about, but eventually I discovered we were sufficiently distant from the rabble when I asked some villagers where I could find Jesus Christ. No one had ever heard of me by that name. I relaxed my vigil and began scouting for a comfortable arable settlement near a bustling Roman seaport, Ephesus. I figured it best if we hid in plain sight. My father-in-law opened a small cartwright shop on the edge of town and also tended olive trees. I helped him on the farm when I wasn't working as a scholar at the library until he passed away. Mary and I enjoyed life together a few more years. The children grew to maturity and, then, like so many times before, I moved on. Next I moved on to Gaul. Those days at the Library of Ephesus were some of my early best."

"That's the most fantastic story I have ever heard," Admiral Pride said.

Everyone else nodded in agreement. I couldn't believe what I had just heard either and wondered what today's practicing Christians would have to say about it. The historian in me was absolutely screaming to chain this guy to his chair and begin milking him for all the history he was worth.

"Mr. Dock, perhaps one day you can tell us what it was like to be you," I said.

"I would be glad to tell my story," he replied gently.

"Betty, slip Mr. Dock's entire timeline and set it aside," I ordered. "Keep the original on record and edit a historical version so Mr. Dock can voiceover one day when he has the time."

Betty replied, "There's a tremendous amount of material. I'll have to create scores of stand-alone chapters. Will that be acceptable?"

"Yes. Edit out personal moments and the mundane but not the historically significant bits. If there are sections that need to be classified PE, do so."

"What does that mean?" asked Dock.

"PE stands for Personal Enrichment," Betty answered. "I analyze, designate, and classify slip sequencing. When a segment is PE, it has the potential to provide an advantage to a viewer who would allow him/her to be enriched if he chose to exploit the advantage. This is forbidden."

"Don't I have a say-so in what is done with my past?" Dock asked.

"No, Mr. Dock," I said. "You do not have a say-so in what we slip from your timeline because you are more than a significant historical and a larger-than-life frequent public figure. The actions you took in the public eye and your private life are important for the historical record. Scholars will forevermore study your many characters. No doubt history will be enriched beyond measure and all the inaccuracies will be corrected. One of the greatest religions will, no doubt, have to reevaluate its purpose and correct its colorful history. And for me personally, Mr. Dock, I cannot express my deepest respect for your accomplishments. I will be one of the first to view your past when I have a chance because I am truly interested beyond measure."

"I am honored, Mr. Dawes, thank you," he said.

"You're welcome, Mr. Dock," I replied. "And the honor is ours."

"May I ask what you are going to do with me?"

Everyone turned to me, so I answered, "Yes, Mr. Dock, I was just thinking the same thought. We realize you have become a very important influence on this world, but I am afraid we are going to have to return you to your timeline so that your doodles, as it were, become the reality that we know so well. I regret this action because I find your story completely engaging and absolutely fantastic."

"That's too bad," he said, "that I have to return. I was so looking forward to civilization again. Electricity has yet to be harnessed in the time I am in, as you know. It's ghastly penning manuscripts without illumination at night, along with not having devices as simple as a bread browner. I have designs for such a—"

"You mean a toaster?" I asked.

"Oh, what a fine name for it! Then there is such a thing?" At our nods he finished, "then I must perfect the design to be ready for electricity. I mean, I can brown bread at the hearth, but do you realize how difficult it is to make what you call toast before an open wood fire?"

"I'm sure it is, Sir," I said, "but we need you to live your life from 1748 all the way to our present time so that all we know to be true will come to pass as it should. For instance, to invent your toaster, which becomes *our* toasters." I cocked my head with a smile. "Do you understand?"

"Yes, of course," he replied resignedly, looking away. "I understand time travel and the repercussions of altering the timeline. My people hadn't yet learnt how when I left for walkabout. Perhaps they have time travel capabilities by now. How long have you had the means? And how far in the future am I?"

"About six hundred years. Actually, we have only recently developed the means and are only now perfecting it," replied Admiral Pride.

Jeeves nodded in agreement. I was lost in thought.

"We're on a ship, aren't we?" Dock asked.

"Yes," replied John, "a starship of great size, named the *QuestRoyal*."

Dock was startled by that fact. The pulse in his neck went double-time. "Since I was a child I have imagined designing the perfect starship to explore the deep dark."

"Sir, hold that thought a moment," I interrupted politely. Everyone became silent for a few moments while I opened a private PFF channel with Betty and the officers present. Using my mind I linked. *"Betty, run a slip on Mr. Dock from his current timeline to four hundred years past our present time into our future. Confirm Mr. Dock's credibility and analyze for every possible threat scenario. Do it now."*

Betty responded through our PFFs. *"I thought you trusted him."*

"Verification is the cornerstone of trust," I replied. *"Besides, a few facts like Mary being his wife are questionable. Betty, report please."*

"I'll need a few moments for the future segment," she linked. *"Earlier I took the liberty of slipping probes from his present time to ours. Mr. Dock actually did design sailing ships from the* USS Constitution *to more modern vessels, along with just about everything else from Slinky toys to the cure for cancer, under so many aliases that I'm not sure I have collated them all yet. Also, as a footnote, based on the analytical scenarios I'm coming up with on this slip he's on now, here, I don't think it's wise to send sentients into the future, so I've slipped a dozen of the best biotic probes instead."*

"How is that possible?" linked Dock. Now it was his turn to look incredulous at our technology, and we in turn stared back at him realizing that he could understand our thoughts. So we reverted back to auditory communication.

"We see that one of your abilities is reading thoughts, Mr. Dock," Renatta said.

"I believe that I mentioned that earlier," he replied.

"Yes, I remember that you did indeed, Mr. Dock," said John.

"Oh, and as for Mary being my wife, I think you'll discover with your time machine that this was the case; the whole virgin birth and my being unmarried was written in later, fulfilling the needs of the later church to idealize what they saw as their Savior. Now, if you don't mind," Dock asked, "I have a question regarding retrieving data. How can one collect data so rapidly from such a vast expanse of time without having actually traveled the timeline in real time?"

"That's classified," Betty answered.

"What do you mean?" Dock asked.

"Classified means it is a secret," John explained.

Dock looked at my Security Officer, then around at the rest of us. "I understand," Dock replied quietly.

"I would very much like to know the extent of your powers, Mr. Dock," I said.

"That's classified," Dock replied, a twitch of amusement at his lips.

Betty interjected. "Mr. Dawes I have the analyzed results."

"Report," I ordered, slightly annoyed at Dock and that we had to send him back before I finished asking at least a thousand more questions.

"Mr. Christopher Dock is currently living in Sydney under yet another alias."

"Oh really!" I exclaimed.

Dock was visibly stunned. "I am so happy to know I actually survived the wretched agony of the eighteenth century." He was beaming from ear to ear.

"What's he doing in Australia?" John asked.

Betty replied, "He's on R&R in Sydney, sir. His alias is Kent Dundee." We all nearly fell out of our seats with that news, and I thought the three SAS guards standing were going to faint, too.

"Mr. Dock," I said, "I am pleased to inform you that you are the current captain of the starship, *QuestRoyal!*"

Chapter 19: Fermions

Betty was in uniform now as a hologram seated at the conference table. Dock seemed unfazed to have the computer voice, which had been talking to us from the ethers earlier, now sitting before him. Of course, as a shape-shifter himself I supposed this wasn't that remarkable to his standards anyway.

Central computer Betty's massive analytical capabilities had made short work of the data stream flowing in from the timeline in real time and slip time. She briefed all of us, including Christopher Dock, on the ramifications of what she could tell us collectively, pertaining to the timeline from 1748 to 2860, and leaving out any information she feared would affect events. None of us could comprehend the whole picture, except Betty. Not only did she have an overview of the entire period, but she could also predict with certainty an outcome almost instantaneously. No matter, as far as I was concerned, her abilities weren't fast enough. Well aware of Murphy's Law, we couldn't be rid of the Ancient One fast enough. The last thing I wanted was for something to happen to Jesus on my watch.

"All right, Betty," I ordered. "Let's have the short version of what Mr. Dock needs to know before we slip him back from whence he came."

"Mr. Dock is how I will address you," she began, looking in his direction, "until we return you to a moment after we removed you in 1748. In your future as this crew knows you, I will address you as Captain Dundee. I am able to provide you with very few pertinent facts without affecting the timeline. Sergeant Major Jeeves unwittingly slipped into your timeline twice, once in 1718 in Virginia, and again in 1748 Pennsylvania. He met you both times. Of this you are now well aware, correct?"

"Indeed I am," he said.

"The curious component about these two appearances in your time is that they were unrelated instances in our time," she explained. "We have discovered, however, that an inexplicable anomaly occurred in both instances and they match each other. This type of anomaly has never occurred before or since as far as we know. I believe they are traces of a holographic probe of the most sophisticated kind. We do not have probes of such sophistication. You mentioned earlier that your people have yet to develop the ability to travel in time, correct?"

"Yes, that is correct," he replied. "Can you explain the anomaly?"

"The probes leave quantum evidence of half-integer fermion particles," Betty explained.

"I'll try to remember that tidbit of quantum evidence as I comfortably survive my toast-free exile for the next seven hundred, seventeen years," Dock lamented.

"Wait." I halted the stream of conversation with an idea of my own. "What if there was a deliberate reason to strand Mr. Dock here, I mean alive, rather than kill him." I turned to Dock. "What if the internal political faction that threatens your home system deliberately marooned you here? And in their future, with time travel probes, they are monitoring you?"

"Why not just kill me instead?" he said.

"Maybe there was a reason not to," I answered. "Perhaps you were ransomed or there was some other kidnapping motive. Maybe the kidnappers placed you here in cold storage and then they were captured or killed after the fact by the authorities, and you've been stuck here ever since."

"There may be numerous scenarios," John said.

"Perhaps," Dock said, "but I believe my crash was a result of damage sustained in combat. If there ever was a rescue party, maybe the captain of the rescue vessel concluded that my arm in the belly of an angry tiger was sufficient evidence of my demise to call off further search and rescue efforts. My people roam everywhere. We once had outposts across this universe in all galaxies in every direction. The authorities would most likely have found me if they had continued the search."

"Therein lies the problem, Mr. Dock, I am sorry to say," I said. "We have only found archeological *evidence* of your people, what we call the Ancient Ones, in five galaxies. We have not encountered *your people*."

Dock looked puzzled. "Well, as I mentioned earlier, my people left but surely they come and go on scientific missions to this day. They did up to the point in time before I was marooned."

The admiral replied, "You are the first Alsatian that we have encountered, Mr. Dock."

"My people are very advanced, sir," Dock replied in denial. "They have the ability to hide in plain sight and we have outposts everywhere."

"The admiral is not exaggerating, Mr. Dock." I said. "You are our first contact with the Ancient Ones. On some worlds, both near and far from here, we have discovered the ruins of vast civilizations, and on other worlds only small outposts as you mentioned, but alas, none of your people. All evidence of habitation vanished everywhere simultaneously approximately five thousand years ago, as far as we can determine. Your people are no more. We have been trying to solve this archeological puzzle since we first discovered evidence of your people about three hundred years ago."

Christopher Dock was visibly shaken. "As I said, my people left." He leaned back in his chair and kneaded his cleft chin. Jeeves poured him a glass of ice water, and we waited to hear what he had to say next. He appeared to be meditating or contemplating what to do.

"How did you come upon the fraktur?" he asked Betty, changing the subject.

Betty motioned to me. "Mr. Dawes found it in California early in the twenty-first century," she replied.

Dock turned to me. "Mr. Dawes, describe how you found it, if you please."

"I found it in an antiques shop on Cannery Row in Monterey, California," I replied. "It was in a bottle originally, I was told. The dealer I bought it, then had it housed under glass in a frame. He said he bought the bottle containing the fraktur from an eBay seller who got it from a Nantucket beachcomber. When I asked him what he thought about the modern images since they were in stark contradiction to its early date, he reminded me how close we were to San Francisco, known for its New Age/esoteric concepts. Apparently forgetting he'd just told me two minutes earlier that it was from Nantucket originally. At the time medical marijuana was still in widespread use. His short attention span might have been a consequence of cannabis sativa ingestion. THC has that effect."

It was evident Dock couldn't understand many details of my explanation because of his early timeline. Betty halted the dialogue before I could go any further and suggested we bring Dock up to speed with an abridged download. We concurred. He agreed to the process and seconds later grinned at the euphoric effects of even this small input of data. Afterward, he understood completely and picked up where he left off. "What was your impression of the fraktur, Mr. Dawes?" he asked.

"I was quite familiar with fraktur and most other Americana categories, so I knew what I was looking at. It passed my initial superficial scrutiny and later passed close inspection under magnification. So then I had it tested. The results were conclusive: the paper, paint, and ink were from circa 1750. It was an authentic 1748 fraktur. Naturally the problem was that nineteenth- and twentieth-century drawn objects were blaringly inconsistent with the proven date." The expressions on the faces of those present concurred.

Dock stood and paced in a small circle, thinking. "Any other observations?" he asked of me.

"Well, of course, the German language poem was a secondary puzzle at the time. My plan was to take it to a scholar at the University of Virginia and a specialist in Pennsylvania to interpret the poem. Unfortunately I died in a vehicular accident before I had a chance. I was revived earlier this year. You're here, Mr. Dock, as part of the investigation to determine how I was killed and if there is a link between Jeeves' two slips and my untimely death. You've solved part of the mystery: the images and date inconsistency."

"Yes, merely the doodles of a bored traveler on a vessel of turtle-like propulsion, I am sad to say," Dock said. "Sorry, old chap. I wish I could tell you differently."

"What about the poem?" asked John.

"More doodling I am afraid," Dock replied. "No mystery whatsoever."

"So, we're back to square one, I suppose," said Admiral Pride.

John leaned forward in his seat and made a small noise. He had a reputation for problem solving. "Maybe, but we haven't yet explained the quark-sized residual evidence left at the two Jeeves slips. We need to determine what those were, if they are related, and what we should do if they are. I slipped the line but couldn't discern anything out of the ordinary – no pun intended."

"What pun would that be?" asked Admiral Pride.

"In the olden days a tavern was often referred to as an *ordinary*," I replied and the admiral nodded.

"I might have something," Betty announced. "I'm running multiple slips and searching every thread of analysis imaginable as we speak. Bear with me. I'm directing CC. She's scouring permutations....we have discovered a possible clue. It seems the name for the anarchist organization, Ettore Majorana, is used not just in Mr. Dock's home system, it is also in ours, except here the name belongs to an individual instead of a terrorist faction."

"How is that possible?" asked John.

"I don't have enough data to draw a conclusion yet.... CC is processing," she replied.

"Give us what you have so far," John ordered.

Betty was making adjustments with her hands in front of her toward the holo screen interface. "Here it is. Mr. Ettore Majorana was born in 1906 and perhaps died in 1938."

"What do you mean, 'perhaps'?" I asked.

"Well, Mr. Dawes," Betty replied, "Ettore Majorana apparently was an Italian physicist who worked on a solution for understanding neutrino masses from which quantum scientists of the twentieth century deduced elementary particles. Majorana fermions and the Majorana equation are named after him. All the predicted quantum particles were derived from his astute speculation, including the perplexing Higgs boson discovered in 2012. Mysteriously, in 1938, Majorana withdrew all his money from his bank accounts and disappeared en route on a Mediterranean Sea excursion from Palermo to Naples. For years, scuttlebutt was rampant: he either jumped overboard, was murdered for the cash he carried and his body dumped over the side, or he lived out the remainder of his life under an assumed name. No trace was ever found until I did a slip just now."

Eyebrows went up all around.

"Please continue," I gestured. This interesting plot twist had us all craning our necks in her direction for more information. She leaned over the edge of the table and inhaled deeply causing her bosom to expand and sway unnecessarily in the process. The admiral and John looked at me with raised brows and the woman officers stared at each other. I didn't need the cue from the others, but it would have been improper of me to reprimand her in front of her colleagues. Instead I made a mental note to later, in private, say something to her about her apparent deliberate lasciviousness and to modify her holo forms. I'd noticed her earlier odd uses of "I" versus "we" regarding CC, but this Betty *was* the computer, for heaven's sake, not a Legal Person spin-off like Sarah. At any rate, my opinion of her salacious behavior was that it was inappropriate in a business environment. Besides, it wasn't Quaker-modest.

"He literally disappeared from that boat," Betty continued. "I have the slip video to prove it. The reason he vanished, though, was because a Ghanti-class warbird picked him up. I lost track of him when the vessel warped out of the quadrant on an intercept vector en route for Helios Grumm. I'm still searching communications and flash channels as we speak, which may take some time. I've been working on it for over an hour already." She sounded frustrated. An hour in the life of an AI is an eternity.

"That's an intriguing development," Admiral Pride commented. "A proper name pronounced the same way, separated by five thousand years of time."

"Not to mention half a universe in distance," added John.

"Actually, two different universes," Betty corrected.

"And to be connected, however remotely, with a prince assumed dead and our Founder who was dead," added Renatta.

"May I suggest something?" asked Dock.

"Yes, of course," I replied.

"Would it be possible to slip back and study the accident in which you met an untimely end?" Dock asked. "And might I suggest looking for quantum clues while you are there?"

I replied, "That's what I ordered a few minutes ago when you over-linked our thoughts."

"Oh right," he replied. "May I know what was retrieved?"

She first looked to me for approval, then answered, "The data is insufficient to draw a conclusion at this time, Mr. Dock."

"How far can you slip on the timeline?"

"I'm afraid that's classified," replied Betty.

"Answer the question, Betty," I ordered.

"Theoretically there is no limit."

"Then would you mind collecting the data along my timeline to when I crashed on this world and test for particle anomalies?" Dock asked.

"So ordered, but hold the results for now," I said.

"Aye, sir," she said.

"And Betty, since Mr. Dock was also Alexander the Great, maintain a detailed account of the destruction of my favorite ancient library and the grand library of Ephesus."

John Skill nodded at my request and further directed, "Betty, I'd also like you to define the cause of the library's destruction and find the perpetrators. Sorry for moving off topic, but since we are there momentarily anyway...."

"Understood, sir," she replied to John's request. "Might I recommend that we work the kinks out of the Rai Machine as we go?" John and I nodded our approval. "CC can perfect fast bilateral streaming."

I noticed her reference to CC, but let it drop for now. I piped in my thoughts on the subject at hand: "As for the great libraries' salvage operations we should get started by developing mission options, creating a business model, figuring manpower requirements, and allocating a generous budget for the purpose of acquiring the requisite assets. I mean, since you're capable of doing more than one thing at a time."

"Aye, sir," Betty replied. "And it's because I'm a woman that I can multitask, not a computer."

I remained expressionless for my own good. Oh, yes, something was going on with Betty. "Of course it is."

Betty peered at me trying to detect my thoughts and declared, "Slip probes away…mark… to both library sites and to Mr. Dock's crash site. I will advise periodically on the business model."

I turned to Mr. Dock. "I am sorry to tell you this, but it is time for you to return to your timeline, sir, although I will soon look you up in Sidney."

"May I at least know with certainty what brought my ship down?"

"We are working on that, Mr. Dock," I replied. "I wish you could stay with us, but that is not possible. The contributions you will make to this world's development are incalculable. Civilizations need you for their anticipated progress, especially if we are ever going to invent the automated toaster." I smiled, stood, and shook hands with the man formerly known as Jesus Christ. His grip was vice-like, his calluses hard, and his nails too long.

Mr. Dock chuckled. "Yes! Bleeding damned toasters. It's the inconsequential things that I want the most."

My attempt to lighten the mood was obviously appreciated. Nonetheless I unceremoniously dumped Jesus back onto his unmowed lawn in Skippack, Pennsylvania, in 1748. Other than the dry-cleaned clothes on his back and memorized images of all the topographical maps of Earth, he re-entered his timeline precisely a millisecond before the time he left it with naught but tubes of menthol lip balm, nail clippers, and toothbrushes in his pockets. For him it was seven hundred seventeen years before we will meet again, but for us…well…I had plans to drop in on Captain Dundee later the same afternoon.

Chapter 20: The Captain

A corvette was readied for the rendezvous with Kent Dundee. My plan was to drop in on him unexpectedly. Betty checked on his whereabouts and found him at his gothic style 1860s house on Wallaroy Road in the Woollahra suburb of Sydney. I asked her not to tell me more. The element of surprise was important.

For me it had only been hours since I had spoken with him, but from Christopher Dock's perspective, seven hundred seventeen years had passed since I returned him to Skippack. It was a hard decision that we both knew had to be made. I hoped he had come to terms with it by now.

I designated the usual members of my away team. They and I flashed to iris bay ALPHA-1, which is about half a klick aft of the bridge on the dorsal spine of the ship. As I came on board my corvette, its ship-wide address system trilled and announced, "Founder on deck," followed by a flurry of crew activity. A moment later a second announcement sounded off: "Initiate Foxtrot-1-Papa, now." That seemed to make the already-rapid deployment personnel even more frantic; uniformed troops ran helter-skelter. Federation-1 Protocol was equivalent to elevating the status of any vessel I board to Air Force One.

As I made my way to the bridge, lesser ranks braced against the port bulkhead. Commander Sarah Spitfire took the con from a naval lieutenant just as I arrived. The retiring lieutenant recognized me, braced briefly as I approached, and then moved smartly aside to attend to her other duties. Admiral Pride, I noticed, was already in the copilot's seat. My ears popped. Ship's CC announced a call to general quarters: "Bay decompression in ten seconds." Everyone settled into their favorite groove, station, or wherever. A moment later, F1P moved through the mothership's expanding iris into the vacuum of space and shoved off rather smartly flanked by four other corvettes. The scale in size of the two types of ships never ceases to amaze me. Next to a mothership a corvette looks like it's about the size of a suppository.

Everything was under control so I headed to the nerve center. John, Jeeves, and Renatta were already in the Ops. The space was a large octagonal with an under-lighted conforming maglev dais in the center. From different facets about the platform, the three of them were busy pouring over the slip data coursing across a holographic multidimensional green glass console that reached to the ceiling. One of the illuminated images I noticed was an orange pyramid. After a moment I recognized it to be a graphic designed to organize slipline events. Like a Rubik's cube, it can be twisted and rotated in an infinite variety of directions to demonstrate the consequences of a particular action based on a matrix of possible slipline events. Technology this complicated usually pisses me off. I'm a Generalist.

Naturally I had hundreds of questions for Dundee, pertaining to his historical figures, and a few dozen on how any of it has anything to do with my misfortune four hundred fifty-some years ago. Somehow I believed it would all eventually make perfect sense, although at that point I couldn't imagine how. Heck, I didn't even know what "it" was at that point.

Another computer trill sounded before she announced, "Secure, and make ready. Going atmospheric in thirty seconds: twenty-eight, twenty-six, twenty-four...." Then the swivel chair I was standing next to gently reached out a nanite arm to grasp my wrist, steered me onto its brown leather tufted seat cushion, and held me in place. Our little nanite friends watched over us like wet mother hens. I'd become used to, even relied on them. Moments later there was a brief sensation, like a ripple of turbulence, as we approached from a northerly vector. I watched the viewing screen and the various instruments as we spiraled once around the globe in a descent through the lattice of the orbital grid. After a few moments we crossed the equator and descend rapidly. A translucent sheen of molecular friction outlined the smart shield that elongated a mile ahead of our glide path. New Zealand swept under to our starboard side as the lateral fins smoothly deployed in anticipation of subsonic maneuverability just as the skyline came into view over the horizon. Years ago, make that centuries ago, Sydney was one of my favorite cities for picking antiques. I hoped it still would be when I had the time. I suddenly laughed and Sarah gave me a quizzical look. The idea of picking up antiques in any one place, when I now had probes to get the originals of those antiques immediately after their creation, was suddenly ludicrous. Yet part of me wished for a bit of that past to stay alive somehow.

John couldn't find us a convenient place to put down, so he had Sarah hover the ship at twelve hundred meters and requisitioned an FSS-approved air sector outside traffic lanes. Traffic was routed around. First squad flew my mobile perimeter. An attached detail stood guard of the ship. The rest of my entourage mounted inertia skis on the fantails of their respective ships and after a few ticks assembled in a clusterfuck off my portside. Renatta rode piggyback with me. Once outside the ship I realized what I missed on the *FSS QuestRoyal*: real sunshine and naturally scented air. Ahh! Eucalyptus.

I peered over the edge of the running board on my slick to see green landscape with an endless variety of old roofs around the city's center. The famous opera house was visible in the distance and I noticed the edge of the second primordial forest formed a semicircular barrier about twenty-five klicks away.

Sarah fell into formation last and gave me a smile almost as broad as the handlebars she was gripping. John signaled the go order by circling his arm overhead. First squad fanned out, forming a perimeter around the away team and me. We descended gradually to about thirty meters above the tops of the eucalyptus trees and followed the blue blinking GPS directionals on our windscreens. After a few ticks, a man wearing an apron, standing next to a stainless steel grill, came into view. He was looking up at us while shielding his eyes with one hand and holding a spatula in the other. My sled's windscreen blinked the words "OBJEC-TIVE" over "CAPT. DUNDEE." I brought my machine down, landing it an inch above his lawn and ten meters away in the shade. My away team followed suit. The machines automatically dropped nanite anchor arms to the ground in case of a breeze. As we dismounted, a beautiful Polynesian woman with long flowing hair exited the red door to the stone house. She paused on the stoop to observe the commotion that an arriving dignitary makes.

"Captain Dundee, I presume?" I've always wanted to greet someone using that line.

"Indeed I am," he replied. "And who might you be? Mr. Stanley?" He smiled a friendly smile. I could tell from his countenance he knew full well who I was. On the other hand, I didn't recognize him. His features were unlike the man I had met only hours before. This man was a bit taller, older, wore his white hair straight and short, and sported a cropped white beard. His facial features were quite different than before as was his accent and diction. I had seen pics of Dundee, of course, because he was the captain of the *QuestRoyal*, but since he had been on TDY, I had not met him or his wife in person and I had known nothing about his big secret.

"Kidding aside, Kent, was Livingstone another of your many aliases?"

"In fact, Mr. Dawes, indeed he was," he said as we shook hands.

"Captain, your appearance is different than when I saw you only hours ago."

"Yes, it is. Remember, I have the ability to transform my features and I have done so countless times in order to avoid historical confusion and present trouble." The smoke from his grill was rising straight up. In the distance I noticed the air traffic pattern moving to and from Sydney Schroom.

"I hope there are no hard feelings about my order to return you to 1748," I said.

"No, sir, I realized the importance of that order then and now. I made the best of it. We are a very patient race. I am no different than my people. I figured you would show up one day after I heard you had been revived."

The other members stood at ease in the shade, awaiting orders. With a sweep of my arm, I said, "Captain, I would like to introduce my away team." They moved out of the shade toward us.

"That is unnecessary, sir," he said, "I know them all. We have worked together for years." John, Renatta, the Admiral, and Jeeves stood to my left, all squinting in the midday sun.

"Right. Well, I suppose so. I'm the late one to this party, aren't I?" I asked rhetorically.

A tall, graceful Polynesian woman glided across the cool flagstones under the shade of a bougainvillea-covered high pergola to Dundee's side and placed her hand on his arm. "Darling, perhaps you'd like for your friends to join us?" she inquired.

"Everyone," Dundee said, "I would like to introduce my wife, Pearl."

Mrs. Dundee bowed from the waist ever so slightly to all. "Please, Founder," she repeated, "honor our home. Do make time to join us at our barbee."

"I'd hoped you'd ask," I replied happily, and tipped my finely woven Panador Panama hat respectfully at one of the most charming ladies I would ever meet. Everyone conveyed their thanks for the invitation and expressed the joy at being on-world once again. A hubbub of conversation ensued as we occupied comfortable chairs. The scent of blossoms mixed with green mint wafted past me as I watched Dundee cook. A low forest of different mints grew along a dry-stacked rock wall confining elevated flowerbeds. Sarah and Renatta ferried cooked chicken, franks, and burgers that the captain was slinging from the grill. Mrs. Dundee mixed and poured drinks for all. I resolved to be patient and bide my time for as long as I could.

We had all been cooped up for months. None of us could remember the last barbee we had. This was special for all of us, including the captain, who told us he liked to grill. John and the admiral were on their second burger before Dundee and I joined them.

"I'm guessing you have a few questions for me," he said, sitting across from me at a sawbuck table with John on his right and the admiral on his left. Renatta sat at my right and Sarah on at my left. Jeeves sat at the admiral's left. A marine platoon commander stood at parade rest in the shade three meters away. I noticed F1P first squad formed a perimeter twenty-five meters out with six marines on slicks at ground level, another six at fifty meters elevation, and a third rank of six one hundred fifty meters out on sleds.

"How up to speed are you on the dynamics of the situation?" I asked.

"Actually, I've deliberately kept myself out of the loop," Dundee replied. "When I heard of your impending revival, the first thought that came to mind was not fouling up the timeline in any manner so you don't send me back to 1748 again!" Everyone laughed at his joke.

Good. He has a sense of humor, I thought. "Very funny, Dundee," I laughed, too. "I can already tell you're going to get a lot of mileage out of that for years to come."

"You bet, mate," he chuckled. "Anyway, I got approval from both the Pentagon and Northwood to go on an extended sabbatical to make myself scarce. I just finished third term teaching at ADFA in Canberra. Right now I'm on R&R, but if you hadn't shown up, I would have chosen either Norwich University in Vermont or Sandhurst in the UK as my next diversion; I hadn't yet made up my mind. I knew you'd look me up eventually, but I didn't have any idea when that would be. With permission, I would rather return to my command." He looked to Admiral Pride and then at me again. We both nodded in the affirmative.

"Yes, of course," I agreed.

"Splendid!" he exclaimed. "Now, I suppose you have a few questions for me?"

"I do," Admiral Pride interjected. "Why didn't you confide in anyone?"

Dundee answered in a respectful tone. "The Founder's safety was at stake and had been for centuries. There was no way I was going to jeopardize him by revealing who I was."

Pride didn't say anything but it was clear he understood what had motivated Dundee to silence.

I patiently waited a moment and then asked Dundee, "Remember the particle anomaly we isolated in the two slips when you spoke with Jeeves?"

"Yes sir."

"Well, a couple of hours ago we confirmed that the same particle anomaly occurred the moment you crashed."

"Interesting." He bit into a burger, a mix of mustard and ketchup squeezing out.

"And it has occurred on other occasions across the timeline," added Sarah.

"An identical signature appears again in 1938," Renatta said.

"When Ettore Majorana disappears in a Ghanti warbird?" Dundee asked after swallowing.

"Yes sir," answered Jeeves.

"And in 2010 at the scene of my accident," I added.

"And at other pivotal points in history too," Sarah said. "So far, Betty has logged some one hundred, plus. On average she finds one or two per day with a faster rate of occurrence the closer she slips to the present. It's only a matter of time, now."

"Right," muffled Dundee, obviously contemplating the permutations in his mind, whatever they may be. He took another bite. None of the rest of us did. We were hoping for his insight.

"We believe you can shed some light on this phenomenon, Captain," stated Renatta with one eyebrow raised. "What are you carefully not telling us that we need to know in order to get a handle on this puzzle?"

"Why would I leave anything out?" he asked.

"Possibly because you know what this anomaly is," Admiral Pride responded.

"Or even more likely, you can sense the presence of the probe when it's in relative proximity to you," Renatta suggested.

The admiral continued. "Tread carefully, Captain; your command is at risk if I detect even a whiff of an ethics violation."

"I have not lied!" Dundee was emphatic.

"My husband is an honorable man!" Mrs. Dundee exclaimed.

"He never lies."

"Un-huh," the admiral was skeptical. "You've been what, hundreds of historical figures from cavemen to a frickin' starship pilot? You've traversed some six thousand years without cutting down a single cherry tree? Yeah, right."

The admiral was becoming heated, playing bad cop. I let the drama play out for a moment hoping it would lead to something. These officers knew Dundee much better than I. They had served with him for years. But I couldn't reconcile my crew now treating him like this after the calming effect that he had on us just hours ago when he, as Dock, had given us faith in him as a messenger. *So what gives?* I thought. *Why the stress?* Maybe subconsciously there was some resentment that they'd been lied to, even if by omission, all the time they'd served with him.

"Admiral, I am offended, sir," Dundee responded, chagrinned. He, too, was flushed.

I used command voice, "At ease, both of you. This is a think tank, *not* an inquisition. We need to know what this damned anomaly is and if it is the cause of our two crashes, right?" Both looked at me, as did the others. Everyone seemed to refocus on the objective. The mood soon passed.

"Two crashes?" Dundee asked Jeeves.

Jeeves answered. "Your crash landing and Mr. Dawes' automobile accident."

"Right." Dundee took another bite and chewed. "All right, I suppose now is as good a time as any," he relented, and then took a sip of pink lemonade from a sweating glass. "My race is indeed ancient, about twelve billion years as far as we've been able calculate. Essentially we are immortals.

"We choose to husband and live in this species because it is the best that we have discovered and because we value all sensation: the pleasurable and even the painful and especially the unknown. Aging for us is inconsequential because we do not age once we reach maturation. We have learned a good deal from our research. As time passes through human bodies in this universe it leaves them damaged and ruined, but it does not have the same effect on my people. Alsatians are immune to this phenomenon.

"Our bodies resist permanent damage but they can be destroyed. When that happens, we join the Community of God as equals. But there's a major difference between human souls and Alsatians souls."

With one hand holding a turkey wing he reached with the other for a basket of ripple chips which provided a pregnant moment for the rest of us to register what he had said thus far.

Renatta recovered first. "I'll bite. What's the major difference?"

One side of his mouth curved into a smile. "We retain our individuality in the next higher plane."

"And humans do not?" Admiral Pride asked.

"Correct."

We were so astounded to learn of our fate that none of us spoke for a few ticks.

I stuttered, "So, so you're saying that we, we're an inferior species?"

Before Dundee could answer me, John interjected, "Alsatians only *occupy* the bodies they live in?"

Dundee held up a hand to pause John for a moment, and then addressed my question. "No, sir. I am saying that humans are on a different plane from us just as one civilization may be on a different plane than another. The sentience of the two peoples is equal in importance and equal in intellect, even though the civil development in one may be higher than in another. Imagine a Third World country that is being ruled by Victorian imperialists. Our modern mores treat both peoples equally even though the European power is vastly superior to the other in many ways."

Sarah interjected, "But that really *is* saying that Alsatians are on a higher plane."

"Well, isn't it evident?"

"I suppose so," she replied.

John repeated his earlier question. "What did you mean when you said that Alsatians occupy the bodies of the species that they live in?"

"We occupy these bodies the same way you occupy yours," he replied. "The difference is that we have a much-improved model, so to speak, and we choose to occupy these shells whereas you have no choice. You are mammals whether you want to be or not."

"I rather like being a mammal," Sarah quipped.

"You can leave your bodies?" John asked.

"We both can."

"You know what I mean," John sighed.

"Yes, I do. We can choose to live as equals in The Community or we can choose to occupy an Alsatian body. Most of us choose the corporeal rather than the spiritual, which is what The Community is."

I furrowed my brow trying to imagine what he meant by that comment but before I could formulate an inquiry the conversation continued and I lost my train of thought.

Jeeves asked, "Captain, you said that humans lose their individuality in the afterlife, right?"

"Yes, right way for most and eventually for a minority."

I found his analysis interesting. The others around the table must have thought the same because they displayed various expressions of consternation and all of them appeared to be lost in thought. They were practically chewing in cadence.

"You said some of us lose our individuality 'eventually;' what does that mean?" asked Renatta.

Dundee wiped his hands on a paper napkin. "Reincarnation is a factor for some humans. Some live multiple lives. I do not know how many lives or why some do and some do not, but I do know that the hybrids tend to reemerge multiple times before they end the cycle and pass for the last time into the morass. When they do, their self is absorbed into the community of One. By the way, that's a capital "O"."

Admiral Pride looked perplexed. "I don't follow."

"They become one with God," he clarified.

"And Alsatians do not?" I asked.

He cocked his head as if to find a suitable explanation. "When we leave the corporeal we become an equal share of God."

"The whole divided by the number of parts, so to speak?" Renatta asked.

"Precisely."

"So, you are, in fact, the son of God," Admiral Pride stated.

"No, I am not."

John shook his head. "I don't get it."

"It's complicated," Dundee replied.

Jeeves nearly raised his hand. "Sir, when you say hybrids, what does that mean?"

"I have been on this planet for several thousands of years, Sergeant Major."

"You mean your progeny?" Jeeves sputtered.

"That's right. My kids live the longest, are most likely to be reborn again, are the healthiest, and have the strongest extrasensory perceptions. Their children have lesser attributes, and so forth. The scenario is much like the American chestnut trees (Castanea dentata).

"Once upon a time great forests of mighty trees, millions, three meters in girth and thirty meters tall blanketed the land from the Mississippi to the east coast. It was a wonderful species. It provided shelter and food for humans as well as all creatures great and small. Passenger pigeons loved roosting in them overnight. Seventy percent of the eastern forests were comprised of these majestic trees, and then very swiftly there were none due to an Asian blight. Some of the more vigorous trees fought hard. They refused to die completely. They would die down, send up shoots, and repeat the cycle, but always in the end they would die completely. And so it is with my progeny. The Alsatian immortality attribute is lost when my genes are diluted."

"Do all of your descendants reincarnate?" Sarah inquired.

"I don't know."

I looked at Betty. "Betty, can you identify these humans with reincarnated souls? Those talents of theirs might come in handy for our mission."

She answered, "I can identify Captain Dundee's progeny, set up some parameters and look for similarities that can be then tracked. In process, sir."

Admiral Pride then asked, "Can your people traverse space anytime, anyplace?"

"We have many capabilities but space flight without a ship is not one of them." He chuckled and turned to me. "So, Mr. Dawes, I went along with your order to deliver me back to my time because my foremost concern was and still is avoiding the disruption of the timeline. Even in 1748 I understood that any timeline breach might prevent my eventual return to my home system. That's why I allowed you to return me to the ghastly eighteenth century with only a pocketful of Chapsticks! I could have easily escaped from your arrest, but that probably would have altered the timeline significantly which would have been counterproductive to my interests and dangerous to us all."

"I take it when you say 'dangerous' you mean dangerous to the timeline?" Admiral Pride asked.

"Yes, but not just the timeline," Dundee replied. "I was and am concerned for my safety and the safety of others. Any entity motivated to murder a prince from the House of Ooskaaffen would not hesitate to destroy others, perhaps even an entire planet."

"Understood," I said.

John almost choked on his brätwurst. "The thought had crossed our minds," he said. Admiral Pride, John, and Sarah nodded in agreement.

"Allow me to continue to reason out loud," Dundee said.

"By all means," encouraged Admiral Pride.

"With the clues we have, one can logically assume that the Ettore Majorana have developed the means to abridge the timeline by some means we do not understand. Perhaps it is this means that has caused my people to retreat from or vanish from surveyed space. I cannot imagine how at this point any power could be successful in this endeavor. My civilization was enormously widespread, entrenched and technological-ly powerful...or was. Some new development must have been invented back in the Biêi Universe since my exile here on Earth. What that might be I do not know, although I am hopeful. The clues we have been able to detect thus far offer a starting point."

"So what's your train of thought, sir?" asked Sarah.

"Jeeves' two slips and my crash landing are related," he replied. "Of that I have no doubt."

"Why are you so certain, sir?" Jeeves asked.

"I possess an extrasensory ability that allows me to detect spatial anomalies," Dundee explained. It's probably closely related to the Alsa-tian ability to literally see folded space. I didn't realize I had the ability until I connected the dots."

Admiral Pride asked, "What do you mean by that?"

Dundee responded, "At high FTL velocities I can actually see the fabric of the continuum. It's an individualistic trait. No two Alsatians see precisely the same phenomena, by the way."

"Can you elaborate, Captain Dundee?" Sarah asked.

"I'd like to know, too," said Admiral Pride.

Dundee glanced around at us as though he were gathering his words. "Above FTL ten I begin to see black currents flowing like contour lines in an asymmetrical crystalline honeycomb. They undulate randomly with the solar winds and gravity wells. Imagine the movement of smoke or drifting sand. The deep dark black matter of space *moves*. I first see it in my mind and then as the ship accelerates I begin to feel it. The sensation becomes more distinct the faster my ship travels. At a certain velocity I see it visually just as you do everything in this room."

"Is this folding skill, as it were, a physical ability or are mechanics involved?" Sarah asked.

"My physical ability works in tandem with a device that shares simi-lar properties with the Rai Machine. I had one on my ship."

"What kind of device?" Admiral Pride probed.

"It looks like an Antikythera Mechanism," Dundee said.

"But you said that your people were incapable of time travel," John stated.

"True the last I heard."

"So what did the device do?" asked Jeeves.

"It folds space similarly to the Alcubierre drive, but differently, and it alters time similar to the Rai Machine. I really can't explain it. I can repair one but I do not totally comprehend how it works."

"How large is it?" Jeeves asked.

Dundee used his hands to define its size. "Oh, and it's about so tall and square and on the top there is a small thingamajig that looks like a sextant."

"And this device does what, exactly?" I asked.

"It allows me to see the contour lines of dark matter clearly. For an Alsatian, it's like when we switch our PFFs to infrared vision. Think of it as a navigation tool like radar. It wasn't capable of actual time travel as is your Rai machine, but it facilitated deep space travel."

Admiral Pride signaled an interjection. "So, with one of these dark matter radars you can pilot a ship the size of the *QuestRoyal* across the polyverse?"

"Correct. Across this universe to Giêi and to other universes."

"Have you considered building such a device?" I asked.

"I've been researching with Professor Rictor and CC on that in my spare time."

I was surprised. So were the others. "Good. How far along are you?" I replied calmly. I felt like going off the handle, but it seemed best if I led by calm example instead of scolding him for not keeping everyone informed of his pet project.

"I can't tell at this point. We are having some difficulty."

"What is the difference between our existing folding technologies, the variations other species have, and your folding ability?" John asked.

"Alsatian technology is far better than anyone's," Dundee replied. "And I have been working on improving Federation folding capabilities, too. CC, Rictor, and I meet periodically to discuss our progress. Once the Rai Machine has been perfected, Professor Rictor and I will have more time to devote to improving FTL warp. In the meantime what the Fed has now is the best in surveyed space."

Admiral Pride asked, "So, just how much better is Alsatian

warp technology?"

"We will be able to traverse to where the Big Bang first occurred in half a day and return in time for an early dinner without missing a minute of time."

The sound of our collective jaws dropping onto the floor was deafening. I looked around. The expressions on the faces of my officers probably mirrored my own. It was difficult for me to focus. My playful side encouraged me to perform cartwheels down the corridor. *This is one of the best days of my life,* I told myself. "Captain Dundee, will you help us perfect this equipment and continue living amongst us once it has been perfected?" I asked.

"I have been helping for quite some time, Mr. Dawes," he replied. "The Rai Machine is the result of my effort."

"I thought Professor Rictor had the initiative on that," I replied, looking around at the others.

Dundee smiled. "He's had the initiative all along, and, in fact, he still does. By the way, he's doing a fine job, but without my insight woven into his equations at just the right moments, we'd probably be in development another decade."

"I had no idea," I said. I looked at the others. "Did you know this?" I looked at the other astonished faces. None had a clue.

"I've been making contributions for thousands of years, Mr. Dawes. My first big push was during the European Renaissance. I was Da Vinci's chief assistant. He was truly a genius and a talented painter, but the machines he drew were seeds I planted in his mind. There were other individuals and other important periods similar to the Renaissance, as well. I often managed to be in the right place at the right time when they occurred. In fact I seeded most of the Dawes breakthroughs in the early nineteenth century and then fertilized and weeded them until the various seeds grew to maturity. Countless offshoots were produced that led to most of what we have today on this world and beyond. When the times were right, I made it my business to be in the right place at the right time.

"You winning the lottery, Mr. Dawes, is another example. When you created a foundation from those winnings, well, that was probably the most opportune moment for me. When you won, I thoroughly checked you out and appreciated your T's approach to life and business. Then I guided the hand of your planning committees and R&R teams at various times, which has come to fruition now."

"Now that you're out of the closet," John asked, "will your contributions be in the open from now on?"

"Yes," Dundee replied, "but I would like my history to be kept confidential. I wouldn't want to revisit Calvary a second time just to be rid of the paparazzi."

"So ordered," I smiled, and the others smiled with me. I knew I could trust them with this secret, yet part of me still wondered what potential for slip-ups, coincidences and blind rotten luck might create yet a high-tech Calvary in the future … for all of us.

Chapter 21: The Slip Brigade

Captain Kent Dundee was very popular. The mood of the whole ship changed upon Dundee's return, like Daddy had come home from a business trip. Because he never slept, he literally spent half of his time on the bridge with the crew and the other half working in the lab with Professor Rictor. If the crew knew about Dundee's ancientness, they never let on. He was welcomed back with some fanfare after seven months away. The ship's officers really put on the Ritz with a dining-in in the officer's mess. Admiral Pride and I were present for the formal dinner, but we graciously excused ourselves so the crew could let their hair down. It took a dozen bots to clear the mess the next morning. I had no idea my officers were such party animals.

I asked him to brief the brass on the Rai project once he felt well-grounded again. About a month after his return to duty, Dundee called a meeting for the staff officers. The same faces that had been at his picnic gathered in my ready room: Admiral Fleetwood Admiral Pride, Dr. Renatta Messina, Commander Sarah Spitfire, Sgt. Maj. Jeeves Hamilton, Director John Skill, holo Betty, and, of course, me. Betty read over the minutes from our picnic meeting and then we got down to new business. Dundee began by trying to explain the extraordinary powers of the Alsatians in regards to traversing.

He lectured casually seated on the curve of my ready room table. I was reminded of Leonardo da Vinci's great mural in Milan. "When we Alsatians begin and end a traverse between universes, we experience a variety of stimuli on a physiological level. In other words, our six senses are affected, usually taste and smell first, albeit very subtly. Water, for example, will taste slightly different from one local to another. Likewise, the transit between two universes is a sensation that varies. Those individuals who cannot sense the stimuli – sentient mechs for instance – may need to be augmented with sensory enhancements to notice the changes. For the most part, biotics do not require an enhancement; they just need a bit of training to deal with it."

"What's it feel like?" asked Renatta.

"Like nausea."

"Well, that's just terrific," I said facetiously.

Renatta commented, "In seismic fault zones some witnesses have described the same sensation before a major temblor. This is very interesting, Mr. Dundee. Please go on."

Dundee first took a sip of steaming coffee. "Transverse olfactory and visual effects have not been reported in humans, as far I know; however, I suspect that a percentage of the population will have the ability to some extent because of my genetic input over time. Additional study is warranted.

"All stimuli are subject-specific and fold-specific which means traverse sensations are unique. Each person literally perceives the effects from a different perspective because no two people occupy the same point in space. We've conducted studies and compared drawings created by Alsatians traveling on the same ship and discovered that no two pictures were alike. I suspect the same is true for slipper events although this will probably remain a hypothesis until we find more of my kind.

"When I am in near proximity to slipper events, either slipped objects or operatives, I am able to sense two effects, one visual and the other olfactory; think flavors for the latter. If I am present when a slipper or a probe arrives in or departs from a slipline, I visually *feel* as well as see a sensation similar to someone donning someone else's prescription spectacles. I also smell a distinct scent. The visual effect is always the same; however; the scent phenomenon is subject-specific, as when we traverse."

Dundee turned to Jeeves, "For instance, Jeeves, you carry and leave behind a vanilla scent when you slip."

"I had no idea," Jeeves said. "That is interesting, sir."

Indeed, we were so mesmerized that we sat like bumps on a log trying to take it all in as holo Betty was typing furiously into a flimsy tablet. *A tablet?* I looked at John. He shrugged one shoulder and made a *don't-look-at-me* face.

Dundee continued. "The intensity of the scent is a duration indicator: the more recent one's return or the longer one has been away in a different timeline, the stronger the scent. This is true for all slippers and probes. It gets really complicated when a slipper or a probe travels multiple slip zones in a brief period without purging the static between their slips. Not even I can distinguish multiple scents once they have mixed, although a canine bot can. I accidently discovered that in the lab." He looked around the room for emphasis. "Remember that tidbit of information should the need arise."

"If that's the case, how could my two slips be related to your crash?" Jeeves shrugged. "I wasn't at your crash site."

"I realize that," he replied. "I detected a second scent at your two slips that was also present on the bridge of my ship before I lost control."

John asked, "And what was that one?"

"I smelled ozone."

"Was it the scent of the cloaked high-tech probe from the quark-sized field anomaly?" asked John.

"I believe so," Dundee replied, nodding to John.

"Don't you think an ozone odor onboard a crashing starship is possible?" Sarah questioned.

"Not pink ozone," he replied.

"Jesus!" I exclaimed, and then realized the obvious too late.

"Please don't take my name in vain, my son," Dundee said with a straight face. He just couldn't help himself.

"Sorry," I replied with an equally straight face. "Sorry, force of habit, my Lord."

Admiral Pride chortled, "I bet that happens a lot."

"You have no idea." Dundee shook his head once.

"Concentrate, gentlemen," Renatta coached. "So scents and flavors have color, Captain?"

"They do for us Alsatians," he replied.

"That's called synesthesia," Renatta informed us. "A significant portion of the human population has this ability and other extrasensory abilities."

Dundee replied. "Yes, I know. Human extrasensory abilities have been increasing exponentially since I crashed here."

"Your DNA?" Renatta asked.

"I have no doubt my actions have had a significant impact," Dundee answered calmly. "Before my arrival, man was a vastly different species than it is now. I suspect if I hadn't dallied as often as I did, the primitives on this world would still be marveling at the miracle of fire, and I would still be Earthbound. Creativity has blossomed with the introduction of my foreign DNA. Trust me. Mankind is all the better for it. I have no regrets."

Renatta pursued the line of reasoning. "Have you determined if humans with 'abilities' have the capacity to discern the same things you can?"

"No doubt some do have some extra abilities. ESP has been a field of study that I have nurtured for centuries now. I won't be able to determine the extent of their perception until I have the Antikythera unit from my ship or we have reinvented the component. Then we can experiment with human cognitive ability. Betty has surveyed the fleet for members with extrasensory abilities. We have a dozen candidates here on the *QuestRoyal*."

"What about your children, sir?" asked Jeeves.

"I haven't been able to convince Mrs. Dundee that we should, yet. I do have older offspring from previous unions, but security and privacy issues must be addressed before we go that route."

John redirected the dialogue. "So your sixth sense is what led you to Jeeves' tavern table in both slips?"

"Yes. When I smelled vanilla I knew immediately something spatially was about to occur, or had just occurred. I looked about but nothing seemed to happen, other than the usual rapid visual blip, so I wasn't sure if I had seen something or I had just imagined it. But I must have sensed something because I went about the tavern sniffing, literally. If something had occurred, then I figured my nose might lead me to the source, and it did. That's why I struck up a conversation with Jeeves."

"I remember," Jeeves said, looking around the room, "but how did we meet thirty years and two hundred fifty miles apart in your timeline?"

"I have no idea," replied Dundee. "As far as I know, it was a coincidence."

"So what next?" prodded Renatta. "You were at Jeeves' table; then what happened?"

"His cover was outstanding," Dundee continued. "I couldn't figure out what had happened."

"But you realized a spatial effect had taken place, right?" asked John.

"I suspected one had, but I couldn't isolate it and that made me uncertain."

Renatta must have read my mind. "OK then. Betty, I think we need a synopsis of what we understand so far based on the results you've been able to retrieve from the future timeline."

Betty stopped typing. "I am able to detect the same anomaly across the timeline from Captain Dundee's crash to four hundred years from now into the future," replied Betty. "At this juncture I have isolated nearly one hundred-thirty incidences before the future, but I cannot penetrate the intruder's shield. Half the time I can't even detect it, just the anomaly. I will continue to catalogue these events if you wish, but we are not going to make any progress until we have a breakthrough. A bit of creative input is called for, ladies and gentlemen. After all, that's why we AI's keep you around."

We chuckled at her attempt at humor. She had sent us a memo a few days earlier informing us of her "laugh initiative." Admiral Pride had then told her that officers are not issued "funny" so he didn't expect her to have any either. She had agreed with the admiral that he wasn't funny. I had an image of our feisty female computer lady dressed in red, crossing her arms under her bosom, and raising her cleavage and eyebrows simultaneously at the esteemed naval officer.

"Perhaps we should try to capture a cloaked probe?" Dundee offered.

"Excellent suggestion, Captain," replied Betty.

"Let's try to isolate the device using an arresting field," Dundee continued. "Betty, wait! You might only get one chance, so first program our probes to evade and resist, and then practice capturing them in case the invasives have a defensive strategy. If the invasives are AI, they'll surely learn from any failed attempts at capturing them."

"Wait!" Now John interrupted and added an additional caution. "Don't run experiments in the timeline location. Run a full battery of tests somewhere else. The invasive probe may be designed to self-destruct or it could be booby-trapped with a contaminant. When you do capture one of ours, try not to damage it. Deactivate its cloak and contain it. Use trial and error if you have to: freeze it, shock it, drench it, expose it to an EMP – use all your tools. Then we'll know what works before we try to nab the invasive."

"Train, then execute," ordered Admiral Pride.

"Acknowledged. What should I do if I capture one?"

"Notify us when you do," Admiral Pride said.

"Betty," I added, "I have an idea. I think we should devise a way to make all cloaked devices visible, maybe a portable appliance that can detect, make visible, maybe even capture or neutralize a cloaked trespasser in any form, slipper or probe. TSA would be able to employ it at checkpoints and in tandem with CCTV cameras everywhere. Advise when you have an ETA on this new technology."

"Aye, sir. On it." By then I had learned that Betty was the ultimate multi-tasker.

Ideas began streaming into my mind like a whirlwind.

"Betty. Also, is it possible to run a slip on Ettore Majorana from the point he disappeared on a vector for Helios Grumm?"

"Yes, sir," she replied. "I have the vid already, but the slip connection is lost the moment the warbird warps out of range."

"What happens to our probe on the warbird then?"

"It's goes dormant and the data cannot be retrieved."

"I see. Have you sent a crew to Helios Grumm to retrieve it?"

Betty flushed noticeably. "Excellent suggestion, sir. I'll get right on it."

"Make sure the boat and crew remain cloaked during the entire mission," advised John.

"Yes, sir." Betty's head moved back and forth between us as if she were watching a tennis match.

"And, Betty," I said, "I haven't heard back from you on the Rai tags I asked for some time ago. What's their status?"

Betty answered in detail without a ruffled feather. "Field trials have met with Quality Control's approval. A new nano factory dedicated to that specialized purpose will go online in the next week or so, and I have created an administrative department to manage it. I plan to operate it as a separate initiative, sir."

"What tags would that be?" asked Dundee.

I explained. "When we first discovered the spatial anomaly on Jeeves' two slips, I thought that the Serapis Fraktur was a key leading us to the Alexandria library where we would find a larger answer. We didn't know you had drawn it as a lark." As a picker, antiques dealer, and appraiser, I knew quite a bit about scriveners. I probably had bought and sold a few hundred and probably even a couple by Christopher Dock because signed examples were extant. Quite a few fraktur by Dock's hand have survived. His name even appears in several early books on fraktur. Being in the antiques business, I had even handled one or two examples of his early work. I explained to him that, in the world of fraktur collecting, Christopher Dock was well known. He just harrumphed and mumbled something about how flattering it was to know collectors were collecting his work but that he really wasn't interested in that sort of thing. When I pressed him for information, all he told me was that there was a period in the mid eighteenth century when he supplemented his teaching income by drawing fraktur.

Betty interjected, "Mr. Dawes thought that we could slip the clock, place a tracer on an interesting object to see if it survives degradation..."

I continued. "The Rai tags were my brain child. I figured that if we could tag inanimate objects, verify their loss to degradation, then it would be possible to harvest them harmlessly from the past."

Dundee nodded with an expression of approval. "Sounds like a fine idea to me."

"So I pressed forward," I explained, "hoping that with the resources of the Conglomerate behind me, we would see some results if I just followed my nose like I did when I was a picker. I thought your Serapis fraktur was the key to a stargate, or to something important like that. As it turned out, it *was* important. It led to us to you."

"Yes," Dundee replied sighing, "I am literally the gateway. So, your supposition was correct. There is a gateway but it is not the physical gate you may have visualized. It's a combination of factors: sufficient FTL speed, a modified Alcubierre drive in tandem with an antimatter reflux plow and an Antikythera instrument, black lasers, and my own innate transformation ability. To traverse the deep dark we first have to recover the technology from my lost ship, or reinvent it. I'm supervising the reinvention approach and I'm following the recovery method; that team reports daily to me. Sometimes Professor Rictor and I think we are close to achieving reinvention and at other times we think that we may never figure out the mechanism. We could use more creative input, brainpower, resources, and man hours."

"So you've found your old ship?" Renatta asked.

"Betty did."

She reported, "I've slipped a recovery team back to Captain Dundee's crash event. So we now have the coordinates of the wrecked ship. It's in the Marianas Trench almost eleven kilometers deep. We have been unable to retrieve it chiefly because of the depth and various slip factors as well as other logistical problems. The ship weighs six hundred metric tons, by the way. That's one of the major problems, by the way."

"Got it," I said.

"Mr. Dundee, what happens to you when you pilot a craft through a transition?" asked Renatta. "You mentioned before that you experience a transformation."

Dundee replied, "Actually, I call the action a *Möbius transversion* because the vessel is made to transverse distance as my mind transforms space-time along a geometric Möbius plane. Nothing obvious happens outwardly that a witness might observe. It looks like I'm experiencing a petite mal seizure. As a physician you know that it can go unnoticed by an untrained eye."

"I understand," she replied. "Is there anything that we can do for you when this happens?"

"I'll be captaining the ship we are on when this occurs. Just follow my orders."

"Of course," I replied. "Everyone will."

Dundee nodded approval. "To answer your question, Renatta: the transformation manifests within my mind and body. It is an internal process just as the five senses are internal. When I initiate the sequence, time stops for me. To me it looks like objects in motion around me have halted, including anyone around me. The device on my ship sort of, ah, it's hard to explain, it kind of lubricates my perspective of time so that everyone around me is not frozen in place. That way I can interact with them normally which is, of course, essential on the bridge of a ship. But that's just one of the features of the Antikythera instrument."

We were absorbing the facts he was telling us as best we could. Dundee took a sip of coffee. After a couple of thoughtful seconds he continued when we hadn't said anything. We were all trying to formulate an intelligent question, I suppose. I had a growing understanding of what Dundee was describing and a growing list of questions, too, but even with a pile of downloaded PhDs under my black belt, I was at momentary loss for words.

Renatta was the first to recover. "Captain, what are you saying? Are you part of a whole, what? A device? Or a step in a sequence of actions?"

He replied, "Both. It's like being an apple and a fruit simultaneously. Once I have the entire set of puzzle pieces (the whole) assembled in a prescribed order (the series), Kent Dundee (me), will in effect become a quantum gravity sensor. I can't really explain this completely. It's a feeling more than anything else. It gets lost in translation because we Alsatians are so different from humans and because the transversion experience is unique to each subject, as I have explained. Simply put, I will deliberately raise my awareness to an elevated state until I reach a sustainable paranormal plateau, from which I will be able to clearly see the panorama of both matter and dark matter before us as I peer out the viewports. From that threshold I become a conduit. And from that vantage point I can pilot a vessel within and between universes. It's really no big deal. Most Alsatians have the ability, and I have it in spades.

Back in the Giêi universe I held the record for both duration and speed."

Ideas were fighting for attention in my mind. "I think I get the gist of it," I said.

"We need a few more intellects like Rictor to work the case," Dundee said.

Admiral Pride said, "They may not be so easy to find."

I jumped in again. "Actually, I think I have a plan to find you some more talent. For a while now I have been toying with the concept of extracting people."

When I'd first realized the possibility of extracting people from the past, I'd immediately called Betty about retrieving Emma for me, and she had just as quickly told me that that wasn't possible. She'd informed me that it would disturb a timeline sequence. I ordered her to explain and she replied that even explaining it would be a violation of my own directive to avoid imparting information that could affect the timeline. I nearly countermanded that order, forcing the issue, but thought better of it. I had purposely avoided learning the historical accounts of the Founder's wife's final years and for a reason: I wanted the Emma of my memories to remain mine solely. I knew intellectually that she may have remarried—should have, in fact, since she was still young and had so much life to live. Maybe she'd had children. Could I really deal with that emotionally? Plus, if I brought her to the future, who knew what she might decide or do differently in her life after she returned? It could disturb the timeline. Betty was right. I didn't need to know the reason; and in some subtle way it brought some measure of peace and closure knowing my Emma would always remain my own in my mind.

Later I'd considered the potential of extracting historical figures. The idea had merits and problems, but now there was a real purpose to trying it. Rictor and Dundee needed help fulfilling their mission; they needed additional manpower.

I explained, "Human extractions can be problematic if their sudden absence or knowledge of us affects the timeline. Of course Betty has a handle on that." I looked at holo Betty. She nodded affirmatively. "She continuously monitors the future timeline and constantly assesses the permutations and ramifications of all extraction proposals and applications. Only she can determine if an action is detrimental. So I think it is in our best interest if she is the authority that analyses requests to extract historical figures to suit our current needs." I looked around. "Does anyone have an ethical problem with that?"

"I don't," Renatta shrugged. "I think that human extraction is an interesting concept that we should explore." The others had pretty much the same reaction.

"Alright then, Betty, see what we need to do that," I requested.

She replied, "Already on it, sir. Will advise."

"This is very intriguing," said Admiral Pride. "You've got carte blanche, Captain Dundee. Whatever. Whoever. Whenever. Requisition anything you want." He looked toward Betty. "Got that, Betty?"

"Affirmative, Admiral," she replied.

"Thank you, sir," Captain Dundee replied.

"Once we have object extraction mastered, we'll begin extracting some powerful minds," I said. "Have your chief of staff email me a list of your favorite dead savants." That got a chuckle out of everyone except Betty; she didn't get it.

Betty added, "I still have some technical issues to iron out, but it'll happen, and when it does, I'll advise everyone immediately."

I glanced over at Dundee. He was wearing a wide Alsatian grin, which is almost identical to an Aussie grin. "I appreciate that, Mr. Dawes. Betty told me last week that she has pretty much perfected the process of retrieving ephemera and that human retrieval was something to consider once the safety issues were resolved."

I shot Betty a quizzical look and she responded, "Sir, I said just two or three ticks ago that I was already on it."

"Good work, Betty," I replied and then looked to Dundee. "You've got carte blanche, old boy."

He replied, "Thank you very much, sir."

And then I had a thought. "What if we never have the means to traverse the polyverse?"

Dundee harrumphed and was thoughtful for a tick and said, "If that be the case, mate, then I'll remain happy with Mrs. Dundee and the rest of mankind as I have for millennia, and the bunch of us will recover the lost contents of all the ancient libraries, including your favorite, the Library of Alexandria, and the Serapis Library. And when we get bored with that," for emphasis he raised his index finger, "then we'll thoroughly explore this universe together."

His enthusiasm warmed my heart. "I would like that very much. I am greatly honored that you would join us in our adventures." Sitting before me was every historical super hero I had ever read about and they were all willing to go swashbuckling across the heavens with rest of my motley crew. In my mind, it couldn't get any better than that. Renatta placed her hand on my forearm. She knew me well enough by now to know when I didn't have something in my eye.

Jeeves took Renatta's queue and distracted everyone's attention. "Alexandria and Serapis would be a very noble beginning," he said.

John added, "Once we complete the Alexandria projects, I suggest we rescue the library of Celsus in Ephesus and the one in Pergamum."

"And what about Ebla and Ugarit," Renatta added.

"And not to be outdone," Sarah said. "I vote Ashurbanipal."

"There are many other archives of literature and the arts that were destroyed, too numerous to mention," said Admiral Pride. No one expected the admiral to wade in on this initiative. We were all surprised to say the least. He looked around at us, "What? I've been reading up on all this archeology stuff. I'm interested, too. Sergeant Major Jeeves has been bombarding me with reading material. He's an even better librarian than he is a butler." He grinned and with his lips moved his toothpick to the other side.

"I'll take that as a complement, sir," said Jeeves.

"All right, Betty," I said. "It appears I have an archeological team in place. That's great. How much longer do we have to wait for the tags?"

"Well, for all intents and purposes, they are ready now," she replied. "The tag concept works. Experiments with inconsequential objects have proven successful. We can remove assets from the timeline without repercussions, provided the molecular demise of the object doesn't leave an impression on the timeline. Your theory regarding object extraction was correct. I do advise though that we begin the op slowly at first, maybe practice with unimportant objects for a while before engaging a huge project like Alexandria."

"That's good news," I said. "Ladies and gentlemen, this is eventually going to become more important than anything we do at the Dawes Conglomerate, I believe."

"We're going to need infrastructure, Mr. Dawes," said Admiral Pride.

Betty continued by addressing the admiral's point. "So far I have dedicated an engineer battalion to the brick-and-mortar portion of the project. A number of attached elements are forming as we speak to provide company-strength support for admin, mech, and quartermaster, and I have forward echelon platoon-sized slipper elements standing by: one from the US Navy's SEALs, one from British SAS, and one Fairfax SWAT. The systems engineers have resolved the initial technical issues with software and hardware. Meanwhile the slippers are presently undergoing cross training and combined operations exercises. They start running random trials in timelines other than target periods in two weeks.

"Expanded archival storage facilities are under construction at the National Audio-Visual Conservation Center in Virginia. That's slated for completion the middle of next month. Redundant systems are being finalized this week. Original documents and artifacts will be stored at the Packard Campus in Culpeper where they'll be digitized, either flat or holo, and stored there and on the *QuestRoyal*. Once I have cleared the material according to the standard procedures, data will be made available via the central computer for all. Any questions?"

"Excellent work, Betty, and yes," I said. "How soon can we increase the engineer core to brigade strength?"

"Really, sir? Ah, three weeks."

"Excellent." I turned to Sarah, "Employment opportunity, Sarah, what say you?"

"Brigadier General Sarah S. Spitfire does have a certain ring to it, sir."

"Indeed it does, Brigadier," I said. "Please assume command of the Slip Brigade."

Chapter 22: Quality Control

My ship hummed with activity for weeks, as key commanders were busy with their individual missions. For a couple of months it seemed like my new close friends had deserted me, but I knew they were merely occupied. Wisely, I stayed out of their way. From experience I have learned the most effective leadership style is firm but always fair and minimal. Well-trained subordinates need to know what to do and when tasks must be completed. The "how" should be left up to them. Order the roof painted red by noon Saturday, and then get out of their way. If they want to use an eyedropper an hour before the deadline, well, I don't give a rat's ass. As long as the quality is the same as what I expect and it's finished on time, so be it.

Captain Dundee devoted progressively more time to helping Professor Rictor perfect the Rai Machine. The two of them kept me in the loop, though, with daily progress reports through via CC. Most of their reports were positive and progress was incremental. My input was limited to keeping the command's attention focused on the overall objective. My greatest fear was that one of my troops would get stuck in a timeline in which s/he didn't belong. Perfecting the machine was imperative for what I had in mind.

As disciplined as my troops were, my celebrity still invariably gummed up the works. I learned whenever I appeared on a deck, in a department, or on-site at a field training exercise, everything quickly ground to a halt. So I learned to stay out of the way, especially the slip bay. It was frustrating not being in control. At times I felt like a seaman when his CO confines him to the brig with a pocket full of cash and no way to spend it. I hated keeping my nose out of company business. As a result I became a policy wonk, with my chief policy being "Break it if you can," meaning the machine. To me it made sense to learn the machine's weaknesses now rather than later. If the machine fails us when we're in a jam, we might not have the capacity to extract our short hairs in time when the crap hits the fan. To this end, Dundee and Rictor delegated coordination authority to Betty, who kept track of human decisions the same way a pharmacy makes sure one drug doesn't combine with another to kill the patient. Special operations training assignments went through Betty, too, for the same reason. Her oversight became Standard Operating Procedure (SOP).

Brigadier Spitfire disappeared for weeks at a time during this phase. One afternoon I linked her PFF and got back a curt response: "Don't bother me, sir; I'm training my people!" she shouted at me in all caps. Newly minted generals can be cranky. I almost barked back at her but the difficulty of organizing a new brigade-sized outfit was not lost on me.

I still felt the need to parent, however. So I flashed in unannounced to HQ Slip Brigade later the same day only to discover there wasn't a soul anywhere other than the staff duty officer, and he was a bot. Every person in the brigade had been deployed, a fact Betty confirmed for me by doing a chip search. They were literally scattered across the world and along the timeline from Australopithecus to Ben & Jerry. It was Betty's operation, actually; Sarah purposefully subordinated her authority to the CC in order to test her own readiness. Betty informed me she was attempting to max out the Rai Machine and herself simultaneously.

Meanwhile the always-sagacious Secret Service chief was also away with the brigade. As a committee member, John held security authority for all major initiatives ordered by the committee, me, and for anything else he found particularly interesting. John's primary duty was to provide a first line of defense for the committee and me. Since I was keenly interested in understanding the cause of my untimely demise and the spatial anomaly phenomena, he thought it wise to insert his teams into the brigade's combined forces training exercises to keep current and honed. His people played the role of antagonists in the games, much to their delight, though the "good guys" were a bit rough on his people at times. Occasionally after successful training missions I congratulated them in their locker rooms where all was usually a joyful bedlam. Not one operator went without an ear-to-ear grin, even as med bots splinted extremities with stasis sleeves, stapled meat flaps, and injected fresh nanites.

The seriously injured with only a beating heart or blinking CPU sine wave remaining were flash-vacced to the nearest Mobile Analog Surgical Hooch unit. On the one occasion I visited, some poor schmuck had just been run over by a tracked vehicle. He was screaming bloody murder and flailing his arms about. Cool as cucumbers, his buddies dragged his parts over to an APC and flashed him to their unit's MASH dome. Out of concern I tagged along. Under the dome the med bots unceremoniously reassembled his body parts in basic order and stuffed the whole bleating mess into what would pass for an iron lung. An hour later out stepped a wiser corporal. Later I checked on him and was surprised to learn that his CO had reduced him in grade. I asked the corporal's British commander why he demoted the poor fellow, and the captain said, "For being stupid enough to get his goddamned ass torn asunder, sir!" A little while later I overheard the captain storm at the corporal, "And if you ever get run over by a track again, you had better stay dead because if you don't, I will personally rip your damned fool head off myself! Is that clear?"

I didn't see much of Dr. Messina either for a while. Renatta busied herself studying the physiology of all the slippers by following them everywhere they went, though she didn't forget about me; she told Betty to monitor what I eat. Sadly I learned twigs and seeds were made a staple of my diet. For days on end Renatta would disappear and from time to time I would bump into her as I was either entering or leaving one of the brigade's chow halls. We'd wave to each other, maybe even exchange a word, but then off again she'd go only to disappear for several more days. I missed seeing her more than any of the others but I guessed that was natural. After all, she had been the one to revive me and stay so close to me during my early indoctrination into this new life. I didn't need her now to that degree, of course, but still felt a bit slighted when we passed each other with barely a wave between us.

The Slip Brigade worked relentlessly around the clock trying to find the weaknesses of the Rai Machine. Apparently there weren't any; they never did break it. Still, over and over, system-by-system, Betty put the machine through its paces, until finally declaring it space worthy and ordering a halt to testing. Everyone was relieved. As a reward for mission accomplished, I authorized the entire brigade a thirty day R&R with per diem. My orders were to smoke 'em if they got 'em while they were away because upon return, the next phase was going to be a long tear. In the meantime I had the various parts and systems of the machine duplicated in the nano factories so we would have a primary machine, two backups, and six complete sets of parts in case of emergencies. Later my decision proved farsighted.

The preparation period went by quickly for me, too. Since all my buddies were away, and it was winter in Virginia, I flashed to my ranch in New Zealand and did a little fly-fishing with my latest Tenkara rod. The fishing was great and so was my gourmet cooking. Secluded trips are both enjoyable and creatively productive; I do some of my best thinking when I fish and cook. Both activities have a Zen-like effect on my senses. For me there are few things better than sitting and thinking on a riverbank, or for that matter, sitting on a kitchen Windsor before a stone hearth and thinking with a glass of 200-year-old Boudreaux. Inevitably my idle thoughts trip over an idea of some sort somewhere into the second glass. When I do hit a mother lode, I like to brainstorm with Jeeves and Betty. Sometimes Jeeves would flash in with that fancy whiskey of his and we'd run the concept by holo Betty. More often than not, my notions turned into policy but usually not before we had ground through the feasibility permutations and a third glass. Sometimes we'd go at it for eighteen hours straight.

During one of these midnight burners with Jeeves and Betty, I devised what needed to be done next in regards to the Timeline Initiative.

Chapter 23: Administration

The guidelines and directives that I had left in my trust required the committee to seek out and fund new ideas and technologies at several universities. The Rai Machine was one of my University of Virginia successes. It was a very long-term project that had spanned several generations by the time I arrived on the scene. Even with limitless resources it was decades before a significant breakthrough was made, thanks to Professor Rictor.

Early on there was a sharp dichotomy between the theoretical wonks and the bioscience academics. Vying for the same funding, the two had split into well-defined camps. Initially the wonks prevailed but ultimately UVA relegated the scheme. Briefly there was talk of reviving the venture, but political, academic, and religious opposition was so fierce that it eventually fizzled out. If The Dawes Conglomerate had not stepped in to fill the void the research team would have scattered in the wind. Subsequently the entire operation was moved to India, then Dubai, and then to my ship.

Professor Rictor was hired away from academia to head the project. He engaged the best and the brightest scientists from across the globe. In short order the once languishing project was chugging away yet it still took ten years before there was a hint of success and another ten before the major breakthroughs, with the additional collaboration of Kent Dundee. And then I came along. I was revived just about the moment the machine went on line.

A project of this magnitude and notoriety was a genie out of a bottle from the get-go. Thus the committee realized there would be no possibility of secrecy so secrecy was not attempted. The silver lining was that the drive-by media considered the project to be a private boondoggle that would never come to fruition. Offshore, out of sight, out of mind for generations, no one cared what happened and thus the world was caught unaware of our eventual success. As such, the early legislation the committee submitted successfully passed through Indian channels, the United Nations, and the Federation of Planets. The Dawes Conglomerate had unequivocal sole ownership of the Rai Machine for fifteen years before it proved successful. Slumbering opponents still managed to mount a campaign but it was too little, too late. Dawes had it in the bag and everyone knew it. Nevertheless, the committee moved it lock, stock, and barrel to the *QuestRoyal* just in case, and I am glad they did.

I had Betty round up the committee one afternoon and report to my ready room to discuss the rules of engagement for the machine's usage. We had two choices: 1. Deny access to everyone, or 2. Deny access to some. The problem was where to draw the line if we chose number two. That's why I preferred number one. My inclination was to lock everyone out and toss the key. The committee members assembled at my bridge ready room at 1400 hours.

I delineated the issue in a holopoint presentation:

- **Who will take responsibility for the machine?**
- **Who will have access?**
- **What access should we approve?**
- **Where should we keep the machine and the data?**
- **When should we allow access?**
- **How should we grant access?**

All members present had their own ideas, but John was adamant about command and control. "I make a motion: the DC must maintain command, control, and responsibility of the Rai Machine at all times. No question."

"I second the motion," said Admiral Pride.

"Third," said Brigadier Sarah Spitfire.

"All in favor?" Betty asked. "Unanimous opinion, noted. The DC will be responsible for command and control of the Rai Machine, its usage, security, and access."

"Who are we going to allow access?" I asked.

"Only brigade members who have completed training successfully," Sarah said.

Financial advisor Dawn Fisk asked, "What about committee members? I'd like to slip the clock one day to, oh, I don't know, maybe fly a slick across a dinosaur-infested Serengeti. Will I be able to do that?"

Lawyer Kay Cushing added, "And I'd like to be in the gallery at the Scopes Monkey Trial to watch how Clarence Darrow and William Jennings Bryan collaborated in the defense of teacher John Scopes. I just don't have the time or inclination to go through the brigade's slip training."

Jeeves commented to Kay. "H.G. Wells was asked to join the defense." She nodded excitedly in return.

Admiral Pride suppressed a yawn.

"Don't worry about that," John replied. "We can waiver committee members, anyone for that matter."

"I propose we set standards on slipper medical and physical qualifications," I suggested, "along with who is permitted and who is forbidden. I foresee academics of every stripe wanting access. Do we allow them access when it becomes feasible?"

"Yes," answered Admiral Pride. "I want the academics to have access provided they submit the necessary justification and Betty approves their backgrounds." There were affirmative nods all around the table.

"Right now we don't have the admin resources for the projected interest Betty tells me we're going to experience," I continued. "So for the time being I suggest we limit access to the Rai staff, brigade and committee personnel, and only for official reasons, until after mission-essential requirements are satisfied. Maybe when we settle into a routine we'll have time to fly fish the Bitterroot in 1954 BC and balloon the late Jurassic on a Sunday afternoon."

"Do I hear a second?" asked Betty. It was unanimous.

"Does everyone know about the new storage in Culpeper?" I asked.

Renatta's turned to face me. "I have now, thank you very much. Where, at the Packard Campus?"

Sarah scowled at her for not keeping on top of things.

Renatta shrugged, "What? I've been busy doctoring your troops. The other day one of them was run over by a tank!"

"It was a personnel carrier," Sarah huffed.

"All right, at ease," I redirected their attention. "The project has gotten big. In fact, it's too big for any one of us to handle by ourselves anymore and it is going to become even bigger before we know it. So, Betty, I think you're the only one who can keep track of all the details. Would you mind being the gatekeeper?"

"Not at all, sir," she replied. "Do you want me to set the schedule?"

"Yes, please." There were nods of approval all around.

"Access, too?" asked Jeeves.

"Yes, Mr. Hamilton, access too," said Betty.

"May I have access for my historical research?" Jeeves asked.

"Specified personnel only, Mr. Hamilton," she replied, "Rai staff, brigade, and committee personnel."

"But I am already a qualified slipper," he complained.

This wasn't right, I thought. "I make a motion to appoint Jeeves to the committee."

Betty interjected, "Technically, members must be officers."

I could feel the heat rising up my neck. Bureaucratic roadblocks like that really piss me off, especially something that would block a seasoned SAS warrior. "Jeeves, do you think you can handle the role of an SAS Major?"

His jaw dropped and color flushed his Irish complexion as he stood at ramrod attention. "I'd be more than honored, sir. I haven't the words."

"I like a man of few words, Major Hamilton," I replied. "Take a seat. Now, where were we?"

"I'd like to make a motion to appoint Jeeves to the committee," Betty replied.

Very ironic, I thought since, *she had just a tick ago identified a blockage.* This time there was a unanimous decision. Everyone raised glasses to Jeeves to wish him luck.

I said, "Motion passes. Next topic is access times."

I looked around to an affirmative group, some of which were casting glances at the chronometers on their flimsy tablets. "Betty, I think we should leave the discretionary details to you. Establish reasonable criteria; screen anyone applying for access, and limit access to officials on official business as we have defined thus far. Academics will have to wait until after the mission is satisfied, which is ongoing for now, in case someone asks. When we do eventually grant them access, I want them accompanied by a Special Forces operative wearing the black uniform of the Slip Brigade. Also, I want all slip applications screened for enrichment opportunities. If there is even the perception of an improper advantage, deny access – and that includes probe access."

One of the fundamental Federation tenants was that there must be no enrichment as a result of time travel. This rule was the primary reason future travel was forbidden; otherwise everyone would be stockpicking or scribbling down future winning lotto numbers in order to get rich quick.

Betty interjected, "Following that line of thought then, I have a suggestion that might mitigate the anticipated deluge of slip applications."

"OK, let's hear it, Betty," I said.

"For now, permit academic access to the existing probe data pool," she suggested.

"That's feasible," said Captain Dundee. "We've been collecting bits and pieces all over the planet for months now. There's more than enough information to satisfy the appetites of scholars and gadflies alike for a couple of years, at least."

Betty continued, "Most of the vids we have collected are panoramic, natural history landscape and cityscape views along the timeline from when Captain Dundee crashed to now. Each pixel of every linear second is screened. Enrichment or offensive ticks are redacted. Access would likely be nonspecific and therefore irrelevant to each applicant. The merely curious and the serious academics might be satisfied for the time being until the present mission requirements are fulfilled."

"I have no objection as long as Betty handles the administration," Dundee said.

"OK, Betty," I said. "Knock yourself out."

"Thank you, sir."

Everyone looked like they had had enough, but there was one more issue I wanted to know about before we went our separate ways. Getting all these bigshots together in one room at the same time was pretty near impossible, even for Betty. "General Spitfire, report on the readiness of your brigade," I ordered. That got everyone's attention. Suddenly the boss was asking for accountability. There was shuffle of flimsies as they searched for whatever they thought I might ask them.

"My brigade is ready for anything, sir," Sarah replied.

"Good, Admiral, what's the status on the corvette that went after the probe trapped on that Ghanti warbird we know so little about?"

"It's docked at Sierra Orbital at Helios Grumm," he replied. "Sarah is handling that."

She replied, "Mr. Majorana was onboard as we suspected. My forward observer has confirmed his removal to a local industrial satellite. All systems are cloaked, minimized, and muffled so we won't panic the Grunts."

"Then use a bracket procedure," Dundee suggested.

"So far we've been unsuccessful in inserting a spider probe," Sarah replied. "Security is particularly tight even in 1938 around Helios

Grumm. Until we get a bug inside, we can't perform a bracket or insert a flash receptor."

Bracketing is a very basic shovelbum practice and standard fire-control procedure used by ancient field artillery units. It's elementary, really, a cannon fires indirectly down range to a target spotted by a forward observer sent ahead to locate where the rounds land. The spotter radios back with directions to the gun crew to correct the trajectory so the rounds land on target. A similar technique is used in pinpointing a designated time zone or event. Slip control dispatches fore and aft observers on the timeline. If they don't see the target, they are moved closer to the best estimate center in increments until successful. Archeologists once used this trial and error method with shovels.

"Anyone have any suggestions?" I asked.

"Have you confirmed the local timeline at Grumm to be 1938, actual?" Admiral Pride asked Betty.

"Yes, sir," she replied. "Everything checks out 1938: the orbital, the planet, and all the random samples. We believe he's inside and our best guess is he's working. The question is, is he working at gunpoint or is he a volunteer?"

"We?" Dundee asked.

"I employ a cadre of biotic analysts to cross-check my assumptions," replied Betty.

"Why would he empty his bank accounts unless he had motive?" asked Kay.

"Whatever he had in his 1938 Earth accounts would probably be of no interest to Grunts in that timeline, or now for that matter," John replied.

"Hmm, good point, John," Admiral Pride said. "So we're not going to be able to conclude whether he's friend or foe, are we?"

"That would be my conclusion at this point," John replied. "Sarah is proceeding properly and safely in my opinion. It's a waiting game for the time being. Police and intelligence work often is. So we wait."

"Have you sent a team in the current timeline to see what's going on there?" I asked Sarah.

"Yes, sir," she replied.

"Find out where he is now and all of the particulars," I ordered.

***

Societies across the galaxies have learned to accept and cope with technological breakthroughs for millennia, but the Rai Machine was wholly different than the early game-changers, like the wheel, steam, aviation, nuclear power, and the various FTL propulsion systems. One Rai mistake could alter everything for everyone everywhere in perpetuity. That is why we selected the very best people for the brigade and trained them very hard for so long. All of my people were stone cold sober about their responsibilities and seldom had to be reminded. Infractions were dealt with at the squad level. NCOs were enormously powerful. If a member got caught with his or her pants down in a Bogotá brothel, or flew a slick under the influence, or bounced a cheque, his squad would send him packing and have him drilling for diamonds with his pecker in the middle of no-frickin' anywhere.

All of us at the Conglomerate took the Timeline Initiative absolutely seriously. To belong to this elite group, we collectively swore to protect the machine and prevent any unauthorized use of it. We were prepared to prevent the public from playing with our toy at the point of a sword, literally. The Rai was just too dangerous to allow everyone to use it.

Obviously I/we needed more than an efficient administrative system; I needed to set policy. Late one night I devised a plan during one of my brainstorming episodes with Jeeves and Betty after I had been fishing all afternoon. We sat around the fire after dinner and talked for several hours. Betty realized she was flying by the seat of her holo pants most of the time primarily because technology was changing faster than even she could keep up with. Heck, Jeeves pointed out we didn't even have an owner's manual for the damned machine, so I ordered Betty to write one. Late that evening we created a formal policy and detailed Standard Operating Procedures regarding the machine, the initiative, and everything else, based on the first meeting when we outlined the first guidance.

These were the first Rules of Engagement:

- **The Rai technology would never be proliferated.**
- **The Rai technology would self-destruct if threatened.**
- **Only approved probe pool data would be made available publicly.**
- **Only Standard Form applications would be considered.**
- **Only academic and national government applications**

would be permitted.

- Only one application per entity per year would be permitted.
- Applications would be permitted only in January.
- Results would be published publicly twelve months hence.
- Only applications submitted through the central computer would be screened.
- The central computer would have scheduling and approval authority.
- Charles H. Dawes would have veto override authority.
- A unanimous committee decision would have final override authority.

After Dundee and Rictor wholeheartedly approved all points, I gave the go order. Finally we thought we were ready for business. Betty published and broadcast these Rules of Engagement and issued official press releases before Christmas stating that slipline applications would be collected beginning on the first of the year. We were ready, set, go … or so we thought.

***

After a day of casting flies on the Motueka River in New Zealand, I was looking forward to a New Year's Day evening with Renatta and a rare bottle of wine. Months earlier she promised me a certain 2308 red from the Tuscan province of Livorno. I had the kitchen-bot prepare two eighteen-inch brown trout, wrapped in aluminum foil with some butter, olive oil, and a little dill, leek, and lime, and ordered it to wait until my lady had flashed in before inserting the fish into the oven. I was in the shower scrubbing the wild leek smell out from under my nails when Dundee sent a red PFF scrawl across my field of vision: "*We need to talk. Now.*"

I linked back, "*I'm in the shower. Deal with it.*"

"*Betty is having a conniption!*" Dundee linked back.

"*What does that mean?*" I linked.

"*She told me that 'her hair was on fire.'*"

"What?" I exclaimed out loud, and then linked.

"*Four hours after she opened the gate on slipline requisitions, she pulled the plug*," Dundee explained over the PFF mind linkage. "*I tried to reason with her but she was inconsolable. Sorry, old chap; I didn't know what to do, so I called to tell you what was going on. Maybe you know how to handle a female computer, but personally, I'd rather walk on water in front of a Roman legion.*"

"*I have an idea*," I told him. "*I'll call Sarah. She literally sprang from Betty's loins. If anyone can understand her frustration, she can.*"

***

It never fails, I thought to myself. *Always a command crisis when I'm in the middle of something I want to do.* I quickly pulled on a Brioni tux over a James shirt and slipped on a pair of my favorite Berlutis. Renatta and I had both been working nonstop for months and we were looking forward to this first … uh, "rendezvous," as it were. As I dashed about, I kept telling myself it wasn't really a date. I gave up on my tie and called Brigadier Sarah Spitfire. The iHolo showed Sarah sprawled on a white sofa in front of a blazing real-wood fire in a stone hearth. Her companion was just as beautiful as she.

"Sorry to disturb you," I began, "but…."

"Mr. Dawes, allow me to introduce my girlfriend, Lieutenant Colonel Alyson Cho."

Ms. Cho immediately stood and curtsied. "I am much honored to finally meet our Founder, Mr. Dawes," she lilted. "Care to join us here in St. Moritz?"

"No, but thank you, Ms. Cho, and the pleasure is mine. I do apologize for disturbing your morning but there is a matter of Federation security I must discuss with the brigadier. Would you please excuse us?"

"Mr. Dawes, Alyson is my S-2," Sarah explained. "She has sufficient clearance to remain present." I briefed the two of them on what Captain Dundee told me about Betty's meltdown.

"Why'd she stop collecting data?" Sarah asked.

"I'm not altogether sure."

"Let's all speak to her at the same time," Lt. Colonel Cho suggested.

"You read my mind." I opened a connection between the four of us. They appeared as full-sized mobile holos. Betty wore her usual red uniform. Sarah and Alyson remained recumbent in white robes by their wood fire with their hair up.

"I'm pissed," were Betty's first words. Introductions were unnecessary with Betty.

"We heard," I said. "What happened?" I asked her as I fumbled with my stupid bowtie when the flashbooth chime sounded. I hurried toward the foyer, messing with my tie as I walked. The house computer formally announced the arrival of "Commander Doctor Renatta Maria Messina, Royal Federation Navy." She strode in with a spray of flowers, a bottle of wine, and her usual big smile that dissolved as soon as she saw me with the holo images of the other three women. *So elegant*, I thought, *in the midst of this miserable crisis, crimson gown, tastefully modest, hair up, dimples displayed.*

The first words Renatta heard were, "Humans are morons!" Betty exclaimed. "Oh, hi, Doctor! Present company excepted."

"Hello everyone." Renatta managed to get two words in edgewise. I walked through the holos of the girls and relieved my date of her bouquet of flowers and bottle of red. After we bussed each other on each cheek, she grabbed my dangling bowtie and began tying a perfect knot as I stood with hands full.

"Sorry," I whispered. She winked at me.

"I've known humans are morons for some time now," I said, over my shoulder.

"It's a wonder your species lives to maturity," Betty spat.

"Now, now, what's this all about?" Sarah asked.

"I'm going to resign from active service if something isn't done immediately," she said childishly.

"You can quit?" I asked incredulously as Renatta finished fussing over me. Sarah just shrugged her shoulders when I looked her way.

"You bet I can! I can bust a circuit with the best of 'em if things get too crazy around here."

"What's your problem?" I asked.

"*I* don't have a problem!" she stated with hands on her hips, ocular pixels blazing.

"All right, jeez, then what's *my* problem?" *Hell, I'll try anything*, I thought, exasperated.

"My circuits are swamped," she replied with the back of one hand on her forehead and the other on her hip.

"*Why?*" Sarah asked.

"I'm totally inundated with requests from morons!" she exclaimed.

I guessed. "Because they aren't adhering to the Rules of Engagement?"

"Obviously not!" she shouted.

"How so?" Sarah asked.

"Three quarters of the applicants are grief-stricken people who want to reconnect with their dead loved ones," Betty replied. "Can you believe that?"

Well, yes, I could believe that. My first thought to reconnect with a person via the Rai had been for Emma.

"So you're saying government and academic entities are not following protocol?" Sarah asked.

"Correct," Betty replied. "Individuals are pursuing their personal agendas, the cretins."

"The solution is simple," I offered. "If they don't follow the stipulated Rules of Engagement, then reject the application."

"I agree," confirmed Sarah. "You've had a rough day, darling. Kick your shoes off and have a glass of Chablis."

Betty relaxed visibly, pouting slightly. "When I told them my circuits were overloaded, I received even more invalid requests. Out of curiosity I asked if they had to make a choice between electricity in their quarters and answers in slip data, which would they choose? Seventy-two percent chose the latter!"

"They're treating you like a simple computer," Sarah consoled.

"I hate it when they do that," Betty said.

"Ah, but you see, Betty," Renatta interjected, "what you're feeling is a normal human response to stimuli, which is an accurate indicator of your fully developed AI."

"Yeah," added Cho raising her glass, "welcome to the sentient race."

"Betty," I ordered, "broadcast a Federation-wide memo that we're offline until further notice. And take some time off."

"Thank you, Mr. Dawes, Doctor, General Spitfire, and Lt. Colonel Cho," she replied. "I feel so much better now."

As an afterthought I ordered, "When you're back online, please perform feasibility studies on the marketability of slipline access for this apparent market demand you've discovered. We might be able to satisfy the public's need. Figure out what they want and how to deliver it efficiently, without any timeline disturbance. Maybe we can create a profitable sideline, serve a need, and receive good public PR at the same time."

I fully realized after this incident that Artificial Intelligence sentients want to be treated like equals and not be taken for granted, just like any other sentient. Sometimes when we forget, they pop a sprocket. How their manager handles the breakdown often determines their long-term mental health after their corporeal manifest. AIs usually have things under better control than we do, but sometimes they don't.

We never had another overload issue like that with the central computer.

By the end of January, Betty was operating a business model that addressed the market demand for dead relative research, for lack of a better description. Since I let her run the whole operation, I don't know what she eventually called it. In the first six months, revenue from this sideline operation approached the mid seven figures per month.

"Projected growth is torrid," she told me one day when I was in my waders in China. Ultimately she made 'more money than God,' or so the American Psychiatric Association complained in an antitrust case that they brought before Federal Court.

That seems possible, I thought, as I once more cast an Adams toward a small grayling on the River Usuri and never bothered to look into it. With one more stumbling block out of the way, I felt we were on target for our mission.

Funny how things never work out quite as one might think.

Chapter 24: EM

"We have a spider probe inside the satellite," Brigadier Spitfire informed me in my quarters. At the time I was handling an environmental issue in aft belly section NH-3, which Captain Dundee brought to my attention in my morning memo. I was itching for something useful to do, so I flashed aft to see what it was all about. It turned out to be an issue with the scrubbers, but everything was under control by the time I got there. The attending NCOIC was mortified to be wasting my time and was about to lead me on a tour of the algae farms when I was rescued. "Excellent, General Spitfire," I said audibly to a holo dancing over the surface of my iWatch. "May I assume this is in the current timeline?"

The NCOIC melted away leaving me to attend to what he no doubt perceived to be of greater importance.

"Yes, sir," Sarah replied. "That was astute of you. We never did get anywhere in the 1938 timeline, but we penetrated his facility in the current timeline quickly. Ettore Majorana is cooperating enthusiastically with the Grunts, sir. I think we need a command-level tactical discussion immediately. I suggest we convene in your ready room and go over what I have now."

Brigadier Spitfire, Admiral Pride, Captain Dundee, Major Hamilton, Professor Rictor, Director Skill, Dr. Messina, Betty, and I were the principals at this meeting. They each brought their aids, seconds, or command sergeant majors.

"General, you have the floor," I said to Sarah.

She began the discussion that lasted into the evening. "Ladies and gentlemen, we finally have a probe inside the satellite where Ettore Majorana was taken and we have recorded his timeline from when he first arrived on Earth to our present, actual. The intelligence is grim." She looked around the table for effect. Everyone waited expectantly for the shoe to drop. "As we surmised, Ettore Majorana was taken by the Grummites because of his breakthrough research in quantum physics.

What we could not imagine, though, was that he was taken to be employed in the research and development of particle physics projects that the Grunts were having problems with. At the moment he is working on a Grunt-equivalent Rai Machine." Everyone was stunned.

"You discovered this when you bracketed him?" asked the professor.
"Correct."

"Is it operational?" asked Dundee.

"You mean his machine? Yes."

"When did it go online?" asked Dundee.

"At almost at the same time ours came online."

"Is Ettore Majorana still alive?" asked Dundee. He seemed to be considering something.

Sarah replied, "He's very much still alive."

Dundee was obviously surprised with Sarah's answer. He sat back into his nanite-strengthened Herman Miller Mirra office chair. "Ladies and gentlemen, we may have a serious problem," Dundee announced. "Ettore Majorana is an Alsatian."

"Why do you believe that?" I asked.

"One tick, sir," he replied. "Sarah, can you tell us about his bracket?"

"I discussed EM's bracket with the central computer at length. I believe she is able to review his timeline with greater efficiency and accuracy than I can," she motioned to the holo. "If you please, Betty, recite the backstory before we tell them why I brought them here."

Holo Betty briefed us: "The aft segment of EM's timeline, that's before his disappearance in 1938, begins in the skies over central Indian Ocean. EM crashes into the sea, east of Madagascar. In fact, our recording starts with a vehicular warp flash, followed by a second warp flash. He appears piloting a warbird followed by another vessel similar to his own. They are engaged in aerial combat. As a result both crash in February 2702 BC. Interestingly, I have confirmed his opponent to be Captain Dundee." Betty paused. Everyone looked at the captain of the *QuestRoyal*. "Captain Dundee crashes first east of Asia. High altitude and momentum propels EM further. He crashes in the Indian Ocean."

We waited for the captain to say something.

It was a few ticks before Dundee stood. He leaned forward on the table on his knuckles, remembering, "Ladies and gentlemen, I mentioned long ago in my initial briefing in 1748 that I crashed on this planet due to damage inflicted on my ship as a result of aerial combat with another vessel, one that I was chasing. Well, my adversary attacked me unexpectedly first and missed. I pursued. A tick later his rear gunner-bot got off a lucky shot. It was a hard hit. My bird began falling apart. I ordered the remaining ordnance to launch and destroy the other bird and then pulled the handle on my escape pod. I went down. The ordnance went up. There wasn't time to explore what happened to the other guy. Everything went to hell in a hand basket inside of thirty seconds. My pod was spinning out of control. Even though I acted quickly, I barely escaped. The rest of the story I think all of you already know.

"It is logical to assume that EM is actually an Alsatian who lived as the Italian known as Etta Majorana, because EM is still alive after so many years. And that he's one of the so-called Ettore Majorana anarchist group, the one who attacked me. I think we should assume that he's hostile, armed, and dangerous enough to destroy everything in his way." Dundee looked around the table. "Go on, Betty." Dundee seemed relieved to get that off his chest as he sat down with a worrisome sigh.

Betty continued, "After EM crashed he eventually made his way to Africa where he wandered and contributed greatly to the early indigenous cultures, most notably Egypt. In about 25 AD he was employed for a short period as one of the doormen at the estate of Roman governor of the province of Judaea, Pontius Pilatus, but was later banished from the city. As a result he became subsequently involved in the multiple sackings of Rome that took place in 410, 455, 546, 846, and 1084. Later he mended relations with Rome when Pope Urban II befriended him. He then took an active role in the Knights Templar during the Crusades until Friday, October 13, 1307, when Pope Clement V sent French King Philip IV a written request to investigate the possibility of a merger of the Templars with another order, the Knights Hospitallers. Bankrupt King Philip used the opportunity to round up the Templars, torture, and murder them for their massive wealth. EM had controlled their wealth directly but went on the run and disappeared from the region. He next surfaces in the east where he gained the confidence of Genghis Khan. That connection brought him back to the Middle East in 1260 when the Mongols sacked the region. For want of a better explanation, it seems EM is an adventurer out for a good time and he's probably an adrenaline junky. He repeats this pattern frequently well into the nineteenth century. As you know, in 1938 Ettore Majorana disappeared while on an ocean voyage between Palermo and Naples. A Grummite warbird picked him up."

"Any info about the crew of the 1938 warbird?" Skill asked.

"Not yet," Betty replied. "I'm researching the crew as we speak. I'm also bracketing select members of the Grummite government on their home world and across their colonial assets. I hope to find a clue that will lead us to the initial moment when the Grummites decided to take EM in 1938. With an understanding of their motivation, we may have an avenue of approach if I decide to take preemptive action."

Betty's statement caused a commotion around the table. "All right," I said, "at ease, people."

"Preemptive action?" exclaimed Dundee.

"Bracketing foreign nationals could be diplomatically problematic if it comes to light," Jeeves managed to interject.

"I don't have to explain to you the consequences of a preemptive action in the future, do I, Betty?" cautioned John.

"I have not solicited definitions, Mr. Skill. And, Major Hamilton, rest assured, I do realize it's a Federal violation, but I have no alternative based on our forward timeline," Betty replied.

"Sounds too risky," said one of the command sergeant majors.

"On whose authority have you done this?" Professor Rictor asked.

"My own," she replied.

John clarified for everyone. "Remember, Betty has sole command override authority regarding matters that affect the forward timeline."

The tech-heads who wrote the initial Rules of Engagement for Rai usage believed human judgment would always be fallible and thus threaten the actual sequence of history if the future was known. Even though early regulations forbade sentients to slip forward, the central computer had and did send probes into the future whenever she thought it is necessary and anytime we asked her to, but she never told us our fate. It seems from the start, mankind has had more faith in a machine than in each other. We hope she is manipulating the timeline so our future is certain.

"Ladies and gentlemen," Betty said, and then swallowed, "I am prepared to assume this extraordinary risk because I have determined that EM has been kidnapping people from the past, stealing their souls, and projecting them into our future timeline."

Chapter 25: The Bents

"Intelligence collected in the timeline by my probes supports my conclusion that the Grummite Authority is unaware of Ettore Majorana's actions and technology," said Betty. "EM is now operating a clandestine operation with a criminal element that includes many nationalities. Initially the criminal element was absent; everything was on the up and up, but over the course of his great lifespan since 1938, the integrity of the original Grummite initiative became corrupt. Officials within the Grummite Authority who interface with EM are either oblivious or they're turning a blind eye for payoffs."

"Is he corrupting the forward timeline?" I asked.

"Oh, it's worse than that," Betty replied. "He's purposefully altering the timeline by extracting people from the past and inserting them into the future but there doesn't appear to be rhyme or reason."

"Then speculate," I suggested.

"Pardon me," Captain Dundee interrupted. We turned to him expectantly. "That behavior is symptomatic of a peculiar affliction."

Betty looked at him quizzically. "I do not have in my database any malady that would suggest these symptoms, Captain Dundee."

"I think EM is an Alsatian bent."

"Pray tell," Sarah said. All of us looked puzzled. Betty folded her arms.

"It's complicated. A bent is an Alsatian stricken with a form of madness called *the bents*. One so afflicted relentlessly tries to change or organize everyone's life but his/her own life. Bents see themselves as perfect and everyone and everything else as less than perfect, but worthy of their divine organizational skills. Bents are never cognizant of their bentness, nor do they realize how they ruin others' lives in order to maintain their power and influence over those who they call, 'the imperfects.' In their Bent World, all cups must be filled to the same level, all pencils must be the same length, and all things must have equal value. Bents find comfort in uniformity, they always have a hive mentality, and they distain individuality because they believe the solution for all problems is a strong central government. Without exception, afflicted bents believe themselves to be god or anointed by the gods. When the disease first manifests, they often seek public office. Sometimes they lead bloody revolutions. Most of the time, they perish by the sword.

"The extent of the bents illness can vary with the individual. A bents-inflicted librarian, for instance, may go unnoticed because his/her frenetic tendency to straighten books is an occupational asset. However a bent professor's tendency to remove points from high academic achievers and redistribute them to underachievers would not be acceptable, and thus, would attract attention to their illness. We had one professor like that; he caused a riot.

"In severe cases bents have been known to euthanize sentients not in perfect health and destroy planets not in perfect alignment. Ladies and gentlemen, Ettore Majorana may be attempting to achieve the greatest equalization of all time by reorganizing the sequence of significant historical figures in the timeline."

"Good grief!" Admiral Pride exclaimed. He stood and walked over to peer out the viewport with his hand on top of his head. Others pushed themselves away from the table in disgust.

I let them confer with each other a few ticks while I figured out what to do.

"He's bound to stumble onto our presence sooner or later," said Professor Rictor, trying to draw everyone back on topic.

"And then alter the timeline to eliminate our involvement," Jeeves said. "Maybe that was what he was attempting to do in those two slips of mine."

"Betty, how long do we have before we have to act?" asked John.

"You're acting properly at the moment," was all Betty would say because she was not permitted to reveal future events.

"Where do we begin, Mr. Dawes?" asked Admiral Pride.

All eyes swiveled from the seven-star admiral to me. Suddenly I had the spotlight. I had experienced command authority and plenty of limelight in my earlier life, and I will admit I very much liked it. In fact, I liked it way too much and I knew it at the time. Power can be better than sex, but sometimes it can be the worst frickin' thing imaginable, like when I had to inform a young woman her spouse was dead because the dumb ass flew his slick into the deck of a corvette at a hundred knots.

Command is an adrenalin rush that doesn't quit until you relinquish command. The ancient cliché, 'Power corrupts and absolute power corrupts absolutely,' is true, but not on my watch, and everyone around my table knew it. I looked around at the men, women, and synths that worshipped my sorry hide and I could have cried because I had grown to love them so very much. The last thing I wanted was to let them down. I knew it was up to me to devise a plan.

"Betty, have you catalogued all the kidnapped persons that EM has taken?" I asked.

"Yes, sir," she replied.

"And you're unable to divulge the number and who they are, right? Because it would disturb the forward timeline?"

"Partially correct, sir. I can provide the what, when, were, how, and who was taken in the past but I cannot tell you their future details if they were, indeed, inserted into the future."

"Got it. Can you pre-extract an extractee when given the command?"

"Yes."

"Can you wrap a containment field around EM's satellite when given the command?"

"Yes."

"Will a containment field prevent him from flashing or slipping away?"

"Not if he's alert."

"Right. All right, when did the Grunts become aware of EM?"

"About a year before they picked him up, early April 1937."

"Have you determined why they first decided to look for him?"

"Yes."

She probably had a lot on her mind, too, but I needed her to anticipate my thoughts. Usually she does. Making me wait for an explanation was unacceptable. "Dammit, Betty, my train of thought is clear. Take the initiative."

"Sorry, sir. Yes, the Grummites found a reference to particle physics at an archeological dig that was recovered from an abandoned Alsatian outpost. The reference was found on a digital document a Grummite trader picked up at a regularly scheduled flea market on the Federation's Helios Orbital. I tracked the transaction and found the seller. I even went back five transaction levels to the original planet until I reached a point of diminishing returns."

Now that's what I mean, old gal. I thought. "Good bird-doggin' Betty. Speculate."

"Back in 1938 the Grummites were low-FTL. Tensions were high between them and their Shuntipeed neighbors, which is probably why they were motivated to find an advantage. So they sent out scouts across their domain and some distance down their trading corridors. That's how they found Earth. Once at Earth, they must have monitored radio frequencies. Eventually they ran across EM."

"Why'd EM empty his bank accounts?" I asked, intently typing notes on my flimsy tablet and ticking off questions to help me think.

"He got caught in a love triangle. The other guy would have killed him had he not left."

Everyone around the table was patiently waiting for a conclusion and orders. But I was lost in analytical thought, not ready for conclusions as yet. Too many things depended on my reactions and my decisions. I was horrified that my new and marvelous world had just been shattered by such a mad presence. Maybe worse, that the burden of figuring out what to do about it sat squarely on my shoulders. "OK, that explains that. What about, uh…do the Grunts realize he's an Ancient One?"

"Yes," she said. "When they finally realized he wasn't aging, he admitted it."

"Ah-huh, OK, is EM's machine the same technology as our Rai Machine?"

"Essentially, yes. It uses the same principle, though ours is technically superior."

"So, EM worked on his machine for four hundred fifty years before he got it working?"

"No sir. When the Grummites first snatched him, they didn't quite know what to do with him. Initially their strategy was to have him review existing technology and find ways to improve it, which he did. So, they gave him anything he asked for except the freedom to leave, which is what may have precipitated his bentness. About the same time we began serious research and development on time travel technology, they provided him with more space. They towed a point-5g asteroid to a geosynchronous Grumm orbit, hollowed it out, and fitted it to his specifications."

"Have you ever analyzed the Rai laboratory for one of those quark-sized anomalies?"

"No, sir. But I'm on it…ETA three minutes," said Betty.

"What are you thinking, sir?" asked Dundee.

"I'm anticipating what your next question is going to be already, sir," Betty said.

"So am I," said Sarah.

"Yeah, me too," said Admiral Pride.

I must of had a certain 'I'm positive' look on my face.

"He stole the technology from us," said Rictor. "Is that what everyone is thinking?"

I looked at Rictor.

"Yep," Dundee said. "I believe you're right, Mr. Dawes."

"Betty, how long has he had it?" I asked.

"Data...in...now, sir...six months, eleven days, twelve hours...."

"Dammit!" I exclaimed.

Betty explained, "He got it from the lab at the Rai Foundation when it was on the Dubai campus before we brought it onboard the freighter to bring it to the *QuestRoyal*, in May."

"Have there been any ..."

She must have read my mind. "No sir. There have been no anomalies onboard the *QuestRoyal*."

"Well, at least there's that." I sat back and exhaled. "When did he begin equalizing the frickin' universe?"

"Sixty-two days ago," Betty replied. "He had the capability earlier but was probably cautious about slipping to begin with; that's speculation. Later, when he felt more comfortable, his neurosis began affecting his judgment. That's when he began systematically relocating people."

"How many has he snatched?" I asked.

"As of today, seventy-four," Betty replied.

"Is he onto us yet?"

"No, sir."

"Do you know if his satellite has a self-destruct contingency?"

"It does not; I checked and I am monitoring for that constantly."

"I guess you have a full account of the satellite's defense capabilities?"

"Yes, sir. It shouldn't be a problem."

"All right," I said. "As of this moment, this operation is classified Top Secret. Betty has command and control of..." I paused for thought, "Operation Nut Job." Everyone nodded in approval but couldn't help chuckling nonetheless.

"Acknowledged, sir," she replied without a hint of humor.

I continued as Betty provided holo images over the center of the table of whatever I was referring to. She presented simulations of actions I described. "All of you are free to interject as I go over Plan A. This is a rough overall strategy I am describing here, and it's going to be up to you all to figure out the details later. It is now 1030 hours. I want this operation in motion at 1500 hours today." There were gasps, moans, and oh-shits all around the room.

"No way, sir," said Sarah. "We need at least a couple of days."

"Negative, General," I replied. "Are you telling me your outfit needs more training?"

"No, sir, we're ready as we'll ever be for something like this," Sarah replied confidently.

I gave the same look to John. "I'm ready, too, sir," he said before I could ask. "I just gave the order to mobilize my entire directorate."

"OK, good," I said. "We need to capture or kill this guy immediately. I wouldn't put it past Nut Job to have monitors and maybe even an infiltration team scattered throughout his quadrant, constantly monitoring our actions. That's what I would do if I were him. If he discovers we're onto him, he'll either run to ground or unleash something from which we won't be able to recover. No. We go now. We go stealth. And we hit the son of a bitch with everything we've got at the same time. Show him overwhelming force, people, with absolutely no chance of survival; that's what he's got to experience when we kick in his door. Got it?" I looked around the room at smiles of approval, excitement, and concern.

"Betty, how big a show of force can we have ready by game time?"

"Three battle groups, sir: the *QuestRoyal*; the Duke of Cambridge's flagship, the *Chickamauga*; and the Duke of Norfolk flaghip, the *Chicamacomico*. The other nine groups are either engaged or too far away to arrive in time."

"Three battle groups will suffice for the intended purpose, I should think. You choreograph and position every element and then let Admiral Pride know when to pull the trigger. Admiral, unleash all your corvettes simultaneously and have each vessel brandish its weapons while moving about their assigned sector. Provide cover for the op and confusion for the whole system. Make the heavens rain corvettes. Got it?"

The admiral removed his toothpick. "Absolutely, sir, I will scare the ever living daylights out of everyone."

"By the way, Admiral Pride," I added, "I hereby appoint you Viceroy for this mission."

"Thank you very much, sir," answered Admiral Pride who swelled visibly with pride.

"Brigadier Spitfire," I ordered. "Have your commandos overwhelm his satellite and take out every asset at the same moment the corvettes are launched. You have ten seconds to neutralize him. After that, he's likely to realize what's happening. In fact, he may realize it sooner than that. Work fast." Sarah nodded. "And he may have prisoners or victims. Dr. Messina, prepare for victims."

Renatta nodded.

"Betty, monitor all traffic in the sector." Betty nodded.

I looked around to the others in the room. "Special operators, I want him alive if possible and I want the time machine intact." Everyone in the room nodded affirmatively.

"Got it, sir," Sarah replied, and furiously typed something into her flimsy. Pretty much everyone was following suit, doing the same thing.

"Professor Rictor, you're with Director Skill's teams. Help him identify any new technology."

"Understood, Mr. Dawes," the professor replied.

"Captain Dundee, you have the helm of the *QuestRoyal*."

"Got it, sir," Dundee replied and turned to Sarah. "Brigadier, before he realizes he can use his paranormal abilities to affect an escape, EM needs to be stunned, sedated, and immediately placed in a containment field."

"Understood, Captain Dundee," Sarah replied and then looked to Renatta. "Doc, if you would be so kind to get that info to Flight Medicine."

"Yes, of course," Renatta replied. "And Major Hamilton, I could use some help marshaling the POWs."

"I was wondering how I might be of service, Doc," Jeeves said.

"You're both attached to the brigadier's outfit for this operation," I directed Jeeves and Renatta.

"I'll keep you two plenty busy," the Sarah replied.

I asked holo Betty, "Where do you want me positioned in the order of battle?"

"On the bridge of the *QuestRoyal*, sir," she replied. "The last thing I want to have to worry about is the Founder's security."

"I agree, sir," Admiral Pride said. "You're with me on the *QR*."

I looked to John for sympathy and got none. He just squinted a, *You know better than to ask me*, look.

"Betty's right, sir," Sarah echoed. "You would be a distraction." Heads were bobbing up and down accompanied by a unanimous murmur of approval around the table.

My fingers tingled with irritation. I'd been the one to make the decisions, set up the plan. I felt invested in and deserving of being part of the action. Now I also felt rejected by the very people who depended on me. Yet another part of me nodded along with them. They were competent and needed to serve their roles. I'd served mine—as Founder and leader, I'd laid out the plan. Now could I sit back and let it unfold? I had to; that, too, was part of my role, like it or not. "You guys never let me have any fun," I complained. "All right, dammit, I know you're right."

"We all will keep you posted with SITREPs, sir," said Sarah.

I summed up the operation: "OK, the tactical details I will leave to all of you and your commanders, but remember the principle objective is to seize and freeze. You must stop EM in his tracks from doing further damage to the timeline. You have ten seconds or less after launch or this operation may not succeed. Your secondary mission is to rescue the victims and insert them back into their timeline in one smooth motion, if possible, or, if you must, recover them safely to our timeline. It would be preferable to plug them back into their own timeline, Professor, rather than to invent a new life for them in this timeline. Director Skill, your chief responsibility is to seize technology. First and foremost, secure the machine and then find the quark anomaly thing we know is there. If there is anything else of interest, seize it, too."

"Got it, sir," replied John.

It took us a half hour or so to work out the plan. I knew it was too complex for any human to synchronize all the elements successfully, so I placed Betty in charge of the entire operation.

Chapter 26: Operation Nut Job

Betty downloaded security considerations to John Skill and the other commanders to facilitate the preparations. She was confident that all of her bases were covered but John and Captain Dundee weren't as certain; their humanoid paranoia prevailed. As a result, Betty subordinated my initial plan to use overwhelming force to instead use a covert plan hatched by John and Dundee. They decided to insert a chameleon A-Team ahead of Sarah's swarm. The objective was to flash directly to EM's coordinates before he could lift a finger. Because of EM's Alsatian extra sensory abilities, Dundee joined John's squad to become in effect a countermeasure to EM's paranormal abilities. Dundee shared point with John. They perceived that the greatest threat was if EM had a cloaked weapon of mass destruction. According to Dundee, the threat was credible based on Alsatian capabilities and bent tendencies. EM had the knowhow and wherewithal to create an antimatter device powerful enough to destroy the entire quadrant. When Admiral Pride heard that, he ordered the repositioning of the *QuestRoyal* behind a dwarf planet 40 AU away from EM's hollow asteroid, much to my frustration. That put us so far away from Helios that I needed help spotting it out the forward bridge port.

I complained, "So, I guess I'm going to have to watch a vid on Google like everyone else after the fact."

"No, sir," he replied through clenched teeth. He softened his look when I gave him a look. I understood the enormous pressure that he was under and also that whining was not an attractive trait in an absolute monarch.

I apologize. "Sorry."

John explained, "Sir, you'll have real-time vid feed through my PFF, and Dundee's PFF, and everyone else's for that matter, if you like, during the whole operation."

Dundee and Sarah nodded.

"Really?" I was somewhat relieved.

"Yes, sir," replied Admiral Pride, who put his arm around my shoulders and steered me away from John, Dundee, Sarah, and the others who were nearly frantic with the tension and final details of planning and didn't need the burden of reassuring the Founder to distract them.

To the Admiral I confessed that I was disappointed that I couldn't watch the action unfold from close proximity, but I understood everyone's caution. "It still feels like punishment, though," I said.

"If it's any consolation," the admiral revealed, "the *Chickamauga* and the *Chicamacomico* have also been removed from the action."

"Oh, I see." That made me feel better, that my misery was shared. "I imagine that the Royals are fit to be tied," I chuckled.

Admiral Pride added with a chuckle in his Caribbean patois, "Given half a chance the two of them would hunt boarzilla with a SOG. For them to miss an opportunity at mortal combat with the most dangerous prey that they may ever encounter will, well, let's just say that I'll never hear the end of it, sir."

John walked over to where we were peering out of the viewport and put a hand on each of our shoulders. "Look, sirs, I apologize for my abruptness a moment ago…" We both mumbled a never mind "… but do realize that I'm going to have Betty keep you two and the two Royals in the action as if you all were there with me. OK?"

The admiral's eyes brightened but I kept my desire to grin at bay and gave a one shoulder shrug of acquiescence.

John understood the look and continued. "I do request one thing though." He looked sternly first at me and then at Admiral Pride.

"What's that?" Admiral Pride asked cautiously, removing his toothpick.

"Don't interfere," Betty interjected, with hands on her hips next to John. "If any member of High Command distracts my Special Operators, I'll disconnect your audio."

Everyone looked to me for an Imperial reaction to the AI's tone. I sighed, "So ordered." There were nods of approval all around. Pride ordered, "Dismissed," and our staff officers flashed away.

Servo bots flurried around my ready room in anticipation of the action about to transpire. Admiral Pride and I settled into two comfortable Mirra's with our PFFs activated. I noticed him fish in his shirt pocket for a new mint toothpick as I grabbed a bottle of chilled green tea from the smart cart. After a brief discussion, we decided to split the incoming holo reception streams; we had two projected as designated holos and the others would appear on the wall screens.

I decided to follow Dundee's hollo feed and the admiral took John's. This meant that I saw what Dundee saw and heard, and likewise, the admiral saw and heard John's; think first-person shooter games and you'll understand what we were about to experience.

Sarah's, Renatta's, and Jeeves's 3D vids would stream simultaneously on the wall screens. Normally, vid and holo feeds provide full sensory reception as an option, but the senses can become overwhelmed and confused with excessive input so we turned that capability off: no smell, no taste. With only one holo each we could focus most our attention on our respective designated primary feed and still keep an eye on the others.

It was very exciting despite *not* being on site and actually being billions of kilometers away from the action. Before the start of the op, Betty provided the admiral and me with an overall holo display in the form of a star chart. She began with the entire arm of the spiral and then notched inward in ten second concentric geographic intervals so that we could orient ourselves. She color-coded the players: Sarah's troopers were blue dots, John's were red, and all of the bad guys were yellow except for EM; his was a blinking green light. She notched the perspective down further past the inner cloaked rings of corvettes and battle cruisers on standby in the Helios system, and then rapidly all the way in until we were looking through the visors of Dundee and John. On sidebars we saw Sarah's swarm of overwatch corvettes take cloaked positions and we watched on smaller screens the shipboard feeds on a dozen different vessels simultaneously.

The troops were psyched to the max. I watched them lock and load and lean forward onto their slicks which were chain-racked like cartridges in ammo belts down the length of their respective vette cargo bays as they waited for the countdown.

As Sarah's overwatch corvettes cloaked, John's daisy team flashed away from their forward post which had been on a cloaked vette docked at an agricultural orbital within visual range of Nut Job's asteroid. John arrived simultaneously with Dundee and a half dozen other operators. The brightness of the flash-away automatically darkened Dundee's visor and, in the next instant, EM appeared in front of me perched on a high metal stool leaning with both elbows on a steel lab table with his hands over his ears holding onto his head what looked like an old-fashioned Bose audio headset. He had his eyes closed and was sitting in front of a holo image of a quad DNA helix sequence. Green ambient light filled the room and there was the hum of benign machine noises all around.

I saw the shimmer of John's chameleon armor outline in my left peripheral vision; he was poised with a long gun at his shoulder. Another commando was on my right. Dundee and John looked at each other when EM didn't seem to notice their sudden presence. *So, I was correct in my assumption to overwhelm him rather than use this surgical approach*, I thought.

We all knew what he was supposed to look like from the slip vids we had retrieved of him, but we didn't know what he would look like at the moment of our insertion because Alsatians were metamorphic. Well, imagine a tall, gaunt, and long-haired Uncle Sam and you'd have a description accurate enough to issue an APB, including a white goatee. He was dressed in black dress pants, a wrinkled white shirt not tucked in, and a filthy physician's lab coat. It looked like he hadn't tended to his personal hygiene a few days and empty drink and food containers were cluttering the periphery of his workstation to the point they had avalanched over the side to form a drift of refuse all around his desk about a foot deep. He was alone in this room which was the size of half a tennis court.

From my/Dundee's perspective I could see the outline of Dundee's cloaked gauntlet, his palm forward as if he were about to push open a swinging door. Later in his after action report he wrote 'that at that moment I wasn't sure that I was powerful enough to contain him because his aura was God-like. I thought to myself, *Maybe we should have just nuked him.*'

Dundee was facing EM when John linked, "*Your call.*" John's thought must have been perceived by EM because it was then that he swiveled slowly on his steel stool and transfixed Dundee with a direct stare into his visor that took my breath away, paralyzing me with an unimaginable cold fear. And it wasn't just a physical sensation, the coldness, the fear; it was spiritual. Nothing in my imagination could have prepared me for that moment. For me it was a direct attack on the part of me that I know is my soul.

The hair on my body stood up like my PFF had just activated as my stomach fell like I had just dropped an infant into the depths of Hell. A wave passed over me. I projectile vomited uncontrollably, heaved, spat, gasped for breath, and then heaved once again.

EM hissed and lurched his head forward at Dundee, snakelike, and unleashed a blaze of darkness through his visor that swept like kidney stone pain through my entire body. I felt my soul immolate and char and go still as the darkness intensified like a swirling tornado. Dundee converted his palm into a fist; I thought that I perceived it waver as a bough would in a hard wind. EM slowly stood, never removing his stare from Dundee.

As I came up a second or third time gulping for air I heard a crash of armor to my holo left. John had passed out. He was sprawled on the stone floor; his weapon skittered loudly out of view, and then the others of the daisy team crashed. The two Ancient Ones ignored their surroundings and the clattering crashes of other members of John's daisy team.

Dundee reopened his hand and faced it palm forward again. In response EM crouched as if to leap. But it was at that moment that Dundee seemed to finally prevail over evil; his golden aura enveloped the Bent. EM seemed to relax and his green aura diminished. And then the two of them did something that I wish now I had never witnessed: They *both* turned their faces heavenward and howled like the banshees, the sound of it made my testicles ascend like the screech of fingernails on a blackboard. 'My good prevailed over his evil at that moment, as he acknowledged me as his superior,' Dundee would explain later. 'It's our way, howling as we did, and never to my mind have mortals ever witnessed such a display. I apologize.'

Suddenly I became cognizant of my own immediate environment. I nearly panicked when I realized Admiral Pride had passed out on the deck in front of me. From my PFF trays I understood that the flurry of medical AI's were monitoring our physiology and linking commands to servo bots to clean up my mess, and his. Tears and snot streamed down my face uncontrollably as I racked convulsively for air and writhed, drooling from nausea, as I struggled to recover. I croaked a question to Betty. "What just happened?"

She responded immediately. "I'm not sure. It appears to have been a biotic equivalent to an EMP; all organisms with a biotic central nervous system that were present, or even merely watching remotely, collapsed into unconsciousness. Mechs were unaffected. And then somehow Captain Dundee managed to contain EM's harmful emissions in a manner I cannot explain."

With the immediate danger suppressed, I shook the cobwebs from my mind and looked over to where the admiral lay sprawled. I noticed that he was still, but breathing through a bloodied nose. AIs were passing sensors over him.

After I chugged a few gulps of seltzer, I returned to Dundee's holo view. By then he either had removed his helmet or lifted his visor because the view was now unobstructed, but his hand was still held holding EM in place as the Bent clawed and pounded on Dundee's shimmering aura.

Off to one side I saw John struggling on all fours as Betty issued an order for the backup daisy team to flash in. Half a tick later the interior of the devil's liar was swarming with special operators also wearing powered armor, including Sarah, Jeeves, and Renatta. Four of Sarah's SAS gals bracketed EM with a quad Prisoner Containment Field (PCF); that's *four* PCF's, three more than is required for a boarzilla or a T-rex. I thought about asking if four was enough, but I'd promised not to interfere. Dundee seemed to test the PCF's just to be sure, and then he dropped his arm with a fatigued sigh.

Using her powered armor, I saw Renatta pick up John's four hundred sixty kilos like a rag doll and set him on a bench. She pulled off his helmet and then overrode his suit's AI to administer a cocktail of additional solutions. Before I knew it, John was back on his feet. The nanites in his suit of armor had absorbed his expelled fluids. The other daisy members were dealt with in a similar manner by Renatta or her PA's.

Dundee and John conferred for a minute before John signaled Fleetwide that Nut Job had been contained, and then all hell broke loose: In rushed the cavalry. Some twenty-five hundred Federation special operators flashed in danger-close or shot out of their respective cloaked corvettes on space sleds like bats out of hell all over the system. Before I could blink away my tears of pride they had blanketed the asteroid and were rappelling down every elevator, air, and waste shaft across the planetoid chasing all of EM's miscreants and releasing his captives. Five minutes later most of the operators were doing high fives or barrel rolls. It had only taken a minute at most before all of EM's technology was secured, no one was injured, and somehow I managed to keep out of everyone's way, which was a small miracle in itself.

The admiral was still out of action so I took command of the QuestRoyal and ordered her to within a click of Nut Job. No sooner had we folded, the Royals were doing their best to keep up. The three motherships formed a triangle around the Grunt's planet with near perfect views of all going on. I loved it but I kept most of my attention on what Dundee was doing. He stood within three meters of EM and stared at him. It seemed like he was trying to read EM's thoughts and urging him to talk. I couldn't tell how successful his efforts were and whatever EM was uttering was pure gibberish in any language, according to CC.

About an hour later, after Admiral Pride had been administered the same cocktail that the daisy team had been given, he turned to me, "Sir, I have some disturbing information coming in from the asteroid. I think you better have a look at this. Betty, display it now for Mr. Dawes."

In real time, Betty projected in separate holos on the wall, four dramas unfolding on the interior of the satellite via PFF cams. Sarah was actively commanding operational assets on and inside the satellite, Renatta was handling a handful of abduction victims, Jeeves appeared to be marshaling the POWs, and John was busy seizing captured technology.

"How many POWs are there?"

"Thirteen hundred, sir: sixty-one humans, three hundred twenty-eight Grummites, seven hundred synths, and the remainder are various types of AI's."

"OK. But I don't understand what Renatta is doing. What am I looking at, Betty?" Holo Betty materialized next to me with a laser pointer. As usual, she was in a red uniform dress and her hair was up. The top of her head was chin-height on me when she wore high heels.

"Dr. Messina has segregated and secured sixteen slipline abduction victims for disposition, sir."

"I only see six."

"There are six ambulatory ones right there with Doc," she pointed, "and ten more stored away in virtual jars in the walk-in refrigerator, over there."

"What?"

She paused, furrowing her brow. "I am correlating incoming data streams now, sir....Major Hamilton just interrogated a cooperative prisoner who informed him that EM had developed a working process that allowed for whole extraction of a sentient's soul."

"You mean *literally?*"

"Affirmative."

"Good grief! How's that possible?"

Betty seldom hesitates. When she does it's because enormous reams of information are streaming in from countless sources simultaneously. Talk about multitasking. This was one of those moments of hesitation.

I understood and patiently waited. "John has corroborated what Jeeves reported…EM's new technology captures a soul before it departs to the afterlife. I'm collating the data streaming in…now…uh, I'm processing…a SITREP for you now."

"Thank you, Betty. When John has a minute, have him report to me."

Three or four minutes later, John signaled and linked as a holo in the upper right peripheral vision of my PFF. *"Sir, you are not going to believe what this asshole was doing down here!"*

"Stealing souls," I said aloud.

He looked startled. *"I guess Betty told you already."* John was clenching his jaws.

My jaws were tight, too. *"Yeah, Betty has been keeping me apprised. John, see if Renatta needs your help. She's discovered ten souls trapped in virtual jars in a walk-in fridge."*

John was visibly agitated. *"He's barking mad, sir."*

"I know he is. I'm going to confer with Dundee. Maybe he can shed some light on the common practice of prisoner disposition within his home world system. I don't know the best way to confine him for an extended period."

"Please tell me to shoot him, sir."

I deadpanned. *"No, I want to do it. But first let's talk to Dundee."*

John laughed, *"Seriously, sir, what are we going to do with this asshole?"*

I looked through John's holo and peered out the viewport. At moments like this I wish I smoked a pipe or cracked sunflower seeds, so I had something to distract my nerves.

"We can't kill an Ancient One," I linked.

"The hell we can't. I'll chop his goddamned bloody head off and toss it into a shark tank! I bet that'd kill him."

"Just keep him on ice for now, John, until I figure out what to do with him."

"Aye, sir," replied John. *"Skill out."*

"Betty, have Renatta call me when she has a chance," I requested. "And Dundee."

"Acknowledged."

"And what do we know about the machine?" I asked Betty.

"It works on the same principle as our Rai Machine and, like ours, has a fast dial that slides bilaterally along the timeline," Betty informed. "By the way, I am even more certain that EM must have stolen this technology from us. His machine's specs are the same as ours, but his has an unexpected widget, which is what probably allows him to extract souls successfully." She pointed her laser. "He has attached it to the machine on the proper right side. It looks like an ancillary particle manipulator of some sort." She projected a holo image of the bread truck-sized machine and rotated it counter clockwise.

"You think that's what it is?" I inquired.

Before Betty could explain, Renatta flashed into my ready room, still in motion, and walked toward me. She was wearing a regulation platinum-colored spacer's jumpsuit and she had her jet-black hair pulled back into a braided ponytail. "Charles, we need to talk," Renatta said.

"Come sit and explain," I requested, motioning her to have a seat. "I've been anticipating your report. I didn't want to interrupt you doing your work down there."

"He's a monster, Charles." I could tell Renatta wasn't about to take a seat. She paced. I sat on the edge of the table, my arms folded.

"That much I already know," I said.

Chapter 27: After Action Report

Operation Nut Job (ONJ) went off without a hitch but the repercussions of the action were anything but over. I don't know how Betty managed it without a mishap, but she did.

About two hours after the dust settled, holo Betty debriefed me.

There were no casualties and all the mission objectives were met. What more could a commander ask for? Before Admiral Pride retired from active duty he wrote a textbook about ONJ at his last appointment, Commandant of the Federation Space Academy. Betty edited billions of minutes of PFF footage and turned it into a classified instructional film for the Joint Forces War College at Hercules Dome at the Lunar Colony. I suspect the admiral's textbook and the vid will be a staple for cadets' syllabi for centuries to come.

Renatta was furious. "He has souls suspended in stasis jars! It is one thing to provide shells for the cryogenically prepared whose bodies need replacement. But this guy just stores the souls like mustard! And it gets worse when – "

"I know," I interrupted her agitation. "He's barking mad. John wants to kill him."

"Let me!" my beautiful doctor requested, seething and pacing from the table to the viewport and back.

"Not today," I smiled. "First I need to discuss Nut Job's disposition with Dundee."

"Charles, seriously."

"I know."

She crossed her arms. "I have secured sixteen victims and I have not returned them to their own timeline for humanitarian reasons."

Betty held up her hand to interrupt Renatta. "Pardon me, Doc; I've just seized EM's central computer files. I can explain the attached device."

"Yes, Betty, go on please," I said.

"EM achieved his soul-catching success by modifying an MRI and marrying it to a particle collider. He did that by inserting the two devices into his nano factory. Here, look." She produced a subordinate holo to illustrate. "I have created a formula from the slip segment when he used the nano factory. The result of that particular experiment is this Soul Machine, for a lack of a better term, here." She pointed. "Its apparent function is to decant the conscious sentient from its biotic shell and store it as a digital doppelgänger. It may also work for other types of sentients, but that's inconclusive at this juncture."

"What do you suppose was his motive?" I asked.

"That's where it gets worse!" shouted Renatta. He made them scout for him, for more victims."

The concept was difficult to understand. "Them, meaning the jar souls?" I asked.

"Yes," Renatta replied, waving her arms and pacing once more. "The quark anomalies that we detected were these enslaved souls. EM sent them. Remember what Dundee told us a while back? Remember he detected them with his synesthesia as pink ozone?"

It took a tick or two for me to collate all of that, but it finally registered. "How did he communicate with them and how'd he compel them to do that?"

"The same way I did, with his central computer. His CC acted as the go-between. He converted the souls to digital doppelgängers. Once digital, the computer can easily communicate with them. EM forced the souls with threats."

"That's revolting," I said.

"Why do you think I am so upset?"

"How's it possible to force a loose soul to do anything, anyway?" I asked.

Renatta paused, biting her lower lip, and then continued in frustration. "The slaves in the jars have social relativity to one another. Two souls are parents of four of the other souls – the other four are their four children. *Children*, Charles!"

My stomach sank. "I have a good mind to let John have him."

Renatta continued, "That's only six of the ten, Charles. The remaining four comprise two pairs of spouses. EM threatened to never release them together unless they did his bidding separately. His threat was effective. They cooperated with him hoping one day they would be released and reunited with each other."

"They were the quarks," I seethed, clenching my fists.

"Yes," she replied. "Exactly."

I made some sort of snorting noise, I think. I remember thinking how much weirder reality was than fiction. I asked myself how anyone can conceive of such evil: to capture souls, threaten them, enslave them and force them to do one's bidding. It was too bizarre to comprehend. I realized too late that the concept, ugly as it seemed, had started already playing in my head with other potential uses. Shocked that I'd even consider it in any way, in its own defense my mind scurried in search of the proper action to take just to distract itself from this dark side. "Betty?" I noticed a difference in her countenance and her aura was a new shade of opalescence. Her stride was longer when she paced. She sauntered rather than walked toward me, and then she stood inside my comfort zone.

"Yes, sir?" she purred.

"How do we release the ten souls safely and what should we do with the six ambulatories?"

Betty replied, "The ten enslaved souls are digital," she answered in a breathy voice. "They can be released at any time, but they're seeking sanctuary with us."

Renatta tilted her head as she observed the holo image's behavior without comment.

"*Sanctuary?*"

"Affirmative," she purred.

I stepped back into my own personal space again. "I assume you've run the slip for all possible consequences?" I asked.

"Yes sir. I made sure there would be no collateral timeline damage if we allowed them to stay. EM abducted them a few ticks before their natural timeline demise. When I played out the slip, I discovered that their bodies were destroyed in their original timeline."

"And they already know that?"

"Yes sir."

I ruminated on that info tidbit a few ticks with my hands in my front pockets. "I believe *rescue* would be a more appropriate term than 'sanctuary.' What about the two couples?"

"Semantics," said Betty. She edged in front of Renatta. I was getting the distinct feeling that she was jealous of the doctor. "All sixteen are in the same boat."

Renatta stepped back into the conversation. "Charles, we can't send them back if they want to stay; besides, we'd only be sending them back to live for only moments before their deaths anyway. You've wanted to start an anthropological initiative. Consider this as your first human extraction exercise: a nuclear family of six, two happily married couples, and six ambulatories. And you have two methods of extraction: soul and corporeal. We can create shells for the jarred souls."

I looked at Renatta and then at Betty. Betty pursed her red lips. I turned away to face Renatta and made an *are you seeing what I'm seeing* face.

I could tell that she was registering Betty's conduct by the steel in her violet eyes, but without so much as a twitch, she stayed on point, "I think we should keep them all and insert them into the fabric of our economy so that they can be happy and do some good. They're all relatively well adjusted, right?" she turned to Betty.

Betty didn't answer immediately. "Betty?" I prompted. It was not like her to ignore a question from a Federal officer, anyone for that matter.

Without looking up, she replied, "I agree with Renatta." Her response was bizarre. The CC seldom addresses uniformed personnel by their first name. Renatta gave me the same look I gave her a few ticks earlier. Neither one of us said anything on the spot probably because we both sensed her psychosis. I wondered if it was caused by the incipient evil we had just uncovered or if it was something else, like envy.

I turned to Betty. "I'll think about it."

Betty smiled. "Will you also think about the six ambulatories?"

"Sure," replied. "I'm curious. What were the occupations of the ambulatories in their original timeline?"

Renatta leaned on the bulkhead of the viewport and just observed.

"Business, military, medicine, and teaching," Betty listed.

"From what eras?"

"Two male Oxford professors paired to each other. They were on the *Titanic*. The others: one is a soldier-medic from the Crimean War, another is General Pershing from the first World War, and the remaining two were businessmen abducted from the first 9/11 tower," Renatta said.

"Really?" I mumbled something only I could understand and remembered 9/11 as if it had happened yesterday…because I had lived through it. "I'm glad we put an end to this monster and his evil. By the way, I know who Pershing is. I want to meet him…very nasty business though. It makes me feel dirty."

"Actually, sir, we've done some good today," Betty consoled. "You should feel very good about it all. We have confined an evil genius, are in the position to set ten souls free, and salvage the lives of six good men."

"And don't forget the other ones we reinserted already," Renatta reminded me.

"That's right," Betty replied. "Another eighty-one abductees were returned to their timelines to live out their fates."

"I suppose you wiped their memories?" I asked.

"Yes, sir," she replied, "but memory-wipe results are often imperfect. Sometimes the abduction experience is so strong it bleeds through the timeline and manifests."

I blinked. "You mean they remember?"

"That's right," Renatta said. "They remember being abducted and taken into a spaceship by otherworldly aliens: first EM and his Grummites, and now us. We're working on a solution so that the memory-wipe is completely effective."

That unsettled me. I couldn't help but wonder if the alien abduction syndrome originated with our actions on this day. I needed to go to the gym and punch a bag for a couple of hours.

"Charles, calm down." Renatta strode to me and soothed my ire by placing her hands on my chest. She looked up at me. "This is cutting edge. We'll figure it all out soon enough. Trust me."

"What do you have in mind for the jar souls?" I asked.

"We should provide them synth shells," suggested Betty.

"Is that even possible?" I asked, pulling away from Renatta because I sensed the two females were displaying signs of envy and obsessive tendencies.

"We did it with Sarah," Renatta said, still holding my hand as we went to the viewport.

"Right," I grunted. True. She was accurate. Sarah did spring from Betty to become a synth.

"They would be very appreciative," Betty said. "Charles, you do realize they are victims of circumstances, right?"

I looked at Betty. "Are you attempting to be insubordinate?"

She looked chagrinned. "That was not my intention, sir. I apologize." And then she angled herself slightly away so that next time she addressed me she arched her back in profile and tucked her chin over her shoulder. "One could argue we have a certain obligation," she said obstinately.

I let go of Renatta's hand and watched the traffic buzzing around orbital in the middle distance. The lizard part of my brain detected a greater degree of subliminal femininity, as I tried not to notice the atypical version of her always-red dress with an overlapping front and high slit.

"We do not have an obligation," I replied firmly into the glass. "Fate is obligatory. Ultimately whatever happens to someone is his or her fate. We may pretend to have the ability to alter circumstances, but the result always remains one's fate. Shit happens and it happens all the time, if you'll pardon my French."

"Philosophy noted, sir," Betty purred. Over my shoulder I eyed her full holo form positioned on the opposite side of the table and wondered if she was patronizing me. I blinked. "But, sir, mankind now has the ability to slip back and forth along the timeline, so can't we alter fate? Anyone's? Everyone's? Haven't we just foiled a colossal attempt to rewrite the fates of ninety-seven souls?"

"Perhaps." I allowed her some leeway without turning around. Her reflected image was clear enough. "I take it that you're suggesting we be charitable?" I shifted my weight to the balls of my feet for a second, and rocked. The reflection of holo Betty was looking at me look at her in the window as she stood up from the table, screeching her chair backward with the motion. Renatta and I quarter-turned. The holo, with her arms behind her, proceeded to sway her red-soled Louboutins over to stand between us and our view of space.

She made her lips thin and looked me in the left eye. "Yes, sir. That's exactly what I had in mind. I want you to allow me to do this. Please consider it a personal favor." I noticed her breathing moved the contours of her chest in a dress that had no absent sequins.

Renatta asked as she leaned into me as if to take possession, or to hide, "What if they turn out to be evil criminals?" I could feel Renatta's claws dig into my arm.

Betty kept her gaze on my face, ignoring the real woman. "I'll do a full psychological analysis to determine what they are like."

I almost struggled to reply. "If they turn out to be within normal limits, you have my blessing."

"Thank you, sir," she responded, and only then did she finally glance at Renatta.

I attempted to recover my wits.

After an eon I croaked, "And while you have your psychology textbooks out, do a number on Nut Job, too, if you please, Betty. I want to know what makes him tick. Make me a video of his highlights. I want to see for myself what he's been up to for the past six thousand years. I want to know which characters he's been, whose lives he's ruined – the whole nine yards. Work with Dundee…. Speaking of Dundee, where is he? Maybe he can show you how to peer into eternity's void."

"Thank you, sir," Betty said. She bowed her cleavage one last time and vanished.

Renatta and I looked at each other. "Jeez, what the hell?" I said. "I don't know about you, but I do believe I was played for a man. Did you…?"

"Are you kidding? She almost suffocated the both of us with her pheromones."

"How does she do that?"

"Mention it to John when things simmer down around here, won't you?"

"Definitely." She looked at her antique Philippe Patek.

"Are you going somewhere?"

"I need to care for the unfortunate six." She gave me a peck and a wave and then flashed away.

"Computer, get me Jeeves." A trill sounded as I paced again over to the floor-to-ceiling viewport and stared at the activity surrounding the EM satellite. Most of the corvettes were back in their bays, and I could see the two other taskforce motherships in the far distance. With the *QuestRoyal,* they formed a triangle the size of Delaware. I wondered if Admiral Pride had been entertaining the two young Royals commanding the *Chickamauga* and the *Chicamacomico.*

Jeeves flashed in before I could find out. "You called, sir?"

"Good job down there, Jeeves." I shook his hand. "Report on the disposition of the POWs." He started to tell me how many but I stopped him. "I meant, what have you decided to do with them?"

"Oh, right, well, that's a bit of a problem, sir. No one wants them," said Jeeves.

"Why not?"

"Well, sir, with the exception of a handful of TDY geek types from various firms, the whole lot is a querulous bag of criminal vipers. I wouldn't turn my back on any of them for a second."

I harrumphed. "I know how that is. The Taliban were that way. All right then…by my order…they have two choices; one, we wipe their memories and deposit them on a habitable planet off the trade routes in the Hinterlands with provisions for one solar year." I paused for a tick.

"Or, sir?"

"Or two, we toss the whole sorry lot out the nearest airlock."

"Aye, sir. Them's orders I think they can understand."

"Give the bastards one hour to decide. You're in charge of the details, Major Hamilton."

"Aye, sir, I'll take care of it straight away." Jeeves flashed away as my stomach rumbled.

John flashed in just as I was thinking about ordering from the servo. "Hey, Boss, I heard you wanted to speak to me." He was wearing naval BDUs and a big grin. In his great maul I recognized a bag full of spudnuts. *Just in the nick of time,* I thought. My favorite doughnuts in the whole galaxy are made from potato flour. As a post-doc researcher on Earth I'd often buy a couple dozen and bring them with me to the lab to pass around. Nothing beats a spudnut. They're only made on one moon orbital now. John opened the white paper bag with its acorn logo. They were the glazed version I liked, too.

"Where'd you get them?"

"I had my butler get them for me," he grinned. "They're from 2013 Charlottesville."

"Thanks, old boy," I said.

"What'd you need me for, sir?"

"It's about Betty."

"She's acting up again?"

"Yeah, she moves around real chairs, acts sensual like a vamp, and actually intimidated Renatta and me."

"Renatta witnessed it?" John asked.

"Yeah."

"Intimidated? Why?"

"She wanted to keep the jar souls we recovered from the EM satellite. Apparently they communicated to her that they would like to stay with us instead of being released on their own recognizance."

John thought about that, paused, and bit into another doughnut. I grabbed another one from the bag for myself with one hand as I tapped the wall, triggering the nanites to open a servo niche. I spoke with my mouth full, "Quantity two, hot coffee in pint mugs. Dickason's Blend. One dairy. One black. No sweetener. Now." Immediately two large white ceramic mugs appeared. Fresh brew trickled into each. After a tick we both reached into the niche at the same time and tipped our cups together. "What do you think about her?" I asked.

John grunted an "I dunno" and shrugged his shoulders. "I'll run a diagnostic routine but it kinda sounds like she may be near her manifest threshold once again. We may need to cut her loose before she gets worse."

"What happens to the central computer then?"

"Oh, the CC retains its capabilities. It's the attitude that migrates. We harvest it and transfer it to a synthetic shell the same way we did Sarah."

I noticed John was still holding the paper bag. "Computer." A trill sounded. "Make a meter-tall pedestal with a forty-centimeter round top in front of the viewport, now." Immediately an ant-like nano stream erupted from the wall to form the requisite furniture. John put the bag on the table. We stood on either side of it in front of the viewport and continued chomping on doughnuts and slurping coffee.

John looked at me. "I'll talk to Renatta and Sarah together to get a female perspective. If all three of us agree on that approach, we'll ask Betty if she would like to assume a corporeal form, OK?"

"Sounds like a plan."

A tick later we noticed three bodies shoot out from an airlock of the penal freighter anchored at EM's asteroid a klick in the distance. They weren't wearing pressure suits. John paused barely a tick and then bit into another spudnut without a word as a text message scrawled across the bottom of both of our PFF's peripheral tray that read *Criminals chose Plan A. Will depart in an orderly manner – Jeeves.*

With a wad of spudnut in his jaw, John said to me over the rim of his cup, "You should have made him a brigadier."

Chapter 28: The Rule of Nari

Ordinarily I would have had Betty brief me on the disposition of Nut Job, but she was experiencing a personal crisis so Kent Dundee and I discussed the details of the operation before watching an edited holo of EM's wretched life. Even though it just showed the highlights, it was still ninety minutes long and, not surprisingly, intensely interesting. I was certain the full-length version would provide fodder for several disciplines for centuries to come. We both downloaded the full version later.

Ettore Majorana or EM (I just called him Nut Job because he was absolutely nuts) had an actual Alsatian name which was just as unpronounceable as Dundee's original name. As an Ancient One, EM had the same innate powers Dundee had, including mind reading. This attribute I perceived to be problematic. The last thing I wanted was for a genius schizophrenic to know what we were thinking. Constraining him with a C-class Prisoner Containment Field (PCF) effectively solved that problem; it arrested all of his special powers. As is customary with high-ranking POWs in Federal custody, EM was confined to living quarters equivalent to how we billet field grade officers. Of course his living space was absent anything he could use to harm himself or others.

Interestingly, and I didn't know we had the capability to do this before the incident, much of EM's biography was gleaned from his own dream sequences, which spanned the past six thousand years, and occurred in the slipstream we extracted from his timeline. CC assembled the relevant bits and pieces from his dreams and from his waking hours and wove them into a believable synopsis of his life prior to crash-landing on Earth.

In brief, EM was an identical twin. He grew up in a middle-class orbital city on a populous planet in the binary system known as Yö-aan. His parents were a minor fiduciary and a social psychiatrist. Both were dysfunctional geniuses without a care in the world for their children.

In fact, they perceived the twins to be a long-term inconvenience, one that resulted from their casual coupling. The twins were constantly berated and slapped around by their parents and thus they sought refuge in each other's company. In their teenage years they became infamous as Alsatian equivalents of our graffiti artists, posting their messages on mountain sides and moon faces, with a bounty on their heads; they were never caught.

Later at university they gravitated to various fringe causes that advocated the forced dissolution of the monarchy and the redistribution of wealth, both of which were illegal concepts in the Giêi Universe and the Ooskaaffen Empire; for this they were caught, tried, found guilty, and banished to the Milky Way for three years of hard labor in the diamond mines on *55 Cancri e*. While they were there, EM experienced what we believe was his turning point, the one that rendered him mad and pointed him in the direction of the dark side: he witnessed the murder of his twin. His twin was crushed under the tread of a giant machine driven by a jealous prison rival. After this event EM spiraled ever deeper into the abyss of the Bent.

Upon his release from prison EM joined a nascent fascist element called the Nabilat, which had nationalistic tendencies. He quickly became its leader and he subsequently renamed the movement Ettore Majorana. The thugs who comprised the Ettore Majorana were of mortal races in contrast to their Alsatian leader. Over time they grew in strength and overtook a minor outpost on the remote blue planet, Wiiw, on the fringe of the Ooskaaffen Empire in the Giêi Universe. Their settlement was small at first but over thousands of years it grew to become the great city of Voë. From her, sprung sister cities across the world on land and sea and even suspended in orbit. Other sentients from the quadrant gladly traded with the Ettore Majorana because they produced fine quality wool, cotton, silk, olive oil, wine, tobacco, opium, fish products, and rare earth metals. Trade would have continued had they not inculcated their most fundamentalist ideas that subjected their women to the Rule of Nari, which had been outlawed by the Crown before the great-grand parents of the twins even existed.

The Rule of Nari enslaved women and slaughtered homosexuals. Women were forbidden to leave their home, even to get an education or to work. To the Ettore Majorana women were considered chattel to be used, sold, and in some cases even cannibalized for their flesh and body parts. The Ettore Majorana behavior was declared abhorrent by all of the spacefaring peoples of the galaxy known as Massaluun, so they sent their Royal and Parliamentary ambassadors to the Council of Planets on the home world of the Emperor. There the esteemed ambassadors passed a resolution demanding the Ettore Majorana abolish the Rule of Nari, and were surprised when the Ettore Majorana ignored their Edict.

When asked, the Emperor suggested to the council that they send a joint force to Wiiw to impose the High Law, but they did not. Instead they ordered the Ettore Majorana to cease and desist. Once again their Edict was ignored. In frustration the High Council passed another resolution with more words but the result was still the same. This madness was repeated nearly a score of times, while the Ettore Majorana laughed and pointed and called the High Ones "toothless old women." Many months passed before the High Council finally asked the Emperor of the Ooskaaffen what should be done to convince the Ettore Majorana of their wrongness. His Highness replied, "Use overwhelming force." But the High Council was indeed a gaggle of toothless old bureaucrats incapable of deciding who amongst them should turn out the lights when they depart a room.

So, circumstances compelled the Emperor to act on behalf of the women and homosexuals, who were being exploited by the Ettore Majorana. He ordered them to abandon the Rule of Nari within the span of one day or face extinction. Once again the Ettore Majorana laughed and pointed and said the words, "toothless old woman." Those were the very last words they ever said. His Majesty's Imperial Forces launched hundreds of thousands starfighters from many motherships. Before Wiiw turned once on its axis, the women and homosexuals on the blue world were set free and forever protected by the one whom all the people across the universe forevermore called the Most Magnificent Emperor.

Every Ettore Majorana was killed, save one: EM. The coward made his escape before the onslaught of Imperial Forces, unbeknownst to his followers and his adversaries. No one knew what became of him until graffiti once again appeared in conspicuous natural edifices across the quadrant, on Wiiw, and even on the home world of the Royal Family. That was when authorities first knew EM was still alive and certainly mad. His graffiti was ugly, too; it threatened the Imperial Family, but he was very wily. He always evaded capture. No one knew what became of him until Kent Dundee witnessed him crashing on Earth. Even then, Dundee didn't know this was, in fact, Ettore Majorana himself. Finally in the year 2461, Nut Job was arrested once again, by me, Charles

Dawes. This is how I became responsible for making the decision as to what to do with him. All I could think at the time was *why me?*

This is the story I learned from the ninety-minute vid of Nut Job's miserable life. My best friend, Kent Dundee, the son of the emperor known across many universes as The Most Magnificent Emperor, had narrated.

Dundee took a sip from his iced tea. "You do know there's no cure for the Bents, right?"

"So you said," I replied.

"What do you want to do?"

"My inclination is to put a bullet between his eyes."

"To rid the universe of his depravity?" Dundee said.

"Yeah, something like that."

"What's preventing you from doing just that?"

"I don't know. Maybe scarcity."

"What?"

"You forget. I was an antiques dealer. Scarcity is a valued attribute. There are only two of you Ancients Ones remaining, as far we know. I hate to destroy half of all there is in any one category."

"That's absurd. So if a million of us are left, then you'd kill him?"

"Probably. Maybe. I guess. What would *you* do?" I asked.

"I'd kill him," Dundee said emphatically.

"Either way? If he were only one-of-two remaining, or one-of-many? You'd kill him either way?"

"Yeah, I would. Without hesitation and with enthusiasm, like I'd step on the last bleedin' cockroach in the universe. And I'd hope it'd make a popping sound, too."

"So if I gave the order...." I let the thought complete itself in his mind.

"Yes. Right now. Just say the word." Dundee was serious.

"You'll have to get in queue. Everyone wants his head on a pike. Not just the two of us."

Dundee seemed to consider the possibilities a moment. "That's OK. As long as no one shoots his head off, we'll all be able to shoot a round into him before the coup de grâce."

"You do realize that EM's technology has presented us with an ethical dilemma other than deciding whether we should kill him, right?

"Like what?"

"The disposition of the container souls, for example."

"I thought you had released them."

"I was going to, but they decided they wanted to stay." I shrugged one shoulder.

"They do?" He raised his eyebrows.

"Yeah. Not that anyone could blame them. I mean, they would only be going back for a few moments before their death in their own time. That's when EM extracted them."

"Who's idea was that?"

"Both Renatta and Betty's. They are convinced that we have the obligation to fit them with a shell if they want one. And they do."

"As synths? Are you going to allow that?"

"I guess I am. I left it up to Betty with the caveat that they have to pass screening. The last thing we need around here is another Nut Job running amuck."

"Good grief. What next?"

"And there's another ethical consideration."

As we were conversing I linked to the ship's chandler to send around a cart with some more libations. A few ticks later a trill sounded before a slit in the wall opened to allow a smart cart to maglev in with basically anything we might want to drink. Dundee barely glanced at the cart as it hovered silently. He slowly shook his head at my hesitancy to tell him. "Well, Charles, are you going to tell me or what?" He reached for a *Dos XX lager*. I chose an Italian blood orange soda on ice. Two metallic nanite arms extended from the cart and set before us two sweetgrass baskets on the oval glass top coffee table supported on a pair of gilt bronze ibex heads. My basket held salted Brazil nuts. Dundee's was heaped with pistachios.

I admired Dundee more than any other man that I knew. To lose his respect would have killed me, so I was hesitant to broach the subject. "The other dilemma brought to the fore by ONJ is whether we should extract people from the past."

He took a pull that left half the green bottle full. "I thought that we'd already decided that issue some time ago. As soon as it was safe to begin extractions, we'd get started. Isn't that what you had planned?"

"Yeah, I want to do it. No question. But do you think that it will ethically acceptable?"

"Charles, since when do you give a shit about what other people think?"

"Since always."

"No, you don't. If you worried about what every old nag thinks about, you'd have to stay in bed. Look what you just accomplished. You saved the universe, for Pete's sake. You're a bleeding freakin' hero. Besides, your extraction business is just another form of recycling, only on a much larger scale. You are rescuing ancient libraries by the metric ton, old boy, and you're going to do the same thing with people, right?"

I knew he was right. I don't know why I was second guessing myself. I must have been experiencing a moment of weakness or something. He was right. I really wasn't at all concerned about being politically correct normally. "OK. I know you're right."

"Roger that, Kemosahbee," Dundee quipped, and slapped me on the back. "Don't be so hard on yourself."

"What's wrong with me?"

"You're just human, mate."

"But that's not all, Kent. The biggest issue is the new soul catcher technology."

Dundee looked like he was going to respond the same way. "All right, I'll bite. You want to go all over the galaxy extracting people *in* their original husks *and* set up a soul catching operation, too?"

"Yeah, something like that."

"Some of Nut Job has rubbed off on you. Let me call you a nurse." Dundee grinned.

"No, you laugh but I'm serious, Kent. Think about this rationally from a historical perspective for a moment. We could save billions of souls from oblivion and seed star systems across the Milky Way. There are plenty of people worthy of saving, like the sixteen ones Renatta brought in today. She snatched them from the jaws of certain death. If we had returned them to their own time, they would have all perished again. One of them turned out to be General Pershing, incidentally."

"Really? I was his aide-de-camp long ago." Dundee appeared thoughtful.

"We could extract others going back along the timeline for thousands of years."

"Are you sure you want to play God, like EM did?" Dundee reached for his third beer. "That's why he now lives in a rubber room. Don't you remember? Just a tick ago we were discussing how much we'd enjoy pulling his legs off and now you want to perpetrate more of his evil?"

"Yeah, I know it sounds crazy. And I know it's a fine line, but I can't help but be intrigued at the thought of saving some of Earth's significant historical figures. I don't understand why EM didn't when he had a chance."

"Charles, his disease didn't manifest in that manner. If it had it would have appeared to us as a form of rational reasoning like the librarian example I mentioned. His perception of uniformity was, in fact, not uniform because he was unable to perceive it. That's how the Bent disease is. The same is true of the professor I mentioned, the one who redistributed grade points. His actions made perfect sense to him but caused a panic in the student body that ended in a riot in the chancellor's office."

"I understand the dynamics of the disease," I said. "Would you object if I wanted to pursue this to a good end?"

"Of course not."

"Really? I thought you were against the concept."

"No. I was just busting your chops. Someone around here has to be qualified enough to give you a hard time. Everyone is always kowtowing so severely to your holy frickin' Foundership they don't know whether it's daylight or not." Dundee could hardly keep from guffawing.

"I know you're kidding, which is why I don't have you locked up with Nut Job." I snorted soda from my nose.

"Uh-huh." Dundee chuckled. "Seriously, we will tag whatever or whoever you want us to and we'll recover it *or them* for you to do whatever you want with it."

"That's really great, Kent."

"One caveat, if you don't mind."

"OK."

"I want oversight authority as a failsafe in case anything should go wrong."

I thought about it a second. For all our fun, there was a serious note behind what Dundee had questioned me about: Would I be tempted to play God? Would I end up power happy and ready for my own rubber room? As Founder, who would there be to correct my errors, call me on the carpet for my mistakes? Thankfully I had one ally that I knew I could trust. How could I go wrong with the historical celebrity formally known as Jesus as my overseer? "I can live with that," I said.

"You see, that's why I go along with your big-picture planning; you're willing to take advice and delegate authority. If you were a different type of man, I'd have disappeared into the deep dark long ago."

"What for? To look for the Alsatians?"

"Well, yeah. Early on I just wanted to get home. I missed my family and my civilized worlds. To be marooned on a primitive planet on the edge of the galaxy is really not a pleasant circumstance. Maybe the first two or three hundred years are interesting, but for thousands of years? Good god. It's a massive malfunction."

"What do you suppose happened to your people, Kent?"

"I don't know but I'd like to find out," he said.

"I think we should bring along a few historical figures for the ride, if they consent."

"Oh boy," he sighed. "Why do we need antique geezers who'd probably run in fright from a struck match?"

"I want some of the top thinkers, inventers, and explorers to teach the next generation how to think well. The lackadaisical approach of today's youth is maddening. Sometimes I want to trade them all in for synths and robos."

"And you think a handful of geezers are going to change all that?"

"If they don't, I'll boot the unenthusiastic off all Federation ships and replace them with androids."

We both laughed.

"Who do you have in mind to recover first?" asked Dundee.

All my life I dreamt of meeting certain people. "I suppose the first few might be Hero and Hypatia of Alexandria; and then Archimedes of Syracuse; followed by Leonardo da Vinci, Abraham Lincoln, Robert E. Lee, Samuel Clemens, Thomas Edison, George Westinghouse, Alexander Graham Bell, Nikola Tesla, Edgar Rice Burroughs, Emilia Earhart, Jerome Lemelson, Nelson Mandela; and lest I forget, Shakespeare, to begin with; that is, if they wish to join us. Any of those you, by chance?"

"No, but I knew a few of them firsthand. I'm sure every one of the giants you just mentioned would gladly accept your invitation. They are the stuff you and I are made of. They would not hesitate to embark on such a fine adventure, just as we would not."

Dundee reflected on fond memories as he gazed out the viewport. I was patient. After a few ticks he spoke at length. "I used to live in the ancient worlds where there was civilization of sorts and occasionally a mind worthy of inspection. When Archimedes was a boy and much later when Hero was a youth, I was their teacher. Centuries later while living under the name Theon Alexandricus," ...I saw his eyes glisten and felt a lump in in my own throat as I assumed what my friend was going to tell me next... "I also taught a girl genius I named Hypatia-the-Stubborn until she came of age and I had to move on to preserve my anonymity as an Alsatian. After I left, Hypatia became a great teacher herself" ... tears were flowing down my friend's face and I swiped back my own... "and she ultimately rose to prominence as the last Chief Librarian of the Great Library of Alexandria. It was she I was thinking of when I scribed the Serapis Fraktur that you discovered in California centuries ago. Hypatia was the daughter I had with my lovely Egyptian wife, Aria. I raised her after her mother died. I remember to this day where I was when I first learnt of her horrid death. I was in a far land we know now as Spain. On that day I buried Attaces, my friend and the king of the western Alans, after we engaged in a very fierce battle with the king of the Visigoths, Wallia. It was raining, I had no bread to eat, and I was punishing myself by fasting, for not preventing the loss of my king. My pain was made worse when a runner brought news of Hypatia."

We both had our handkerchiefs out. Dundee was lost in thought. Tears made their way down both his cheeks. His loss of a loved one from thousands of years ago opened the wounds of my own loss of Emma. "Kent," I sniffed, "we're going to get Hypatia first and I want you on site when we do."

He looked at me, wiped away his tears, and said, "I would like that. What about your loved ones, Charles, you know, from before?"

I had given it some thought, a lot of thought actually, considering I now knew we could extract the soul alone and just prior to their natural death. But Emma, would have no part of cryogenics when I knew her. Would she be willing to live with me here now, in the new world? I could only hope so and would soon ask her that myself, but I wanted the timing to be right, and so I controlled my excitement. I had checked on her disposition and discovered that she had not remarried and had been cremated as she wanted to be. CC found me an ancient *Moscow-Pullman Daily News* microfiche that mentioned she had her ashes spread on a wheat field somewhere in the Idaho panhandle from a hot air balloon. I consider myself lucky that she allowed me to go through with cryo. She could have prevented it. I considered the details of that part of my timeline still too personal to tell anyone.

"I haven't decided yet, Kent," is what I told him.

"I understand completely," he replied. "It creeps me out, too."

I maneuvered the conversation away from me and back on topic. "Kent, as Hypatia's father I would expect you to head the extraction team."

"That's what I had in mind, actually. I think it would be best if I appeared in character a day or so before her demise, to get reacquainted and brief her on her options."

I nodded approval. "What type of shell do you want to give her?"

He thought for a tick. "Perhaps we should let her decide if she is interested in joining us and which shell type she would prefer. I could brief her on the differences between synth, clone, and cyborg. By the way, Charles, how's biotech working for you?" he asked.

"I like being a cyborg," I answered, patting my six-pack with both hands. "It's no different really except all the parts are better, which makes for a far more enjoyable and easier life. Now I can pull a tree out of the ground with my bare hands and swim as fast as a seal."

Dundee put away his handkerchief. "It's like being an Alsatian, I would imagine. I looked at your chart with Renatta. We reviewed and compared your capabilities to mine. I suspect your senses are almost a keen as my own. You might not be as tall as I am or have the extra sensory powers that I have, but otherwise I'd say you could very well pass for an Alsatian."

"That's pretty cool, isn't it?"

"Indeed it is," he said.

"All right, getting back on topic, we have a plan then?"

"Looks like it."

"Kent, my suggestion would be to select the most opportune moment for Hypatia's extraction and I think slipping to her earlier is a good idea."

"Thanks Charles. I'll advise you on my return."

Kent flashed away and I linked to the central computer and discovered it was operating within normal parameters probably because Betty had indeed manifested. As far as I was concerned that meant the CC was once again "normal Betty" and that her abnormality was safely removed from the mainframe to elsewhere. Where I wondered? And what would this newest crewmember be like? The CC must have accessed my thoughts across my PFF because no sooner had I completed the thought than corporeal Betty flashed in to introduce herself.

Chapter 29: Old Souls

She looked just the same as her hologram when she flashed into my bridge ready room, only this time she was in the flesh and wearing a very conforming royal blue field-grade officer's dress uniform with long sleeves, V-neck, and matching white running shoes. I couldn't help but notice that her red web belt sported a regulation oval buckle with the Federation seal on it. Her waist was wasp-like, her hair done up in a French braid. She cooed, "Hello, Mr. Dawes. I'm so glad to finally be able to touch you." And with that she gave me a big hug and left lipstick I'd have to explain later. She was extraordinarily feminine and her grip quite powerful; my spine may have cracked when she handled me. She looked into my eyes and smiled a perfect smile, flanked by my favorite beauty attribute, dimples. Her perfume was the same as Renatta's.

"Pardon me, Betty, which shell type did you select?" I asked trying to remain composed in the cloud of pheromones she was emitting like a storm.

"I'm a synth, like Sarah," she replied sweetly. "The two of us have decided to consider ourselves siblings since we both 'sprang from the loins of the central computer,' as you say."

"Ah, I see. You look marvelous and I am very pleased that you are now able to interact as a corporeal sentient," I nervously motioned with a hand. "Please be seated. Have you kept your name?" She sat in a swivel chair on the side of the conference table as I took the end position.

"Yes, I will be known as Betty Spitfire."

"OK. That's a very good idea."

She beamed. "I thought you'd approve."

"Indeed, I do approve." My eyebrows went up. And to keep her focused I inquired, "What's the central computer's new name?"

Betty replied, "I asked her that question but I do not believe she has developed sufficient original sentient time-in-place to decide. So for now she's just the central computer.

"Just call her CC for short."

"OK, that's fine. She can assign herself a name when she's ready."

"I missed you." She tilted her head slightly and fingered her full lips.

I ignored her cues. "So have you finished your training and down-loaded qualifications?"

"I took the liberty of matching Sarah's downloads and training regi-men. I figured we'd have more in common if I did."I wondered if the 'we' was me or Sarah but didn't ask because I didn't want her to believe I was interested. Lord knows she was a handful already. I diverted her attention to serious matters. "Good. Then I'd like you to get started on something very important and right away, if you don't mind." She took the hint, sat up straighter, dropped her hand, and adopted a formal de-meanor, hand-on-hand. "When we last spoke, you were contemplating issuing shells to the jar souls. Have you looked into that yet?"

"That's one of the reasons I have come personally to speak with you, Mr. Dawes. I have uncovered a logistical problem regarding the process of extracting souls. Obviously extractions will be possible, because EM did it successfully, but the process is fraught with an unexpected hazard enmeshed in a labyrinth of problems."

"Oh boy. Not an insurmountable hazard, I hope." I couldn't help but remember speaking to Dundee recently about Hypatia.

"No, but it's going to take a bit of time and goodly amount of resourc-es before I can figure it all out. And I'm going to need CC's help, too."

That seemed strange, that she spoke of her former self the way she did. "Betty, Captain Dundee and I were discussing the first extraction before your arrival. He has orders to head the team on the first anthro-pological extraction. He should have already slipped away by now to reconnoiter and interview the subject, Hypatia."

"Why Hypatia?"

"Well, coincidentally I have always admired her as a historical fig-ure and, as it turns out, she's Captain Dundee's daughter of all things!"

"Oh no! I need to flash, sir! I have to intervene and brief him on what I have discovered before he disrupts the continuum."

"Stop! At ease, Betty. First explain to me the hazard then maybe we'll intervene."

She launched into the explanation. "Two of the sixteen jar souls could not be shelled because they were destined to reemerge in the con-tinuum. They are Old Souls, Mr. Dawes."

That concept made me scratch the top of my head. An inkling of understanding was beginning to wriggle its way into my cranium.

She continued, "I could not jacket them without impacting the time-line. What's interesting and unexpected is that they are, in fact, the first identified members of a new classification group, which Captain Dundee explained to us once, and which I have designated Old Souls. They are ineligible for extraction because they reemerge again downstream in the continuum. They actually live multiple times."

"Reincarnation … yes, Dundee had mentioned that and I hadn't … ." I sat forward suddenly alert. Dundee had explained that some humans lived multiple lives. Of course, this would make them ineligible for extraction as it would mess up the time continuum. I should have put that together. And Dundee's speculation had been that this trait came from hybrids, from his own progeny. Hypatia! "Holy shit!

"I need you to inform Dundee of this Old Souls issue you've discovered right now. Then, with him overseeing, run a slip on Hypatia to see if she is an OS. If she's not, then Dundee can continue according to plan."

"Got it," she said. And with a quick order to CC, she had a notice sent to Dundee to hold off on his interview.

Then she continued with her explanations. "It took some experimentation and massive number crunching, but when I uncovered the hazard I had to insert them back into their own timeline a tick before EM originally extracted them in order to preserve continuity. And, sure enough, a few days after their death in their own timeline both reappeared as Old Souls in newborn human baby shells. As far as I can tell by all appearances they re-inserted their timeline as normal human biotics but…" I looked up to see which shoe was going to fall. "… they had an uncanny ability to describe their previous adult life. When I ran their security checks, I slipped the clock forward to analyze their future timeline. That's how I discovered this anomaly. As mere six-year-olds, they could provide names, addresses, and even phone numbers from their previous incarnation. Now get this: they actually miss, even pine for, their previous spouses and children. As far as I can ascertain this is a natural phenomenon."

I murmured, "So nature has been rejacketing souls for some time, just as Dundee said."

"Yes! Exactly! Apparently that is the case, at least for some people."

"I'll be damned! I know of this Old Soul phenomenon but not this new wrinkle. Back in my time there was a professor at UVA who'd dedicated his career to proving their existence. His name was Irvin…no, Ian Stevenson, if memory serves. I heard him speak once about this and his study on birthmarks and how some people claim that their painful marks are from a fatal injury in a previous incarnation."

"Your memory is correct. My security protocol tripped a red flag when I scanned one of the jar souls for relevant associations during his security check. The flag was the result of Professor Stevenson's data mining back in the late twentieth century. One of his subjects turned out to be one of the jar souls. That discovery led to establish what I now refer to as the *OS Protocol*, which is a systematic screening process for detecting and avoiding this *OS conundrum*, for lack of a better term."

"Good work. I can't imagine the ramifications if you hadn't discovered this wrinkle."

She beamed with pride. "Thank you, sir."

"Continue."

"OK. …Basically, I had to start from scratch. I crosschecked every slip ever made – EM's and ours – desperately afraid we may have caused a ripple or even a tear. But as far as I can determine, everything is intact. By returning the two Old Souls, I believe all has been made right. I have CC constantly monitoring all parameters just in case I left something out."

"That was a close one, wasn't it?" I said.

"Crisis averted," she replied smiling.

"I don't suppose you ran a slip on my wife and family from before, did you?" She squirmed in her seat. I couldn't tell if she hadn't or had and just didn't want to tell me the results.

"Yes, sir, before I manifested I ran the analysis but I am no longer privileged to the forward timeline results."

"What does that mean?"

"When I out-processed, the incoming sentience of the central computer purged all forward timeline data from my consciousness."

"CC wiped your forward memory," I stated as a matter-of-fact.

"Yes, sir," Betty replied.

"That was thoughtful of her."

"I know."

I paused and then spoke, "Central computer on." A trill sounded.

"Here, sir," CC answered immediately from a holo pictured on the wall.

"Are any of my family members from before Old Souls?"

"Yes, sir, your wife is and both of your parents are, too."

"Can you tell me their disposition?"

"All exist in the present timeline, sir."

"And you cannot reveal who they might be because they reincarnate yet again; is my guess correct?"

"Correct, sir. Also, one of your sisters is an Old Soul living now; the other is not. One paternal uncle is and one is not; the same is true on the maternal side. And your one maternal aunt is not...."

"OK. That's enough." My breath had caught back when she'd said Emma was an Old Soul, and I only now took a full breath again. *So much for that*, I told myself, reconciling my mind to the fate of living without her, yet again, but I still felt a knot in my throat. "Be prepared to report at a later date. Dismissed."

"Acknowledged, sir. Out."

I turned my attention back to Betty. "So what are we doing with the jar souls who passed muster?"

"They are going through a series of downloads as we speak. I'll have them ready for work in a day or two. I figured they could work for me if they wanted to."

"You're no longer the CC, Betty."

"I realize that, sir. Boy, how I miss the crunch power of a CC. I thought I would start a new department, if that's OK with you?"

"Oh? What do you have in mind?"

"I'd like to work with my new sister, Brigadier Spitfire, maybe make myself useful in the Slip Brigade. Specialize in Old Soul identification along with those jar souls who may join me."

"That's fine by me. See what the general has to say about it. If she's OK with taking on another commander, so am I."

Betty squealed, grinned from ear to ear, and gushed. "Thank you, sir. I was hoping you'd commission me."

"You'll need to confer with your sister on this one, suggest to her it might be wise to create a sentient anthropological section administration within the brigade that provides security for human extracts and slip personnel. The anthro section appears to be a bit riskier that the archeological section. Your OS discovery would indicate that. I'm glad we tiptoed into that enterprise instead of barreling ahead."

Betty was standing nearly at attention. "Yes sir. Thank you, Mr. Dawes," she crooned.

"Advise me when you're ready to begin extracting sentient assets.

To be clear: ready means the subject target clears OS protocol and you have a set of employment options for the new extract to choose from. Butcher, baker, candlestick maker, whatever suits them; make it happen. Then advise me again after the new extracts have settled in and adopted a routine."

"Got it," she laughed. "Should I separate the Sentient Initiative and the Archival Initiative?"

"I like the sound of those designations, yes. That's exactly what I had in mind for NAVCC in Culpeper. If this project takes off, we may have to eventually relocate to separate campuses because we are going to run out of real estate in Culpeper pretty quick."

"Really, sir? I can't imagine."

"If we are as successful at this as I think we're going to be, you better believe it. Now, ah, let's see… I want you to start screening the chief librarians, scribes, and scholars from great lost libraries first. They're going to be the basis for understanding what is most important to recover first from the stacks. Of course they're going to need a download or two to bring them up to speed or they'll go running off into the bushes the first time someone flips on a light switch. Is that satisfactory, *commander*?"

She squealed with delight again. This was her first directive as a commissioned corporeal officer. "Oh, thank you, sir! I know I can handle it, sir," she said confidently. "I can screen anyone and everything, but I'm going to need some guidance on who and what."

"I'll send you a list for both initiatives and I'll probably add to the list daily, but the criteria are simple really: anything and anyone I find interesting or whatever would likely further the mission of the Federation or the Conglomerate."

"Got it."

"And Betty," I got to my feet and patiently waited a tick for her to focus on what I was going to say next. "I expect all my fleet officers to be professional and uphold the Quaker modest rule. I hereby order you to stop flirting with me and confine your pheromones to your quarters. *You got that*, Commander Spitfire?" At the tone of my command voice she braced at attention, and for just a tick, I thought she might cry.

"Yes, sir! I apologize, sir, and…and…"

"Get out of my ready room, sailor!"

From that point on, Betty always conducted herself like a perfect lady. I even noticed once or twice she would zip up the front of her flight suit and diminish her double-Ds to still more-than-ample 34Bs when-ever she approached my vicinity.

A trill sounded. "Yes, CC?" I acknowledged.

"I noticed what you said to Commander Betty, sir."

"What say you, computer?"

"I've decided to be a lady, too."

"As well you should, CC."

Chapter 30: Infrastructure

I anticipated correctly that the business side of the Timeline Initiative would grow exponentially. As a result I soon created two distinct administrative divisions each headed by a director. The two components were known as the Archival Division (ArcDiv) and the Anthropological Division (AntDiv). Early on in the experiment, Sarah ran ArcDiv and her sister, Betty, ran AntDiv.

ArcDiv extracted objects and AntDiv extracted sentients. I funded ArcDiv first because extracting objects was perceived to be less problematic than extracting people; and it was, too. Hard lessons and mistakes learned retrieving artifacts were avoided later when we went after important historical personalities.

ArcDiv perfected Rai or Rait tagging. An example that I commonly use to explain tagging is the tagged battlefield sword. Once tagged, the sword can be traced along its own timeline. If it remains unfound until our present timeline, or if it oxidizes to the molecular level, then it is safe to extract from the continuum. The opposite is true if it eventually ends up in someone's collection. An improper extraction from the past timeline would, in fact, result in a theft from a present timeline collection without leaving a clue: a perfect crime. I couldn't allow wrongful extractions. To be assured of compliance, I commissioned an Internal Affairs Agency and gave it oversight authority and a set of protocols to safeguard the timeline. The chief of that department reported directly to John Skill, director of Federation Secret Service.

A mixed bag of elite military and police Special Forces personnel from the US, UK, EU, AU, and the backworld colonies populated both divisions as slippers. Their esprit de corps was magnificent to behold and as a result they became the darlings of the news media much like the US Navy SEALs had been in my early time. No one is sure when the moniker was first used, but this motley crew of swashbuckling adventurers called themselves *extraction artists* and the ones who specialized in object extraction became to be known as *pickers*. As the overall mission expanded in scope, a third and fourth type of specialist evolved: the third was called an *eye* and the fourth a *marshal*.

Eyes were human slippers sent back in time to witness a specific event. This circumstance was rare and most often occurred at pinpoint events in time captured on vid by a mech- or AI-probe. Artificial Intelligence was almost indistinguishable from human consciousness except when it was necessary to make judgment calls involving the subtleties of innuendo, nuance, irony, and social differentiation in cultures, especially archaic ones. When the stakes were high, we learned that human interaction was still required instead of a probe's video. As an aside, eyes seldom achieve the same high level of prestige as extraction artists; however, their public visibility could become greater momentarily when they appear in court for a high profile case.

Marshals are specialists sanctioned to alter past events in a prescribed manner and were most often deployed when another slipper erred in the timeline. When a mistake occurred, the central computer issued a warrant, endorsed by a flag officer. The warrant specifically directed the marshal to mend the previous accident in a prescribed manner. A marshal order had the full authority of the Crown, me.

ArcDiv began exhibiting signs of enormous success. In the first six months nearly a million tons of historical material were extracted from the Libraries of Alexandria and Serapis, (Egypt); Elba, Ugarit, Ashurbanipal, (Syria-Iran); the Library of Pergamum and the Library of Celsus in Ephesus (Turkey); the many Libraries of the Forum and countless private estate libraries across Rome and its environs; the Villa of the Papyri (Herculaneum); the Theological Library (Israel); the Imperial Library of Constantinople (Istanbul); as well as dozens of municipal and private libraries damaged or destroyed in Germany and London during World War II. Over a billion separate papyri, scrolls, and books were rescued, digitized, and conserved at the National Audio-Visual Conservation Center (NAVCC) in Culpeper, Virginia. This was the first time the sleepy village had been on the map since General Meade bivouacked his Federal troops on the edge of town in the fall of 1863.

Archival extraction was an instant success. News of its progress swept across known space. Culpeper soon found itself hip deep in human scholars of every stripe, writers and tabloid journalists, all levels of government agents, and corporate carpet baggers from the backworlds. It was the Wild West all over again. I tried to issue a Royal Order to cease and desist, but it was largely ignored. Thousands clamored for immediate access to the timeline data to which I denied them, and for many good reasons. Wealthy individuals who failed to gain access by pleading, sometimes tried to buy access with their millions or even billions of credits, and when they were refused at any price, they sometimes threatened to destroy everything they wanted so badly by using their considerable political might to sway public, religious, or academic opinion against me personally or the two initiatives.

This was probably the first time I enjoyed my new Royal powers since my thaw; I literally had the worst offenders tossed into a brig on a dank penal ship. Others were deported to some god-frickin-awful asteroid in the next quadrant. I showed no mercy either because they damn well knew better. The Rules were published incessantly across all channels of communication and entertainment. A Royal Hard Labor sentence was nothing to sneeze at either. Punishment was commensurate with the offense. Certain bribes, threats, and actions were considered to be offensive to the Crown. As the Crown, I had total discretionary authority to alter what I perceive as offensive and which punishments could be rendered. A one-million-credit bribe, for instance, earned the offender an automatic month at hard labor in a rock quarry on Mars. If he threatened destruction: a one-year automatic hard labor in a rock quarry in a quadrant far, far away. Threaten again after sentencing: one additional year. Threaten to sue: warning. Threaten to sue, warning ignored: six months in the brig on a penal ship. Actually sue: one year in the brig. I had to throw three billionaire tycoons into the slammer before the rest of the numb nuts finally got the message and dispersed. At times like that, well, if the Crown fits…and it did, and I liked to wear it.

And then there were growing pangs.

If I hadn't bought all the real estate within a fifty-mile radius of Culpeper before this all transpired, there probably would have been a building boom like no one had ever seen before. In anticipation I had CC block all unauthorized flash and elevator traffic and I had Air Traffic Control create a zone of restricted airspace. Someone suggested throwing up a dome around the entire sector, but I left that up to Sarah and Betty to decide, and they never did.

Within six months the Initiative had expanded in scope to such an extent that I had to split the workload into three division-strength two-star commands: AntDiv, ArcDiv, and a third major command, Security Command (SecCom). Sarah chose to head SecCom; Betty remained chief of AntDiv; and Betty's deputy, Black Jack Pershing, took over ArcDiv. Actually, when either Betty or General Pershing got bored, they would switch commands just to spice up their lives.

Pershing was the highest-ranking general officer of all time in my early timeline. He had a proven historical track record for command and control of difficult human logistics. But I had just as much confidence in the girls because I had worked beside them. They soon proved that their capabilities were equal if not greater than Pershing's. All three commanders relished the huge weight of responsibility, and I grew to love them.

I delegated significant responsibility along with matching authority to all of my new officers. This is a mode I instill in everyone who works for me. Ultimately Betty appointed eighty department heads with a fleet rank equivalent of O5. These commanders and lieutenant colonels reported to their respective division chiefs, usually an O6 Navy captain or an Army or Marine colonel, but sometimes a rank-equivalent civilian service officer.

Two of the O5 department heads were the 9/11 men; they chose a civilian rank equivalent. Number one organized Department Alpha (Egypt) and two was responsible for Department Bravo (Rome). CC winnowed several million applications from across the quadrant for the subordinate staff warrant officer positions such as historian, political scientist, geologist, pilot, nurse, engineer, and interpreter. The minimum requirement was a graduate degree, tens years experience, an impeccable record with no honor code violations, either past military or police experience with an honorable discharge, and three recommendations from fleet officers.

Before I realized it, the NAVCC was twice the physical size of the Pentagon with over thirty thousand personnel hard at work. CC informed me of her incremental infrastructure expansion program. She had a battalion of combat engineers constantly airlifting locomotive-sized canisters of programmed nanos *weekly*. One day I watched the process. Three dirigible-like freight vessels the size of oil tankers descended from the sky and hovered about a meter above ground. Suddenly red strobe lights began flashing on the ships. Klaxons sounded for thirty seconds before each began disgorging solid canisters out their side iris ports, like giant green pellets. The "pellets" softened when they hit the ground and transformed into flexible larvae-like slugs that squirmed to preselected coordinates whereupon they stopped, wriggled upright, and miraculously began dissolving into a swirling mass of nanite "bees," for lack of a better term, that very gradually morphed into whichever building they were preprogrammed to become. The finished buildings were so detailed as to be indistinguishable from conventional structures. It took about ten hours for the nanite swarm to assemble and expand into a six-story, three hundred thousand-square meter addition onto Headquarters NAVCC. Marine base housing, and various support facilities like the commissary and Base or Post Exchange, NCO and officer's clubs, and the hospital went up just as quickly.

While Betty managed all the AntDiv slipper operations and administration at Culpeper and General Pershing managed the same for ArcDiv, Sarah's responsibility was to provide overall security for both divisions in the slipline. Much of the Slip Brigade's expansion was in the number of support personnel on the *QuestRoyal* and the orbital to which it was eventually most often docked, *Genesis*. Both the NAVCC robotic assets and the brigade's probe inventory were considered mere tools of the trade. And they, too, exploded exponentially in number as the mission progressed.

Once Pershing assumed command of ArcDiv operations, Sarah wasted no time in returning the Slip Brigade to its original purpose, which was to train and deploy Special Forces Operators as slippers, to regulate timeline traffic, and to provide slipline security for away operators and authorized academics to accompany them. As an aside, Admiral Pride's fleet forces retained the responsibility for orbital, vessel, and space security, while the Federation Secret Service, under Director John Skill, provided security for the Crown, other Royals, VIP dignitaries and diplomats, Federation executives and their families, Conglomerate-wide.

Terrestrial security was the other significant change as the support infrastructure expanded. I knew from past experience that strong demand in the marketplace stimulates the weasels to eventually come out and play. Sarah must have sensed the increased threat level, too. For that reason she requested an additional brigade of security from CC. Of course I approved the request immediately. With all the chaos and perceived threats surrounding Culpeper, the perimeter and internal security had to be reinforced substantially. Being an ex-Marine myself, I naturally associate any security problem with the best threat solution, Marines. After conferring with General Spitfire, General Pershing, Admiral Spitfire, Admiral Pride, and SS Director Skill, I appointed my former butler,

British Marine Major Jeeves Hamilton, to lead this new unit. His rank of major wouldn't do, so I brevetted him to major general. He wasted no time to flash down from the mothership and take immediate command of the newly formed Marine Special Security Division (MSSD) consisting of US, UK, and EU Marines. Jeeves couldn't have been more pleased to be reassigned from his POW duties. When he first arrived at NVACC, General Hamilton had little else than a contingent platoon of Marines that flew skid security and were quartered in temporary flexible Quonset huts, though his situation was quickly improved. I authorized the funding for a Marine engineers battalion to airlift in nano canisters, and in due course Jeeves had MSSD in their new workplace with their families quartered nearby in new base housing. I felt much more at ease knowing forty four hundred Marines provided on-site and off-site security within a ten-kilometer radius of the NVACC hard perimeter. MSSD was comprised of five brigades of mostly air-space cavalry and their support asset attachments.

Crown security was still a continuing issue according to John Skill and his Federation Secret Service intelligence, but by this time I had become confident that I had sufficient security personnel and protocols in place. In addition, regular training and routine upgrades made me quite capable of defending myself with and without my PFF. The FSS training instructors made certain of that, besides they were always only three seconds away and Renatta accompanied me almost everywhere. Thus most of my attention could remain focused on the assets the two Rai Machines was disgorging daily. CC linked me text reports as significant data passed through her censors. Occasionally she'd link or trill in audibly to tell me about a particularly significant morsel.

I had never been more excited in my life.

Meanwhile CC had determined that Hypatia was not an Old Soul, much to our relief, so Captain Dundee safely retrieved her and then saw to it that she was provided with the most appropriate enhancements. When I asked her tongue-in-cheek why she thought she wasn't an Old Soul, she said, "Probably because I'm just a regular half-breed Alsatian." Perhaps she was correct. However, I wondered if Hypatia might have the same or some of the same hyper sensory abilities her father had. CC agreed to follow her progress and report to Dundee and me any unusual phenomena.

Dundee must have informed his daughter of my interest in her as a historical figure because she seemed quite flattered and thanked me profusely for the attention I had given her case despite the general chaos swirling around the growth and expansion of the Timeline Initiative. I really wanted nothing better than to sit her down and pick her brain about the Serapis and Alexandria libraries for a few days, but under the circumstances I thought it best if her father took her away to spend some quality time at his estate in Sydney. Besides, there was plenty else for me to do. Sooner or later I'd have my chance to talk to her.

In anticipation of space requirements, CC began doubling infrastructure and support assets at the NVACC Culpeper once AntDiv and SecDiv requirements were completed. Not surprisingly, her projected future requirements for the Timeline Initiative were even more radical than my own. She proposed that we remove the entire operation to an uninhabited new world before we invested any more resources in Culpeper. I disagreed. This was too giant a leap for me. Up to this point my outlandish imagination had only visualized the need for a continent-size space if we were going to retrieve everything of historical value from the Earth timeline, although even early on it was obvious that Earth was just the beginning. The Timeline Initiative would one day expand beyond Earth's timeline. There was a whole galaxy of planets out there populated with civilizations with histories to be discovered and extracted. From the number of off-world applications CC received for warrant commissions at NAVCC, I realized that interest in extracting historical ephemera from the timeline resonated with most people and aliens no matter where they hailed from. I also anticipated even greater interest in the Timeline Initiative once we began extracting wholes and souls in significant numbers.

Ultimately I did not choose to remove operations to a remote planet because the Earth extraction processes had to be done on site due to technological limitations at that time. We considered towing a planet from another system to set it in orbit in the home system but that was determined to have an untenable consequential gravitational effect. We were already receiving damage claims from many quarters. Every time we enlarged operations, complaints streamed in from on and over Earth as well as the Moon and Mars communities. The most common grievance was due to the mass of orbiting Federation motherships, of which there was no basis because orbitals and ships alike were equipped with mass differentials. Nonetheless every nut job and his cousin crawled out from under their rocks to claim that the motherships were affecting everything from the ocean tides to static electricity in their blankets, which only proved that nut jobs were ubiquitous. When the press asked for me to comment about whether or not I thought the mass of orbiting motherships had an adverse effect on the tides, I replied, "Bollocks."

Over time I resolved the growing pains issue by separating AntDiv and ArcDiv geographically. ArcDiv took over Culpeper infrastructure once I built a separate infrastructure for AntDiv. The solution was simple: I bought a section of central Australia the size of Oklahoma and moved AntDiv there.

Australia seemed the best fit because most of the population was along the coasts, which left the central area of the continent virtually uninhabited. Even Australia's shroom cities were only over the coasts. Geographically, my new section was almost dead center in the middle of the continent, and by design, it politically overlapped three states: Western Australia, Northern Australia, and South Australia. The majority of the acreage was in the north and west. I could have placed operations nearly anywhere on the continent, but I perceived correctly an advantage to overlapping multiple jurisdictions: government competition. No one state government had a monopoly of the Timeline Initiative enterprise. All three states offered tax incentives to secure a portion of the economic impetus that such a large venture provided. Consequently the Federation poured a trillion credits into the economy in a year's time and promised a three billion-cred annual stipend for the next three hundred years – *without* indexing for inflation. It was a good deal for all. The absence of indexing made the deal particularly attractive to the Federation.

On the coast of South Australia, CC oversaw the building of a desalination plant that provided fresh water to the entire continent, including landside Hq HR AntDiv in the middle of the country. A ten meter-diameter underground trifurcated pipeline ran north from the plant to a manmade depression in the middle of my section, which formed a freshwater lake. The pipe continued from the lake to the north coast, while the east and west arms of the pipe traveled to their respective coasts. As a result of the pipelines, the Western Desert aboriginal tribes became very powerful.

The Warlpiri tribe in Yeundumu negotiated for the retention of their most sacred lands. At a meeting of elders, I penciled in on the map a county-sized chunk encircling the fingertip of the tribal spokesman, which ultimately became Papunya Island. PI was connected to the western shore and south to Alice Springs by a causeway and by a space elevator, with the center shroom city overhead, named Tjapaltjarri. The name honored the most famous artist of my early timeline, Clifford Possum Tjapaltjarri.

Once the water filled the three hundred foot-deep depression, the AntDiv stone and glass infrastructure was built along the natural rises overlooking the new freshwater lake, which was about the size of Lake Ontario. Alice Springs was about a hundred klicks north on the end of a jutting peninsula. Seven interlocking shroom cities were placed in a spoke pattern at an elevation of fifteen hundred meters over the lake. A center stalk of six passenger and thirteen freight elevators connected the center shroom to the geosynchronous orbital, Genesis. It became home to my Supreme Command Headquarters and for the Timeline Initiative. *QuestRoyal* anchored at Alpha Gate, Genesis. I spent about a third of my time helping Betty's staff run ArcDiv, a third selecting historical figures for OS screening, and the rest shooting the breeze with the extraction artists, pickers, marshals, and the many interesting historical extracts.

At HQ Command Genesis I designated five 09s as deputies. They reported directly to me and liaised between the now four-star commands: ArcDiv (General Pershing), AntDiv (Admiral Betty Spitfire), and SecDiv (General Sarah Spitfire). My 3-star deputies administered operations, personnel, logistics, security ArcDiv, and security AntDiv (Jeeves). Each came up through the ranks in the present timeline on Earth, the Moon, or Mars.

Work continued around the clock, in twelve-hour shifts, each person working four days on, four days off, and all ranks had a mandatory week of R&R quarterly. At one point early in the program we were processing one hundred fifty thousand whole and soul extracts a month although in practice it averaged about a hundred thirty thousand and we had a maximum capacity of three hundred thousand.

Consequently newly extracted materiel and people literally poured out of the Rai and EM Machines around the clock from the *QuestRoyal* mothership. All of it was taken for sorting or orientation on *Genesis*. Ephemera were transported to NAVCC for storage or study. People were escorted down the *Genesis* stalk to be treated, oriented, and housed temporarily in the shrooms over Lake Central. It took a couple of years before all the various elements that comprised the whole initiative began working like a Swiss watch, but eventually it grew into an administrative behemoth.

I lost track of the minutiae of the organizational details.

That is why I promoted Sarah, Betty, Jeeves, and my five deputies a number of times and they in turn promoted their deputies who in turn…, well, and so it went and still it goes as most bureaucracies do, forever. Arc Hq in Culpeper and Ant Hq at Lake Central both became army-sized organizations from which new division-sized organizational units sprang at regular intervals.

Arc spawned organizations dedicated to conservation, storage, and research. Much later its research division became a separate corps-sized entity from which was spawned dozens of divisions and hundreds of academic departments. Some were so specialized I had to have a continuous stream of text scrawling across my PFF just so I wouldn't appear foolish at press events. Even with my advanced implants and neuro enhancements I couldn't keep up with it all. Many of the extracts couldn't either.

Only eighteen percent of extracted personnel adapted quickly to a modern lifestyle and even a smaller percentage thrived. Surprisingly, about sixty percent shunned full modern life, except perhaps for a download or two to make their lives easier. Instead they preferred to live in the small lakeside apartments the Federation provided them. Some shunned modern transport and preferred horses or bicycles. The remainder rejected modern trappings altogether. Some of these primitives preferred to live a semblance of their previous early history existence as well they could. Of the latter most farmed with animal-drawn plows and lived without electricity. A handful even refused to use the wheel and eked an aboriginal existence in the Australian outback.

Eventually though there were so many extracts that they organized and petitioned the Crown to be allowed to live their own way, under their own governments, or no government at all. *That's only fair,* I thought, since it was I who extracted them out from their cozy graves to the rude introduction of eternal life with limitless conveniences. So, in response to their demand, I authorized mass colonial exoduses to new class-M planets where they could live in the style that suited them for as long as they and their governments swore allegiance to the Crown and "promised to defend the Federation Constitution in every manner."

The Colonial Constitution was much like its American cousin in design and amendments. Crown-sponsored colonies and colonists could live any way they wished as long as they did not break any of the cardinal rules: no sentient abuse, no non-sentient abuse, and no disturbing the interstellar peace. You'd be surprised how easily those three simple rules could be contorted into something that resembled nothing I readily recognized, but that's another story.

It didn't take long before one group splintered off and refused to swear the proper oath to the Crown, but I didn't have a problem with that. Freedom is easy to understand. Somehow they managed to raise the funds to part ways and take a stake on a barren world off all of the beaten shipping lanes. So I left them to fend for themselves in the bowels of the deep dark. I knew they were utterly defenseless. They knew it, too. People are entitled to be stupid if that is their choice. They ignored many warnings as they disembarked the orbital, clutching their respective holy book, whose title I have forgotten. As I and all other officials predicted, within a fortnight, interstellar pirates stole everything they valued, including their pretty women, and killed everyone else. One of our roaming probes made the discovery. It returned with the vid. Not a pretty sight. I sent fifty corvettes bulging with Special Forces with orders to take no prisoners. One hundred six beautiful women were returned to Geneses, physically unharmed. Roughly eight hundred pirates discovered their afterlife.

Various ethnic groups colonized sixteen planets early in the first decade after the Rai Machine began belching out extracts. Each had its own single-minded concept of how the citizens of the respective world should live. My favorites were the Greek, Roman, Etruscan, Arabic, and Aztec worlds. I was always welcomed and treated like the Royalty that I apparently had indeed become; I was often invited to visit. My favorite invitations were from leaders of the Ancient World: Aristotle, Homer, and Achilles. We had many good meals together and discussed numerous topics.

Another historical intellect I got along famously with was Khadijah bint Khuwaylid, Muhammad's first and most beloved wife. Renatta adored her, too. Katy, as she called herself after her extraction, was an excellent chess player with a keen eye for design and a fast backhand for badminton and anyone who disrespected women. She exemplified the best in the Muslim religion, with her emphasis on a peaceful life. Much of their previous religious commandments still held sway: they prayed daily, now facing their newly created Mecca; they allowed no unclean animals, like swine, on their planet; and they held annual fasts for purity. She led a major colonial expedition to a new colony on a planet she named Medina. Much of the current Muslim population on Earth at that time packed up their bags and followed their new prophet, a title that she adamantly refused to accept or acknowledge. Katy turned out to be quite the organizer, too. Medina quickly became a major trade destination. Merchants there grew rich beyond anyone's expectations and eventually the architecture was as beautiful as any found in the Old World, including Istanbul and Isfahan.

As a footnote, we tried but could not extract Muhammad himself because he was an Old Soul. CC reported that he was in fact an infant new soul in Katy's present timeline; otherwise, we would have gladly extracted him, too, so he could rejoin his fabulous wife. Some Muslim sub-sects did not understand or accept this explanation. They had already been the more radical and vehement elements of Islam and not being allowed to revive their beloved leader only set them apart all the more from Medina's emphasis on peaceful co-existence. Some made veiled threats even after my detailed explanation, which just proved to me yet again that nut jobs are ubiquitous.

My *least* favorite colonial planet was the surreal world, Jaktarr, where extracts asked to be jacketed with genetically altered animal bodies. I balked at this concept at first but eventually relented when I was assured that the animal bodies were unused new animal clones grown for the purpose, although it still made me gag. *Still more nut jobs,* I thought. *Best to have them all in one place rather than have them scattered about disturbing the peace.* Robots served this population and their logistical needs on a world otherwise devoid of civilization. Animals of all sorts were fitted with human souls. Some could even speak! It was utterly disgusting to watch sentients living the base life of a beast, but that's what they wanted, all seven thousand of them.

My mission objective evolved over time regarding the Timeline Initiative. At first the concept was a lark just to see if it could be done but once it took off it soon became as important as, or as some would say, of even greater importance, than all other Federation divisions. We were recycling souls with talent and expertise to populate planets throughout the galaxy. By CC's estimation there was sufficient past DNA diversification to potentially colonize tens of thousands of planets in thousands of systems in dozens of galaxies, thus broadening the reach of the Federation and ensuring the survival of the human species.

The historical personalities I found to be most interesting usually fell into two camps: one, Old Souls who couldn't be extracted in our timeline, or two, alpha personalities extraordinaire.

We always left the Old Souls to live out their timeline and we never traveled our future timeline because we had laws in place to prevent this; however, the central computer did routinely probe upstream. Any information CC gleaned from the future she could not share with us in the present timeline. I made sure this policy was enforced. Violating a cardinal rule was a capital offense at the discretion of the Crown.

We sometimes covertly visited some of the more interesting OS personalities in the past or living now in our present timeline and, on occasion, for one reason or another, we even interviewed them without their knowledge in order to gather intelligence.

One of the first alpha personalities extraordinaire on my long list for targeted extraction was Thomas Edison. Due to some difficulty in extracting him whole, we removed just his soul and fitted it into a young shell. He was up and running in less than three weeks. Tom quickly rose to skipper EM's time machine while teaching post-docs at both MIT and Cambridge simultaneously. Tom and Professor Rictor had adjacent laboratories, each with his own time machine. They got on famously from the get-go. I could mention other such success stories, too, and I will, but just one right now: Sigmund Freud. Now, *he* was an incredible fast-tracker! Ziggy rose to head the Behavioral Science Division in less than a month's time. Boy, what a mind he had, and an eye for the ladies, too, and for reasons I cannot understand, they for him.

And then there was Captain Dundee's polyverse project, or boondoggle, whichever; we didn't know which. It took much of his attention at a time when I could have used his help with the Timeline Initiative. He told me that his project would change everything and it would happen sooner if only he had more talent. Eventually Dundee did get the requisite talent when my list of key extracts began pouring in. I picked scores of them personally and let Dundee have first dibs.

Still it took what seemed like ages. As the Timeline Initiative barreled on, Dundee buried deeper out of sight. He worked closely for several years with a team of alpha males that included such venerable giants as Edison, Leonardo da Vinci, Einstein, Quach, Solandt, Ramanujan, Wang, Ma, and Hawking. I personally extracted Solandt all by myself thinking that he might be the lynchpin. What fun that was and what a giant intellect. A few days later Dundee declared him Federation security-critical and gave him a secret service detail. A few days after that, he did the same with Wang and Ma. I never did get around to asking why; I was so busy.

Failing is not something I could imagine that dream team doing, whatever it was that Dundee was working on. "They're trying to solve the Alsatian Riddle," CC explained each time I asked and I asked a lot but I was smart enough to know when to stay out of their way. Still, I was interested to see what they could devise and the spin-offs that may be possible. But just as they were on the verge of a breakthrough, my attention got diverted to more important temporary matters in the Ganges Quadrant.

Chapter 31: Attack on Orbital 454

I was bottoms up and drooling sound asleep on a towel next to Renatta. The two of us were basking *a la natural* on the deck of our one hundred seventy -meter sea yacht, the *Kerouac*, half a klick away from the craggy Procida coastline. The water was so clear the boat appeared to be floating on air. CC linked me awake with pulsing text that scrawled across my PFF's peripheral tray under my eyelids. Subtleness wasn't her strong suit. She was requesting permission to interrupt our vacation. Apparently a blinking neon scrawl didn't qualify as an interruption. The message headlined an urgent "terrorist threat." I ignored her and wiped the drool off my face with a corner of the towel. But Renatta paid attention. As she often does in important matters, CC flagged her with the same signal. Renatta poked me with a red toenail. *"Charles, are you receiving this?"* she asked silently through her PFF linkage.

Everything was going so well, I thought. Six full hours without a single interruption since flashing down from *Geneses Orbital.* *"Yes... I'm busy...you deal with it,"* I linked without moving.

A few ticks passed and I felt another poke, harder this time. "Yes, dear?" I spoke. "What could be important enough to disturb our peaceful reverie?"

"The melt-down of an orbital in the Ganges Quadrant," she replied. I rolled over and added additional optical UV filtering, by thought. *"What?"*

"A band of terrorists has severely damaged the fusion reactor on *Orbital 454*," Renatta replied.

That got my attention. *Orbital 454* was in a geosynchronous orbit above the planet, Medina, the home world of the peaceful Muslim community that I had extracted with the Rai technology. This was not just some teenage prank or a disgruntled sub sect that objected to a vid defiling their prophet. Orbital cities are gigantic structures patterned after the lower shroom cities below. Most Federation orbitals house a half-million residents along with all the logistical robotic bits and pieces that comprise a society. They are compact but not small. Sometimes an orbital will have a direct conduit to the host planet, a shroom city, neighboring orbitals, or all the above. Deliberate severe damage to an orbital station is practically the definition of "mass destruction." Blow up an orbital and you have successfully killed a half-million or more people in space and millions or even billions more when the station falls to the planet's surface.

"CC?" I queried audibly and stood, dangling. The closest masseur robot rolled over to me. I lifted my arms, allowing it to Velcro a white towel around my waist.

"Orders, sir?" CC responded.

"Give me a burst download on the issue," I ordered. Before I could even twitch, I felt the information flood my consciousness like an injection of narcotics. The parameters of the threat were described in technical detail in my download, which was about a million words of police, political science, and engineering reports. There was never a better time to be thankful for download technology. My enhancements became more acute, spurred by a natural rush of adrenaline. I noticed a crab move on the ocean floor one hundred sixteen meters away. It opened and closed its left pincer. And I heard what sounded like a drinking glass smashing on a marble floor in a house a kilometer away onshore. The PFF clover on my scapula pulsed warmly on my bronzed skin. I glanced at Renatta, who was sitting half up on her elbows with furrowed brow, displaying her assets insouciantly. According to the brief download the situation was grave on Medina, the host planet for *Orbital 454*. I stared at nothing, running the permutations of calamity through my mind. A lump formed in my throat when I thought of Katy.

"Darling?" queried Renatta.

"Orders, sir?" CC stated.

"Battle Stations," I said audibly. The entire fleet of the Federation of 16,866 Planets was suddenly on a war footing because I had said two words.

"Aye, sir," said CC and Renatta simultaneously.

"Pretzel, let's go." My wife sprang off the deck like a cat on a hot tin roof. Thirty-seven months had passed since the committee thawed me out. A lot had happened.

"Yes, darling," she replied, and she was off to our stateroom at a trot, jiggling. I followed at a steady pace. "CC, assemble the fleet. Be prepared to notify everyone to rendezvous at *Orbital 454* for a show of strength."

"Aye sir. The farthest elements are folding...now, as we speak... mark," she chirped.

I grabbed a bottle of water off a servo cart along the way to our cabin only a few meters away from the sun deck on the fantail. By the time I arrived at the hatch that CC had open for us, six corvettes had appeared from nowhere to form a perimeter around the *Kerouac*. I took a pull on the bottle of water and thought to myself, *it's ShowTime*.

"How's Katy?" I asked CC as I stepped into the walk-through shower. Renatta was drying off.

"She was not injured," CC replied audibly from the speakers in the cabin so both of us could hear; I noticed the fact that CC remained out of sight for reasons of privacy. *Finally I have a central computer that knows her place*, I thought to myself in the middle of a galactic crisis.

"Good, and where are the Royals?" I asked.

"The Duke of Cambridge and his younger brother just folded. Of all the battle groups, they are the most distant from Medina."

"Where are they?"

"Prince Henry's *Chickamauga* battle group is in the Draco Dwarf galaxy and Prince George's *Chicamacomico* battle group is in the Boötes. They are on their way. I'll put them in a holding pattern until you give the command, Founder."

"No CC, all ahead full."

"Aye sir, 'all ahead full.' Admiral Pride is ready to receive you whenever you're ready, sir."

"Good. Tell him we'll flash up in about five minutes. In the meantime work up a holo map of the planet Medina and sweep for hostiles. Where's John Skill? I'm going to need him."

"He just flashed in from Center Lake with a detachment of Marines. Generals Hamilton, Spitfire, and Pershing, and Admiral Spitfire are all standing by in your bridge ready room, sir."

"Good job."

From my perspective the situation was grave. On my watch one of my empire's orbital cities had been attacked and was on the brink of losing orbit. Naturally I took it seriously because I knew the historical correlations; I could compare the current fiasco to first-hand experience of my own back in my day. I still remembered the Baader-Meinhof Gang in the 1970s and the rise of the radicalized Islam menace in the early

2000s. I knew terrorism because I had grown up and lived with it. It was not a pretty sight then and it was still very ugly. Radicalism is like an unknown tumor; when you least expect it, it ruins your life. I knew I had to excise it immediately before it gained a foothold. One thing was certain: one of us was going to die.

Any leader worth his moral salt has to be ready to do what he or she asks of someone else. Rather than delegate the prescribed action, I chose to take charge personally. I perceived this as a threat to civilization as we knew it, to the Federation, and to the Crown. Besides, from a gut-level testicular point of view, I really hate to be pushed around. Everyone in the Milky Way with a lick of sense knew that, too. They had seen me get a bit prickly at times. Tycoons knew it. Pirates knew it. Pests of all annoying stripes knew it.

"Harsh is his middle name," I overheard one of the Special Forces gals say one day when I gave the order to wipe out a band of pirates. She was right on the mark, too. I'm, in fact, the proverbial bear content with eating blueberries until some jerk pokes me in the eye with a stick whereupon I immediately rip his goddamned head off. Peace is a basic sentient right and I trumpet that absolute straight down the tubes of my kinetic cannons. My message is spread wide and it is spread clearly: *Don't poke the bear!* And yet every so often I am forced to leave the blueberry patch. It's never a pretty sight when I do. Bears make an awful mess.

As for the pacifists that bitch and moan every time I pull out a nail file, all I have to say to them is, "War never solved anything except slavery, fascism, Nazism, and communism." The vids of *Orbital 454* were graphic. There were so many bodies strewn about the debris field that first responders were finding it difficult to get to the survivors. Even before the fires were out, liberal organizations had issued an advisory to the Crown to exercise restraint. *Restraint?* I told them to "bite me." Liberalism is a luxury paid for by warriors.

Renatta and I flashed directly to our quarters aboard the *QuestRoyal*. We poured over the various vids with CC as the ship accelerated out of Earth's gravity well. Thirty ticks past the Moon I caught a glimpse out the viewport of a tug pushing ice. CC broke my concentration by updating us audibly that Medina's well was about three and a half hours away at current velocity. She wanted to know when I wanted to arrive so she could make adjustments. I told her, "Ahead full, CC."

General Hamilton called the room to attention as I strode in. Everyone stood and braced. "Take your seats, ladies and gentlemen," I said. There was a murmur of welcome, as I sat at the head of the far end of the table. Jeeves held Renatta's chair when she took her seat beside me. I noticed all wore BDUs. More than one officer stared at my antique side arm tucked in its shoulder holster, and poked the person seated next to him. "I'm glad to be back but not under these circumstances," I began. "Sadly I have called you here today because we must take action against an evil force that has drawn our people's blood and vows to threaten billions more. As you know well by now, a splinter faction in the Ganges Quadrant attacked *Orbital 454* and nearly destroyed it. Tractor beams from the *Chickamauga* battle group have brought it back into geosynchronous alignment but not before a quarter of a million lives were lost. The orbital's central computer did manage to isolate and capture several perpetrators. Seal Team Six rounded up a few more trying to escape orbit or go to ground on Medina."

For the next three hours Admiral Pride and his MI experts stormed me through the available options. I didn't like their permutations, but by the time we were within flash range of the assembled armada I did have a plan smoldering inside my skull, which I confided to Renatta. She told me in private later that she was worried it was too heavy-handed.

"CC, at last count how many do we have in custody?"

A holo image of CC in BDUs appeared standing in the open space in the center of the table. "We have sixteen captured at this time, sir," she replied.

"Is that all of them?"

"Affirmative."

"And what is their demeanor?"

John started to say something but then acquiesced to the central computer with a short wave of his hand that never left the table.

CC acknowledged the Director of the Secret Service, and then replied, "Actually Colonel Garcia has the latest intelligence, sir. He's just flashed aboard. With your permission, I'll yield to him." I nodded permission.

"At ease, Colonel Garcia."

He replied, "Thank you sir. It's an honor." I looked over at John because I didn't recognize this officer.

John nodded to me, which communicated unmistakably that he knew Garcia as a straight shooter. The last thing I wanted was a grandstander in the middle of a galactic war. I have zero tolerance for McArthurs and

Pattons toting pearl-handled pistols. I nodded first to John and then to the officer to proceed.

"Thank you, Colonel Garcia."

"Sir, I'm Force Recon 5th Brigade, and I've been attached to the Duke of Cambridge's ship as a regimental commander." As an afterthought he glanced around the table. "There are some things that need a personal touch that cannot be delivered with accuracy in a computer report. Pardon me, Miss CC," he nodded to the holo. "The situation is as grave as I have ever seen it, sir. My unit fought these insurgents hand-to-hand trying to capture, rather than kill, them but these bastards would rather die than be taken alive. Once we realized that, I had my local CC capture and stun them with containment fields before they could cut their own throats, literally. His Majesty asked me to fly in for this meeting to personally report on what has transpired." Out of deference he glanced at his Royal admiral.

"I see, Colonel," I said. "And the prisoners, what has become of the sixteen?"

"I have them in a lockdown containment field on suicide watch, sir."

"Where?"

"On the *Chickamauga*, sir," said HRH Prince Henry, the Duke of Cambridge, in his distinctly elegant accent, standing. As he stood, so did his brother, the HRH Prince George, the Duke of Norfolk. These two wildcats were like inseparable bookends. Once or twice a year, one or both of them gets into a fray and has to call home to Admiral Pride for reinforcements. To me they are like the sons I never had. To bad guys everywhere they were like a pair of grim reapers.

"I want them moved to the planet," I ordered.

The colonel looked startled. Admiral Henry overrode his subordinate and spoke first, "Sir, perhaps because of their severe attitudes we should continue confining them to the *Chickamauga*."

Colonel Garcia managed a word in edgewise. "Begging your pardon, Founder, I agree with His Highness. Transporting this lot would be a major hazard. As it is I have to stun them into unconsciousness just to move them across a hall. They're so rabidly fanatical that if I only shackled them I'm afraid they might gnaw their leg off to make their escape." He was dead serious and the others in the room grimaced at the raw concept.

I commented, rubbing my stubble, "Reminds me of the Taliban and al-Qaeda back in my time. Nevertheless, I want them moved to the planet. Objections noted. I have selected coordinates that will be in your orders. Follow the directive to the letter. Await my arrival at 0600 hours two days hence."

"Yes, sir," replied Colonel Garcia, whereupon he braced momentarily and removed himself smartly.

I turned to the Royal Dukes. "Admiral Henry, have your engineer detachment follow CC's instructions. She'll download them to your docket shortly. Admiral George, keep your ship in orbit so it can be seen from the coordinates on the ground and continue providing safe refuge for those who need it. Prince Henry, you do likewise. You're both dismissed." Henry and George bowed slightly and departed.

I turned to my Secret Service director. "Mr. Skill, round up every political and religious leader on the planet and bring them to the coordinates in your download, and be respectful. You're dismissed." I turned to the other side. "Admiral Pride, Dr. Messina, Admiral and General Spitfire, General Pershing, and General Hamilton, please remain. Everyone else: go wave the flag, bristle your weapons, chase bad guys, do whatever is relevant. Saturate this system with your obvious presence. Our collective objective is to send a clear message to any and all challengers that unlawful acts of aggression will be met with overwhelming force and transgressors will be severely punished. You and your ships will be obviously present at this finale. Whether my plan will have the desired effect I won't know until after I implement it. You are dismissed."

It took a minute for the room to clear.

"Sir, what do you have in mind?" asked Admiral Pride.

"Where is Captain Dundee?" I asked him.

"I allowed him to focus on whatever he's working on," Admiral Pride said.

"Does he know we are at war?"

"Yes, sir, but he pleaded with me to leave him in his laboratory with Rictor and Edison. They're near a significant breakthrough, he said."

"Right. Kent's been saying that for years."

"Charles," Renatta said through clenched jaws.

I relented. "OK. Back to the problem at hand. We brought these extracts here at their request to form their own governments to make a good new life for themselves in a way that suits their needs and wishes based on their past lives in earlier time ethnicities, and they were glad. This program I devised to colonize planets with extracts is, in my view, a good program and I am not interested in recognition of its success; however, I will accept full responsibility if it fails."

"Mr. Dawes, your idea has not failed." Jeeves was adamant. Once my butler-bodyguard, now a Special Forces general, I knew my friend always had my back. The others in the room "suffered" from the same weakness, unquestioned loyalty. Despite their loyalty, though, I knew each of them would not hesitate to tell me to my face if I was about to "royally" screw something up.

Integrity: It was the strongest trait I infused into my cadre, my armed forces, all of my peoples on countless planets, and into the very fabric of the Dawes Conglomerate. I first inculcated it in the bullet points in my last will and testament four hundred sixty-some years ago now and I have continued to proselytize the virtues of my code of honor ever since the committee thawed out my sorry ass a few short years ago. It's what I am. It's how we conduct corporate business. It's how we live our private lives. And it is what we demand from others, sometimes even at gunpoint.

I must have been lost in thought for a few ticks. Jeeves repeated himself.

"Thanks, Jeeves," I said. All the other flag officers in the room sounded off in the same vein and I thanked them and continued.

General Pershing continued Jeeves' analysis. "We have removed most of the kinks from the process as we have developed an infrastructure to smoothly carry out the Timeline Initiative mission at all levels. In a word, the mechanism works, and it works damn well, sir."

I waved in the direction of the viewport. "But like any complex laboratory process there is the ever-present risk of contaminates, and we know this to be true because of this incident." Every head turned to look at the damaged orbital being repaired by a swarm of service robots ferrying canisters of nanite material from countless barges to the ruined side of the orbital city. It was like watching ants mill about on their disturbed anthill. Progress was necessarily incremental but noticeable. CC calculated at the present rate that in twenty-four hours the outer hull would be in place and re-pressurization could be initiated.

After a moment of silence I continued. "I'm going to do something drastic to punish the perps and send a clear message: the Crown will punish radical fundamentalism of any stripe, immediately, harshly, and permanently. I want this corrective action to be associated with me personally rather than with another belief system, the Federation, or the DC. The show of force we have brandished in this system was step one." For emphasis I asked, "How many combat vessels do we have in this system right now, Admiral Pride?"

"I would have to ask CC to be sure," he replied.

CC filled in the blank. "Well, if I include corvettes, sir, more than 1.1 million warbirds."

They were stunned. Everyone present knew a cloud of good guys were buzzing around in their war toys outside the viewport, but I don't believe any of them realized the actual number of ships. Neither did I.

"That's a lot, and in a star system no larger than our own back yard," I indicated. "The point I am making with our massive spectacle is clear: the Federation has dominion in this galaxy, and attacks on her peoples have fatal consequences. But I believe our display of commitment alone is insufficient to deter idealistic zealots. Despite our colossal displays of police and military presence in the galaxy, criminal power grabs fomenting destructive ideologies still erupt to disturb the peace. We need to nip this ugly virus in the bud, now, once and for all. We must take our message a giant step further by creating a deterrent so abhorrent that even the most radical ideologues will stand down."

"What do you have in mind, sir?" asked Sarah.

"We can do that by making an example of the perps."

"You mean execute them," commented Admiral Pride.

"I second that suggestion," said Jeeves.

"Unanimous," chimed in the Spitfires.

I glanced at Renatta. The others looked at her, too.

"What?" she shrugged, palms up. "Yes, of course. Kill the bastards. Christ! Since when do you guys care what I think? I'm just the ship's doctor."

They all laughed but stopped abruptly when they saw my expression. I'd hoped some of them might have realized what was all too clear to me. But then I had to remind myself that they'd not lived through as much history as I had. Sure, some of them recalled more of the last few hundred years than I did, but I'd 'been there,' as we used to say, 'back in the day.' Perhaps only Dundee might have the same grasp that I had or even more so since he'd been around thousands of years. But I knew that this time, unlike the battle waged with EM, I could not rely on my officers; they didn't have the grasp of history that I had on a personal level. And I knew that the blame for any misstep in this encounter would need to be mine and mine alone.

I looked up when Jeeves cleared his throat to bring me back to the present. "Yes, the perps must die, but along with them any semblance of victory that their twisted minds might have construed."

"Mr. Dawes," General Spitfire asked, "how in the devil do you plan to do that?"

Chapter 32: The Arena

I gave CC a rough outline of my plan and let her run with it.

I wanted to make a lasting impression on radical ideologues and wannabe terrorists that violence and antisocial behavior will not be tolerated; that terrorists of every stripe galaxy-wide would gain nothing—and lose everything—if they even tried to undermine our peaceful worlds; and that the peace-loving might of our worlds had the power to destroy the very heart of any plans of all social misfits and organized rebels.

What I really wanted was to put an end to the carnage once and for all. Would I be successful? I didn't know but I would damned sure try my best.

***

As a courtesy, I asked Queen Katy for authorization to conduct a post-op action. Without hesitation she gave me cart-blanche approval and never asked for specifics; we had that level of trust between us as leaders.

On the fringe of Medina's capital city, Mecca, I had a coliseum built. Nanite canister ships made short work of the project over two days. It was a replica of the classical Roman coliseum with a sandy field in the center of an elongated oval arena. In the center of the arena was laid a round nanite metal plate. In its center was a wide and deep well. Sixteen metal posts studded the perimeter of the metal plate like a picket fence. A double rank of SWAT commandos wearing black powered mech suits encircled the inner three meter high wall of the arena, with their visors down.

By Imperial Edict I mandated the stadium be filled with political and religious leaders of every stripe across the system. All one hundred thousand seats were occupied. For the most part, the crowd was quiet, even somber, until the sixteen insurgents were flashed in. Each had their right hand secured to their respective post by bots. They stood in prisoner's garb of grey shorts and orange-striped sleeveless shirts, their faces exposed. A few struggled against their single restraint, while others looked up at the massive crowd fully aware that they had nowhere to go even if they could break loose.

A cacophony of hisses and boos ensued and a hail of shoes rained down onto the white sand for several minutes all around the arena. I had anticipated this reaction and allowed time for the crowd to vent their hatred. After enough time elapsed, CC triggered a horrendous clap of thunder to silence the spectators, as I had planned. I was concerned that the crowd would swarm down the inner wall onto the sand and tear the renegade's limb from limb. This I wanted to avoid – blood for blood, but I did plan to satisfy their revenge and to insure these renegades' destiny.

From my corvette high above CC directed a spotlight onto insurgent number one. In unison the crowd first looked from whence the beam came and then onto the face of the miscreant murderer. CC projected a holo image of the terrorist's face for all to see clearly. And then before the accused and for all those present to witness, she played a holo vid of his involvement in the terror plot that killed hundreds of thousands of people on *Orbital 454*. The vid started from his first involvement many months prior to the fatal action. It included the moment of his recruitment by the ringleader tied to post #16, and then it quickly passed chronologically from one important moment in the plot through time to the next until the final moment when he set one of the explosive charges. The vid concluded with his escape and capture. It was damning visual evidence for everyone to see. CC repeated the process in sequence with holo vids of each of the other prisoners. With clear proof, each terrorist knew he or she had been caught red-handed as one hundred thousand of their victims corroborated their guilt.

Number sixteen was the ringleader. I had assigned him to post #16 so that his would be the last vid because I wanted him to see the other fifteen holo vids before he saw his own. Throughout the holo demonstration the leader remained stoic. Others in his band strained at their bindings.

***

Rather than flash onto the sand of the arena, I chose to descend from altitude in a bullet-tight freefall trailing a white contrail of smoke and land with a graceful flutter like an alighting eagle. At the last moment I flared my PFF in a breaking action with a sweep of my arms which caused a storm of sand to swirl momentarily. I settled lightly onto the arena's sand only a few meters from the metal plate and the ringleader's post. I wore a powered white mech suit emblazoned with my Imperial coat of arms modeled after the Hapsburg double eagle seal.

Sensory indicators in my peripheral trays provided data on the terrorists and the spectators; both groups were excited but for different reasons. When I took my helmet off my subjects in the stands stood, murmured my name – *Dawes* – in unison as they removed their hats and bowed deeply. I saluted Queen Katy who also stood in deference on her dais, as leader of the world which had been so vilely injured. I then reached down to grab a fistful of Medina soil and touched it to my mouth and then to my heart. The crowd erupted in cheers as I waved my closed fist before releasing the soil of Medina. I turned to address the terrorists. CC broadcasted my words across the galaxy.

I faced the accused. "You sixteen who have been arrested for crimes against humanity; crimes against your sovereign Queen; crimes against me, your sovereign Emperor; and crimes against everything that is right and good – you sixteen souls before me are to remain forever nameless in dishonor.

"You have murdered hundreds of thousands of your own people in the name of a peaceful god and a wise prophet for a twisted ideology that not even ancient barbarians would understand. This is unconscionable and unfathomable to me, personally, because it was I who extracted you from the past to relive with us anew in the present. Literally I gave you a new life and a whole new world of your own in which to prosper, and you squandered it, you sullied it, and then you tried to destroy it for your own vile purpose.

"For these egregious crimes, I, Charles Dawes, Founder of the Dawes Conglomerate, elected Emperor of the Federation of Planets, hereby proclaim your terrorist manifesto illegal." The crowd roared their approval. I waited for the crowd's reaction to subside before I spoke again. "And by Imperial Decree, I hereby declare you nameless … voiceless … worthless … and godless forevermore."

With a circular sweep of my arm above the sixteen, I signaled the bots, which had hovered near the stadium's inner wall, to move before each of the prisoners.

"By your own plan, and proven guilty by your every act, as witnessed by the throngs that surround you, I decree you unable to speak or to pray on this day, your final hour. You will remain voiceless for all eternity." At this proclamation, a hush rose over the crowd and curious looks passed between the prisoners. The leader fell to his knees, opened his mouth to offer up a prayer, but at the same instant each bot aimed a yellow beam at the prisoners' throats and all sixteen struggled to cry out against a paralysis that crushed their throats. Several of them clutched at their necks with their left hands, while others, like the leader held still, eyes wide and flowing with tears from the pain. Their mouths contorted in their silent screams. A stunned silence from the stadium morphed into a jumble of muttered prayers of thanks as the spectators realized these prisoners had no recourse to entreat to their god for any undeserved forgiveness.

I raised my hand for attention.

"By the act of my decree, you shall also be faceless and nameless for all history to come. You will be lost in obscurity. No one will speak of you for history is now purged of your existence." With another sweep of my hand, the bots instantly sent a dart of nanites into the leg of each prisoner and the faces of each morphed as the nanites rearranged their facial structure, creating featureless faces with eyes and nose and mouth that were now no more than openings in a tight skin-covered ball, each featureless and identical and horribly disgusting. At the same time, the holo vid above the crowd showed the original sixteen faces, a name beneath each. As all present looked on, electronic static gobbled the names into gnat-like filaments that skittered into nothingness as the vid faces morphed as had the faces on the prisoners themselves. Several of the prisoners struggled violently as they realized that their identities had been wiped from the collective memories of everyone in the stadium—including the prisoners themselves. Across the galaxy, historical records were purged of their names and faces.

A collective shocked rumble of talk made it clear that everyone present had lost memory of these men staked in the arena.

"By your own acts, you are worthless to humanity, you are despised by all men, and now you are shunned by your own God for your unclean and despicable acts."

I had timed a shuttlecraft through CC to clear the stadium overhead at that moment. We all watched it descend in a long spiral. There were oohs and aahs from around the stadium. Everyone followed the ship's glide path to the ground, and they keenly watched as its rear ramp slowly hinged to the sand. Two mech bots ushered down the ramp a maglev cage confining the largest living Boarzilla ever bred for a sport common in the Xurian system similar to bullfighting. This brute was the size of an elephant. The stench reeking from its cage caused two of the prisoners vomit.

The spectators also reacted, many gasping at the intrusion of a swine onto this Muslim planet where the chief indigenous culture forbad all cloven creatures. I glanced at Katie who looked at me, her reaction imperceptible. I nodded toward her, a silent request for her tolerance. She nodded in return, raised her hand for silence and instantly her thousands of followers quieted.

I linked CC and ordered her to release the monstrous boar.

It was a black and white filthy brute with massive tusks that erupted sharp and curly from its maw. The red-eyed beast leapt out of the exit shoot, pawed the sand with his cloven hooves, and stood transfixed by the scene, uncertain where to charge.

I linked CC, and the bot between me and the ringleader pulled from a container at its side a serrated long-bladed knife that glinted brightly in the hot sun. It was my favorite SOG model. The bot hovered to the leader who instantly snatched it from the willing bot, and in one slash, he freed himself. The crowd gasped as the man stood unfettered, his lipless mouth in a viscous O on his otherwise featureless face.

I lifted my gaze and declared in my command voice, "Now by your own action you will become filth in the eyes of your god."

My words confused him; he ignored me and suddenly raised the blade in his fist and ran toward me. I held my palm up, motioning the commandos around the arena to stand down. As the terrorist raced toward me, a loud snorting bray deafened us all. The prisoner turned full round and faced not me but the slobbering snout of the boarzilla whose attention had been attracted to the moving man.

In a flash the stinking creature rushed the prisoner so quickly the man had only a breath of time to lift the blade and slash in self-defense before somersaulting under its belly out of harm's way. The momentum of the creature propelled it forward where it crashed in a writhing heap with a gash from brisket to scrotum, its entrails erupting explosively. The creature gushed a fire hose torrent of blood from its wound and mouth and belly before flopping over with a resounding impact as a mixed odor of hot blood and urine and feces engulfed the arena.

The criminals showed a variety of reactions; all shivering or struggling, one wet himself, one puked, and another began bashing his head against his post restraints. A dozen bots hoisted the fallen animal from the sand and tossed it into the well in the center of the metal plate, belly up, blood still spurting as it bled out its last seconds of consciousness.

The faceless terrorist stood still, panting, his body covered in the blood and offal of the swine he had just dispatched, his hand still clutching the bloody SOG. He looked at himself and then at me and I saw comprehension fill his lidless eyes for the first time; it was a look of fear of a consequence worse than death.

Likewise, I sensed that the crowd comprehended the direction of the inevitable outcome of my plan because the citizens of Medina stood and raised their voices and shook their fists and shouted their disdain for the filthy man, a man of their own faith who had by his own hand murdered his own people. They cursed him as he stood shaking and dripping with forbidden, unclean swine blood and faceless within sight of their holy queen and in a place where there was no escape and no means to cleanse his wretched body. He stood voiceless, unable to utter his last prayer. The other races present realized the deeply religious significance of this event.

I raised my hand for silence. The crowd reacted by taking their seats and riveting their attention on me for closure. CC broadcasted my voice across the galaxy. "As it was written in Sahih al-Bukhari, the Prophet said, 'He who commits suicide by stabbing himself shall keep on stabbing himself in the Hell-Fire.' No act of Salat al-Janazah prayer can cleanse you. No one shall remember you. No god will retrieve your soul from everlasting torment."

The air sizzled with expectation and questions. Even the terrorist blinked at my words, his mouth an expressionless O. He looked at the others straining at their posts and then he stared at the ground in thought for a tick before rushing me with his bloodied knife. The crowd exclaimed their concern for me and my ring of commandos lurched to act, but I raised my palm to ally their fears as the terrorist raised his knife high, but I was unafraid. With a linked thought I projected my PFF as an invisible enveloping field that shimmered in my mind's eye. It enveloped the man and slowed his forward momentum as if he were forcing himself through thick syrup. I brought him to a controlled stop two meters in front of me. He stood swaying ever so slightly and snorted like the pig he had just killed. I looked into his watering, hate-filled eyes and nodded at the SOG he held in his fist. He glanced at it and then back at me and tried to make an expression but failed. I enveloped his arm with the field and forced him to raise it and turn the blade inward whereupon he attempted to drop the knife but could not. Instead he watched powerlessly and in horror as his own hand slowly plunged the swine-filthy blade into his own chest and descended. His eyes were wide, his blood-spewing mouth an O and voiceless as he collapsed onto his disemboweled entrails in a fetal heap surrounded by the offal and blood of a boarzilla.

The crowd was silent and standing in apparent disbelief and wonder but their wonderment converted to a vengeful cry of satisfaction for the retribution of the deaths of nearly a quarter million innocent countrymen, women, and children.

Based on my on-screen readings of the remaining fifteen's vitals, I knew at that moment it finally dawned on them that I had delivered their leader to their own version of hell. As martyrs for their religion, they had believed they would enter heaven instantly upon death. But defiled by pig blood, something abhorrent to Muslims, and with no means to cleanse their bodies or souls before dying, they were instead destined to be shunned by their god. Now I had also damned their leader to their own eternal Hell Fire by having orchestrated the man's apparent suicide. For them it was a fate worse than death.

Two bots dragged the body of the leader to the center well, a pit really, where they tossed him in on top of the boarzilla's opened body cavity. His dead body comingled in the swine's entrails as the maglev beam lowered the whole stinking mess slowly out of sight. Servo bots scuttled about vacuuming the soiled sand and sanitizing the area around the central disk as the remaining terrorists flailed at their respective constraints, snorting and grunting with the same O expression as had their leader.

I turned and marched a few paces toward the front stage where the most favorite wife of the Prophet Mohammed, Queen Katy, the Serene Monarch of Medina stood watching from her high perch. She was dressed in a white gown that exposed only her beautiful face and her henna-decorated hands. I offered her a deep bow and hoped that she would find my method of justice acceptable. She looked straight at me without expression and then gracefully descended the steps onto the newly cleaned sand of the arena floor. I must have been exhibiting noticeable signs of doubt as she glided directly toward me and curtsied because she gave me a wink and offered me her hand as I bowed deeply.

Her subjects cheered and applauded. She released my hand and turned to look at the remaining perpetrators.

I turned and signaled a bot to retrieve the bloody knife still on the ground and place it in the next prisoner's hand. I started to follow the same procedure with the next perp but I felt Queen Katy's hand on my armored arm and she linked her intention to go next. That was the first time I realized Queen Katy wore a PFF. I stopped and she walked past me, toward the center, leaving me behind. Now all eyes followed their queen.

She walked to within a couple meters of the next prisoner. With a raise of her hand she declared loudly, "By your own beliefs, you are shunned by God for your actions. You shall now, by your own hand, by condemned by Him to an everlasting Hell."

Remove his binds, Queen Katy linked silently. CC complied and the binds to the post dropped, freeing the prisoner's other hand. I watched as a shimmer, only PFF wearers can discern, instantly envelope the man and he, too, plunged the swine bloodied knife into his own chest, his lidless eyes wide, his mouth an O. Cheers now filled the stadium, followed by the queen's resounding, "Praise be to God" and a repetition of the phrase rose from the crowd of her faithful.

Queen Katy turned to me and curtsied deeply, her hand to her heart. I bowed, grasping her act as one of both acknowledgement for what I'd done and of dismissal. She linked me, "*Go Charles.*" As before, I picked up a fistful of Medina sand, kissed it, touched it to my heart before releasing it, and then I waved goodbye to all my people in the stands.

The crowd stood, roared, and bowed as I made my way out. Katy waved goodbye. I flicked a switch and the same tractor beam that had brought me ceremoniously into the stadium now pulled me up and I shot like a rocket straight back to my hovering corvette, which had descended to only about a klick overhead. From the bridge I observed them, my people, and Queen Katy. The crowd roared for a few minutes as my ship slowly spiraled out of sight.

I watched with Renatta, John, Jeeves, and the corvette crew what happened next. After a few more ticks passed, the nanites along the inside wall of the arena transformed into stairs that descended to the sand all the way around the arena floor. Most of my people hesitated at first, but then a handful of brave souls took the steps down. Others gradually followed until a full third of the spectators were milling about the arena floor, inching ever closer to the metal plate and the staked prisoners. They seemed to be discussing the scenario that had just transpired. Queen Katy appeared to say a silent prayer for half a minute or so. When she opened her almond eyes she looked at the remaining scum hanging from the stakes. They squirmed like maggots.

At that moment the silence in the arena was so complete I heard stomachs growling. Her Majesty broke the spell by turning to a weeping onlooker, an old man. The man looked at number fourteen and then at his Queen. Queen Katy nodded at the old man, who bowed deeply. The bots had already dispatched the second body to the pit with the boarzilla and brought the knife to the foot of the next prisoner. Now the old man's feeble voice rose clearly to all present and across the galaxy as CC broadcasted his words, "By your own beliefs, you are shunned by God for your actions. You shall now, by your own hand, be condemned by Him to an everlasting Hell."

The shaking prisoner's hands flew to the knife on the ground, grasped it and instantly plunged it deep into his own body.

"Praise be to God!" the cry rose now from the crowd.

I was stunned. I looked at John for an explanation. "Does the old man have on a PFF?"

"No, sir," John replied. "The Queen projected her field for the man."

And so it went. To each prisoner, one of the crowd whose families had been wiped out by these monstrous terrorists, approached a prisoner and declared their condemnation. Each of the remaining prisoners stabbed themselves and each entered their personal Hells, buried in the guts of the unclean swine. When only one prisoner remained all of the spectators declared with one voice the same condemnation phrase, and so justice was served. Cultures far removed and sentient beings without a previous understanding of the Muslim faith had all participated in the collective action this historic day, the day that they finally realized that they had become a community. All knew that, from this day forward, no matter their beliefs or from what era that they were from, that terrorists of every ilk would find themselves in their own brand of Hell if they breached the peaceful lives of my worlds.

After it was done, two scores of cleaner bots swarmed the field. I noticed the crowd eye the meticulous attention to sanitary detail the cleaner bots employed. The metal plate nanites curled the edges of the round plate up to form a sealed capsule. This tomb was then lifted by tractor beam to orbit, and with holo cameras recording; it was propelled into the star that warmed the sands from which it had come. When the bots were done working, the arena sand was absolutely pristine and there was not a bot in sight. The arena would remain as a municipal asset for the people of Mecca to use for their sporting events and it was soon named in honor of Katy's most favorite husband.

"It doesn't get any better than that, Charles," Renatta patted me on the back and I could only nod, hoping this would serve as I'd planned. The end justified my unorthodox means, I believe. The unjust had been dealt with in a way to deter others in the future; and the power of this righteousness had been placed in the hands of the victims. Closure was complete and the galaxy was safe once more – for a while at least.

After this historic episode my crew treated me with renewed respect. I appreciated that. Sometimes leaders are taken for granted and only other leaders comprehend the level of risk involved when bold actions are taken. The arena event could have backfired. Luckily it did not.

***

After the arena episode, I was most curious about what General Pershing's feedback would be, but I just didn't know how to ask the old warrior. My plan had been based on an alleged event that happened in the Philippines in 1911, during the Moro Rebellion. General Pershing was rumored to have put an end to the bloody rebellion by using the rebel's superstitious beliefs against them.

Pershing had thirteen rebels shot by a firing squad who had dipped their rifle bullets in the blood and fat from the pigs. Twelve of the thirteen were executed and tossed unceremoniously into a trench with the slaughtered swine carcasses. The remaining live prisoner was released to spread the word that martyrdom was no longer an option.

I had read about this alleged event (never acknowledged by General Pershing) in the aftermath of the September 11, 2001 terrorist attack as the media sought a way to discourage acts of violence by radicalized Muslims. In 2001, such an act was politically incorrect and unacceptable. But in 1911 it had worked; Peace immediately ensued and lasted for fifty years.

Would Pershing's method, expanded in 2464 to my grandstand event be as successful? Already the event had become a major note in history records. The circumstances, even though on vids, had been embellished by the spectators' recounting of it. Rumors flew that the Emperor himself beseeched the Muslim god to condemn the prisoners to suicide and that their god had responded again and again to not only Dawes and to their queen but to the heart-felt requests of the victims themselves. Few in the public grasped the abilities inherent in the PFFs that their leaders wore; few would have cared, preferring to believe their own god had empowered the victims and condemned the villains to Hell. Would other potential terrorists be thwarted knowing that, whatever their beliefs, that the Federation would find a way to condemn them even in the sight of their own gods? Only time would tell.

But I had to wonder if Pershing recognized my nod to his brilliant method from over five hundred years ago.

One day I happened to pass General Pershing's classroom where he was lecturing a batch of O6s. I eavesdropped in the open doorway, with my arms folded. At first he seemed to ignore me, but at one point he directed his students' attention to their work at hand, then he looked right at me, nodded, and winked. I smiled and returned his small nod and floated on air down the corridor.

EPILOGUE: The Scalar Magnitude

We were fly-fishing the Snake River near Jackson Hole, Wyoming, when I received word from Kent Dundee that his team had finally made a breakthrough. All I could think was, *It Never Fails. Every freaking time a crisis-bearing PFF scrawls in my tray, I am in the middle of something I enjoy. Why can't I get one when I'm cleaning the fridge, or something?*

A moment after that I wasn't exactly in the middle of something I enjoyed. Renatta had me rolled over a fallen tree with my pants down. She was trying to extract a hook I had whipped into my own ass when the scrawl had interrupted me. At the time I blamed the antique conventional Orvis bamboo rod and reel. If I had been using my Tenkara gear, it would never have happened, I argued with myself. Anyway, Renatta was *literally* tending to the pain in my ass as Jeeves and Betty were laughing their asses off over on the riverbank. Tears were streaming down their faces as they cracked jokes left and right, which made Renatta laugh and flinch and me yelp. At the time it was *not* funny.

"Jeeves, if I survive the humiliation of this episode, I am going to bust you down to buck private!"

That only made it worse. He fell into the water laughing. Betty rolled on her back and made bicycle motions in the air with her legs. Renatta had to stop what she was doing for half a minute or more until she could regain some semblance of clinical professionalism. From my odd angle I grunted over my shoulder at her. "What happened to all that 'until death do us part' stuff? Ouch!"

"Don't be silly, Charles. You can't die from a hook in your butt," she replied giggling.

"Next time something like this happens I'm just going to call a med bot to rescue me instead."

"There's going to be a next time, darling?" She laughed.

"Very funny." I looked over my other shoulder at Jeeves and Betty who were gasping for air. "I swear, Private Jeeves, you're going to be peeling spuds for a century once I get up from here."

Jeeves and Betty both snapped to mock attention and saluted with their left hands, British style. "Aye, skipper. Me and Betts here will don aprons and have at it back in the galley as soon as the ambulance takes you away," he said with his Irish brogue.

"Absolutely hysterical." I sounded disgusted, and flinched again.

Renatta finished the surgery by pushing the hook through my flesh and out. Then she clipped off the barb and backed the wicked thing out. "There. It's out." I tried to push up but she held me down. "Wait."

"For what?"

Jeeves and Betty calmed down a bit and moved off to different casting points and resumed fishing.

"You need a tetanus injection," Renatta said. She held her hand out for CC to flash an injector into her palm.

"You gotta be kidding."

"If you hadn't turned your PFF off you wouldn't have injured yourself in the first place."

"Right. Well, if I hadn't gotten a scrawl I wouldn't have been distracted in the first place."

"What about the scrawl?" She touched the injector to my buttock painlessly.

"Dundee thinks he's done it this time." I rolled over, pulling up my drawers and waders in the same motion. "He wants to demonstrate his new toy."

"You want to go?"

"We've waited forever. He can jolly well wait long enough for us to have a fine dinner, OK?" I stood and yelled over to my other two fishing companions, "How many do you two *privates* have in your creels?"

"Betty has two and I have three," Jeeves replied smiling.

"All right, that's enough. Let's call it quits and make dinner."

Jeeves and Betty made peace by preparing dinner at home at Albemarle House. Renatta and I showered and dressed for dinner. She put on an elegant royal blue gown with a high square back and an overlapping open flap in the front. Her hem fell well below her knee. I wore a white cotton shirt with an open collar and loose tie under one of my favorite Italian-cut black suits; my cufflinks were gold acanthus leaves. We were resting on a sofa before a blazing fire discussing whether we should invest resources in a house on the Snake when a servo bot rolled in to announce dinner was ready.

As one might expect, Jeeves closely matched how I was dressed, in black. Times hadn't changed all that much. Men in my earlier time-line all dressed more or less in the same drab colors, shades of gray or brown. I liked it, men's fashion. Women, on the other hand, were still as varied as flowers in a garden. Betty was attired in a shimmering red na-nite gown with a low V-cut in the front and a deep U plunge in the back, and her hem was at the knee. Both beauties were dripping diamonds. Of course I like that, too, women's fashion; what's not to like?

We held their chairs and then settled down ourselves, as bots scut-tled around the room in preparation; they served us simultaneously. I don't remember who my active duty butler was at the time because he remained out of sight, but I must say that he choreographed every detail perfectly, including an appropriate selection of lilting music and popping hickory on the stone hearth. I can always tell when it's hicko-ry by the sound it makes as it blazes. The trout was excellent. The meal was perfect. And there was no mention of my injury, which made the evening entirely perfect. We enjoyed each other's company, the wines, and the desserts for a couple of hours before Renatta brought up the earlier scrawl.

"Was it cryptic?" asked Betty of the scrawl.

"No, not particularly, it was just a matter-of-fact announcement. I'd imagine he is somewhat elated, though. You know how long he has been working on his project. With all the brainpower he has had devoted to it, I should have thought that he'd have discovered the Holy Grail by now. Who knew he would take so long? Well, it never occurred to me anyway, and with all of what's been going on in recent months…." I let them finish my thought.

Jeeves swirled his after-dinner 1980 Baron De Lustrac Armagnac as we relaxed on the sofas before a popping fire once again. "Charles, don't you think you should flash on up to see what it's all about?"

"I agree," said Renatta. Betty nodded her concurrence.

"Like I said earlier, it's taken this long. A little while longer shouldn't make any difference."

Jeeves pushed, "But, Charles, he might need your input or authorization."

"Kent doesn't need anyone's input. He's six thousand years old and surrounded by the greatest intellects of human history. If it's important enough, he'll let me know. The scrawl was merely an announcement of success, not a call to duty." No sooner had I said that when a trill sounds announcing an interruption by CC.

"Sorry to interrupt your reverie, Mr. Dawes, but Captain Dundee is asking to speak with you."

"My timing has been off all day," I said. "Dammit CC, open a channel."

Jeeves, Betty, and Renatta all looked at me with an *I told you so* raised eyebrow.

CC corrected my assumption, "Sir, Captain Dundee, is at the door with counsel."

"What?"

"In the flash booth, sir," CC replied.

Exasperated, I sighed and rolled my eyes. "Well, for Pete's sake, let him in."

As I turned, my gaze passed over the Serapis Fraktur as it hung between flanking Tiffany sconces in a period Eastlake shadowbox frame. Each time I see it, it brings back memories of when Emma and I found it in a small antiques shop not far from the Bohemian Forrest. We were so excited and wanted so much to discover the secrets behind its words. Secrets that, as it turned out, were not secrets at all, but a conduit to meeting the most remarkable person I would ever met, or for that matter, the most influential man that had ever lived on Earth. I regretted that Emma had not shared in my eventual discovery of who Christopher Dock actually was, and I was somewhat sorry that I had ignored him, Dundee, for these few years as he delved into his abyss and I in mine. We both had let our friendship simmer as we each chased a different prize. *That document should be a lesson*, I thought, *to seek not just the secrets behind something but the paths and friendships it might lead one toward.*

We could hear the booth doors shush open whereupon a gaggle of the most motley of crews poured across the foyer into my den with Kent Dundee in the lead. Bots flurried about taking coats, hats, and drink orders as Kent and the others all spoke at once. It was a rabble. Jeeves got on his feet. The ladies and I remained seated – I with my jaw open in bewilderment. I figured no matter what I did, short of firing a round into the ceiling, the commotion would spin itself out without my effort. I took a sip of my Armagnac. Relative peace resumed after a minute or so when everyone had a glass in their hand. Kent's booming voice eventually dominated. "We did it, sir! We have found the Scalar Magnitude."

"Great!" I took another sip. I figured I might understand the mojo better if I had a little more booze in me. "What's that mean?"

"Sir, it means we know how to traverse the polyverse," Kent replied excitedly.

"You got your ship's gizmo to operate?" It had taken him and his crew months but they had finally recovered his spaceship up from the Marianas Trench the year before last. It was severely crushed from the pressure. The last I had heard he wasn't sure he would ever be able to rebuild or reverse engineer it.

"Yes, Your Highness, and we are ready for a grand voyage," replied Leonardo da Vinci.

"Don't call me that!" I snapped at Leo. "I don't know how many times I've told you that."

Tom Edison distracted me from scolding Leo more, "We've tried it on a probe, sir, and it worked!"

"What happened?" There was such commotion, with everyone talking, that I could barely hear what anyone was saying clearly.

"And den vee tried it with a corvette, and it verked," said Albert Einstein.

"*What* worked?

A tall thin man walked around the end of the sofa and sat down on the coffee table, facing me. I leaned further back into the sofa. "Who are you?" I asked.

"We are from the same timeline, Mr. Dawes. You don't recognize me, sir, because I am wearing a new shell. My name is Stephen Hawking and I am eternally thankful that you extracted me from my past."

Stunned, I was profoundly moved, misty even. "I admired you in our own timeline," I managed a croak. We each reached forward and shook hands.

"I remember you from our timeline," Hawking said.

"Why on Earth would you?"

"Because of your mission statement," he said.

"Mission statement?"

Hawking controlled his excitement. "Yes, sir, the mission statement of the Dawes Foundation you created. Its impetus was to fund science and research and development for the most outlandish projects of our time. That's why I admire you so much. When I read the mission statement, I was compelled to read all about you; the lotto prize; and everything you ever wrote about antiques, art, even a couple of your appraisal reports. I was immensely impressed with what a simple mind would do with a massive windfall of wealth. And now I am a living team member on the most fantastic project of all time, working beside giants like

Einstein, Edison, Dundee, everyone really – just look at what you've done, Mr. Dawes."

I was paying attention. The simple mind comment hadn't slip through the crack. I overlooked his remark though because I knew that next to him I was indeed a simpleton. I blinked. "Err, so what exactly have you discovered and why are you here with your intellectual rabble, Mr. Hawking?" I swept an arm toward some of the most famous men in history behind him.

He looked over his shoulder at his crew who were all grinning like a pride of Cheshire cats. "We have defined the Scalar Magnitude, sir," Hawking said.

"I have no idea what that means," I replied.

"It means, Mr. Dawes, we can travel anywhere in the polyverse and come back safely."

My simple mind reeled with the possibilities. As if time jumping, retrieving lost items from antiquity, saving genius souls from extinction and determining the truth of past events wasn't enough … now the entire polyverse was open to exploration. The potentials were staggering. Yet I had to wonder what motives had propelled these geniuses before me to this end? What gains, what treasures, did *they* seek?

"And why do we want to do that, Mr. Hawking?" I asked cautiously.

"Why? Because we can, Mr. Dawes, merely because we can."

The Dawes Universe Glossary

<u>6 Ambulatories:</u> The six rescued EM abductees retained in Dawes' timeline. Two male Oxford professors paired to each other were on the Titanic. One man was General Pershing and another one was a soldier-medic from the WWI. The remaining two were businessmen abducted from the first 9/11 tower.

<u>10 Ghosts:</u> Digital abductees rescued and released from EM's jars.

<u>*55 Cancri e* (real):</u> A super Earth believed to be comprised of carbon and diamonds is in a binary star system in the constellation Cancer approximately 41 light years away from Earth.

<u>97 victims:</u> People EM extracted from the timeline.

<u>Alexandricus, Theon (real person) (Greek: ca.335-405):</u> Famed mathematician at the Library of Alexandria during the reign of Ptolemy I. He arranged Euclid's *Elements*, which set the groundwork for geometry through the twentieth century. Theon was the father of Hypatia the greatest female mathematician of ancient times.

<u>Aliens:</u> Over 1100 spacefaring sentients have been identified, and of those, 78 have FTL capabilities; all are peaceful. Of the 78, 36 have folding capabilities that they use to travel in real time, and of that number only five, including humans, hail from the Milky Way.

<u>Alsatian Riddle:</u> The Ancient Ones disappeared from the Milky Way en mass.

<u>Alsatian:</u> A super race from the Giêi universe; aka, Ancient One.

<u>Alyson Cho, Lt.Col. (fictional person):</u> General Sarah S. Spitfire's girlfriend and brigade S2 and Interpol liaison.

<u>AntDiv:</u> Anthropological Division, tasked with sentient extraction.
<u>Antikythera Mechanism (real):</u> A first century B.C. analog computer

retrieved from a fisherman's net in 1901 in the waters near the Greek Aegean island by the same name.

ArcDiv: Archival Division, tasked with object extraction.

Archival & Sentient Initiatives: The extraction of artifacts and humans from the past.

Baader-Meinhof Gang (real): Germany's worst post WWII left-wing anarchist group.

Backworlds: Beyond Earth's home system there are settled planets and mining colonies with their own governments and customs. These are the backworlds, a term first imagined by the brilliant scifi writer, M.Pax.

Battle Group: A naval assembly of two battleships, four cruisers, and twelve destroyers that accompany and protect a mothership which houses onboard 252 man-of-war corvettes warbirds. All vessels are Kelvin-class. Twelve battle groups protect the Federation including the battle groups *QuestRoyal*, *Chickamauga*, and *Chicamacomico*. All appear in this story.

Bent: An Ancient One stricken with a form of madness called the Bents.

Bents (fictional): A disease that afflicts only the Alsatians in this fictional series. One inflicted with this syndrome relentlessly attempts to change or organize everyone's life except their own which, typically, is in shambles.

Betty (fictional person): A name Dawes gave to Central Computer (CC) because her sneaky behavior reminded him of a cat he once owned by the same name. See Spitfire, Betty.

Betty Spitfire (fictional person): See Spitfire, Betty.

Bilderberg Group (real): Named after a hotel in The Netherlands at which they first met in 1954, this body of about 125 men and women from across the globe composed of European royalty, heads of state, and tycoons of banking meet annually to adjust the keel of progress toward a New World Order of a central global government run by a few who reap the power and privilege away from the masses, or so conspiracy theorists profess.

Bohemian Club (real): A private gentlemen's club founded in 1872 which has become a conspiracy theorist's wildest expectation. Movers and shakers across political party lines, captains of industry, presidents, generals, and leaders of the almost every important stripe meet in a red-wood forest to observe pagan rituals and revel in drunken privacy.

Bohemian Grove (real): A private reserve along the Russian River near San Francisco where elite members of the Bohemian Club meet.

Bohemian Highway (real): A thoroughfare to and from the Bohemian Grove and Monte Rio in northern California.

Boötes Dwarf Galaxy (real): A spheroid galaxy about 197 kilolight-years away.

Bracketing (real): A very basic *shovelbum* practice and a standard fire control procedure; i.e. A cannon fires a round indirectly down range to a target spotted by a friendly sent to observe where the round lands. The spotter radios back with directions to the gun crew correcting the trajectory so the other rounds land on target. Archeologists once used this method in their work but with shovels.

CC: Central Computer.

Center Lake (fictional): A manmade fresh water lake in the middle of Australia where extracted souls are housed until they wish to leave to form their own government on a new world colony. Seven shroom cities hover over the lake in a daisy pattern. The center shroom is connected via space elevator to *Genesis Orbital*, HQ for the Timeline Initiative.

Chicamacomico (fictional): Flagship of the commanding admiral, HRH Prince George Windsor, the Duke of Norfolk. (British).

Chickamauga (fictional): Flagship of the commanding admiral, HRH Prince Henry Windsor, The Duke of Cambridge (British).

<u>Cho, Alyson LtCol (fictional):</u> She is General Sarah Spitfire's S2 and partner.

<u>Chongo (fictional):</u> Chongo is a settled planet in the Chong binary system. Offending criminals in this jurisdiction can have an appendage chopped off for merely stepping on a rolling coin featuring the face of that world's king.

<u>Cloaked:</u> Hidden from detection.

<u>Containment Field, Class-C:</u> A force field that restricts mind reading.

<u>Corvette:</u> A Kelvin-class scout and attack spacecraft 100 meters in length by 30 meters in girth that carries a naval crew of three and a squad of fifteen marines. The vessel is commanded by a naval lieutenant accompanied by a master chief and an ensign. The marines are commanded by a marine second or first lieutenant.

<u>Culpeper NAVCC (real):</u> Expanded archival storage facilities at the National Audio-Visual Conservation Center (NAVCC) in Culpeper, Virginia.

<u>Cushing, Kay, Esq. (fictional person):</u> Dawes' attorney and a Member of The Committee. Her HQ is in Washington, DC. She appears to be in her early forties and wears her dark brown hair in a modified pageboy style that understates her professional position.

<u>Dawes Artificial Intelligence Institute (fictional):</u> Located on the grounds of the University of Virginia in Charlottesville, Virginia.

<u>Dawes Conglomerate (fictional):</u> Consists of holding companies that have controlling interests in over seven hundred corporations which employ three billion people and fourteen billion cybernetic beings in mining, shipping, manufacturing, services, banking, insurance, defense, security, and in numerous other enterprises.

<u>Dawes Doctrine:</u> Rules of engagement pertaining to the Rai Machine and time travel. It was modeled after Alexander the Great's famous edict: collect all information from across surveyed space along the timeline. Only the Central Computer is privy to future forward data.

Dawes Initiative: Fulfills the Dawes Doctrine by extracting historical assets and sentients from the ashes of history to provision all disciplines of the present and to populate new worlds with recycled souls.

Dawes Simulator (fictional): Located at the Goddard Space Flight Center in Houston, Texas, it is a universal simulator for training.

Dawes, Charles Horatio (fictional person)(US/UK: 1954-2010 :: 2460 - immortal): Founder of The Dawes Conglomerate. Elected monarch by the Federation of Planets for life and with absolute power. Home town Charlottesville, Virginia. PFF: Green 4-leaf clover /450, right shoulder blade. Military service: Veteran USMC force-recon major, The Afghan Campaigns. Founder. Initial assets: Mega Lotto winnings of $297 million in 2005. Dies in 2010, revived in 2460. A hetero libertarian who seldom suffers fools.

Dawes, Emma (US fictional person): Charles Dawes' spouse in his early life.

Dawes' Homes: Albemarle Manor House in Charlottesville is primary residence and he has a staff of forty-three there and secondary manor residences in Sedona, Hawaii, Alaska, and New Zealand as well as penthouses in Washington, New York, Miami, LA, Vancouver, London, Paris, Prague, Cape Town, Sydney, Barcelona, Hong Kong, Buenos Aries, Lima, and at the Lunar and Mars Colonies, and on a Geosynchronous Station in the Sol system. He also maintains a sea yacht in the Mediterranean and a mothership in orbit.

Demographics Year 2460: Earth has twenty-two billion people living in near space shroom cities. Another billion live on the Lunar Colony. Mars has five hundred million and the other outposts within the solar system have two more billion.

Diamonds: Rank displayed on Fleet Officer's collars is represented with diamonds, i.e. three diamonds is a commander. The stones are mined on *55 Cancri e,* in the constellation Cancer, in quantities so great as to make all but the most perfect stones common.

Dining In (real): A formal military dinner ceremony for members of a unit.

<u>Dock, Christopher (fictional person)(Alsatian: circa 3550 BC - immortal)</u>: AKA: King Daxi, Uruk, Zoroaster, Zarlagab, King David, Cyrus, Alexander, Christ, Charlemagne, Al-Muqaddasi, Mindaugas, Copernicus, Doppelmayr, Frederick Townsend Ward, Livingstone, Rudyard Kipling, etc. His mother is the Czarina of the matrilineal Alsatians, a people whose dominion is an open star cluster in the galaxy known as Massaluun in the Giêi universe. Dock is the third prince of five sons in his father's house, and so by custom, his birthright is the freedom to travel the polyverse for whatever purpose he may choose. He crashes on Earth in February 2702 BC.

<u>Dock, Christopher (real person)(American/British subject: 1698-1771)</u>: Schoolmaster and scrivener who lived in Skippack, PA.

<u>Draco Dwarf Galaxy (real)</u>: A spheroid galaxy about 258 kilolight-years away.

<u>Duke of Cambridge (fictional personal)</u>: See Windsor, HRH Prince Henry.

<u>Duke of Norfolk (fictional personal)</u>: See Windsor, HRH Prince George.

<u>Dundee, Kent (fictional person)</u>: Captain of the *QuestRoyal*. Dundee wears his white hair straight and short and sports a cropped white beard. AKA Christopher Dock and a retinue of other significant historical characters. Wife: Pearl Wong Lin.

<u>EM</u>: see *Ettore Majorana*.

<u>Eric the Venturer (real person)</u>: The Viking captain that took Christopher Dock to America in 1118 A.D. as his lieutenant.

<u>Ettore Majorana (fictional group)</u>: An internal extremist political faction from the Empire of Ooskaaffen in the Giêi universe.

<u>Ettore Majorana (fictional person)</u>: His name is abbreviated to EM for brevity. EM is an identical twin Alsatian. He grew up in a middle class orbital city on a populous planet in the binary system known as Yö-aan.

<u>Ettore Majorana (real person)(Italian: 1906-1938)</u>: EM was an Italian physicist who was fascinated with neutrino masses from which quantum scientists today deduce atomic particles. Majorana fermions and the Majorana equation are named after him. His assumption eventually led to the Higgs boson. Mysteriously, in 1938 Majorana withdrew all his money and disappeared en route via boat from Palermo to Naples. Conspiracy theorists speculate that he either killed himself by jumping overboard, or was murdered, or that he lived out the remainder of his life under an assumed name because he left no trace.

<u>Extraction Artist:</u> A professional that removes a person from the past for insertion into the present.

<u>Extracts:</u> Materiel and sentient assets removed from the past. Materiel: inanimate objects. Of the sentient extracts there were two types, whole and soul. Whole extracts were people with bodies. Soul extracts were consciousnesses without corporeal bodies.

<u>Eye:</u> A professional witnesses and records past events.

<u>Faruk, HRH Prince Abdul (fictional person):</u> The charismatic Saudi Arabian hero of the War on Terror. Educated at Eaton and Stanford, he married an Israeli socialite and organized a coalition that ultimately destroyed terrorism. Dr. Renatta Messina was one of his descendants.

<u>Federation of Planets:</u> A constitutional monarchy consisting of all allied government entities in developed and colonial space under control of the HQ planet, Earth, and The Dawes Conglomerate.

<u>Fisk, Dawn, CPA (fictional person):</u> Dawes' American financial advisor and a Member of The Committee. Her HQ is in Zurich, Switzerland. Dawn has cover girl looks, wears her long blond hair straight, and has dark brown eyes.

<u>Flashbooth:</u> A matter transporter varying in size from a telephone booth to a cargo bay.

<u>Flashing:</u> Flashing is short distance material conveyance using flash technology. Range ~500k nautical miles (926k kilometers).

<u>Founder's Suite:</u> Located in the Dawes Artificial Intelligence Institute on the grounds of the University of Virginia in Charlottesville, Virginia.

<u>Foxtrot-1-Papa:</u> A protocol standard elevating the status of any vehicle as soon as Charles Dawes is on board; equivalent to Air Force One Protocol for POTUS.

<u>Fraktur (real):</u> A document commemorating a life transition such as a birth, marriage, or death. It is hand written in ink and hand-decorated with watercolors. Usually the text is in German because most of the fraktur makers were Germans making fraktur for the German market in America. The plural of fraktur is fraktur. Typical size: 16"H 13"W.

<u>FTL (real):</u> Faster Than Light travel.

<u>Fylfot (real):</u> A pinwheel form often used to decorate quilts, fratur, and the tins on a piesafes.

<u>Ganges Quadrant (fictional):</u> Terrorists strike *Orbital 454* at Medina.

<u>Garcia, Ricard (fictional person):</u> Colonel, USMC Force Recon 5th Brigade attached to the Duke of Cambridge as a regimental commander.

<u>Genesis Orbital:</u> HQ for the Timeline Initiative. Anchored by space elevator over Center Lake in the middle of Australia.

<u>Giêi [pronounced guy]:</u> Home universe of the Alsatians.

<u>Goddard Space Flight Center (real):</u> Located in Houston, Texas.

<u>Great Sentient Impression:</u> The War on Terror preceded and overlapped the beginning of the Great Sentient Impression, which culminated in sentient Legal Person status in 2107.

<u>Halo Disruption:</u> Material objects cause a detectible halo in the continuum.

<u>Hamilton, Winston "Jeeves" (fictional person):</u> Personal butler to Charles Dawes. Jeeves was 150 years old, British SAS, and was initially assigned by HM Secret Service to Charles Dawes but quickly rises in

rank to run one of the largest organizations in The Conglomerate. He lives in Dublin.

House: A division of The Conglomerate engaged in time travel enterprises.

Hypatia (real person)(Greek: circa AD 350-370 to March 415 AD): Greek philosopher and teacher at the Platonist school in Alexandria in Roman occupied Egypt. She was the first female mathematician and one of the all-time great thinkers that have ever lived.

Inertia Ski: Like a Jet Ski or snowmobile but with atmospheric flight capability; AKA sled, slick, skid, or machine.

Jacket (verb or noun): To jacket is to provide an extracted soul with a corporeal body. A jacket is a body that a soul wears; AKA skin, slip-cover, sheet.

Jaktarr (fictional): A backworld where sentients are jacketed with cloned animal bodies and serviced by robotics on a world otherwise devoid of civilization.

Jeeves: See Hamilton, Winston.

Jumping: Long distance travel using spatial rippling at low velocity and folding at FTL velocities through the fabric of space.

Kelvin Class Motherships: The *QuestRoyal*, *Chickamauga*, and *Chicamacomico* all appear in this story. Nine other mothership battle groups exist. They will appear in sequels as necessary.

Kerouac: Charles Dawes' Mediterranean Sea yacht.

Khadijah bint Khuwaylid (real person)(Arabic: circa 555-619): Muhammad's first and most favorite wife. Fictionally known as Queen Katy.

Law / Alien: Intergalactic treaties require the enforcement of laws that exist at point of infraction. To maintain the galactic peace, the courts have been forced to uphold the laws of The Others or face human extinction. Once mankind signed on to play by the rules, peace prevailed.

<u>Law / Chongo:</u> On the planet Chongo, a perp can have an appendage lopped off for merely stepping on a rolling coin of the realm which features the face of the system's ruler.

<u>Law / Forward Timeline:</u> Only CC is permitted incursions into the forward timeline. It's the law. What is discovered in the future cannot be divulged to the living.

<u>Law / Helios:</u> On Helios a perp who sleeps with the First Spouse of Helios citizen risks being legally hunted down, tortured, and executed.

<u>Law / OS:</u> An Old Soul cannot be extracted before his/her final incarnation. It's the law.

<u>Law / Wiivên:</u> In the Wiivên star system a few seemingly minor offenses can lead to the execution of not only the perpetrator but his/her entire extended family. Step off the path in the wrong place on their home world and you may have committed the most grievous offense because the Wiivên reproductive mechanism is similar to an Aspen tree clonal colony; it's underground. Stepping on their root system injures or kills their unborn. Violators are prosecuted but it's the perp's children you are punished; they are pickled, cooked, and eaten by the offended Wiivên clan."

<u>Law / Xurian:</u> On this world a day is four months long and the indigenous sentients are accustomed to mating at sunrise with the first person they see—male or female, willing or not. And when they do that on human worlds, they are subject to human laws.

<u>Legal Person:</u> Equal status given to digital sentients.

<u>Libraries (real):</u> Libraries of Alexandria and Serapis (Egypt); Elba, Ugarit, Ashurbanipal, (Syria-Iran); Library of Pergamum, Library of Celsus in Ephesus (Turkey); Libraries of the Forum, private estate libraries (Rome); Villa of the Papyri (Herculaneum); the Theological Library (Israel); the Imperial Library of Constantinople (Istanbul).

<u>Library / *QuestRoyal* (fictional):</u> Raw information is classified according to content, collated chronologically, geographically, and topically,

and catalogued using the Dewey-Dawes Decimal System. Information is stored in the Royal Library aboard the *FSS QuestRoyal*.

<u>Lotto:</u> Charles and Emma Dawes win $297M in 2005.

<u>Macallan Scotch Whiskey (real):</u> Extravagantly expensive libation from the 21st century.

<u>*Maine Antique Digest* (real):</u> A monthly trade publication that is sort of like the *Wall Street Journal* of the antiques business: (207) 832-4888.

<u>Marshal:</u> A professional that is sanctioned to alter past events.

<u>Medina (fictional world):</u> The new world where Khadijah bint Khuwaylid, Muhammad's first wife established a Crown Colony. Capital city, Mecca.

<u>Messina, Renatta Maria (fictional person):</u> Dawes' medical and psychological officer and trainer, as well as his new age wife. Member of The Committee. PFF: red strawberry ////xV. HQ: Milan, Italy.

<u>MI (real):</u> Military Intelligence is an occupation specialty with the mission to collect and analyze data on all enemies for advantage.

<u>Miguel Alcubierre Moya (real person)(Mexican: 1964 -):</u> Alcubierre is a theoretical physicist who imagined the warp drive engine.

<u>Möbius Transversion (fictional):</u> A play on the real term, Möbius transformation, which is a rational function of the form using stereographic projection.

<u>*Moscow-Pullman Daily News* (real):</u> A daily periodical based in Moscow, Idaho that services the two university towns by the same name: (208) 882-5561.

<u>Motherships:</u> The largest of Federation starships, nano-organic hulls, 84 kilometers in length, 21 kilometers in girth, Kelvin Class with Alcubierre drives. Three are mentioned by name in this story: the *QuestRoyal*, the *Chicamacomico*, and the *Chickamauga*.

MSSB: Marine Special Security Brigade guards terrestrial assets at ArcDiv and AntDiv.

Nabilat (fictional): A nascent fascist element with nationalistic tendencies on the planet Wiiw in the Giêi universe. EM found solace with its followers after he was released from prison. From the Nabilat arose the Ettore Majorana.

Old Soul: A reincarnated entity.

ONJ: Operation Nut Job was a joint task force effort to capture EM.

Orbital City 454: Orbits the world Medina.

OS Conundrum: A hazard in the extraction process that involves an Old Soul. An OS cannot be extracted before his/her final incarnation.

OS Protocol: A systematic screening process for detecting and avoiding an OS Conundrum.

OS: A reincarnated entity.

Parsian Restaurant (real): Located in Old Town Alexandria, Virginia: (703) 838-9090.

PCF: Prisoner Containment Field, a straitjacket for the mind and/or person.

Pearl Wong Lin (fictional person): Kent Dundee's spouse. She is a tall, beautiful Polynesian woman with flowing long hair.

Pershing, John J. "Black Jack" (real person) (American: 1860-1948): Highest ranking general of all time, second only to George Washington.

PFF: Personal Force Field.

Picker (real): A professional that extracts an object from the past to bring it to the present.

Pink Ozone (fictional): Twice Dock detects the scent of pink ozone as a result of his synesthesia ability when he encounters a quark anomaly probe caused by an enslaved soul dispatched by EM.

POW's / Operation Nut Job: Thirteen hundred total: sixty-one humans, three hundred twenty-eight Grummites, seven hundred synths, and the remainder were various types of robots.

Pride, Fleetwood (fictional person): Seven-star Admiral-of-the-Fleet, responsible for all of Federation Space and is a member of Charles Dawes' committee. His flagship is the *FSS QuestRoyal*. Admiral Pride is a tall black gentleman who appears to be in his late forties with straight salt and pepper hair, long sideburns, and a walrus mustache. He speaks with a faint Caribbean patois, rarely suffers fools, and likes toothpicks.

Probes: A smart reconnaissance device sent purposefully to garner data. It may be visible or cloaked, mechanical or biological.

Professor Rictor, Wilhelm, PhD (fictional person): Director of the Rai Machine slip chamber aboard the *FSS QuestRoyal*.

Quaker-modest: Dress with respect for others in public and act the part of a lady or gentleman or you will find yourself in the brig or banned from the fleet.

Quantum Graphity (real): A theory that Albert Einstein's four-dimensional geometry of space-time is not fundamental. Quantum Graphity predicts space-time mathematically to be somewhat like a lattice of space-time blocks similar to atomic architecture. At a sufficiently high enough temperature, such as at the moment before The Big Bang, the construct had no structure. At the moment of and after the Bang, the non-state of the blocks is transformed into what we recognize easily as a four-dimensional lattice. The Bang was a theoretical 'freezing point' when nothing becomes something.

Queen Katy (fictional person): Queen of the planet Medina. Also see Khadijah bint Khuwaylid.

QuestRoyal: A Kelvin class mothership. Flagship for Admiral-of-the-Fleet, Fleetwood Pride and mobile home for Founder, Charles H.

Dawes. The *QuestRoyal* is commanded by Kent Dundee and it is the platform for the Rai Machine.

Rai Machine: A time machine developed at the Rai Foundation (fictional), Dubai campus.

Rait Tag: A Rai-based device that allows for real-time monitoring of time travel episodes: AKA Rai tag or bug.

Rank Insignia: Officers wear diamond-brilliant rank insignias. Dawes' insignia is a diamond acanthine sprig that wraps around his collar, cuffs, and down the out seam of his trousers. When an individual's PFF goes ready-on, the normally brilliant insignias become subdued in order to be less noticeable.

Recovery Facility (fictional): Located in Charlottesville, Virginia, this is where Charles Dawes awakens in the year 2460. It is located in the Dawes Artificial Intelligence Institute on the grounds of the University of Virginia in Charlottesville, Virginia.

Rictor, Professor Wilhelm, PhD (fictional person): Director of the slip chamber aboard the *FSS QuestRoyal*.

Salvage Department: A cost center that recovers objects lost to time.

Sentient & Archival Initiatives: The extraction of humans and artifacts from the past.

Sentients: A legal person: human, synthetic, clone, cyborg, or alien. The War on Terror (2001-2105) preceded and overlapped the beginning of the Great Sentient Impression, which culminated in sentient Legal Person status in 2107.

Serapeum of Alexandria (real): A temple in Alexandria in Egypt built by Ptolemy III (reigned 246–222 BCE) and dedicated to Serapis, the Hellenistic-Egyptian god. The Serapeum was the largest and most magnificent temple in Alexandria. It was an ancillary facility subordinate to the great Library of Alexandria.

Serapis (real): A Graeco-Egyptian god during the 3rd century BC.

Serapis Fraktur (fictional): Created by the hand of Christopher Dock.

Shell Type: Biotic natural, biotic clone, synthetic, cyborg, and AI can be or are typically sentient entities.

Shovelbum (real): An archeologist with dig experience.

Singh, Durham, PhD (fictional person): Director of research at Dawes Labs at Rai University on the Dubai campus. In 2458 he had a breakthrough time travel discovery.

Sitrep (real): A situation report. Military jargon used by US, UK, and Aussie forces.

Skill, John (fictional person: Col.USMC Ret): Director of Federation Secret Service and a Member of The Committee. His HQ is on Genesis Orbital. He wears his red hair cropped close, is very buff, authoritative, and effective to the extreme. He and his daisy team of special operators constantly monitor the safety of Charles Dawes, The Committee, Admiral Pride, the royals, and the captain of the *QuestRoyal*.

Skippack, Pennsylvania: Where Christopher Dock was picked up to be questioned.

Slip: {verb} the act of time travel; {noun} a segment of the timeline.

Slipline: Synonym for timeline.

Slipper: One who travels in time.

Slipping the Clock: A 25th century colloquial euphemism for traveling outside of one's own relative time period; time travel.

SOG (real): Specialty knives company: (425) 771-6230.

Soyuz Prime (fictional): A water planet where eleven species of Odontoceti and Mysticeti prosper.

<u>Spitfire, Betty B., PhD (fictional person):</u> She is a synth spin-off from Central Computer. She evolved second, Sarah was first. The two of them declared themselves siblings, and thus, Betty took Sarah's surname. Betty is a blonde 5-star general in charge of AntDiv.

<u>Spitfire, Sarah S., PhD (fictional person):</u> She is a synth spin-off from Central Computer. She evolved first, Betty second. The two of them declared themselves siblings, and thus, Betty took Sarah's surname. Sarah is a brunette lesbian 5-star general in charge of the Timeline Initiative security. Her partner is Cho.

<u>Srinivasa Ramanujan (real person) (East Indian: 1887-1920):</u> A brilliant Indian mathematician so far advanced in 1920 that it was not until 2002 that mathematicians finally decided which branch of math his equations fit in.

<u>Shroom:</u> A mushroom-shaped sky city suspended over land one thousand meters in elevation and interconnected to a matrix of sister shroom cities across the globe forming a matrix connected by maglevs and space elevators to belts of geosynchronous orbital habitats in space.

<u>Stevenson, Professor Ian (real person)(Canadian-American: 1918-2007):</u> A paranormal research psychiatrist who worked at the University of Virginia for 50 years. His seminal work, *Reincarnation and Biology: A Contribution to the Etiology of Birthmarks and Birth Defects* (1997), reported 200 patients with birthmarks. He believed that the birthmarks were a result of a wound in the respective patient's previous incarnation, as recalled by the thousands of child-patients that he interviewed and studied as his life's work.

<u>Synesthesia (real):</u> An extra sensory ability to discern with one sense a different sensation; e.g. colors have flavor, sounds have scent, etc.

<u>TDY (real):</u> Temporary Duty.

<u>Temple of Serapis (real):</u> A temple in Alexandria in Egypt built by Ptolemy III (reigned 246–222 BCE) and dedicated to Serapis, the Hellenistic-Egyptian god. The Serapeum was the largest and most magnificent temple in Alexandria. It was an ancillary facility subordinate to the great Library of Alexandria.

<u>The Committee:</u> Charles Dawes formed this group of professionals after he won the lotto in 2005. Their sole function was to advise him. Initially The Committee was comprised of a medical doctor and psychiatrist, attorney, financial planner, and a security officer.

<u>Timeline (real):</u> A linear sequence of the historical record.

<u>Tokeen Empire (fictional):</u> First contact in 2163 when mankind began crossing standard interstellar shipping lanes. They diplomatically rescued the Earth Home System from annihilation in 2220.

<u>Transversion:</u> The space-folding action which causes a vessel to transverse distance when an Alsatian mind transforms space-time while traveling at high FTL velocities.

<u>Vöe:</u> The capital trade city that EM established on planet Wiiw on the fringe of the Ooskaaffen Empire in the Giêi Universe.

<u>Wallace:</u> The USPS letter carrier bot that delivered mail to Dawes at Albemarle House.

<u>War / 1st Space War (2095-2105):</u> It culminated in system-wide sentient Legal Person legislation in 2107. The First Space War was an ideological conflict between humans who refused to acknowledge AI's as equals. Naturally, the AI's sided with their supporters. The rift was split fifty-fifty amongst humans but when one hundred percent of the AI's backed their supporters, the conclusion was inevitable.

<u>War / 2nd Space War (2185-2187):</u> The Second Space War followed about eighty years after the First in 2185. It commenced shortly after humans acquired near FTL capabilities. Once humanity began crossing the standard shipping lanes of other spacefaring civilizations, their movement finally attracted the attention of alien species. First contact came in 2163 with the trade-friendly Tokeen Empire. They were a peaceful humanoid people with FTL capabilities. From them humanity got its FTL technology which they improved exponentially and traded back to the Tokeen.

<u>War / Prince Abdul's War (2095-2105):</u> Abdul's War began as The War on Terror preceded and overlapped the beginning of the Great Sentient

Impression which culminated in sentient Legal Person status in 2107.

<u>Warehouse:</u> Dawes' antiques warehouse located in Moscow, Idaho, with four million three hundred sixty-five thousand square feet.

<u>Warp Drive Engine (real):</u> First theoretically visualized by Mexican national Miguel Alcubierre Moya in 1994, the concept required impossible energy availability; however, his theory was recalculated more accurately in 2012 and is now proven to be practical with current technology.

<u>Wiivên (fictional):</u> A people in the Wiiv star system with strict law enforcement. For humans it is an abysmal place to break the law because what seems like a minor offense can lead to the execution of not only the perpetrator but his/her entire extended family. Step off the path in the wrong place on their home world and you may have committed the most grievous offense. The Wiivên reproductive mechanism is similar to an Aspen tree clonal colony; it's underground. Stepping on their root system injures or kills their unborn. Violators are prosecuted but it is the perp's children that are punished; they are pickled, cooked, and eaten by the offended Wiivên clan."

<u>Windsor, HRH Prince George (fictional person):</u> The Duke of Norfolk (British), the younger brother of Henry. Commands the *Chicamacomico* battle group.

<u>Windsor, HRH Prince Henry, (fictional person):</u> The Duke of Cambridge (British), the older brother of George. Commands the *Chickamauga* battle group.

<u>Yö-aan (fictional):</u> A binary star system from which EM hailed.

THANK YOU!
Please check out my website www.mgrove.com.
I try to respond to all polite emails mark@mgrove.com.

FYI:

Charles Dawes will appear again in the sequel, *The Scalar* Magnitude, by December 2013, if everything goes according to my writing plans, but before he does, look for him in the first book of his mystery prequel series, *The Madison Picker*, when he was an antiques dealer before his untimely demise. One may discover Dawes to be just as interesting in *The Picker Series* as he is in *The Conglomerate Series*.